Last of the Aerial Gunfighters

By

Paul Corrigan

ISBN 0-9743792-0-4
(Previously published by First Books
ISBN 1-4107-4998-3)

Library of Congress Control Number: 2003095758

Printed in the United States of America
Naples Florida

Cover Design by Michael Cheauré

Acknowledgements

Officers in Flights Suits, New York University Press by John Sherwood, contains a superb characterization of the USAF F-86 pilots and their environment in Korea. This reference helped me in developing the dialogue between John and his F-86 compatriots.

I must also express my appreciation to the F-86 jocks at Kimpo AFB, Seoul Korea for the many hours of hangar flying we engaged in during my visits from the USS Philippine Sea. They were most helpful to this frustrated fighter pilot.

Paul Corrigan

Dedication

To Nancy, my wife of 27 years, without whose
love and support I never would have made it.

And

To the F-86 jocks in MiG Alley whose
protective umbrella shielded the UN forces
from the MiG-15 deluge that would have
otherwise occurred.

CHAPTER 1

USS Cabot
Gulf of Mexico
Monday, 26 June 1950

It all happened in the blink of an eye. Up in Primary Flight, a cubicle perched on the side of the island overlooking the flight deck, Ensign John Sullivan watched, his heart in his mouth, as the Bearcat tried to climb out of its predicament. John dropped the grease pencil that he was using to log the successful landings for the Air Boss, and leaned forward, his face pressed against the windscreen.

Commander Mike Moran, the Air Boss, threw his stogie in the butt can, and jumped up out of his chair to watch the plane's struggle. "Oh, no," he muttered under his breath, his ruddy face set hard and grim, as the Bearcat clawed for altitude following the late wave-off. As the plane slowed in its climb, the monstrous four-bladed prop bit into the air at full power and torque quickly took control, the engine trying to rotate the blades in one direction and the airplane in the other. The plane lost the contest and rolled inverted to begin its nose-down drop to the sea. It did not break up much on

1

Impact, but just kept going down, its high density responding to the call of gravity.

The ship's 1MC announcing system barked the message throughout the ship. "Plane in the water! Port side! Plane in the water! Port side!" On the carrier's hangar deck, the duty boatswain's mate ran to the sponson where the motor whaleboat was on alert. The davits were swung out, the crew jumped aboard, holding onto their individual lifelines, and the boat was launched into the choppy sea. The destroyer plane guard had already begun its race to the scene, its bow cutting the seas as it accelerated to full speed.

"My God! What happened?" John stared, his mouth agape, at the oily green slick where 302 had crashed. There was no sign of the pilot, but the rescue helicopter continued its fruitless search, hoping the pilot would pop to the surface. "302 is Andy's plane! No - not Andy!" Words expelled in anguish.

"He's gone, Mister Sullivan. He's gone. If he hasn't cleared the cockpit by now and reached the surface, he never will. I'm sorry." Moran shook his head, and looked at John sympathetically. "He was a friend of yours, wasn't he? An Academy classmate?"

"One of my best friends," John replied sadly, as he struggled to control his emotions. "What happened, sir? It was all so fast! One moment he was almost to a cut position. Then he got a wave-off, and torque rolled. Why?"

"I'm sorry, Mister Sullivan - shit, let's not stand on formality at a time like this. It's John isn't it?"

"Yes, sir."

"Well, John. The Bearcat's a bitch to control at slow speeds. All engine and prop, little stubby wings, and a miniature cockpit. A big fellow like you couldn't even get in it. Built to deck launch, get the kamikaze, and back aboard. No endurance. She'll torque every time when she gets low and slow, and full power is applied." Mike paused, studied John's anguished face, and continued. "It's hard to determine for sure from here what happened initially. You need to be on the LSO's platform to really see it. I think he anticipated the cut - spotted the deck. Tried to land the plane himself, and as all of you've been told time and time again, only the LSO can judge the timing, when to cut the power and land the plane. You know what that means?"

John did not answer. He kept staring at the slick, where the plane had hit the water, hoping somehow his friend would pop to the surface.

Moran spoke gently. "He's not coming up, John. He never got out of the plane. They either surface in ten or twenty seconds, or they never come up. I'm sorry, young man. Your friend's gone."

"How will I ever tell his wife," John said softly. "How will I ever. ."

"It's tough, kid, I know. The Notification Team will make the first contact with the widow, but I'll get you and his other buddies ashore in time to see her shortly thereafter."

"My wife and his wife, Ann, are best friends. It will tear my Sylvie apart, too."

The door of PriFly opened, and a comms messenger handed Moran a message. He read it, and then looked at John.

"I'm afraid the bad news all comes at once, John," he said, and held the message up. "You might as well know this right now," he waved the message, "because your wife will already know it when you get home. This is a message from the Admiral, directing us to meet with him tomorrow about accelerating carquals. It seems that the North Koreans are ripping the South apart. That border incident reported on the news yesterday? Now it's a full-scale invasion. Truman's directed MacArthur to intervene. We've got ourselves a war, son. We sure as hell do."

John said nothing. He looked at the Air Boss as though somehow two tragedies couldn't occur at the same time. Moran studied John's face for a moment. "You going to be able to handle this, Mister Sullivan? You have a lot of anguish written on your face."

John stiffened his shoulders. "Yes, sir, I can handle it."

Moran clapped him on the shoulder, "okay, John, good show. Now let's get on with it, and qualify the rest of the Bearcats." he paused. "And thank you for your help keeping track of the landings for me. I'll get someone else now."

Commander Moran leaned back in his chair, put his feet up on the ledge below the Plexiglas, and pulled another stogie from his shirt pocket. He turned around and opened the door to let the breeze in. The flight deck was quiet, and Mike had some peace for an hour or so. He had eighteen years in the Navy, including combat time in

World War II, with one more tour to go to make his twenty and retire. He figured he'd never make captain, and was satisfied with his career.

A burly looking man, Mike was short and stocky with powerful forearms and thighs. He looked every inch the gladiator that he was, a title earned as middleweight boxing champion at the Academy, and later the Pacific Fleet. His complexion was ruddy with a pattern of boxing scars webbed around his eyes, nose, and temples. Mike's blue eyes had a youthful twinkle. The flaming red hair of his youth now sprinkled with gray still retained its boyish curl. Mike was not a handsome man, but he exuded power and sex and the women loved him. For all his pugilistic appearance, he was friendly and seldom raised his voice, but young pilots quickly learned that the pleasant voice could have a big bite when he quietly, but effectively, chewed out a young pilot.

Mike lighted the stogie, and enjoyed the evil smell that emanated from it. With the door open, it was tolerable. He took another puff, his face softening as he thought about the young pilots who were qualifying that day. They were so eager to do it right.

I love these kids, he grinned - and then sobered, *but they really don't know what's ahead for them. Today they tasted death - they'll taste a lot more, especially with this Korea thing breaking. Their spirits are down right now, but they'll rebound, and become their usual carefree, brash, and noisy selves again. Just wish I could be with them, helping train them, rather than riding this rust bucket, doing coequals.* He paused and then mused, *but, they'll make it - and I like this young Sullivan. He's okay.* Mike stuffed out his stogie, and left PriFly to pump bilges, and get a sandwich.

Ready Room 2
USS Cabot

The three Academy ensigns sat together four rows back in the Ready Room, their thoughts turned inward as they grappled with Andy Sloan's death. Three NavCads, also due to qualify in the Corsair, gathered together in the front, talking quietly among themselves, respecting the feelings of the ensigns and their need for privacy.

John Sullivan, Brad Masters, and Guy Branch were a disparate collection of personalities and physical characteristics.

John was a tall, well-built athletic young man whose six-foot three-inch frame carried his 190 pounds of sleek muscle easily. His three years on the varsity crew at the Naval Academy, rowing twelve miles up the Severn every Saturday left him fit and trim. His Celt heritage had given him a head of thick, dark hair that tended to be a bit unruly, and clear deep blue eyes that reflected his good humor and easy-going attitude. However, when his Irish temper was aroused to anger, those same eyes could become steely cold and piercing.

Raised in a blue-collar community in Columbus, Ohio, John's first love had always been flying and airplanes. As a child, he loved the tissue and balsa wood airplanes that he built and attempted to fly. His favorite World War I Spad biplane seemed to have acquired its own burning desire to fly because it always did so well.

Endowed with a superb physique and the body coordination that goes with it, John had a natural flair for flying, and an intuitive understanding of the spatial movement of objects in flight around him, an understanding so essential to a good fighter pilot.

Brad was one of John's closest friends, suave and debonair, smooth with the ladies, and a social asset at any gathering. He was a handsome dog with classic Greek features and curly black hair - a regular Adonis. Women couldn't resist his charm.

Brad was also a superb pilot, one of the few chosen to attend the new Jet Training Unit that was just beginning to produce a pitifully small number of pilots for the Navy's embryonic jet community.

Guy Branch was a solid Midwesterner - the type that the corn country of Nebraska produced in quantity. His body was stocky, his face friendly, and his actions deliberate. He had sandy hair and light gray eyes that sparkled when he smiled. Guy was an excellent pilot who controlled his airplane well. While his spatial coordination was excellent, Guy lacked the imagination and aggressiveness to be a really good fighter pilot.

The three men plus Andy Sloan were inseparable companions at the Naval Academy, and again during the past year as they learned to fly. Sloan's choice of Bearcats instead of Corsairs disappointed the other three pilots as it had split him away from them.

John put the back of his chair in the full rear position, and let his head lie heavily against the headrest. His face, a grim mask, hid all the emotion churning inside him.

I still can't believe it, John murmured, shaking his head. *I can't believe Andy's gone. I keep thinking he's gonna walk in at any moment, and tell me it was all just a bad dream.* John wiped his face, and rubbed his eyes with his knuckles to get rid of the nightmare in his mind.

Brad rolled his head to one side, and looked at his friend. "How you doing, buddy?" he asked gently.

"Aw, Brad, I just want to turn the clock back, and do some things over again. I saw him in the passageway just before he went to ops. I was headed for PriFly, and he stopped to talk a minute. I cut him off because I was in a hurry - to get where? To PriFly to see him die! Shit! Damn me!" He ran his hands over his face again, and turned to Brad. "Sweet Jesus, Brad. I want that time back to do it over again."

Brad could see some of the despair leaking through John's mask. He couldn't hide it all. "Hey, John. Don't lay a monkey on your own back. It wasn't your accident."

"Yeah, but I could have given him more time when he needed it." he paused, and then shrugged, "Well, too late now, I guess," he said, trying to get rid of the sense of helplessness that was weighting him down.

The door of the Ready Room opened to admit two LSOs, the Senior LSO followed by Joe Ward, the one who had waved Andy. The Senior LSO, a lieutenant two-striper, took a position in front of the chairs, his feet planted wide, his hands on his hips, and his eyes arrogant and intimidating, all business.

"Okay, guys," he began, "we had a bad one up there this morning, and I don't want a repeat of it. Ya hear me? Sloan did it all wrong. Spotted the deck, and then couldn't control his plane on wave-off. Frankly, his responses to the situation were poor. Joe had no choice, but to wave him off."

His comments about Andy caused John to glare at him, and he mumbled under his breath. "Yeah, man. He looked good when he went by me! The LSO's creed, isn't it? The LSO, of course, couldn't possibly have made a mistake!"

The Senior LSO heard him, and now stared menacingly at John, unaware that John and Andy had been so close. "Just shut up, smartass! I don't need advice from any goddamned nugget! Your buddy bought the farm because he wasn't too smart!"

John roared up out of his chair, his face livid with anger. "You son of a bitch!" he yelled. "You're talking about my friend - a dead man! Now you shut up, or I'll break you in two! Have you no respect - you asshole!" he glared, his body taut with rage, his hands balled up into fists that opened and closed emotionally.

Brad reached up and pulled John back to his seat. "Hey, John. Easy, boy. Cool it," he whispered, trying sooth him.

Joe Ward intervened. "Okay. Okay everybody. I waved Andy, and I'm going to wave you guys, The debrief of what happened upstairs belongs to me," he looked angrily at the Senior LSO. "The debrief is mine. You can stay if you want, sir, but I'm giving it. Okay?"

The Senior LSO shrugged his shoulders, picked up his logbook, and departed.

"Okay. Here's what happened, guys - straight from the horse's mouth. Andy spotted the deck. I didn't have any choice, but to wave him off. He was headed for the ramp. Instead of concentrating on me, he looked at the deck and tried to land the plane himself. You've heard it a million times. Don't spot the deck!" He looked at them for a minute trying to reestablish the rapport with them that had been destroyed by the Senior LSO. Seeing he had their attention again, he continued, "Let's not let Andy's death be in vain. Learn the consequences. For God's sake, guys, concentrate on me. I won't let you down!" he paused again to let the message sink in.

"Now you know the routine. I've waved all of you ashore, and I have confidence in your ability. Otherwise, you wouldn't be out here. Let's just keep it cool, and get the job done. Okay? Any questions? Anything bugging you?" The room was silent. "Then I'm going back to the platform. If you have any problems, for God's sake cancel yourself out, and then see me. Don't take chances." Joe looked hard at John, knowing how distraught the young man was. John's face was impassive, etched in stone. He said nothing, but he had visibly relaxed somewhat from the earlier incident. Joe smiled at him. "Stay cool, John," he said, and headed for the door.

After the LSO departed, the pilots again retreated within themselves to come to grips with their feelings about the accident.

John sat quietly, slowly unwinding from the anger that had overwhelmed him earlier. His grim mask gradually disappeared to be replaced by a morose look of inadequacy. Then, slowly but surely the fighter pilot mentality began to take hold of him again. Fighter pilots die! Good friends die! It's part of the culture. Live fast; die quick. No regrets.

Why did it have to be my best friend the first time out? Why Andy? He sucked on his teeth, and then shrugged philosophically. *No choice now, but to deal with it. Got to control my emotions. Accept it. Yeah, accept it, or I'll never fly for long. That worm of fear will begin to eat at my guts - growing bigger - ever bigger - 'til I can no longer deal with it. Then it's get out and go sell insurance instead. That's it, buddy. That's the way it is.*

Guy interrupted his thoughts, leaning over the seat in front. "Jesus! What a way to go. The poor son of a bitch didn't have a chance. God, it happened so fast. One moment you have it under control; the next moment you're dead - or dying in an aluminum coffin with a burial at sea." Guy shuddered.

"Enough of that, Guy," John replied. "We can't think that way, especially now when we're waiting to do the same quals. If we let it, it'll eat us alive, and distract us from the job at hand. We need all the concentration we can get right now."

"Yeah," Brad jumped in. "Look at it this way. He never knew what hit him. Not a bad way to go. The only better way is to be making love and have an elephant sit on top of the two of you." he laughed, turned, and looked at John to see if his face was free of stress. "Enough morbid talk, buddy. I'll be so scared I won't be able to fly. And I'm fearless!"

"You're too handsome to be scared, Brad," John laughed lightly, the heavy tension broken. "Yeah, with all those good looks, Brad, when are you going to trap Pam?"

"Trap Pam? You crazy? These Pensacola beauties trap aviators - not the reverse," Guy snorted. "She'll run so fast that Brad will catch her. Just like it's all planned. You're a goner, man!"

"Okay, Fearless, you gonna get six traps in a row?" John poked Brad, the crash and death of Andy Sloan now relegated to the world of unspoken topics - as if it never happened.

"Sure, why not," Brad replied. "I like the way the Corsair handles. Stable man - very stable. The only problem's that damned cowl flap sticking out the side of that long damned hose nose - The Hose Nose. A good name for the bird! You sit so far back that you can't see the LSO on the straightaway. You've got to time your approach so you're not long in the groove. Roll out of your turn and get a cut. That's the way you do it."

"Well, why not just close the cowl flaps," John chuckled.

"Sure, and overheat the engine so that it quits, and you go in the drink. No thanks, asshole," Brad responded, flipping John a friendly finger.

John laughed, "Don't you know, Brad? You could get killed doing this shit."

The emotional level of the Ready Room had returned to normal.

"Corsair pilots - man your planes!" the squawk box boomed out.

Flight Deck
USS Cabot

"Bad scene, sir," the plane captain said to John as he approached his aircraft. "Didn't it shake you up a little?" He looked carefully at John for signs of fear.

John shrugged. "Can't let it bother you - can you?"

The plane captain gave him his helmet, plugged in his g-suit and radio, put the shoulder straps in place for John to buckle, and tapped him on the top of his helmet to signify "okay".

Wouldn't trade it for the world! John thought, watching the flight deck activity.

"Clear all props and exhausts! Start engines!" cried the bullhorn.

The big props of the Corsairs slowly began to turn, and the engines belched and popped, spewing white smoke as they caught with a roar, sending a blast of prop wash astern that could blow the unwary over the side or, worse yet, into a turning prop.

The launching officer signaled a one-finger turn-up for a deck run. John added power to the engine, checked his mags, and gave an okay thumbs up. The launch officer signaled two fingers maximum power, and then leaned forward, pointing down the flight deck. John added the rest of his power, and released his brakes. As the plane started to roll, John felt the intense thrill that came with the plane's thrust towards the abyss in front of him. The bow passed under him, and he was out over the sea, feeling the heady buoyancy that comes with becoming airborne.

LSO Platform
Flight Deck - USS Cabot

Joe Ward had been waving planes aboard for two years. The Senior LSO stood behind him on the LSO platform that protruded from the flight deck on the port side about the position of the first arresting wire. Outboard of the platform a steel mesh safety net went down under the platform itself to rest against the hull of the ship. The net provided safe haven for LSOs when pilots forced them to jump off the platform. One jump, frequently head   first, and the occupants would roll down the net to rest against the ship's hull.

A vertical canvas screen protected the LSO platform from the twenty-five knot wind over the deck required for the planes to get aboard. It gave the LSOs the protection needed to stand upright with legs spread and arms extended to give the signals to the incoming pilots. The LSO wore a tight-fitting canvas helmet with earphone receivers and a lip mike on a boom. Three-inch wide red stripes ran vertically down their brown cotton flight suit from shoulder to ankle, and a similar yellow stripe ran out the arms from shoulder to wrist. When the LSO took his stance on the platform, legs spread and anchored, arms extended from the shoulders, there was no doubt that the pilots could see the cross, formed by the vertical red and the horizontal yellow stripes.

The noise on the platform was horrendous. The wind that buffeted the canvas screen carried all the sounds from the flight deck; the roar of engines at full power as the planes raced down the deck to take off, and the scream of the arresting gear as a plane engaged a wire and was dragged to a halt by the powerful engines. Overlaid were the ancillary sounds of tractors, bull- horns, and starting units, all contributing to the cacophony.

"Here come the Corsairs," announced the LSO to no one in particular. "I sure hope they do a little better."

"Gear down, flaps down, hook down," the spotter announced.

"Clear deck, green flag, cleared to land." The Senior LSO barked the remainder of the litany. Joe picked up the Corsair at the 90 with a Roger and continued to hold it most of the pass.

"Look at this guy ride the railroad tracks," Joe admired the approach.

"Solid. Solid. Who is he?" the Senior LSO asked.

"This is the guy who almost punched you out in the Ready Room for bad mouthing his best friend. Shouldn't have done that, buddy. I waved him a number of times ashore. He's good. Now getting a little high. I'll give him a high dip to ease him down. Whoops, the little shit beat me to it. He didn't need the signal, just eased it down himself."

Inside the cockpit of the Corsair John sat back on his tailbone and squirmed to get comfortable. "Damn! I'm just an RCH high - about ten feet. Ease it down, lad. Just drop the nose an RCH, then right back up to proper attitude. Good."

"Looks like he needs a little more bank to increase the turn rate," the LSO commented. "I'll give him a couple seconds to correct."

"Damn! This guy's good. Every time I get ready to give him a signal - he's already doing it. Maybe we should make him an LSO?"

"Not a bad idea, Joe, but he's still too inexperienced." the Senior LSO responded.

"Here he comes. Rolling into the groove right at the cut position."

Suddenly, Joe waved his right arm and paddle sharply across his chest. "Cut!" he announced, and John responded to the signal by cutting the power. The Corsair dropped to the deck, catching number four wire.

"Okay pass. Damned okay. Now let's see the rest of them come aboard." Turning to the talker, he added, "give him an okay, four wire in the book. Good pass. I hope the rest of them do as well."

John quickly got his six landings. The others took a little longer with a couple wave-offs, but no close calls. All the Corsair pilots qualified, and the tension in PriFly subsided considerably. The Air

11

Boss took the remains of his stogie out of his mouth, looked at it, made a vile noise, and threw it in the tomato can spittoon. He turned to the phone talker, "Tell the LSO to get them debriefed, and then get them ready to launch to the beach."

The catapult officer pointed his extended arm down towards the bow and - WHAM! The hydraulic pressure released from the accumulator, the piston slammed forward, the hold back ring broke, and John roared down the track. The bow of the ship disappeared under him.

"Wow! What a kick in the ass!" John shouted, as he experienced his first catapult shot. He slapped the gear and flap handles to the up position, and snapped into a port turn, climbing to 3000 feet to wait for the other Corsairs launching behind him.

"God! This is the life. I just made my qualifying landings, and I'll get my wings next week." John cried out exuberantly, as he maneuvered the Corsair around some fluffy white fair weather clouds. *I know Andy Sloan's dead, and I really hurt for Ann. I probably should be more solemn right now, but I can't. It's different when you fly.* He looked over the long nose at the sleek cowling around the Pratt & Whitney R-2800 engine. *That ole P&W baby! It purrs just like me - so happy to be up here, away from all the earth's problems. Nothing around but unlimited sky and the white cotton clouds. No death. No grief. That's for those on the ground!*

John watched the second Corsair leap off the carrier's bow and begin its climb to join him. Then the opposite cat came to life and punched off the third Corsair. *Wish we had time to do a little tail chase. Fly around those clouds ducking in and out, a couple loops, a few rolls - maybe even a Split S. Great Fun!* He leaned back like a kid with a new toy and watched as the second Corsair slid into position, followed shortly by the third and then number four.

The rendezvous complete, John rolled out to the north towards home plate at Corry Field.

Another fifteen minutes and I'll be on deck at Corry, then home with the bad news.

Officer's Club
Mainside, Pensacola

"It's your bid, dear," the lieutenant commander's wife said with a sigh, impatient to get the game moving. Her husband was the Administrative Officer for the naval base, and she was very much aware of her position in the hierarchy of officer's wives. This afternoon, she was disappointed to end up at a table with "three young twits" The conversation was always so boring.

Ugh! These Navy wives get so serious about this game. Sylvia Sullivan lifted her heavy dark hair up off her neck, fanned herself, and then let it fall back into place, her pretty young face wrinkled in concentration as she tried to decide what to do with her bridge hand.

One year as the wife of a fighter pilot and Sylvia loved it. All the excitement and glamour, with a new adventure happening every day. Sure made Worthington, Ohio seem like history. Nevertheless, those years with the good sisters at St. Mary's of the Woods, and all the drilling in the social graces by her mother had left Sylvia a contender with the best of them. She was charming, outgoing, and without guile, but she had an impish streak a mile wide. She shifted her cards around one more time to see if they looked better. They didn't.

"I bid one club." Sylvia announced at last.

The lieutenant commander's wife gave an exasperated sigh of relief. All that time for only a one-club bid! Really! You'd think she had a grand slam. This afternoon would be a long one.

Sylvia's partner was her best friend, Ann Sloan. Ann was everybody's darling - a petite blonde with a natural beauty that needed little enhancement. Wholesome and good-natured, she always had a ready smile, and tried her best to please other people. Everyone simply loved Ann Sloan.

The fourth at the table was Pam Jones, Sylvia's guest, and the steady girl friend of Ensign Brad Masters, John's roommate at the Academy and squadron mate. A willowy brunette, Pam was a stunning local girl with noticeable assets, which she exposed in a two piece bathing suit every Saturday and Sunday afternoon for the admiration of the boys on the white sand beaches of Pensacola.

"One no trump," Ann replied to Sylvia's initial opening bid. The opposition passed. Sylvia bid two hearts, followed by Ann's two spades. Ann closed the bid out at three no trump.

13

Sylvia laid her hand down and got a nod from Ann. Then she sat back in her chair to watch the play. She was bored, bored, bored! She could think of a thousand better things to do. Frankly, she'd rather be at home with her handsome young husband, maybe playing house together. It was a delicious thought, and she dwelled on it for a few moments until the play of the cards caught her attention. Ann was going to make her bid. She laughed to herself, and looked at Mrs. lieutenant commander whose lips were pursed in a sour grimace. *I'd like to stick my tongue out at you!* Sylvia giggled under her breath, as she mentally did just that. *Whoops! Better be careful or I might accidentally do it.* Instead she ventured, "Well, girls, today's the big day for the guys, that final step, carrier quals, and then the wings of gold. John could hardly wait to get out the door this morning. Even forgot to kiss me."

"Brad was over last night. He seemed sort of blase' about it all." Pam offered her thoughts on the subject.

"Game and rubber!" Ann gleefully chirped, pulling in the last hand.

"Andy was nervous this morning," She frowned, as she collected her winnings. "You know - after they sent him to the beach when he couldn't get aboard last time out. I just hope he makes it this time!" she added with some concern. Suddenly she stilled and shivered, wrapping her arms around her shoulders, her face gone pale.

"My God, Ann! You alright? You look like you're going to faint," Sylvia jumped up and quickly ran around the table to her friend.

"I don't know what came over me. I just suddenly felt a deep chill." She smiled weakly at her friends. "But, I'm okay, now."

"Looks like we'll have some real celebrating to do tonight." Pam said. "I'm meeting Brad at the O'Club as soon as he calls and says he's back. I hope y'all will be there, too."

"Umm, John and I may be a little late, Pam," Sylvia giggled, again thinking about playing house as soon as John got home.

"Okay, Sylvia. We all know about you and your stud husband. But, can't you wait?" Ann teased her friend.

"Well, girls, this conversation is getting to be a bit much," Mrs. lieutenant commander gave a weak attempt at a smile, rose from her chair, and departed, leaving the three young wives in a fit of giggles.

"Oh, let the old biddy go," Pam laughed. "Hers is probably all dried up anyway!"

"Hey - quiet girls!" Ann shushed them. "They're liable to throw us out."

"That's okay. We're ready to leave, and go see what's happening in the real world." Pam giggled.

"Not to change the subject," Sylvia said, "but what do you girls hear about this Korea thing? It was on the six o'clock news last night."

"I heard something on the radio yesterday afternoon," Pam interjected, casually looking into her compact, obviously totally unconcerned about world events.

" John says it's nothing to worry about," Sylvia continued, "He says they're always having little squabbles along that border."

"Yeah, but one announcer said it looks like a heavy attack by the North Koreans," Ann replied, soberly. "Andy said there may be trouble."

"Well, it won't affect us, girls," Pam closed the subject. "Let's go out and get a coke by the pool."

"I'm out of here!" Sylvia laughed, picking up her purse.

At that very moment Edgar R. Murrow was on the air with a special news analysis, reporting the scope of the North Korean thrust across the 38th Parallel, belatedly recognized now as a full scale invasion - and Truman's response to it.

1750 Cedar Lane
Pensacola

"Oh, my God, it's war, and John will be in it." Sylvia whimpered, as she listened to the newscaster droning on about the fighting in Korea. She had been prepared to handle the hazards of flight - but war? A whole new dimension of fear had now been added to her life. All the lovely days of June Week, the wedding, their honeymoon, and the fun of flight training were blown away by the stark reality of war. Sylvia sat in the living room looking out the window, stunned by the rapid turn of events. She watched panicked, as John's car pool, a battered wreck of a car, pulled up in front and dropped him off. Sylvia ran to the door, wrenched it open, and threw herself into his arms. "Oh! It's so terrible." she cried out in anguish.

"Yes, it is, darling," he responded, not sure which terrible thing she was talking about, but fearing the word on Andy was already out.

"You'll go over there and get yourself killed, and where will I be? You should have gone multi-engine! Those bastards will be safe, and you'll die!" she sobbed.

John didn't know what to say - what could he say?

Sylvia looked at him through her tears, as if he didn't understand her "The war, dummy! The war in Korea! It's on the news. The North Koreans invaded and we're sending troops," she almost screamed, her face reflecting her terror.

"I heard about it on the ship, but I don't know any more than you do, Syl," John replied, holding her to him and quietly trying to calm her. "How big this war is, and how much fight the Koreans have, I just don't know." He tipped her chin up, and looked at her frightened face. "Aw, they're probably just some small time thugs who can be handled easily," he said to soothe her, not at all sure that he believed it himself, but wanting to.

But Sylvia was not consoled. Her cheeks were wet with tears that continued to fall. "Hey Honey! Sylvie! Get hold of yourself! Listen - I'm afraid there's more bad news, darling. Sit down, please."

Sylvia looked at John, wiping away her tears with the back of her hand, as she sank onto the sofa. *Jesus, how the hell do I tell her?* *he* worried. *She's already hysterical from the war news. I don't know if she'll come completely unglued when I tell her about Andy.*

John sat down beside his distraught wife, and took her hands in his. He drew in his breath, and took the plunge. "It's about Andy, Syl. He got a late wave-off for being too slow and settling at the ramp. He tried to correct, but rolled over and crashed into the sea. The plane went straight down."

Sylvia looked at him not comprehending what he said. "Is he alright? I mean - will they wash him out, or .."
She stopped in mid-sentence when she saw John shake his head sadly, his eyes shiny.

"He's ...He's?" she swallowed hard, as the reality began to hit her.

"Yeah, Syl," John said quietly. "Andy's dead. He went down with the plane."

The room began to spin. Sylvia took a sharp breath, her face went white, as she felt the nausea rise in her throat. She closed her eyes, and began to shake again, tears flowing from closed lids. "Oh, God, no!" She moaned, rocking back and forth. "No, not Andy, please God! No, not him." She looked desperately, pleadingly at John. "Are you sure? Oh, John, not Andy." The words came out in a torrent. Suddenly, Sylvia stilled, gazed unseeing into the distance, and whispered. "Ann knew. She knew."

"Oh, Syl, she couldn't have. There wasn't any word until we came ashore."

"Oh, no, John, Ann knew," Her face was determined. "We were playing bridge at the club and she got a sudden chill." The voice sank back into a whisper. "She knew."

John swallowed, at loss for words. Gallows humor in the Ready Room, the brave front that was expected - these he knew how to deal with. But, this emotion - Sylvia's grief and fear - he couldn't seem to handle it. He felt helpless.

John gripped Sylvia by the shoulders and shook her gently. "Sylvia. Sylvia. Listen to me. You are an aviator's wife now, and aviators do die. I told you that before we were married. We talked about it. It's dangerous, but that's the way it is. It's our life now. You've got to accept it." He paused, and watched her face for a moment.

"I know you'll worry about me and my flying even more now, but you shouldn't because I'm good at what I do. I'm not going to do anything stupid, because that's what causes accidents. I'm also very lucky. That's a plus in this business. I have luck! So have faith in me. Come on, sweetheart - get hold of yourself - for me and for Ann - for all of us."

Sylvia looked sadly into John's concerned face, as if trying to memorize his features one by one. "You're right. I know you are. It's just so hard to face up to it. Thank God, it wasn't you. Give me a second to wash my face, and we'll go do what we must."

The street and driveway in front of Andy's house were filled with cars. John parked a half block away and he and Sylvia slowly walked back to it. In the fading light of day an evening drizzle had begun to fall on the somber scene.

"Come on, John, or we'll get soaked." Sylvie said softly, as they ran for the porch to join a dozen other Academy graduates standing together in the gray twilight.

"Our first loss, John," one of them declared.

"How's Ann and where is she?" Sylvia asked.

"In the bedroom, Sylvie."

"John, just stay here until I see how she is. I'll come to get you if she can handle it."

"Is that necessary, Sylvie?"

"Yes - yes, it is," she shot back. "You're alive and Andy's dead. I know how I'd feel, watching the other guys walk around. Why my husband? Why not someone else? Please, just stay here, and I'll call you. Get yourself a drink." John didn't need to look for a drink. Guy Branch handed him a stiff scotch on the rocks, and Brad came up to put his arm around John's shoulder.

"Bad show, John. It's only the first. Can't fly and not have people get hurt," he turned his beer up and drained it.

"Sure cuts deep, John," Brad gloomily interjected. "Andy was such a nice guy, but Guy's right. You can't do these kinds of things and not hurt people."

"Yeah, but maybe there's a better way to do it. Carrier operations haven't changed much since the days of the Langley. We still do it the same old way. Somebody in the Ready Room was talking about the Brits experimenting with something called the angled deck. They said you can land, miss the wire, and take off again."

"Bullshit! I'd like to see how they do that," Guy added skeptically.

A tall, trim aviation cadet in perfectly tailored tropical whites mounted the porch steps in company with another cadet.

"Mr. Sullivan, you don't know me, sir. I'm Aviation Cadet Larry Duncan, a friend of Andy's," he said. "And this is Cadet Dave Herbert. Dave and I are three classes behind you. We've been playing bridge with Andy in the Ready Room, waiting for flights and we"d like to pay our respects to his wife."

John offered his hand to both and shook his head. "Ann may not be up to seeing you guys at the present time. My wife is in with her, and she'll give us a reading shortly. She didn't want me to go in either until she reviewed the situation. If you can't see her, just leave your card with condolences on it. And please call me John."

Larry blushed and replied, "Jeez, I'm sorry. I don't have a card."

"Here. Put your name on the back of mine. The fact that you were here is the important thing." John handed him two cards.

"Thank you, sir. You're Academy, aren't you, Mr. Sullivan - John? Andy's classmate?"

"Yeah, I'm a Ring Knocker," John chuckled. "It's nice to go through flight training as an officer."

"Funny to hear you say Ring Knocker, sir. Most Academy graduates don't like to be called that."

John laughed and knocked his ring twice on the banister, "Why not? I think it's funny. Well, Ring Knockers we are, Larry. Like it or not." John held up his glass to them. "Here's to the Navy. Bottoms up." They all toasted and drank.

Moments later, Sylvie came out, and touched John's arm. "Ann's too upset, John. The doctor's in there now, and he's going to knock her out so she can sleep. John, there's a small Florida Room around the side of the porch. Stake it out for the men, and leave the living room for Ann and the wives. Send someone to stock some booze and ice. The wives will be bringing food tomorrow to put in the dining room. Okay? Will you organize that for me, sweetheart? I'm going back in the bedroom to keep an eye on Ann until she's asleep."

"Sure, Sylvie. C'mon guys. Let's check the liquor stock and then go get what we need." John was surprised at how Sylvia was taking charge, considering her earlier hysteria.

The men returned with beer, coke, a couple fifths of scotch, pretzels, and peanuts - whatever John could buy with the cash he had. Talk in the Florida Room turned to what some reporters were now calling Korea - a Police Action - but, what the aviators knew was really a war in the making.

"I heard some news just before I came over here." Guy said. "AP's reporting that the ROK Army's in full retreat."

"We'll be in it, that's for sure," Brad interjected. "But as for me - give me the east coast. I'm a lover, not a fighter."

John grunted, "Even the lovers will be in this one, Romeo."

"What kind of action do you think we'll see?" Guy asked.

"Who knows? Except for what the AP news said, I know nothing about Korea. We'll just have to wait and see."

"What if the Russians come in?" Brad asked.

"The Communists are behind all this, Brad. You can be sure of that," Guy added. "If the Russians come in, it'll be the start of World War III."

"Hey, don't be ridiculous, Guy." John laughed. "That'll mean the atomic bomb! And the Russians are scared shitless of that! Damnit! Let's not ask for more trouble. We've got enough as it is."

"Well, hell! We don't need a war right now. I don't want to have Koreans shooting at me," Guy grumbled, pouring another drink.

"Ain't going to be no turkey shoot, old man," Brad snorted.

"Gee, it's such a shame about Andy," Guy began again on the subject that they were all avoiding. "He was a nice guy."

"Yeah, he was," John replied. "I'll miss him."

"Here's to Andy" Brad added, and raised his glass. The other three followed, and the four downed their drinks. With that, the subject closed down as quickly as it had come up. The aviators simply refused to talk about what had happened. It was over and done with.

Sylvia came into the room. "She's knocked out, and the doctor said she won't rouse before noon." She turned to Brad, "Pam really wants to stay the night with Ann, Brad. She said for you to go back to the Q, and she'll call you." Sylvia looked at John, "Ann's mother called, and her brother will be on the morning plane. I'll meet him at the airport. Other relatives will follow later in the day. So, let's close it down for now and go home."

"Alright, Sylvie, but first I want you to meet these two gentlemen - Larry Duncan and Dave Herbert. They know Andy from the Ready Room and came to pay respects."

"Hi guys, thanks a lot for coming. It will be important to Ann later."

"Thank you, Mrs. Sullivan. We thought a lot of Andy, and know you and John did, too. Who knows - the way things are happening maybe we'll see duty together somewhere down the line."

"Well, maybe so. You guys look like hot aviators." Sylvia smiled. "And please call me Sylvie. I'm not old enough to be a Mrs. Sullivan."

"Yeah, she's only fourteen," John cracked and took Sylvia's arm as she went down the steps.

"Seem like nice people," Larry said.

"Yeah," agreed Dave.

Neither John nor Sylvia spoke on the short drive home. John parked the convertible in their driveway, and Sylvia got out without saying anything. She looked in her purse, found the house keys, and went inside without waiting for him. She hung up her jacket, went straight into the kitchen, and returned with two large whiskies - neat. Turning to John who was hanging up his coat, she handed him a glass, and raised hers.

"What did they say in that movie? Here's to the next man to die! I guess that's the way it will be." She tipped up her glass, drained it, and gasped for air.

"Hey! Don't do that Sylvie. You'll feel like shit tomorrow." John said, reaching out for her.

"I don't have to wait until tomorrow to feel like shit! I feel that way now," Sylvia retorted, her eyes filling. "Bottoms up, husband dear. I'll pour you another." She went back for the bottle.

"Okay, what the hell. Why not?" John angrily tipped his glass up, drained it, and held it out for another. Sylvia got the bottle of whiskey, poured another round, and set the bottle on the coffee table. Then she turned to face him. "Okay. Why John? Why? Why! It's such a waste! Am I going to live out my life wondering if you're the next one? The next to die? Smash your plane into the sea or the desert?" She downed the second glass of whiskey, stood up, and threw the glass across the room where it hit a lamp, shattering both. She then sank back onto the sofa, and put her face in her hands.

"Take it easy, honey. Hey, I know it's tough and you worry about me. But, this is my life, Syl. I can't stop flying! You know that."

She raised her head and looked at him. "So what, my husband. I didn't realize before that death was so much a part of this life, or that I'd have to live on the edge of it. I don't want to lose you, not ever! I simply won't lose you!" Sylvia went to the cupboard, got another glass while John cleaned up the mess. When Sylvia reached for the bottle to pour another, John stopped her because her voice was beginning to slur a little.

"Enough, Syl! What's done is done. Leave it alone. You can't change it."

Suddenly she stopped crying, and smiled grimly. "Okay, Big Guy. If that's the way it is." She grabbed John by the hand, pulled him off the sofa, and headed for the bedroom, stopping at the last second to embrace him. Her eyes blazed as she looked at him desperately. With a yank she tore off her blouse, scattering the buttons, and flung it to the floor.

"Okay! So, screw me, Mister Pilot! And screw me hard! Do it good, so I can forget the flying - forget the war - and forget death!"

John looked at her, astounded at the language that had exploded out of her mouth.

"Sylvia! Honey! You've never . . ."

"Well, I am now, Mister Pilot! So let's just see how good you really are!"

She snorted, as the lacy bra dropped to the floor, and she threw herself against him, wrapping her arms around him.

"Screw! Screw! Screw! That's how I feel with my world collapsing around me!" She pressed her breasts against his chest, and then stepped back, her eyes blazing with the fire of anger and emotion that she couldn't control.

"So screw me, Mister Pilot! Make me know that you're still alive - not lifeless on some slab or twenty fathoms under the sea!"

12734 Summit Drive
Worthington, Ohio

The phone was ringing off the wall as Bernice Houghton ran to answer it, dropping her pruning shears on a chair in the patio as she flew by.

"Houghton residence."

"Hello, Mother, I need to talk to you. Gotta minute?"

"Sylvie, what a pleasant surprise! How are you?" Sensing an upset, she added, "Did you and John have a fight?"

"Oh no, Mother, it's far worse than that. You remember Andy Sloan?"

Bernice could hear the tears being sniffled back.

"Yes, of course I do - and sweet Ann. I remember the wedding."

"Well, Andy's dead, Mother. He died at sea when his plane went in." Her voice cracked.

"Oh, no! Poor Ann! Oh, my poor children! And you - what about you, my darling? Are you holding up okay? This must be terrible for you."

"I'm okay now, mother, but it's been so hard. Really been awful. I never thought much about this sort of thing happening. It always happens to someone else. It hadn't touched me. Now, here's death at my door. I look at John, and see him lying cold and dead! My dreams are terrible!" The tears broke through.

"Sylvie! Stop that! You're a married adult now, and you need to be able to cope with these things. And, you will, Sylvie! You will. Your father saw this coming, and when I asked him to discuss it with you, he only said - Let her have her fun. She'll have to face it soon enough - So be brave, Sylvie dear. Try to be brave."

"I'm trying, mother. I really am, but it just cuts me in my guts. I'm sorry about using guts, but that's the way I feel."

My Sylvie has learned lots of new terms from John her mother mused, and then said, "how's John taking it?"

"He's a tower of strength - at least on the outside. He feels it deeply I know, but he won't let it get to him, or let anyone know it's getting to him. None of them will. It's part of the code" The thought of losing John enveloped her again. "Oh, Mother, I need him so! The thought of . . ."

"Enough, Sylvie darling! Enough of that," Bernice said forcefully. "You want me to come down for a few days?"

"Sure, I'd love it, Mother. But, like Dad said, I have to face it. I have to face a lot of things. Just let me call you and talk whenever I'm down in the dumps."

"Call collect, Sylvie. I know an ensign's pay isn't much."

"Okay, Mother, I'll do that. I've got to go. Love you. 'Bye."

Bernice slowly hung up the phone. *Franklin was right. The first loss would tear Sylvie apart. We'll call back together when he gets home. He'll know how to handle it.*

1750 Cedar Lane
Pensacola, Florida

"What are you going to do this morning, honey?" John asked, as he zipped up his trousers and tied his shoes.

Sylvia sighed, "Oh, I don't know, my darling. I'm just so depressed about Andy. - and poor Ann. What will she do now? I know it's an awful thought, but I wonder if she'll ever get over it and remarry."

"Lots of pilot's widows frequently marry another aviator. They've become so accustomed to the camaraderie, and the fast pace of life that the idea of marrying a banker just doesn't seem all that appealing. So they simply marry another aviator," John replied, buttoning his shirt.

"Just how many aviators can one widow go through?" Sylvia asked sarcastically, as she studied her nail polish.

"Funny thing, Sylvie - only two." He said matter-of-factly.

"Why two?" she snapped back at him, in a tone indicating she expected a punch line.

"Because after two, she's bad luck. No one will touch her."

"You're serious!" Sylvia said stunned.

"There are guys that think that way, Syl." John sighed. "Fighter pilots are a superstitious lot."

"Well, I think that's a terrible thing to do - to label a woman that way!"

John shrugged and gave her a crooked grin. "I'm going to Mainside to fill out forms and visit the detailer. I'll be back this afternoon with my assignment. Maybe we'll do something great to celebrate - that is, if you're a good girl." He patted her rear.

"Make it an East Coast outfit," Sylvia said gently, unconsciously straightening his tie. "I want you alive, not dead."

"Oh, Syl, c'mon! This war will be over before you know it. Stop worrying."

After John left, Sylvia stood quietly looking out the kitchen window while she drank her coffee. It all had seemed so simple yesterday. Marriage to a handsome man with a glamorous exciting job - a wonderful, adventuresome life that would keep her away from damned Worthington, Ohio. Now a friend has died, and John was probably off to fight a war. War? Back in college some of her professors had said that the atomic bomb had made war obsolete. Part of her believed it. Sylvia sighed heavily.

Administration Building
Mainside, Pensacola

John sat outside the office of Commander Barney, the Aviator Assignment Officer for the Training Command, waiting his turn to be interviewed. He kept wondering to himself what kind of assignment he would get. West Coast? East Coast? A fighter squadron? A damned utility squadron towing targets? No way! He wanted the Jet Training Unit, but that was out of the question. The students had already been selected for that plum.

Damn Brad anyway! He got it and I didn't. Well, the best thing for me is a fighter squadron with one of the air groups. Deploy on a carrier. Deploy to Korea. There's a war going on and I need to get in it. Sorry, Sylvie. That's the way it is, honey.

"Mr. Sullivan, Commander Barney will see you now," announced the secretary, smiling at the handsome young ensign. In a fifteen minute interview John received his assignment: the pilot's pool at North Island, San Diego, for assignment to Air Group Eleven and the carrier USS Philippine Sea. Not bad for starters, John smiled as he left the Administration Building, got in his car and headed for the Club for a quick beer and a private celebration before going home.

Officer's Club
Mainside, Pensacola

A heavy paw gripped John's shoulder. He turned to see Commander Mike Moran sliding onto the adjacent barstool.

"Buy you a drink, John?" Moran asked.

"Yes sir, glad to have another," John replied, as he stood up in deference to the senior commander.

"Sit down, John. Relax! What are you drinking?"

"Ballantine ale, sir."

"Two Ballantine's, Tiny," Mike said to the massive bartender who was wiping the bar top near the two aviators.

"You're going to tell the young ensign just how it is in the Navy?" A deep gravely laugh followed. Clearly, Tiny and Moran were old acquaintances.

"You got it, Tiny! And please bring us some nuts. How's the missus?"

"She's okay. Jus' got a little rhum'tism."

"Tell her I asked about her," Mike smiled and Tiny returned it. Ritual completed.

Having taken care of the logistics, Mike turned to John. "How's it going, Tiger? Are the troops recovering from Sloan's accident?"

"Yes, sir. But, it's still quite a shock. He was the first one of our class to go. Until now, I guess we all thought we were immortal!"

"Yeah, I know what it's like. When you're young, you really do think you're immortal. Even during the war, we thought like that," Mike reminisced, as he took a sip of beer. "or at least we talked like that. Now another real war. You'll grow up fast."

"Growing up when and where I did - during the Depression and the War - I never had much time for being young."

He studied John for a moment, and said, "You're a serious-minded young man, John, aren't you? And, you're good at what you do."

John didn't know what to say to that compliment. "Well, thanks, sir. I guess I am. I probably take things more seriously than my buddies. Sometimes, they call me grandpa." he laughed.

Mike said nothing, but snapped his fingers to get Tiny's attention. Tiny had two more on the bar with a pair of sparkling clean glasses in three seconds.

"Not for publication, John, but I'm leaving the Cabot for a new command. I'll be Commander of Carrier Air Group Eleven."

"The CAG for Eleven? That's great, sir! I just got the word that I'm going to the Air Group Eleven pool at North Island." John brightened.

"I know," Moran chuckled. "I asked for you. As I said, I like the way you fly, and the way you handle yourself. Now that we're going to war, I want the best or at least the better pilots. I think you're one of them. And I'm stealing the LSO, Joe Ward who waved you during quals. You know NavCads Larry Duncan and Dave Herbert?"

"I met both of them at Sloan's house the night of the accident. Larry seems like a nice guy, but he shouldn't play poker." John laughed. "You can tell what he's about to say just reading his expression."

"That's him, John," Mike smiled. "He can't hide an emotion, but he has an intuitive mind that quickly grasps and analyzes everything he sees. He's an above-average pilot, but not spectacular. He has potential, plus he's good company to have around. He'll keep people loose."

"Dave Herbert is a likable guy, but seems just the opposite, sir. I can't read him at all."

"Yeah, he reminds me of a big cat - cool, aloof, but deadly. I think he'll take risks, but always a calculated one. Anyway, I got both of them tagged, plus the LSO - and you too!" Laughing, he rose from his barstool, and put a five-dollar bill on the bar.

"Keep the change, Tiny."

John began to protest that Mike had picked up the whole tab.

"Forget it, John. I'll get you at the bar in Dago." He said as he and John headed for the parking lot together.

"Tell me - how are the wives taking it?"

"Taking what, sir? The war? Or Andy's death?"

"Both."

"Well, sir, this flight school routine has been a lark for them. They know they married hot shots, and stepped into a ready-made social organization. They never realized - or at least never thought much about accidents happening. It always seemed to happen to someone else. As for war, well, I guess it's just like the accidents. But, what a double whammy. It hit my wife hard, although now she seems to have rallied. But, when she hears I'm going off to war, it might hit hard again. Nevertheless, I think there's steel there. I sure hope so anyway."

"John, the women who are strong will adjust and take the risks in stride. Some actually like the idea that their men live dangerously. It gives them a sense of perspective. They can't talk about the bullshit - like crabgrass and diapers - because tomorrow their husband may be dead. The others will piss and moan, bitch and whine until their husbands divorce them or get out to take a nice safe job in an office,"

27

he snorted. " Then the husband gets pissed off and resentful because all his friends are still living the life he had to leave. It's not a good scene."

John stopped at his parked car, saluted, and said, "Thanks for the beer, sir - and the conversation."

Mike extended his hand, "Take it easy, John. I'll see you in San Diego."

But, instead of moving away, he paused. "One other thing, John. You're a good pilot who could be a great one. But, there's one thing about flying that you need to be aware of. You need luck. I've seen excellent pilots die because luck wasn't on their side at one moment in time. We all know that when we land safe, no matter how skilled we are - we've beaten the odds. Lots of times we do it because we're just plain good, but more often than not luck has more to do with it than anything else. So, just hope you never come up snake-eyes, son, and pray that if you do, it's not a bad situation." Moran drew on his cigar, and smiled. "The philosophy class with Monsignor Moran is over. Go home to your wife and give her the bad news. See ya in San Diego, John."

CHAPTER 2

2739 Cedar Lane
Pensacola, Florida

"Hey, babe, you look great," John said appreciatively as he ogled Sylvia who was putting on the last touches to her makeup. It was the big day - graduation from flight training. The ceremonies would be held at Mainside in an hour. For the big event Sylvia was wearing a simple print dress with a pleated skirt that swished when she turned. She had her dark hair done up in a ponytail arrangement that was so popular with the young wives. When she left the house, she would also be wearing a flowered bandeau hat and white gloves, as was the custom for formal occasions like the awarding of the coveted Navy wings of gold.

"Here, darling. Fix the clasps on my collar," John said as Sylvia finished applying her lipstick. He leaned towards her while she worked at putting together the tight choker collar of the service dress white uniform. Sylvia got two of the three hooks in the high collar put together, but the last one was a bitch - made even more difficult by the distraction of John running his hands around her derriere.

"Damnit, John. If you don't stop that we'll never get to the ceremony!" Sylvia growled, playfully.

"Why don't we just skip it, darling," he teased. "I'll call in sick and we'll crawl back in bed, and do some good things together," John replied, now running his hands around her breasts.

"Stop it, John!" she complained, but the offer was still tempting.

"Okay, okay! But are you interested in a date, a little celebration later?" He said, his hands still roaming.

Sylvia patted his collar, brushed his shoulder boards, and gave him a quick inspection. "You'll pass. And I don't think I look too bad either," she said with a final look at herself in the mirror. "Let's go!" She started towards the door. "Well, Big Guy - do I have plans for you tonight? Yes, but until then," she grabbed his ear, and twisted it playfully. "Keep your cotton-picking hands to yourself!"

Sylvia was very satisfied with herself. She had two bottles of champagne on ice, a slinky white satin nightie, low cut in front with a slit up the side, and dinner reservations at the club. *Yes indeedy, I have plans for you, Johnny boy - lascivious plans for the new naval aviator*, she thought to herself as she walked to the car. *But I'll have to get him out of the O'Club and away from his buddies before they get wrapped up in their flying and drinking. I'd rather have him sober, but come to think of it he's pretty damned good when a little tipsy too!*

Mainside
Pensacola, Florida

The Commanding Officer of Mainside, Captain John Broka, rose from his seat and approached the microphone. "Ladies and gentlemen, may I present Vice Admiral Ralph Towers, Commander, Naval Air Training who will present the wings and diplomas to the new aviators."

"Thank you, Captain," the Admiral began, looking over his half-rim glasses. "Ladies and gentlemen - and particularly the new aviators of the class of 23-9. Gentlemen, you are the first class to graduate since the North Koreans invaded South Korea. For you it is a time of heavy responsibility, a time of great challenge, and also a time of great opportunity. Many, if not most of you, will become involved in the war - now officially known as a Police Action," he chuckled and the aviators guffawed." War or Police Action - call it what you will - you are going to get shot at. Frankly, your business is flying and killing. You will have the opportunity to test your skills and test your mettle in combat. How well you do will strongly influence your future life - first as a man, second as a naval officer, and third as an aviator. Your character will be changed by combat. Make certain the change is for the better.

"Now, we all know the news of the war on the radio is sparse. Frankly, the people don't want to hear about it. So I'll give you an update. Some of this is sensitive - keep it to yourselves and your loved ones." He looked down at the intelligence summary and continued.

"The 24th Army Division arrived at Pusan on 2 July from Japan. First contact with the enemy was made about ten miles south of Suwon. The First Cavalry joined the 24th. These two divisions plus the four ROK divisions, which are badly beaten up now, form the Eighth Army under Lieutenant General Walker. They have been unable to stop the North Korean advance thus far because they still do not have the tanks necessary to counter the Russian T-34's. They are now forming a line of defense 35 miles from Pusan, and their armor should be arriving shortly. Without the armor it is questionable whether they can hold that little piece of real estate, but Walker has been directed to do so at all cost. The First Provisional Marine Brigade has been formed and will embark shortly for Korea.

"Naval aviation has been making its mark. On 3 July the Valley Forge, in company with the British carrier HMS Triumph, bombed the North Korean capitol of P'yongyang and has been carrying out interdiction and counter air strikes against railroad bridges, rail yards, airfields, and roads.

"Two jet pilots off the Valley made the first air combat kills of the war. Lieutenant junior grade Plog and Ensign Brown of VF-51 each shot down a NKAF Yak-9 prop fighter, and then destroyed two more on the ground. The Boxer will deploy shortly, giving us two first-line carriers on the line. I also understand that we will soon deploy two escort class carriers with Marine squadrons embarked.

"Gentlemen, there's a big fight brewing out there for you." The Admiral surveyed the new aviators with a steely eye, paused, and then said, " Let's give you your wings, and let you get on with the fight. As my aide calls your name please come up and receive your diploma and gold wings. We'll leave it to the wives and girl friends to pin them on. Would everyone please hold the applause until the last man has received his wings."

FASRON 4
NAS North Island

"Gentlemen, welcome to Air Group Eleven pilot's pool. I'm Commander Mac Demmler, the Acting CAG for this rowdy outfit. The new CAG, Commander Mike Moran, will report in two weeks. He's coming from the Cabot at Pensacola where he was Air Boss. Some of you new guys may know him."

John turned to Guy and chuckled, "Mike Moran is one tough son of a bitch, but he's fair. And he takes care of his men. I talked to a lot of the flight deck people on the Cabot. They really like him, and I heard he's a damned good fighter pilot."

"Before we get into the training program we have laid out for you, Lieutenant Alfie Joyce, one of our new air intelligence officers, will give you a rundown on what's happening in Korea. The briefing is secret. Alfie, it's all yours." Mac sat down.

"Gentlemen, the defense of the Pusan Perimeter is strengthening. The First Marine Provisional Brigade has arrived, as have two CVE's, the Sicily with the Marine Black Sheep Squadron embarked, and the Badaeng Strait with VMF-323 embarked, both flying Corsairs. They will provide close air support to the Army as well as the First Provisional Marine Brigade. It seems the Air Force has forgotten how to do close air support." Ribald comments about Air Force pilots emanated from the audience. " A Marine night fighter squadron, VMF(N)-513 flying the powerful F4U-5N Corsairs is now at Itizuki for defense of Japan. Also the Boxer is now on station with the Valley Forge. Any questions? Back to you CAG."

"Okay, guys," the Acting CAG said, sitting on the edge of the table and draping one leg over the front. "We'll schedule you for two hops a day by division. Some of you have never done a division takeoff from a tarmac - or a division landing for that matter. As you have observed already, North Island has two active runways - one east-west along the north side, and one north-south on the west side. They're used mostly for jets and transports. The entire area between them and the hangars and shops is paved in blacktop, called the tarmac. You can have as many as eight planes landing on the tarmac at once. So pay attention. Remember, a mid-air collision can spoil your whole day! So could a ground loop on landing!" Chuckles and comments from the audience.

"You enter the pattern going up the Strand north from the destroyer piers, fanning out as you go to get spacing, and then straight in to the tarmac. Okay? Any questions? Monday we'll do a cook's tour of the area and let you see landings and takeoffs from the tower."

Mac Demmler stood up, straightening the creases in his uniform. "Enough for today. It's Friday afternoon and time for a little Happy Hour to get to know each other. What'll it be? O'Club or Mexican Village?"

"Mexican Village! MexPac!" the aviators roared, laughing and talking as they gathered their papers, dumped the cigarette butts, and straightened the briefing room.

"MexPac it is then," the Acting CAG laughed. "But I wonder how much you'll really get to know each other and how much time you'll spend trying to make out with some of those ravishing beauties! I have some papers to finish up, but I'll see you in an hour."

"Hey! What's the Mexican Village?" John asked Guy as they headed for the parking lot and their cars.

"The Mexican Village has the best - literally the best, John! The coldest drinks and the hottest women, the biggest tits any place south of LA, and the best bodies! A real body exchange. All the local girls go there, husband-hunting, of course, but there also are the imports - tourists from all over the U.S. who have heard about the Mexican Village and just want to fuck a fighter pilot on their vacation!" He laughed.

"You got to be shitting me, Guy," John shook his head.

"No shit, John! Maybe I shouldn't take a nice married guy like you there! Too much temptation. You'll just get in trouble."

John chuckled, "I can handle it, but I'd better call Sylvie and tell her that I'll be late."

2739 Maple Drive
San Diego, California

"Oh damn! It's the phone," Sylvia said, wiping her hands on her apron and shoving the pie she was making into the oven.

33

"Sullivan residence," Sylvia answered, balancing the earpiece with her shoulder as she continued to clean up the kitchen counter.

"Hi honey, it's me. I'll be a little late. Everyone's going to Happy Hour at the Mexican Village. I'll be home by seven."

"Where's that, John?"

"It's in Coronado near the ferry landing. They tell me it's a bar and restaurant and apparently popular with the aviators," John said, omitting Guy's comments about big tits and fucking.

"Okay, sweetheart. I'll see you then."

Mexican Village
Coronado, California

The Mexican Village was located two doors up from the landing leading to the ferry slip, a convenient place for drunks to stagger across to the ferry for San Diego, or for the not-so-drunk to drive their cars to the line waiting to embark. The front of the building was narrow with two small windows and a large green double door also with small windows. The doors swung open and closed constantly with the comings and goings on most nights.

The Village was in full swing when John arrived and entered through one of the green doors. As soon as his eyes became accustomed to the gloom and the smoke, he saw a long bar, extending deep into the room on the right, crowded with aviators and good looking women happily chattering and laughing. The wall on the left was lined with high-backed booths which provided some privacy. They were already nearly full with patrons. Mexican hats, banderas, and swords festooned the dingy stucco walls and baskets of tired plastic flowers hung from the overhead's arched beams, giving the feeling of a back room in a cantina where people played and enjoyed themselves - even if it was sort of frowsy around the edges. The room was laden with smoke, further darkening the already dimly lighted area. The waitresses were pert, beautiful and well endowed. They wore peasant blouses pulled down over one shoulder with full swinging skirts gathered up above the knee to expose more leg.

The atmosphere was naughty, the ambiance raucous, and the crowd fast and noisy.

John and Guy elbowed their way through the crowd and found more Air Group Eleven aviators about halfway down the bar.

"Hey John, Sylvia give you your liberty card?" one of them yelled.

"Not a problem," John called back.

"Did you tell her about the Village, John?" snickered a bachelor. "If she knew you were here, she'd cancel that liberty card fast. Deceitful, John. Very deceitful." The other guys roared and made snide remarks.

"Not really. When I told her I was coming here, I didn't know what it's like! You all told me it was a restaurant, and it's listed in the phone book as such." John smiled innocently and rolled his eyes to the ceiling.

"But I told you about the Village, John. You're waffling," Guy laughed and drained his glass.

"Yes, you did but I considered the source. All naval aviators are ten percent truth and ninety percent bullshit!" John smiled and lifted his drink in a toast to lying naval aviators.

"Some husbands are even less truthful than that, John, especially when they're talking to their wives!"

"Hear! Hear!" Air Group Eleven roared.

2739 Maple Drive
San Diego, California

Sylvia sat on the couch watching *I Love Lucy* after finishing her pie which was cooling on the counter top

You know, she said to herself. *John owes me a night out! Why don't I just clean up, jump in a cab, and go to this Mexican Village Restaurant, and after Happy Hour we'll go to dinner - like we used to do in Pensacola! All the guys would go to Happy Hour. Then when it was winding down and most of the drunks gone, we wives would join them. Why not? We had such fun then!* She jumped up, dropped her dress on the way to the bedroom, shed the bra and panties as she entered and went straight to the shower. Twenty minutes later she was in her new shirtwaist dress, had a new face on, and a cab on the way.

"Yes ma'am," the cabbie smiled, as he opened the door for her. "Where'd you like to go?"

"The Mexican Village Restaurant in Coronado, please."

35

The cabbie, a grizzled veteran of the San Diego streets, gave her a funny look for a second, closed the door, and walked around the cab to slide into the driver's seat.

Maybe this is one of those Navy broads who cheat on their husbands when they are deployed to WESPAC. Funny - she doesn't look like one though. Too fresh looking, he murmured to himself. Being part psychiatrist, part psychologist, and part father confessor, the cabbie felt sure in his judgment that she was not the type.

"You sure it's the Mexican Village you want to go to, ma'am?" he volunteered, looking in the rear view mirror to judge her response.

"Oh yes, please. Happy Hour is in progress, and my husband's already there," Sylvia replied happily.

"Does he know you're coming, ma'am?" the cabbie rolled his eyes upwards to express his disbelief.

"No. I'm going to surprise him."

I'll just bet you will. You'll do that for sure, little lady, the cabbie mumbled as he turned into Old Town to access 101 and head for the Coronado ferry. *You'll surprise the hell out of him. I hope he's behaving when you get there, lady.* He grimaced and shook his head at the foibles of the young.

"You really shouldn't do this, lady. You really shouldn't," he said aloud to Sylvia. "Why don't I take you to the El Cortez? They have a nice restaurant on the top floor. You can call him from there and have him meet you."

"Oh no," Sylvia replied. "We always meet at Happy Hour. Maybe we'll go to the El Cortez after we get together at the Village."

"It's your funeral, lady," the cabbie shrugged his shoulders and stopped talking.

Mexican Village
Coronado

Moose Flanagan was feeling no pain as he ordered another ale, putting his foot on the bar rail and shoving for space. "I got the best spot here," he announced to his FASRON buddies. "I can watch the front door and pick off any new pussy as it comes in." He leered at the faces around him.

"Moose, you need to go back to the BOQ and sleep it off. C'mon. I'll drive you," one of the FASRON troops offered.

"Yeah, in a minute, but let me look at one more before I go," he grinned.

At that moment Sylvia came through the main entrance, looked around timidly, and then headed towards the back looking for John.

My God, this is a really rowdy place and look at some of these women, she said hesitantly to herself.

Her thoughts were interrupted by a large meaty hand which put a vise-like grip on her wrist and pulled her to its owner, a large beefy man with pig eyes and a flushed face.

"C'mere, darlin', and talk to the ole Moose. You are really something else!" He grinned, blowing his beery breath in her face.

"I'm sorry, but I don't know you! Please let go. You're hurting my wrist," she replied, struggling to free herself.

"Oh my God! Where's John!"

Instead of freeing her, Moose pulled her up tight to him and gripped her around the waist with his other hand. "C'mon, honey. Loosen it up. The ole Moose won't hurt you. I just want a few kisses, a little feel, and maybe a little..." he leered down her dress. "Maybe a little more." He pinched her fanny.

"Let me go!" cried Sylvia.

"Let her go, Moose," his buddy said anxiously, but the other FASRON troops were laughing and commenting as Sylvia struggled to break free.

Sylvia finally lost her temper. "You let go of me, you bastard." She yelled and pulled free of the waist restraint, and was trying to free her wrist without success.

"John! John! John! Help me!" She screamed as tears came to her eyes.

The blow traveled only eighteen inches, the right fist striking Moose in the jaw just below the temple, knocking him flat, and stunning him. John was on top of him in an instant, grabbing him by his belt and shoulders and hustling him towards the door which opened to admit a startled new CAG Eleven, Commander Mike Moran.

"Hold the door for me, sir, while I rid the premises of some trash."

CAG did as bidden and John threw Moose out on the sidewalk. Moose landed on his face.

An angry crowd of FASRON aviators had gathered near Sylvia who was trying to smooth her dress from the fall that happened when John hit Moose.

The Air Group Eleven troops who saw that John was involved and in trouble moved forward menacingly.

"Would you mind telling me what that was all about?" CAG said calmly.

"That clown had hold of Sylvie and wouldn't let her go."

"Sylvie?"

"I'm sorry - my wife. Sylvie, this is CAG. CAG, my wife, Sylvie."

"You brought your wife here, John?" CAG asked incredulously, his face reflecting astonishment.

"It was a misunderstanding, CAG."

"And you better get your ass out of here, swabbie," a FASRON aviator barked. "And take your little sweet patootie with you. We don't need women like that in here."

"No one throws an Air Group Eleven aviator out while we're here," Guy yelled, as the murmur of violence grew.

"Alright guys," CAG interjected. "You've had your fun and no one's been hurt. Let's just settle down to some serious drinking. Okay?"

"Just who the hell are you, buddy," a FASRON troop piped up.

"Sorry. I'm Mike Moran, Commander, United States Navy, and the new CAG for Air Group Eleven. Any more questions before we settle down?"

"Settle down, bullshit!" some one in the rear of the FASRON crowd chirped up. "Maybe I ought to just kick his ass."

CAG heard him and shouldered his way though the crowd. "Sailor Boy, if you want to step outside and kick my ass, you're welcome to try. I'll be glad to take my stripes off and keep the Group Eleven guys quiet. But in all fairness I need to warn you - I was middleweight champion of the Pacific Fleet for five years running. Undefeated. You still think you want to try me?"

"CAG, if you need help, Air Group Eleven is standing by," Guy yelled from the far side of the bar.

38

"Not necessary, men. Now let's get back to our drinking."

"Hey Sylvie," one of the Eleven aviators called. "Come on over here, we'll take care of you, baby - and bring that dippy husband of yours with you."

Everyone laughed and the tension broke.

"John, let's get out of here and go to the O'Club," CAG said, taking Sylvia by the arm and steering her towards the door. "I'm meeting my wife, Peg. Please join us for dinner. I wanted to talk to you anyway when I checked in, John, and this is as good a time as any. Besides, Peg will want to meet Sylvia and talk about the ways of fleet aviators and their wives. As you just saw, life's a lot different here than it was in flight training."

"Oh CAG, we'd love to," Sylvia replied for both of them, giving him a warm grateful smile.

"Good. I'll meet you there. We'll take both cars."

Officer's Club
North Island

Peg Moran was pushing forty-five, but didn't show her years. An Irish colleen with curling reddish brown hair that framed her face, a turned-up nose and an ever-smiling mouth, she radiated an inner beauty and serenity that was apparent to all. She was everything you'd expect in a senior officer's wife - gracious, kind, considerate, and able to cope.

Peg grew up in Lincoln, Nebraska, as had her husband, Mike. They went steady in high school and later dated at the Academy, Peg traveling the long distance to Annapolis. Mike gave her a miniature his second class year and they became engaged. Peg was a perfect foil for Mike. She knew how to handle the junior officers' wives, all of whom adored her, and she knew how to deflect the amorous attentions of men drawn to her by her charm and verve.

"Peg, this is Lieutenant junior grade John Sullivan and his wife, Sylvia. John'll be with us in Air Group Eleven."

"Welcome aboard," Peg smiled and offered her hand. "Sylvie - can I call you Sylvie? Sit here next to me, so we can talk together. I know these men will soon be out in the wild blue yonder - making like airplanes with their hands." Peg patted the chair next to her for Sylvia to sit and then mimicked the men by waving her hands around.

"Fly boys," she laughed turning to Mike, "Where'd you run into these charming young people?"

"Well, Peg, as you know, I was planning to stop for a few minutes at Happy Hour in the Mexican Village. I arrived just in time to hold the door for John to throw out a misbehaving aviator."

"My goodness, John! You didn't! Why?"

"He was molesting Sylvie."

"You didn't take Sylvie to the Mexican Village, did you, John? Shame on you, taking a nice young lady like Sylvie to that place!" She waggled her finger at him.

John blushed and Mike smiled at his discomfiture.

"Aw, it wasn't his fault, Peg. Sylvie decided to surprise him, thinking it was a restaurant."

"Oh Sylvie," Peg interrupted, and smiled at her, "You never go to the Mexican Village without an invitation, and certainly not without an escort on your arm when you enter!" Peg smiled at Sylvie. Mike chuckled, John looked somber, and Sylvia blushed in embarrassment at her faux pas.

"But, not to worry, dear! A natural mistake," Peg continued and took her hand. "We'll have lunch together at the O'Club next Wednesday noon, and I'll introduce you to all the social niceties of a fleet community of wild carrier aviators."

"Shall we order, Peg?" Mike asked.

"Of course, dear."

After dinner was finished, Mike ordered a brandy for himself and John and a creme de menthe for the ladies.

"John, my job right now is to put together a top Air Group Eleven team. I've gone over your record and talked to your instructors at Pensacola. I want you in jets as soon as possible."

John's eyes lighted up. "Thank you, sir. I really want that."

Mike continued. "However, it's not easy. Assignments to the Jet Training Unit at Olathe are few and far between, and the Training Command controls them. It will be years before the waiting list drops down. The only other way is to get assigned to a squadron already flying jets. I can't swing that with a fighter squadron, but an old shipmate of mine has command of VC-61, the Pacific Coast photo recce squadron. We will have a detachment assigned to Air Group Eleven. I want you in it."

"Aw CAG, c'mon! I don't want photo recce! I want a fighter squadron!" John complained, exasperated at the unexpected turn of events.

"Listen to me, son. Do you want to fly jets now, or wait three years - maybe five, and maybe never make it because of circumstance? A bird in the hand is worth two in the bush, believe me. Besides, I want you in jets, and I want you in that detachment. Do one tour in Korea on the Phil Sea in recce, and I promise you, I'll get you into a jet fighter squadron for your second tour. This week you and I are going up together and dogfight. I want to see personally if you measure up to my expectations. If you don't, the deal is off."

He pulled a cigar from inside his jacket.

"Alright, CAG, you're the boss - but only one tour in photo recce." CAG's offer of a jet fighter squadron in a year perked John's sagging morale.

"I promise you, John. And, John, you'll need to do a lot of learning on your own out there at Miramar. VC-61's training program leaves something to be desired. Their training for recce is great, but their basic flight and tactics stink. I want you to call my Ops once a month to schedule a check flight with me. Also as soon as I can, I will periodically schedule you for a week with VF-112 to learn some fighter tactics. Neither skipper will like it, but that's the nice thing about being CAG. They don't have to." He laughed and lighted his cigar.

Sylvia and Peg had been silent during all the male dialogue. Peg looked at Sylvia and said, "That's enough of this man talk. Let's talk about boy and girl things." She paused and looked at John.

"John, you'd best pay attention to Mike. He's been around carrier aviation a long time and knows what he's talking about. And most important he's still alive. Follow his example, and do us all a favor!" she smiled at him.

"One final word, Peg and I'll shut up. John, we have two young ensigns fresh from the training command reporting in this week - Larry Duncan and Dave Herbert. Do you remember them?"

"Yeah, we talked about them at the O'Club at Mainside. I met them. Nice guys, but I've never flown with them."

"Well, I'm also sending them to VC-61 to become part of your detachment. I'm still looking for an O-in-C."

"What's an Oh In See, CAG?" Sylvia asked, and thought. *There's so much I have to learn. I really am naive.*

CAG laughed, "Sorry Sylvie - an Officer in Charge, sort of like a Commanding Officer of a very small unit."

"Sounds like oink! I thought it was a pig farm," Sylvia giggled.

"That's the way, Sylvie," Peg laughed her warm laugh. "Don't let those guys get ahead of you." She turned to Mike and added, "Mike, are you quite finished with this Navy stuff?"

"Okay, Peg darling. Okay," Mike sat back in his seat and physically yielded the floor to Peg.

"Sylvie, what are your hobbies, besides beating John at tennis?" Peg smiled mischievously at John. Sylvia had mentioned it during their visit to the ladies' room. John blushed, not knowing what to say. Sylvie smiled at him, then pushed her hair back, and let it fall again, happy to be one up on him.

"I like designing women's clothes, modeling, and presentation of fashion. I won some awards in retailing in Columbus, Ohio. My college had an outstanding program."

"Good," Peg responded. "I have contacts in San Diego. I'll help you break in, if you like. You'll need something like that when these guys are deployed and you get lonely. My hobby is floral arrangements, and I work part time for a florist. It keeps me busy, and I enjoy it as well." The two women smiled at one another.

Naval Air Station,
Miramar, California

The advantage to the Navy of Miramar was its isolation. Other than Camp Elliott, a broken down Marine facility in caretaker status, there was nothing else on the mesa, and the Navy was buying up the surrounding land as fast as it could in order to control the area beneath its flight patterns and thereby prevent encroachment and later complaints. Even then, the Navy wanted to make Miramar its Fighter Town, but it had a long way to go in 1950!

When John arrived at VC-61, he learned to his dismay that he would still have to fly props for four additional months. The squadron did not have enough jets and, therefore, only pilots with three months to go until deployment were allowed to check out in them.

"When you're ready, John," the Operations officer told him in the Ready Room over a cup of coffee, "we'll put you on the flight schedule, and send a mechanic out with you to make sure you don't over-temp the engine when you start."

"Sounds like you're more concerned about the airplane than the pilot," John retorted.

"You got it, buddy. Jet planes are in short supply. Pilots are a dime a dozen! That's a joke, son." But John wasn't so sure.

The CO, Randy Green, cornered John by the coffee maker in the Ready Room as John was finishing a cup before his Corsair flight. "Have you heard the news, John? The Eighth Army has broken out of the Pusan Perimeter, and the Marines have landed at Inchon. Maybe the war will be over by the time you get there." He poured his coffee.

"Where's Inchon?" John asked.

"West of Seoul," came the reply. "The news said it was a real military coup. The tides there are among the worst in the world. But they're ashore and established, headed for Suwon where they'll link up with the Eighth breaking out from Pusan. The gooks are in full retreat." He paused for a moment and then asked," How you coming on your jet checkout?" Without waiting for an answer, he swallowed his coffee and walked out.

John chuckled. "Too many G's. His mind's going. But, Sylvie will love the news. No more war worries. Personally, I'm sorry to miss the action, although I'm happy to see it ended."

As John prepared for his first jet flight, he asked a lot of questions of the qualified jet pilots in the Ready Room, and he got lot of answers - quite different answers to the same question, and frequently wrong answers. The knowledge of jet aircraft and jet operations was abysmally slim.

Naval Air Station
North Island, California

Every month John went to North Island to fly with CAG, first in F4Us and later in the F9F Panther after he had qualified in it. They did section tactics, division tactics, and dog fighting.

"Look at that little shit trying to turn inside me," Mike grunted laboriously through tightened lips as he pulled 4g's to counter John's maneuver. His face sagged from the increased body weight, but the high-pressure air entering his G-suit squeezed his abdomen, thighs and calves, and kept him from blacking out. "A little more experience and he'll begin to whip my ass. At my age I'll have a hard time pulling the extra g's to counter him. But I'm still smarter," he wheezed through his teeth as he whipped into a high-speed reversal, and almost threw the Corsair into a snap roll and spin. It put him on John's tail in the fatal six o'clock position. "Rat-a-tat tat. Gotcha, John." CAG laughed.

They landed the two Corsairs on the tarmac and walked to the line shack to fill out the Yellow Sheet. "I just got briefed on Korea, John." CAG said. "Want to hear the latest?"

"Sure. Are we at the Yalu yet?" John asked.

"Almost, but there are disturbing reports of Chinese volunteers operating with the North Koreans. Intelligence is worried, but the Mighty Man in Tokyo says it's not a problem."

"Sylvie was so happy when she heard of the North Korean rout after the Inchon landings. All she can think about now is that the war's over."

"Don't let her get complacent, John. This thing's not over yet."

Officer's Club
NAS North Island

Sylvia arrived late for her luncheon with Peg. Greatly embarrassed she hurried across the dining room to the terrace.

"I'm so sorry, Peg. The damned ferry was late!" she said as she slid onto a chair and smiled her apologies.

"Not to worry," peg laughed and waved to the waiter. "Let's be sinful and have a glass of wine." The logistics satisfied Peg sat back. "Okay, tell me. How did you manage to end up in the Mexican Village?"

Sylvia looked at her like a naughty child. "John called me and said he was going to happy hour at the Village. I thought it was a restaurant- bar – sort of like the Club- and decided to surprise him."

"Well, surprise him you did, sweetie! MexPac is a pretty rowdy spot. Nice girls don't go there."

Sylvia laughed. "So I found out! The taxi driver tried to talk me out of it, and I should have listened to him.

The wine arrived and was poured. Peg raised her glass. "Here's to Air Group Eleven. God protect them all." After a sip she continued. "Okay, tell me about yourself and how you and John met."

"Well, I'm a spoiled brat from a very waspish bedroom community north of Columbus, Ohio – beautiful and well-bred – Worthington, Ohio."

Peg chuckled, "Spoiled you probably are. A brat – no way! Untutored in the ways of the big city – or at least carrier aviation – definitely yes. And it's my job to educate you. Where did you go to school?"

"Daddy wanted me to go to Vassar, but Mom wanted me close to home. So I went to Saint Mary's of the Woods, a girl's finishing school run by the good sisters. A damned good liberal education with a lot of cultural polishing. They had a great program in fashion design and marketing. As I told you before, I did well in it."

"Yes, and it will be helpful here when the men deploy and we are left to keep ourselves busy. Now tell me how you and John met."

"Daddy brought him home for dinner on short notice. My mother had a fit. Interfered with her girl plans. Then when she learned he was an Irish immigrant, well . . . .."

"But he's not an immigrant?" Peg interrupted.

Sylvia giggled. "To my mother, all Irish were poor illiterate immigrants. And when she learned he was raised in Columbus near Timken Roller Bearing in an Irish-Wop working class neighborhood, well. . . . But Daddy prevailed and my mother just loves John now."

"Tell me more details. What a story, Sylvie."

"Well, Daddy met Midshipman John Francis Sullivan on a train returning from Washington, D.C. on business. John was going to Columbus for his summer leave from the Academy and Daddy offered him a seat in the crowded club car. Daddy was impressed with John. You see Daddy used to be a dollar-a-year man with the Navy in World War II, and greatly admired servicemen. When he learned that John was Chief O'Connor's grandson, he invited him to dinner."

"Chief O'Connor?"

"John's granddad was Chief Inspector John Francis O'Connor -

"How Irish," Peg murmured. "The Chief was a man of great integrity and well known in Columbus circles. Daddy is a prominent banker and had occasion to meet with Chief O'Connor and knew of his reputation." Sylvie paused to take a sip of her wine. "John was raised in his grandparent's home- and yes, they were, in fact, Irish immigrants. Grandfather O'Connor came over from County Cork when he was seventeen - and not an ignorant Irishman either, Peg. According to John, he was educated in a Capuchin monastery. You should see his beautiful handwriting – flowery with flourishes. A monk's script for sure."

"I'm fascinated," Peg interrupted. "but we'd better order."

After the order was taken and another glass of wine served, Sylvie continued. "Grandpa O'Connor was also a physically powerful man. Large build, like John, and tall. He used to tell tales about life in Cork- how he single-handedly hewed a six foot cross and mounted it by himself on the peak of the chapel. Claimed he used to carry hundred kilo bags of flour from the mill to the monastery, That's two hundred twenty pounds, Peg. Hauled it ten clicks on his back."

Peg laughed. "The Irish have a way with words – and tall tales too."

"That may be, but it's no tall tale that he was picked up at Ellis Island because of his physique to lay ties for the intercontinental railroad. He drove spikes across most of the west and then joined the Seventh Cavalry in Montana."

Peg roared. "Now don't tell me he's the sole survivor of Custer's last stand!"

"Oh Peg," Sylvie giggled. "It does sound like that!"

"Tell me now how your mother was sweet-talked into having him for dinner and then letting him marry you."

"Well, you know how John is. He can be so charming."

"Yeah and a line of Blarney too. Must have kissed the stone in Ireland – as my Mike would say."

"Oh Peg," she stopped a moment and the chuckled. "It wasn't all John's personality. It was Daddy. He didn't want me marrying some local yokel and settling down in the provinces to raise babies. He knew that Academy graduates were socially accepted everywhere and the old school tie could open many doors. Once Mother recognized that John was not just some ignorant Irishman . . . .."

"If there really was such type." Peg interrupted

". . .and then met John, he was tolerated initially and finally accepted despite his mother. My mother couldn't abide her. His mother opposed the marriage because she thought John should care for her first and then maybe marry some good Irish-Catholic girl when he reached thirty-five."

"A lot of them thought that way," Peg agreed. "Fortunately, Mother Moran was not like that. But what about John's dad?"

"It's a sad story. He was Comptroller for Fisher Body and contracted tuberculosis."

"Oh my . . ."

"Fisher Body sent him to a sanitarium in Santa Fe. The doctors gave him six months to live. He outlived them all – his doctors and nurses. John's mother was petrified of the disease, even after it was arrested. She refused to join him and moved in with the grandparents. They eventually divorced. It was John's father that got him the appointment to Annapolis."

"So there's no dissension in the ranks?" Peg asked.

"My mother absolutely loves John. So does my dad. John's mother tolerates me, but I love his dad and he thinks I'm great."

"Let's have at the salads," Peg said as the waiter brought their lunch. "And then I'm going to tell you about carrier aviation, carrier aviators and their wives. It's a great group of people. You'll love them to death." Peg paused. "Not a good choice of words, huh? But we accept death as something we live with." She looked carefully at Sylvia. "Mike tells me you've already had your baptism of fire."

"Yes, I have." Sylvia replied softly. "John's best friend was killed at Pensacola during carrier qualifications."

Paul Corrigan

CHAPTER 3

Naval Air Station
Miramar

After three months of Corsair flying, the great day finally arrived for jet checkout. John was up early for a last minute look at the handbook. Sylvia fixed him a hearty breakfast. " You can't fly jets on an empty stomach," she intoned. "I envy you the excitement and the thrill that you're going to experience. I know you'll do well and have fun, but, personally, I'm just as happy to stay at home, and be here when you return." She said, setting the table for him. "I'm no Amelia Erhart, but I guess there are some women who really want to fly - maybe even be fighter pilots."

"God no, Sylvia! Women fighter pilots? It would scare me shitless to have one on my wing!"

Sylvia came out to the car to wish her husband good luck. The car was a 1947 Studebaker with the rounded rear window that completely enveloped the rear seat - old and decrepit transportation for John to drive to work while Sylvia kept her beloved Green Hornet.

John took the two-lane highway through Linda Vista instead of the freeway because it was direct and much faster. He parked his car at the Administration Building, and went to his office to change into flight gear, which was more primitive than it is now, even though it performed similar functions. John wore the ultimate sign of the jet jockey, the g-suit corset and leggings under a dark green, skin-tight, nylon flight suit which was very sexy. It was also very dangerous because it burned and adhered to the skin when it melted. After a few tragic accidents, it was replaced with fire-retardent cotton. The sexy image disappeared, much to the chagrin of the jet pilots. The helmet consisted of two pieces and looked like an old World War II cloth helmet over which was strapped a hard shell. It was years before the one piece molded plastic helmet like the football players wore came into inventory. A simple Mae West with the bag of shark chaser over the heart, a dye marker, and a weak water-initiated flashing light completed the ensemble.

On his way to the line shack to check the Yellow Sheet that contained the maintenance history for his plane, John ran into Lieutenant Bob Dufoe, the VC-61 Operations officer.

"We've assigned you Peter Peter 61, John," he said. "It's been a good bird the last four flights. You should have no problem." Peter Peter was the squadron call sign of VC-61, the large PP on the rudder distinguishing the west coast photo recce birds. "Remember it's just another airplane," De Foe continued, "Go try it out. You'll like the quiet of the jet with the engine in back of the pilot. And it's a real thrill with the speed and the g-forces. You can't make a decent turn without pulling two or three g's."

John did not want PP-61 because it didn't have as much power as the dash 2 model. "Hey that's great, Bob! But, how about a duece instead?" John responded. "I'd really like an F9F-2 with the 5,000 pound thrust of the Pratt & Whitney. These runways are awfully short for jets, and this is my first try at jet flying."

"Relax, Lieutenant," De Foe laughed. "All you have to do is kick the tire, light the fire, and brief on Air Force Common. "

" Air Force Common?" John raised his eyebrows.

"C'mon, John. Get with it. Air Force Common - the Guard channel, Lieutenant. The Emergency channel that the Air Force weenies garbage up with useless chatter."

John looked dubious. De Foe chuckled, "a little nervous tiger? Don't be a candy ass." But, he saw that his light banter was not helping John relax.

"Aw, it's not a problem, John." The Ops Officer, exhibited great confidence in his opinion. "You'll never notice the difference between the prop and the jet. When you get to 105 knots just ease back on the stick, and she'll fly off on her own. Wait until you see her climb! Good luck." He gave John a healthy slap on the back and headed for his office.

John stopped in the line shack to check and sign the Yellow Sheet, see what prior gripes there had been, and what Maintenance had done about them.

"Mr. Sullivan, it's the big day for you isn't it," said the Chief who was the line supervisor, as he handed John the clipboard with PP-61's Yellow Sheet attached. "Have you met Petty Officer George Slade? He'll help you get settled in the plane and get the engine started."

"Hi, George. Don't worry. I won't break your plane," John quipped.

"Hello, Lieutenant. Well, the bird's ready to go. I'll walk around it with you and point out things. Then I'll help you start the engine. It's really no problem. Just keep an eye on the tailpipe temperature. If it soars, shut the engine down. Wait five minutes to clear excess fuel, and try again."

"Okay George, have you checked the fuel low points for water?" John said, as he walked around the plane and visually inspected it.

"Yes, sir. You have full tanks including tips. The step is down, sir, if you'd like to mount up."

"Okay, let's go," said John, putting his foot on the step and raising himself into the cockpit. He slipped the parachute harness over his shoulder, snapped the crotch straps and chest buckle, and checked the emergency oxygen bottle embedded in the parachute on which he sat.

George plugged in the g-suit, connected the radios, and put John's helmet on him. He signaled for the power unit to be started.

"Okay, hit the start button. When the RPM reaches eighteen percent, bring the throttle around the horn and you should get an immediate rise in the tailpipe temperature. If no temp after five seconds, shut down. If the temp goes to maximum limits, shut down. Try it, sir."

51

John pushed the start button, watched the RPM rise to 18 percent, moved the throttle around the horn and got a light off. Temperature increased to the normal operating range.

"Alright," George smiled at the young aviator. He tapped John on his helmet, and lowered himself off the step.

John signaled for the chocks to be removed. "Miramar Tower. Peter Peter Six One for taxi, local VFR flight plan."

"Roger, Peter Peter 61. You are cleared to runway two six. Altimeter 30.01. Winds 280 at 10."

"Peter Peter 61, Roger that. Request runway 29 instead." John asked, hoping to get the longer runway.

"Negative," the tower replied. "26 is the active."

"You son of a bitch," John growled to himself. "You just want to show who's the boss."

As John completed the take-off check list, he remembered a problem he had with the elevator trim setting. The handbook said nothing about the proper elevator trim setting for take-off, and most of the experienced jet pilots dismissed it, saying, "use whatever you want." Lacking any better ideas, John set the elevator trim at zero degrees.

"Tower, Peter Peter 61, Ready for take-off."

"Peter Peter 61, tower. Cleared for take off number one, runway 26. Altimeter 30.01."

"Rog, tower. Rolling."

The jet accelerated slowly at first. In the cockpit there was the whine of the air conditioner, but otherwise complete silence. John marveled at the lack of noise, no heavy foot pressure on the right rudder to counter torque, and total visibility of the runway. When the aircraft velocity reached 105 knots, John eased back on the stick. Nothing happened. *Maybe I need a little more flying speed.*

At 110 knots John eased the stick back again. Again nothing. The aircraft seemed firmly planted on the runway and was not about to fly. The end of the runway was rapidly approaching. John had no choice. He literally yanked the bird off the runway against heavy forward stick pressure, and the bird flew.

Exhilarated, John immediately raised the landing gear and the flaps. Suddenly, nose of the plane pitched sharply down, and John was looking at the runway approach markers coming at him.

"Peter Peter, are you in trouble?" came the voice of the tower operator.

Uncertain what caused the tremendous pitch change, John gently eased the stick back watching the response. The plane flew low over the runway markers, and between two groves of trees as he picked up airspeed, and then he climbed - all the while grumbling, "Was I in trouble? You bet your sweet ass I was."

Now angry at the lack of response by the pilot, the tower operator assumed the maneuver was deliberate. "Peter Peter 61, you're on report for flat-hatting on take-off. Report to the duty officer upon landing."

At this point John could care less. He now had control of the bird, and was rapidly departing the airfield. Climbing at 4000 feet a minute, John marveled at the plane's response, its maneuverability, power, and rate of climb. A few slow rolls - not supposed to be done on the first flight - steep chandelles pulling almost vertical and then rolling off on a wing, and some 4-g turns convinced him that he was in a new world - a wonderful new world of jet flight!

After an hour of playing tag with the clouds in between the serious business of practicing slow flight, stalls, and landing configurations, John paused to analyze what had happened on take-off. Obviously the trim setting was very wrong - maybe as much as 1-2 degrees. The heavy nose-down trim kept the plane firmly on the runway until John overpowered it. The nose-down rotation when the flaps were raised was an enigma to him. He had nothing in his experience to relate it to. He was to find out later that the F9F flap system lacked a bungee arrangement that compensated for the large change in wing camber as the flaps came up.

"Miramar tower, Peter Peter 61. Over the point. Landing instructions."

"Roger, Peter Peter 61. Cleared to runway 26. Report at the break."

"Peter Peter 61. Can I have runway 29?"

"Negative, Peter Peter 61. 26 is the active."

John pressed his mike button. "Tower, you're one big pain in the ass."

"Say again PP-61," the tower came back.

"I said you are one big pain."

"Roger that," the tower replied.

John laughed to himself. "Fuck you, Miramar. I don't need the extra one thousand feet anyway," he said, setting the bird down fifty feet from the end of the runway, and turning off at the first intersection.

2739 Maple Drive
San Diego, California

John arrived home riding high. Sylvia met him at the door with a glass of champagne, a bunch of roses, and a hot kiss. "Welcome home from the wars, Sir Knight. The chastity belt is unlocked." She giggled.

"EF or FF?" John asked, leering down the front of her dress.

"We are going to dinner first. No FF. We have a reservation at the club in forty-five minutes - just enough time to shower and change - and that's all!" Sylvia replied, primly lowering her lashes. She then grabbed him by the ass and pulled him to her. "You big hunk, I love you. Now don't make me horny or we'll never get to dinner. John, stop that."

John reluctantly stopped running his hands over her tight buns.

Officer's Club
NAS Miramar

The Peter Peters of VC-61 had staked out a section of the bar. John and Sylvia were welcomed with handshakes, kisses on the cheek and some loud guffaws about John's take-off.

"Hi Sylvie, what do you think of the old man now?" one of them hooted.

"I think he's pretty hot stuff," Sylvia gaily responded, easing into a spot opened for her at the bar.

"We all saw your take-off, John. What were you doing out there? Looking for gopher holes?" Chuckled a pilot named Mike.

"Naw, he was just showing off for the tower. Are you still on report?" shouted another.

"I talked to the duty officer after the flight," John replied, looking quite serious. "He was very understanding when he learned I would share the gopher count with him. He went Able Sugar about the chance to get a gopher count." John laughed.

"You'd better get him out of here if you're planning to go to dinner," said a wife of one of the lieutenants. "Give them another hour of bar flying, and you'll never get him to dinner! You'll have to pour him into the car."

"Hi. I'm Ray Hale," said a short funny-looking man as he came up to John and Sylvia. "You're John Sullivan, and you checked out in jets today. How did it go?"

John looked at him, smiled, and turned towards Sylvia, "Honey, this is Ray Hale. Ray, my wife Sylvia." Sylvia acknowledged the introduction and Ray murmured a "Glad to" response .

"As for the flight," John continued, "I had a few problems, but it was a wonderful experience. You can really soar in a jet."

"I just checked in," Ray said "And I'll be joining you on the Philippine Sea. The skipper just assigned me as Officer-in-Charge of the detachment. Next week it's my turn to check out in the Panther."

"Congratulations on the OINC position," John said, shaking his hand.

"Oh good," Sylvia grinned mischievously. "That means you'll be the Oink of the Peter Peter barnyard detachment on the Phil Sea."

"Huh?" replied Ray.

"Just ignore the remark, Ray." John replied dryly, looking at Sylvia with feigned disapproval.

That's one up on the naval aviators, she told herself, smiling innocently at the two men.

"There's a lot to learn about jets. It's a different kind of bird," John offered for openers.

"All I need to know," Ray replied, "is how to start the engine, and where the stick and throttle are. What else do you need to know? It's just another airplane."

"I don't know," John replied, uncertain of his jet knowledge. "It sure seems different, but maybe it's just my lack of flight experience. They don't call new aviators Nuggets for nothing, you know."

"Do they call you Nugget, John?" Sylvia asked aghast.

"Not to my face," John laughed.

"Ray, is your wife here?" Sylvia asked, changing the subject.

"Nope," Ray replied. "I'm divorced and happy to be so." He grinned and looked at Sylvia, appraising her. It made her strangely uncomfortable, and she took John's arm.

"Well. We'd better get over to our table, Mister Nugget," she laughed and steered him towards the dining room.

"A pleasure to meet you, Ray. We'll see you around." John waved his arm as they left.

The O'Club dining room was small but cozy. The tables were formally laid out and there was soft piped music. Dinner was Steak Diane with a large tossed salad and a baked potato. For dessert they had baked Alaska, a specialty of the house.

John and Sylvia talked about the future and their plans. John would make one cruise on the Philippine Sea to Korea in photo recce, and then upon return he'd get transferred to a fighter squadron with CAG's help. Then another tour to Korea; and finally shore duty, hopefully at the Naval Post Grad School in Monterey.

"Just as long as we don't have to move too often," Sylvia sighed. "I get comfortable in a house, and it begins to feel like home. I like this house we're in now. I'm going to stay here until you're finished with Korea."

"Okay, honey, whatever you say. Why don't we go home and I'll bite your neck. Maybe a little feel in the car," he smiled, as he signaled for the check.

Sylvia frowned at the offer and replied, "I hope I get more than a bite on the neck, and a feel. Not much of an evening from a Stud!" She laughed as she picked up her purse, and rose to leave. Outside the club she pulled him to her and said, "A rather skimpy offer, Mister Nugget. Put your hand in my panties as we go through the gate. Let's shock the Marine guards!" she giggled wickedly. "Do you remember when we did that back in Pensacola? That Marine guard got an eyeful! Besides, I'm horny as hell! I was never like this in Worthington! You've corrupted me." She threw her head back laughing, and then kissed him, and pulled him towards the car.

After passing through the gate and turning on the radio, Sylvia put John's hand back in her panties. The soft music filled the car. Sylvia laid her head back and felt the heat of John's exploring hand flowing up through her lower body.

"We're going to do it right in the middle of the floor when we get home, Mister Nugget. You can start undressing me as we go through Linda Vista. When we pull into the garage, I want to be completely naked," she giggled.

"Just hope a cop doesn't stop us before we get there," John laughed, but he accelerated at the thought of a naked Sylvia.

"We interrupt this broadcast to bring you a special news bulletin," the radio announced.

"Oh shut up," Sylvia said to the radio, reaching to change the station, but she wasn't fast enough. The announcement had already begun.

"We have a special Associated Press report on Korea. The United Nations Command reports that the Chinese have crossed the Yalu in regiment strength and have penetrated far south. Their total strength is unknown at this time. The Eighth Army is under heavy attack on three sides, and the Marine Third Division is pinned down in a place called Chosin Reservoir in the mountains northwest of Hungnam. The Pentagon is concerned about the Marines' ability to extract themselves because the Chinese hold the mountain heights along the valley route out of the Reservoir to Hungnam. We will provide another special report as we get additional information. Now returning to our music."

Sylvia took John's hand out of her panties, and turned the radio off. She moved closer to John, her gray eyes large, and her face white with shock. She bit her knuckle and whispered. "Oh God, John. I thought that was over," as tears trickled down her cheeks.

Naval Air Station
North Island

Helmets tucked in the crooks of their arms, their oxygen masks dangling from one side, the two jet pilots sauntered across the ramp and headed for the line shack to sign in. Their yellow life vests partially covered their skin-tight dark green flight suits which were soaked with sweat from their recent exertions in air combat maneuvering. The g-suit bladders on the legs and abdomen showed prominently through their tight flight suits, and the air hoses that connected the system to the plane's air pressure dangled from their left sides, like the misplaced tail of a mongrel dog.

"You done good, son," CAG smiled at his wingman, John. "That last reversal almost got me, but you need to do your yo-yo's quickly and positively. No lollygagging to telegraph your maneuver."

"I'll never get you, CAG. You're too damned good."

"Yeah, you will, son. Before long you'll whip my ass," Mike paused, looked at him, and squinted. "I have plans for you, John. I think you've got what it takes to become an ace. So I want you to have the opportunity to achieve it in this war." Putting a hand on his shoulder, CAG stopped John, and looked him in the eye to emphasize his belief in him.

"Changing the subject. I've arranged for you, Larry, and Dave to go out next week on the Phil Sea to observe carquals. I think it will help you when your turn comes."

USS Philippine Sea
At Sea Off San Diego

The flight of four Panthers swept down the starboard side of the Phil Sea at 100 feet in a tight right echelon formation, led by Lieutenant junior grade Ralph Bonner, a classmate of John's. Ralph had gone through Pensacola in multi-engines and was assigned to VC-61 flying R4Y's, the Navy photo version of the Liberator bomber of World War II. Ralph decided he wanted to fly jets and convinced the C.O. that he could make the transition, a most unusual one since he had never landed aboard a carrier before.

The flight of four passed by the bow of the carrier on a course parallel with the ship. Ralph looked at his wingman, kissed off, and sharply threw the plane into a 60-degree, 3g bank, turning downwind to port crossing the bow of the carrier. He cut the throttles back to 60 percent, dumped the speed brakes, and at 180 knots airspeed put down the gear, flaps, and tail hook. The maneuver was sharp and impressive.

"Nice break," said the Air Boss.

"They look good," agreed CAG.

The LSO, Joe Ward, picked up Ralph at the 90 with a Roger signal.

Good position, good airspeed, he mumbled approvingly.

Ralph proceeded to fly a solid approach. A nice rollout onto the centerline of the flight deck, and a cut by the LSO who mumbled to himself, *Okay. Good pass.*

Then it happened. Ralph pulled the throttle back to idle in response to the cut, and dropped his nose to start down to a landing - but he dropped the nose too much, executing a maneuver that all LSO's feared - diving for the deck.

"Oh shit!" the LSO exploded.

"Oh shit!" the Air Boss echoed, reaching for the crash alarm.

"Oh shit!" thought John, standing behind the Air Boss.

The only one who didn't say "Oh Shit," was the pilot, Ralph, who didn't know yet that he was in deep trouble. In a fraction of a second, however, he realized what he had done as the jet landed nose wheel first. The main gear followed hitting the deck, and bouncing as the nose of the plane rotated upward into a flying attitude. It became airborne again, headed upward over the Davis barrier towards the planes parked forward.

The crash alarm screamed, "Bee-bop, bee-bop, bee-bop."

Over the bullhorn came the Air Boss' voice, "Crash! Crash! Crash! Clear the flight deck."

"Oh shit!" Ralph finally said, and jammed the stick violently forward trying to get the nose wheel back on the deck to engage the barrier, but he was too late. The jet sailed over the top of the barrier, as Ralph slammed the throttle full forward, now trying to get enough thrust and airspeed to clear the planes parked in front of him. The engine spooled up slowly - it seemed like forever, but the power began to take hold as he passed the forward edge of the island in a climbing attitude. He almost made it. As he climbed and turned to avoid a Panther spotted on the port catapult with wings folded upward, his right main landing gear struck the tip tank and wing tip of the parked jet, tearing the gear loose. Remarkably, he remained airborne!

"You talk about luck! I thought for sure he would go into the pack or over the side!" the Air Boss heaved a huge sigh of relief. "But we're not out of the woods yet, CAG. What do we do with him now?" He pinched the tip of his nose.

"Peter Peter 51. Your signal Dog. Orbit the ship at 500 feet. Do not - repeat - do not attempt to raise your landing gear or flaps. Your starboard main gear is damaged," the LSO instructed Ralph.

"I recommend we send him to the beach," CAG said.

"I agree," parroted John, and got a dirty look from CAG for breaking into the conversation.

"I don't think so, CAG," the Air Boss replied. "I think we should try to bring him aboard as soon as possible. He may have damaged the main spar in the wing. If so, it could fold up on him at any time."

"It's your decision, Air Boss. Let's see what the Old Man says." The Air Boss turned and depressed a button on the squawk box.

"Attention on the flight deck," the bull horn roared. "We're going to bring the injured Panther aboard. Clear the flight deck forward of all planes and personnel. I want all Yellow Gear - the starting units, the tractors, all the support equipment - lined up three deep in the center across the flight deck ten feet beyond the run-out distance of the barrier wires."

"You think that'll stop him?" CAG asked, his face showing his skepticism.

"If we're lucky," the Air Boss replied through a grim smile as he turned to the talker. "Tell the LSO we're bringing him aboard. Try to cut him a little left of centerline to counter his skid to the right due to the damaged gear."

Mike reached into his pocket, pulled out a long black stogie, put it in his mouth, and picked up the mike of the VHF radio. "Ralph, this is CAG. You made a good approach, boy, until the last second. Keep your cool, son and we'll bring you aboard. You can handle it. Your signal is Charlie now. Enter the pattern downwind. Joe Ward will wave you. He has some special instructions."

"Ralph, this is the LSO. Listen carefully. Give me a pattern as good as the last one. I'm going to bring you aboard about five knots slower. So watch your airspeed. Try to line up a little left of centerline, and when you get your cut try to hold the starboard wing up. For Christ's sake don't dive for the deck again like you did the last time! We want you in the wires or in the barrier."

"Okay, Joe, I'll do my best," Ralph replied grimly as he adjusted the throttle, wiped the sweat from his forehead with sweat-stained gloves, and prepared himself emotionally for a period of intense concentration.

Ralph's approach was good all the way from the 90. It was a Roger pass to a cut a little left of center and five knots slower than normal.

The port gear touched down at the number four wire, but despite Ralph's efforts, the right wing dropped onto the flight deck with a thud and the tearing of metal. The nose swerved right, placing a heavy lateral force on the nose wheel, which collapsed, lifting the tail hook off the deck. The hook could not engage a wire, and without a nose wheel strut the plane could not engage the Davis barrier

"Bee-bop, bee-bop, bee-bop," the crash alarm sounded as the Panther plowed into the yellow gear, spewing parts and pieces in all directions, and pushing the nose left so that the plane was again headed up the centerline. The Panther's port main landing gear collapsed to the sound of tearing metal, and the bird slid up the flight deck on its belly.

Reacting in sheer terror, Ralph slammed the throttle forward to 104 percent maximum engine thrust. The engine responded, as the plane continued to slide forward towards the bow on its belly, spewing a cloud of debris. The engine reached full power just before the plane arrived at the centerline elevator forward. It went off the bow and disappeared from sight.

"Right full rudder!" cried the Captain to the helmsman as he attempted to avoid running down the jet. "All engines emergency stop," he yelled to Main Control on the squawk box as the annunciators rang up the engine signal. Suddenly the Panther reappeared in front of the bow, clawing the air as it attempted to climb out of a near-stalled condition.

"I'll be damned! The lucky shit is airborne! He's going to make it! I didn't think it was possible!" CAG exploded through his cigar, which he now removed from his mouth, looked at it as though it was somehow responsible for the good fortune, stuck it back in his mouth, and smiled broadly.

"Lucky, lucky, lucky," the Air Boss added, shaking his head as his entire body sagged into the chair in utter relief. He then sat up straight and reached for the radio mike.

"Ralph, I'm sorry we were unable to trap you or get you into the barrier. We have a flight of four Panthers just arrived from the beach. The flight leader has you in sight and will rendezvous with you. Your vector is 080 degrees, eighty miles to Miramar. They're expecting you and are foaming the runway for a belly landing. Your signal Bingo. Destination Miramar. Good Luck, son."

In the cockpit Ralph heaved a sigh of relief. A wheels-up landing at Miramar was a piece of cake, compared to what he had just been through. He wiped the sweat from his face with his sleeve, pulled his gloves off, unhooked one side of his oxygen mask, took a pack of Camels from his arm pocket, and fired up, rubbing his face in the process to restore circulation.

"Peter Peter 51, this is your escort, Eagle 103. Hold your heading while I check you for damage."

103 slid under the port wing of PP-51 and slowly moved from port to starboard, inspecting for damage.

"Peter Peter, you have a problem. While damage to your flaps and wings is minimal, you have a bad leak of clear fluid, streaming from your belly. I think it's jet fuel."

"Yeah," Ralph replied. "Yeah, I just noticed it. I am really losing fuel. I can actually see the gauge dropping. I'm now less than one thousand pounds, down from the 2000 I had at the 180 on my last approach. I don't think I can make Miramar. Maybe I can dead stick it if I run out of gas."

"Peter Peter. This is CAG. You have too much damage and not enough experience to risk it. If you can't make it with the fuel remaining, eject. I repeat - Eject! We have a helo in the air, and the Coast Guard is launching another from North Island."

"You're right, CAG. I'm now down to 500 pounds and dropping rapidly."

"Punch out while you still have power, Ralph."

"I'm switching my IFF to Emergency and going," Ralph replied through clenched teeth. He reviewed the ejection litany. PRE-POS-PULL and then he executed it, pulling the pre-ejection lever which jettisoned the canopy and pulled the safety pin on the ejection seat. The air stream blasted him and ripped the outer shell of his helmet away from the inner cloth helmet as he positioned himself by aligning his spine vertically. He then reached up and pulled the face curtain. The seat exploded upward, clearing the tail and tumbling. When he was certain he was clear of the plane, he unbuckled his seat belt and pushed away from the seat. Finally he found the parachute D ring and pulled it. The chute blossomed and the long manual process of ejection was over.

Ralph plunged into a moderate sea and came up gasping for air, but clear of the chute which was billowing and threatening to pull him along after it. He hit the snaps at each shoulder, releasing the chute, pulled the lanyard to inflate the Mae West, and got a mouthful of water as a three-foot wave rolled over him.

He was heaving in on the line connected to the parachute seat pack where his one-man life raft was located when the Phil Sea's helo entered hover above him, generating wind and spray. The horse collar quickly dropped down on its cable. Ralph slipped it under his arms and the crewman began the retraction.

With Ralph safely aboard, the helo headed for the naval hospital at Balboa Park.

Naval Station
Miramar

John was seated in the Ready Room reading Grampa Pettibone and chuckling at the stupid things pilots do to get themselves in trouble. Grandpa Pettibone was a legend, the old and not so bold flyer, who called pilot's faux pas the way he saw it with colorful language to warm up the monologue. John laughed as he read about the Corsair pilot who ran out of gas after a series of ridiculous escapades dodging thunderstorms and trying to maintain Visual Flight Rules in instrument flight weather.

"Jumping Jehoshaphat!" Grandpa growled. "Another case of get-home-itis!"

The door of the Ready Room opened and Ralph entered and went to the coffee bar.

"Hey Ralph," John called. "How come you don't speak to me?"

Ralph turned and looked - recognition slowly dawning on his face.

"Oh. Hi, John. Sorry I didn't see you there. Preoccupied, I guess."

"How you feeling, Ralph?" John asked.

"Okay, I guess. A little depressed. I just turned in my wings to the Skipper."

"Hell no, Ralph! Tell me you didn't do that! Except for one error you flew a superior pattern."

"John, let me tell you, lad, I used up all my luck the other day. I was so lucky, I can't possibly have any more! I'm out of luck and that means I'm out of this game, or it will get me soon." Ralph looked at John steadily for a long moment, then set down his coffee, and left.

Two months later a driver on Interstate 5 lost control when his black cat jumped out of his wife's lap and landed on his chest. The car swerved across the median and hit Ralph's car head on. The other driver was not scratched. He got a $300 fine and a six months' suspended sentence for reckless driving. Ralph got a shiny new bronze casket and his wife the NSLI insurance.

"This one's really good, George," Joe Ward said to his LSO understudy, as John turned in from the 180 for a practice approach in the Field Carrier Landing Pattern. "I waved him in Corsairs on the Cabot in Pensacola. Six perfect passes. If he's as good in jets, watch him and learn how to do it. He's all yours, George," Ward said, handing him the paddles and reaching in his chest pocket for a pack of Lucky Strikes.

"LS/MFT," Ward added as he inhaled his first drag deeply and exhaled through his nose.

"Yeah, Lucky Strike means fine tobacco," George replied. "It also means a good case of lung cancer at age 50." George was a non-smoker and a firm believer in its hazards.

"Naw, George. That's medical mumbo jumbo." Ward took another drag.

"Here he comes," George interrupted as John passed through the 90. "Looking good."

"Yeah, look at his attitude carefully, George. See - he's slightly cocked up. Not much - about 112 - 115 knots airspeed. Now look at the leading edge of the wing and see its relationship to the leading edge of the elevator. Gives you a good check point. Each LSO has them - their own - developed over time. You should work on it."

FCLP was flown ashore using a regular runway as the simulated carrier deck to teach the pilots the patterns, altitudes, and approach speeds used in actual carrier operations. The only difference- and a big difference - was the lack of a ramp, and the blue ocean to intimidate the novice. Miramar was a good place to do FCLP. There was nothing but flat mesa with runoff gullies. The thermals were not bad, and the ride not too bouncy, but doing four hops a day with the canopy open and no air conditioning was very enervating.

The sound of the jet engine increased as the plane approached the runway and crossed the threshold. George gave John the cut and turned to watch the plane land, marking the spot where he touched down. The jet roared as the engine spooled up for take-off, executing a touch-and-go landing. As soon as the noise subsided, George put both paddles in one hand, swatted a fly that was pestering him, and said, "he landed a little long. I cut him too late."

"Good call, George. You're getting the feel of it. About a half second too late. He would have caught the number eight wire, but that's too close to the barrier. Keep working on it- you're improving. I'm going to let you wave a few aboard the carrier the next time we're out, but I'll continue to call the cut for you for a while longer."

George and Joe idled while the planes were flying their upwind pattern. "Hey, remember the Lucky Strike Hit Parade on the radio with Snooky Lanson? The top ten songs each week," Joe smiled at his trip down memory lane.

"Yeah, and the parody when they switched from a green pack to a white pack because they couldn't get materials. Lucky Strike Green Has Gone To War! Great marketing."

"Here comes the next one. Larry Duncan in Peter Peter 61. What's the name of the other guy in Peter Peter 67?"

"Dave Herbert. Duncan's kind of rough but he'll smooth out. Herbert's pretty good. Not as good as Sullivan though. VC-61 put together a good team for Air Group Eleven."

"I hear CAG had a hand in it. Sullivan's a protege' of his." Joe stopped to think for a second and then said, "I think these guys will need about ten more FCLP sessions ashore and they'll be ready for the boat."

John usually went home dogtired. It took a cool shower and some TLC from Sylvia to bring him around.

USS Philippine Sea
At Sea. Off San Diego

John rolled his Panther into a port turn off the 180-degree position as he began his sixth and final approach to the Philippine Sea. He had completed five near perfect traps with no wave offs, and was ecstatic over his performance.

"I've got this program wired," he chuckled. "I'll ace this one - one final pass and I'm jet qualified!" He checked his air speed, added a little power, and a tad more bank to bring the plane around towards the centerline of the flight deck.

"Just an RCH more power," he grinned, thinking of Sylvia's reaction when he told her what the three letters stood for.

"Looks like another good pass," Joe Ward commented to his understudy, George, as he picked up John with a Roger.

John rolled out onto centerline at 112 knots and a little high. He dropped the nose slightly, executing a high dip maneuver back to proper altitude.

A flight of four Panthers roared down the starboard side at 100 feet and flashed into John's view, momentarily distracting him.

"Good pass," the LSO mumbled, and gave him a cut. John cut the power and dropped his nose to start down towards the deck beneath him.

"Oh shit! Too much," John yelled aloud, pulling back on the stick to correct the mistake, but the jet's momentum continued to carry it down to the deck, landing nose wheel first.

"Damn!" screamed the Air Boss, hitting the crash alarm.

For a fraction of a second John saw everything in freeze motion like the individual frames of a motion picture. He could hear the crash alarm and saw men forward as they looked at him momentarily, frozen in fear, and then started to turn, their legs arcing over one another as they twisted and ran for the safety of the catwalks.

At that instant the tail hook made an in-flight engagement of the # 5 wire. The plane engaged the wire a foot off the deck, and slammed down hard on its main gear. The tires exploded, and one wheel shattered, but the gear did not collapse. The hard landing jarred John, and put heavy compression forces on his spine. He would hurt for months.

"Thank you, God! That was the nicest trap I've ever had!" John mumbled a prayer as he raised the tailhook. The yellow shirts attached a tow bar, jacked a dolly under the shattered wheel and dragged the plane forward. After he shut down, John gingerly raised himself up in the cockpit. His back hurt like hell, but he could move okay.

"After five great passes, I don't believe he did that," CAG said ruefully, pulling a stogie from his pocket.

"Complacency, Mike. Complacency sure as hell. The five great traps went to his head and he got careless. One lucky son of a bitch!" the Air Boss added, looking out over the sea at the next plane now at the 180 position. "Well, let's get on with it."

"John Sullivan, you shouldn't have done that - but learn a lesson, you lucky SOB." The LSO muttered. He turned away from watching John's plane being towed forward and began to focus his attention on the next bird now at the 90.

Ready Room #1
USS Philippine Sea

John entered the Ready Room and was greeted with the usual ribald comments that aviators use to hide their feelings about the hazards of flight.

"Hey John, that there air-ri-o-plane is not a pogo stick, you know."

"Another one like that, John, and you'll be playing a harp."

"No way, buddy," interjected another. "With his reputation he'll be shoveling coal down below."

"You trying to make Sylvie a widow?"

"Don't worry, John baby! I'll marry her."

The door opened and CAG entered on the last remark. A piercing look and a frown from Mike and the Ready Room immediately quieted.

"You almost bought the farm, son," CAG said sympathetically, taking a seat next to John. "But, having done it once and gotten away with it, you'll never do it again, believe me. Remember what I said about luck at Pensacola? You had a pair of snake eyes going for you up there, and the bet was on your life," he paused and then smiled at John. "But, one die took an extra bounce and came up six instead of an ace, to give you a lucky seven. Very lucky, John. Just remember. Watch out for the snake eyes on the big event. They can kill you. No matter how good you are, it's that one careless moment that gets you." Then he smiled. "So cheer up, lad. By the time the Phil Sea deploys, the ship will have the new eleven-foot high barricade to replace the Davis Barrier! Even you can't get over that! In the meantime, take Sylvie out to dinner, the best medicine right now for you."

"You're right, CAG. I know better." John said, humbly looking at the floor.

CAG got up, gave him a friendly tap on the head, and left.

2739 Maple Drive
San Diego

Sylvia lay on her side asleep, her breasts slowly rising and falling to the metabolic rhythms of her body. The dinner at Anthony's had been delicious. Sylvia didn't know what had prompted the big event, but it had been fun, and she'd enjoyed it. John had been particularly tender all evening, especially with his love making.

John was now propped up in bed with a heating pad against his bruised spine trying to read a book, but his mind wouldn't concentrate. It kept coming back to the bad landing.

Why? He kept asking himself. *Why did it happen? The four jets going into the break distracted me, but that shouldn't have done it. I just wasn't giving it my full concentration. Admit it, John. You thought about other things coming around in that approach. Complacency kills - as the safety poster in the Ready Room says. And you were complacent, hot shot! Asshole!*

And after you dumped the nose - what did you do that saved you? Not a damned thing! Yeah, you caught a wire, but it wasn't any skill of yours that did it. Luck! Nothing but pure dumb luck! But for luck you would have been just like Ralph - except you had six jets parked forward while he had only one. You'd never have made it, and Sylvie would have been a widow.

He looked down at her tenderly. *She's strong and tough though. Probably'd marry another fighter pilot. She likes the excitement and the camaraderie of naval aviation. Ordinary living would be dull after this!*

Learn a lesson, John. You'll never get another reprieve like that. John smiled, removed the heating pad, threw the extra pillow on the floor, and immediately went to sleep.

Sylvia sat curled up on the living room couch with her legs tucked under her, her face drooping in a hang dog expression, a lost little puppy with big eyes and a hurt paw.

I will not cry! John needs all the support I can give him. But the tears seeped out anyway.

John finished packing his sea bag, hoisted it onto his shoulder, and carried it to the door, where he dropped it with a thud next to the B-4.

"There! Finito! I am ready to mount my steed and go slay dragons," he said lightly, trying to get a smile from Sylvia as he snapped the elastic on his skivvies.

"Oh, I forgot one thing," he remarked, turning towards the closet. He reached up on the top shelf and removed a device that looked like a metal bikini with a small lock on it.

"What is that thing, for God's sake?" Sylvia asked, perking up for the first time since John began to pack.

John smiled evilly and handed it to her. "It's your chastity belt. Try it on to see if it fits. I'll try to slide my dong inside it by going up your thigh to test it. I don't want some VP weenie figuring out how to bypass it."

Sylvia cracked up and laughed for the first time that evening. She smiled at him. "Oh John, you're so crazy! Where did you ever find that silly thing?"

"A new store in town called Fredericks. They've got some crazy stuff in there. This thing reminds me of a story. Want to hear it?" he teased.

"No, but tell me. You will anyway, you darling nut."

"Well, it seems the Earl was headed off to the Crusades. He called in his chaplain, gave him a key, and said, 'This is the key to my lady's chastity belt. You're the only one I can trust with it. If I die in the wars, you are to unlock it and set her free.'

" 'Yes, my lord. I will take good care of it,' the Chaplain promised him.

"The Earl was about two miles down the road with his entourage of knights, pendants flying, when a rider approached them at full gallop from the rear. It was the Chaplain, his cassock flying out behind him

" 'Chaplain, what's wrong?' the Earl asked after the chaplain had reined his steed to a halt, the steed digging its rear legs into the earth, as the Chaplain pulled its head upward by the reins. 'Is my lady ill?'

" 'No, your grace. She's just fine, but you made a bad mistake.'

" 'What's that?' the Earl said with concern.

" 'Sire, you gave me the wrong key!' wailed the chaplain."

John laughed heartily at his own joke.

"Oh John, you are so bad," Sylvia replied laughing, again with tears - this time tears of joy -rolling down her face. Suddenly she stopped, smiled at him and said, "Well, Sir Knight, the chastity belt is unlocked. See if you can do it to me better than the chaplain would have - if he had had the chance, that is." she giggled and pulled him down on top of her.

"Do it to me, John. Do it until there is no baby juice left in you. Screw yourself dry, and then do it some more. I want all of you before you go."

John lifted her in his arms, carried her to the bedroom, and stripped the chemise off of her in one quick motion.

"God, you are so beautiful, Sylvie. I'm going to miss you." He buried his face in her hair and took in her scent.

"Just shut up and love me, John," Sylvia whispered, her nipples erect, and her body eager for him.

They lay quietly in each other's arms, their bodies glistening and sated. Sylvia rolled towards John, wrapped her hand around his balls and gently massaged him, teasingly.

"Come on, Flyboy. One for the road," she said, nipping his lip and slipping her tongue in his mouth.

"I don't think I can, Sylvie" John moaned, his body denying what he had just said. They had One for the Road.

The Philippine Sea sailed from the North Island pier for Korea on a gray morning in early January. The Naval Air Pacific Fleet band played lively tunes on the pier as the ship prepared to leave. But it was a somber occasion, especially for the pilots who were beginning to feel their mortality. In three weeks they would be under fire. Wives were crying and couples were embracing as the crew slowly pulled away from their loved ones and boarded the carrier. Sylvia and John talked quietly their emotions totally spent the night before. John finally gave Sylvia a hug and a kiss, slowly releasing her, and went up the brow. Her eyes frantically searched for one last glimpse of him, before he was swallowed up in the sea of dark blue uniforms that massed along the edge of the hangar deck; but her vision was blurred with tears.

Ten minutes later the brows came down, mooring lines were cast off, and with one long blast on the whistle the huge ship got under way. Six tugboats pulled it away from the pier, spun it around so that it headed down channel, and with six loud farewell toots, the tugs cast loose. The Phil Sea headed out of port for Korea. The band did its best to keep things lively with "Anchors Aweigh", but it was a lost cause.

CHAPTER 4

USS Philippine Sea
Sea of Japan

Three weeks later John got his first glimpse of North Korea about 0700 on a bright clear winter's morning. The Phil Sea was about forty miles offshore, and the rugged, uninviting peaks could be clearly seen, gray and dirty with flecks of brown at the lower elevations, snow-capped at the top. A cold shiver ran through John, both because of the biting cold wind, but more at the thought of what was coming.

This afternoon I'll be flying through those mountains and around those peaks, and there will be people there who want to kill me. He pondered for a moment, then shrugged and said to himself, *So what! I'll fly smarter, and luck will be with me. I feel it in my bones. I'll not be foolhardy, but I will be aggressive.* With that thought he went below.

John's first flight was a routine recce of sections of the North Korean rail network. The Navy's principal mission since the MLR had stabilized near the 38th parallel after the retreat from the Yalu, was to interdict the road and rail system to stop supplies from reaching the Chinese troops at the MLR. This meant cutting the tracks, dropping bridges, attacking any trains caught out of the protecting tunnels, and attacking trucks found camouflaged along the roads or in the narrow valleys. But, most traffic moved at night, and

73

jets simply could not operate at night off the carrier. Therefore, the carrier had a fighter detachment of F4U-5N's to operate at night. The squadron was VC-3, but they soon became known as UDT-3, which stood for Underwater Demolition Team 3, because every pilot had ditched at least one plane.

The Ready Room was full of pilots preparing for flight. The ticker tape screen announced the weather, the divert field's bearing and distance, and the position and intended movement - the PIM of the carrier force. The duty officer had the plane assignments and the deck spot from flight deck control. The YE code for the day was given out. The YE navigation system emitted a different letter signal in Morse code for each octant of a circle centered on the carrier. The code changed daily. This was the only navigation device available to the pilots although the ship could direction find on a plane's radio signal as an emergency measure.

The squadron duty officer called attention as Commander Vic Towsan, the skipper of VF-112, entered the ready room.

"Carry on, men" Vic said. "Today's the big day. Let's not try to win the war in one day." There were some twitters, some chuckles, and laughs, and a few guffaws, depending on the anxiety level of the individual. "Take a steady strain, no showing off, no low pull outs, no revisits. Consider it a training day. There's not a single target assigned today that's worth an airplane, much less a pilot. Okay, the lineup. Jim you have the Combat Air Patrol. No indications of MiG activity. John, you've got the recce - Wonsan to Hamhung. Watch the 88's at Hungnam. Ray, you've got Green Four Tare recce. Watch it at Yang Doc. Stay above 4000 feet. That place is loaded with triple A. Divisions two and three have the rail cutting missions north of Wonsan."

Towsan looked around at his pilots. They all seemed ready. "Any questions? Everyone got a poopy suit on? The water temperature is 50 degrees. You'll last about five minutes without your exposure suit! Poopy bags for everyone. That's an order. Okay? They'll call you to man planes in a few minutes."

The poopy bag was a large rubberized bag that fit like a large balloon about the body with seals at the neck and cuffs. The bag's feet went completely into the boots that were worn over it. The original poopy suit was large and ungainly, and difficult to position comfortably in the cockpit. Pilots didn't like them because they were afraid that the suit might hang up when trying to exit the cockpit in an emergency, or that the air would accumulate in the lower extremities, and turn them upside down to drown in the water. The new bags were a big improvement. They were form fitting with a tight seal across the chest, and rubber boots integrated into the unit.

Towsan noticed John, sitting inconspicuously in the back of the ready room, and frowned at him. "Lieutenant, where's your exposure suit?"

John looked like a kid caught with his hand in the cookie jar. He flushed and replied. "Skipper, supply ran out of the size that fits me, and won't have one until the COD aircraft arrives. That's three days of no flying. We're here to fight a war. I'll take my chances."

"Didn't you hear me, John? I said poopy bags for everyone. No poopy bag, no fly. Sorry. Dave Herbert will take your flight for you. But I'll do this for you," he smiled. "Some new suits are due on the COD in three days. I'll give you first choice. Okay?"

"Yes sir," John said sourly, as he glumly got up and left the room. The last word he heard was, "Pilots man your planes!"

Three days later John got his poopy bag, and was put on the flight schedule. He had a routine mission to recce the rail lines north of Hamhung.

"Hey, John, you flying today?" called Jim Moore. "It's so nice to do it in style with your brand new latest model poopy suit by Dior. The rest of us have to fly with those ratty old poopy bags. Really hurts my image. I'm glad no women can see me in it." He laughed.

"Fuck off, Jim. It'll take more than a new poopy suit to clean up your image," John chuckled. "But I have to admit this new job does have a nice cut to it. Not baggy at all like that potato sack you're wearing!"

"Pilots! Man your planes!" squawked air operations over the announcing box. The pilots picked up their helmets, knee boards, and map cases, and headed for the catwalk. They exited the inside passageway into the bright sunshine to another catwalk that ran alongside the flight deck.

"At least, we don't have lousy weather to deal with," John said to the pilot behind him.

"Yeah, I don't like instrument flying around mountains," the pilot replied.

As they climbed up out of the catwalk, John noted that his plane Peter Peter 69 was spotted on the port cat. John would be first to launch.

Jim Mason, the plane captain, greeted him. " Good morning, sir. A great day for flying. "

"Yeah, as long as some gook doesn't bag me," John laughed.

"You'll be okay, sir. I have my good luck charm." He pulled out a rabbit's foot as they started their walk around the plane, John checking various items. "The plane's ready. Full internal tanks, tips also full. Oxygen 1800 pounds. No outstanding gripes. Low points drained. You're ready to go, sir."

"Okay Jim, thanks for the good work." John mounted the step to the cockpit. Jim helped him strap in and connected the g-suit, headphones, and oxygen mask.

"Clear all intakes and exhausts! Check for debris about the deck! Start engines!" announced the Air Boss from his small tower located three levels up on the side of the island.

The jets began to whine; the props coughed, sputtered; and came to life with a deep-throated roar. The ship leaned sharply to port as it turned into the wind. Only the chain tie-downs kept the aircraft from sliding over the side.

"Launch aircraft!" shouted the air boss. The catapult officer put two fingers in the air and rotated his hand in a circular motion. John went to full throttle, the holdback ring constraining the jet.

John checked his instruments, put his head firmly back against the headrest, tightened the grip on the throttle, and saluted. The catapult officer moved his arm in a sweeping arc from over his head downward towards the bow, at the same time bending his right knee so that his fingers touched the deck. The catapult supervisor hit the valve releasing the hydraulic fluid. The holdback ring parted and the aircraft accelerated to 115 knots in 88 feet and was airborne. An immediate turn cleared the jet wash from the carrier's bow, gear and flaps came up, and the aircraft was on its way to its mission over Korea. Well almost! The radio that was working fine before the launch was now dead. John triggered his mike, "Imperial, this is Peter Peter 69. Radio check." No answer.

John continued his climb as his wingman rendezvoused on him. It was Jim Moore in Eagle 112 who pointed to his helmet where his receivers were located and gave a thumbs up and then down to ask about John's radio status. John replied with a thumbs down, and turned the lead over to Jim who took them to the DOG circle at 20000 feet to await recovery since the flight could not go over the beach without operating radios.

John's approach was perfect, catching number 4 wire. As he taxied out of the gear and cleared the landing area, the radio suddenly came to life and he could hear other pilots loud and clear. The flight deck yellow shirts taxied John to the number one elevator and spotted him below on the hangar deck for maintenance. The radio mechs checked the plane over, found no discrepancy; and put the bird back in a "UP" status.

On two succeeding flights John had the bad luck of being assigned Peter Peter 69 again, and each time the radio quit on take off and reactivated itself on landing.

John was furious. Other pilots were beginning to look strangely at him, and some even avoided him. First, he couldn't fly because some supply puke left him without a poopy bag - the only pilot in the Air Group not to have one. Then on three successive flights the radios wouldn't work, and he had to abort, only to have them work again on deck!

John cornered Chief Watson, the leading mech for VF-112. " Chief, You've got to find out what's wrong with the radios on Peter Peter 69. You absolutely must. Other pilots are beginning to wonder about me."

"Lieutenant, we stand down tomorrow for refueling and rearming. That will give me time to put my best people on it - but it will be a bitch to find. Something must be shorting out due to catapult acceleration on launch, and then moving back to unshort when the bird catches a wire and decelerates on landing. It must be a wire going through a bulkhead that is moving slightly and shorting out. In the meantime we'll keep the bird in down status so they can't assign it to you."

"Thanks, Chief. You find it and tell the world about it - and I owe you a bottle of whiskey when we get back to Yokosuka."

"Okay, Lieutenant. Make it Red Label, if they have it. But don't worry. I'll find the problem."

The day after replenishment Peter Peter 69 was put in a "UP" status after an antenna wire was reinsulated and secured where it went through a bulkhead. Chief Watson broadcast the results to the entire ready room that John had really had a problem.

The four photo pilots sat in the back of the Ready Room facing each other in two sets of high backed ready room chairs that formed a mini-ready room for the recce pilots. The talk was about nothing in particular. Ray, who had the next mission due to launch in one hour, was studying the map of the Hamhung area when Chief Watson entered and dropped into the chair next to him.

"Commander, we have a problem with 59. I'm downing the plane, and will have to scrub your mission."

"What's the problem, Chief?" Ray asked.

"The fuel control is surging about two percent. While that amount is flyable, it's also an indication of potential problems that are more severe. The surge could suddenly increase to a point where it is uncontrollable and the engine could flame out. I want to change it now."

"Aw, Chief. A little surge never hurt anyone," Ray replied, grinning. "Down the bird after my flight."

"I'd rather do it now," Watson persisted.

"No dice, Chief. Not until after my flight."

The flight was uneventful. The engine continued to surge moderately, and Ray sat happily in the Dog pattern waiting for a Charlie signal.

"PP 59. Your signal Charlie now."

Ray reduced power, dropped his nose, rolled over on his back into a semi-split S, and screamed into the break at 350 knots. On the downwind leg the engine began to surge again. It was barely noticeable and Ray ignored it, but by the time Ray reached the 90 position the surge was up to four percent and increasing, making it difficult for him to hold his airspeed.

Listen to that engine surge, the LSO muttered. *I think I'll work him a little fast.*

Ray did not respond to the come-on given by the LSO. As he rolled into the groove, the engine RPM suddenly dropped five percent, and Ray rapidly began to lose airspeed and settle at the ramp.

"Wave off! Wave off!" the LSO called and Ray responded with power, but it was a late wave off and Ray was slow, made even worse by the surging engine. PP-59 rolled into a climbing turn to port trying to clear the eleven-foot barricade located forward of the arresting wires, and headed over the side of the flight deck. Ray's hook engaged part of the horizontal nylon strap forming the upper portion of the barricade. The strap snapped under the force, but the plane lost substantial airspeed in the process. Ray tried to hold his altitude but didn't have enough airspeed. PP59 continued now nose down over the number two deck edge elevator, its tail hook engaging some of the safety netting around the side of the elevator, further reducing the airspeed. The aircraft then disappeared over the side - only to reappear again in a near-stalled condition, its wheels inches above the waves. Ray fought to gain more airspeed without losing altitude as the plane continued in level flight. Unable to get off the backside of the power curve, the F9F was effectively in irons. It couldn't climb without more airspeed, and it couldn't gain airspeed without dropping the nose and going into the water. Eventually one big surge of the engine to 107 percent gave it the extra boost needed to start accelerating and climbing out of the hole it was in.

"Phew! That was close," Ray laughed into his mike. "This damned engine is really surging! Hope it doesn't flame out."

The Air Boss turned to John who had the F9F advisor's watch in PriFly. "What can he do, John?"

"Tell him to shift the fuel control to emergency," John replied, wondering why Ray hadn't done it before this.

The answer came back quickly after the Air Boss had relayed the instructions.

"How do I do that?" Ray asked.

"My God, he doesn't know!" John exploded. "Tell him there is a switch with a red safety cover on the left hand console behind the throttle quadrant. Activate the switch to put the fuel control in emergency."

With the RPM stabilized Ray's second approach was uneventful.

Ray entered the Ready Room, threw his Mae West in a chair and plopped down into a chair.

"You damned near bought the farm, Commander!" Chief Watson exploded, his face red with anger at the stupidity.

"Why didn't you go to emergency earlier, Ray" John asked.

" I didn't know how to. Never did understand what that switch was for." Ray laughed

"Ray!" John retorted exasperated. "It's in the Handbook."

"Handbooks are for Nuggets," Ray replied

"Well, Commander, that's one good engine that you cost us," Chief Watson growled through clenched teeth. "The engine went to 107 percent, and that means an engine change. The plane will be down for three days - all because you were too damned lazy to read the Handbook." Watson glared at Ray for a full minute, then turned, and stomped out.

"I think he's mad," Ray laughed. "These goddamned mechs think they own the airplane."

"Read the fucking Handbook, Ray," John snapped at him, as he rose and stomped out too.

Over Hamhung
North Korea

Ray Hale had an easy mission. It was his twentieth and that would give him his first air medal. He was assigned recce north of Hamhung with instructions to look for telltale signs of truck traffic turning off the main road to hide in the valleys and under trees. The discoloration of the soil where the trucks packed it down as they left the road was very visible from the air even when no tracks were present. Ray was cruising at 1000 - 1500 feet, doing 250 knots. He had his cameras set to oblique so that he could get 30 degree stereo. His air conditioner was on because he really didn't expect any flak in the area. Lieutenant junior grade Jim Moore was the VF-112 escort in Eagle 102, flying at 1000 feet above and behind Ray where he could observe flack and keep Ray in sight.

Suddenly there was a loud bang and Ray's cockpit quickly filled with smoke. Through the haze Ray could see the red glow of a warning light in the general direction of the fire warning lights.

"I'm hit and on fire!" Ray shouted into his mike. Jim saw the canopy separate from the plane. A fraction of a second later the seat ejected and cleared the plane.

"Mayday! Mayday! Peter Peter 59 ejected twenty miles northwest of Hamhung," Jim shouted into his mike, and turned the

IFF to emergency. It seemed to be happening in slow motion. Jim saw the seat reach its maximum trajectory and begin to fall. He saw Ray kick out of the seat, but he was dangerously low, The chute pulled out and began to stream just as Ray hit the ground.

"Station calling Mayday, this is Yo-Do angel. We are launching Angel One Five. Identify yourself and say again location and condition of pilot."

"This is Eagle 102. Twenty miles northwest of Hamhung. The pilot of Peter Peter 59 said he was hit and on fire. He then ejected, but he was too low, and his chute didn't open in time. He's dead, but the plane is still flying, and I see no signs of fire. What shall I do?"

"Roger Eagle 102. We'll take it from here. You are cleared back to Home Plate."

Ready Room #1
USS Philippine Sea

"I don't know what happened," Jim said in the debriefing with CAG, the skipper of VF-112, the squadron intelligence officer, and Chief Watson. "I saw no flak, no enemy action, no damage to the airplane, no smoke, no fire, and the plane kept flying for ten minutes - still in horizontal flight until it crashed into the side of a mountain."

"You're sure there was no fire," Commander Towsan probed.

"Yes sir, I'm sure. I checked the plane close up. No external damage, no fuel leaking. There was some smoke in the cockpit, but no sign of fire, and the skin wasn't blistered as it would have been if there had been an internal blaze- say in the engine compartment."

"What do you think, Chief?" CAG asked.

"It's strange, sir. Based on what Mr. Moore has said I don't think there was a fire, but what the hell was it?" Watson brooded for a minute, while the others waited for him to speak.

"That fire warning light bothers me. We've had no reported cases of false alarms with the system," Watson mused some more, and then turned to Moore.

"Mr. Moore, what other red lights are there in the cockpit and where are they located?"

"Chief, there's only one that I can think of. The radar altimeter low altitude warning light, and. . ." Moore paused as recognition flashed in his mind. "And it's right below the fire warning light.

Jesus, you think that's what he saw? What about the smoke in the cockpit?"

"That's easy," Watson replied. "The Panther has a history of hydraulic line failures many of them in the plenum chamber where the air conditioning system gets its bleed air. A failure there would fill the cockpit with hydraulic fluid, vaporized into smoke. It looks just like smoke, but a pilot can tell the difference by the smell if he removes his oxygen mask. Now, Mister Moore, when does the low altitude warning light come on?"

"You set a marker on the dial and when the altitude drops below that the light comes on. I used to set it twenty-five feet below my altitude for night FCLP, and most guys set it at one thousand feet and leave it there for routine flying."

"And what was Commander Hale's altitude?" Chief Watson continued to probe.

"He was about 1100 -1200 feet before the accident. Then I noticed that he was losing altitude. Do you think ..?"

"I think it's a plausible story. Maybe even most likely if we rule out fire," CAG interjected.

"I think so too," the Skipper of VF-112 chimed in." But we'll never know for sure. Thanks a million, Chief. I think you put it all together."

The Air Boss and John sat in PriFly waiting for the next recovery. The flight deck was spotted already and everything was quiet.

"I need something to keep me occupied, John. Maybe I should take up big black stogies like CAG."

"Jesus, Boss. One is enough," John laughed.

"What do you think of the accident, John?"

"I think Chief Watson has it right. Unfortunately, Ray didn't know his airplane. Witness the surging fuel control that almost put him in the drink two weeks ago. He simply refuses to study the Handbook. In my opinion he panicked when he saw the smoke and the red light. There were many things he could have done quickly, before he made the decision to bail out. For example, loosen his oxygen mask and sniff the smoke, turn the air conditioner off to see if the smoke goes away, crack the canopy to clear the cockpit of smoke, and when all else failed, zoom to altitude before he bailed out. It's fairly common knowledge that 1000 feet is the absolute minimum altitude for bailout in horizontal flight, considering all the manual steps involved with ejection. I'll bet you a hundred dollars that Ray didn't know that. I read in Aviation Week that the Brits are working on a ground level ejection seat, called Martin-Baker, but it'll be a long time before we"ll see it operational."

"Well," the Air Boss added pensively. "It was bad luck - just plain bad luck."

"Not really, Air Boss. He had some bad luck for sure, but he made most of his bad luck himself. Ray was a natural born pilot, but he didn't know his airplane, and it killed him."

Four VF-112 Panthers roared into the break. The next landing cycle was beginning, and Ray Hale was forgotten.

Yokosuka, Japan

The flight deck of the Phil Sea was spotted for "Operation Pinwheel" to assist the ship in making its turn into the pier from the channel as it entered Yokosuka harbor. The harbor area around the pier and turning basin was very narrow, and not designed for a thousand foot carrier.

In "Operation Pinwheel", the propeller planes were spotted on the bow and stern on either side of the flight deck facing inward. The planes were manned and started, and then controlled by radio to provide additional athwart thrust to the carrier from their props turning up at full power. The pilots didn't like it, and CAG screamed that the engines were for combat, and not to be worn out maneuvering the ship. To no avail, Pinwheel helped the Old Man turn the corner.

Once the brows were in place, there was a mass exodus of the crew. Some to sightsee Tokyo, some on tours, many to geisha houses. Some old timers kept a Japanese girl in a home away from home. Considering the state of the Japanese economy, it was not difficult to find a lovely young girl to play house with for eight months, and then turn the arrangement over to a friend on the relieving carrier until the first carrier returned again.

Most aviators going on liberty started out in the "fleet bar" at the naval base Officer's Club, to adjourn later in the evening to the Komatsu, a high-class geisha house that catered to aviators. The "fleet bar" was a large room in a isolated portion of the O'Club. The furniture and other fixtures were dilapidated, the management apparently believing that one shouldn't waste money on rowdy destructive aviators. The pilots in turn felt that they contributed handsomely to the financial well-being of the club, and should have better accommodations.

John, the squadron LSO Mike Turns, Larry Duncan, and Dave Herbert had spent the afternoon in the "fleet bar" sopping up Bud from the neck, laughing and joking about the missions, and arm wrestling, the result of which Mike Turns was proclaimed champion.

"What are we going to do for dinner," asked Dave Herbert. "Want to try the Pi Loo in town?"

"I don't feel Japanese today," John replied. "No raw fish or sake for me."

"How about something to eat at the Komatsu," suggested Mike Turns.

"I may poke it but I sure as hell won't eat it," laughed Larry. "That's worse than raw fish although it smells the same." He wrinkled his face and held his nose between his thumb and forefinger.

"You guys just don't appreciate Asiatic delicacies," Dave replied chug-a-lugging his beer.

"Okay, guys. Why don't we just eat here in the dining room." John suggested. "Personally I just want some dinner and then go back to the ship."

The four aviators entered the dining room of the O'Club to the hostile glances of the members of the local establishment. As in all wars, there are the combat troops and the rear echelon weenies who think the war should not disturb them. It was said that General Mark Clark, Commander of the Fifth Army in Italy, threatened to send a battalion of combat troops to Naples to clean out that "nest of Vipers" if the local provost marshall didn't stop harassing Clark's combat troops on R&R in Naples.

From the corner of the dining room came a shout, " Who let those jet jockeys in here?" It was Joe Laskie from VA-113, the Spad squadron.

"God, I thought I smelled some dead fish in here. Did you guys just come back from the Komatsu?" retorted Mike Turns, the LSO.

A supply corps commander took offense and intervened. "You aviators have no business in here. We'd like to keep our dining room quiet and respectable. Since you can't behave, go back to the fleet bar."

"The fleet bar, the fleet bar, there's no place on earth like the fleet bar. Aviators should not go far. . . from the fleet bar," singsonged Mike Turns in a loud off-tune voice.

"There once was a man named Alstair who liked to make love on the stair. The banister broke, he quickened his stroke and finished her off in midair." recited Dave in a monotone, with a big smile on his face.

"Okay guys. Let's settle down and get a table. Sorry, Commander, we just got in from Korea, and we're a little wired." said John apologetically.

"Well, Lieutenant, this dining room has had enough. Please return to the fleet bar." He glared at John

"We'll quiet down, sir," John repeated. "And we'd like something to eat."

"You will not stay in here, Lieutenant. You wore out your welcome. I'm ordering you to leave now." The Commander, still seated, was rapidly working himself into an apoplectic fit. His face was flushed, his jaw twitched, and his eyes protruded bug eyed.

"I don't take orders from supply corps weenies in comfortable rear echelon jobs," John flared, as his Irish temper took hold. He turned to his buddies, "Look at him. He seems greatly overheated. I think we need to help him cool down."

"Indeedy, very overheated," Mike added with a look of mock seriousness on his face.

The commander continued to fume, not realizing the precariousness of his position. "Will you get out of here!" he roared as the entire dining room stopped eating and began to watch the dispute

"Now, Commander, just calm down," John replied, holding his hand up as if to stop him, with a devilish look on his face.

"I don't want to calm down. I ordered you out of here," he yelled and with that each aviator grabbed a leg of the commander's chair and hoisted him up over their heads. Now concerned, one of the station officers went to find the shore patrol officer in the Fleet Bar.

"Yo-oh-heave-ho," in step, the four sang the Volga Boatman chant moving at a dirge-like pace. The commander continued to scream for them to put him down and leave the premises. Through the

French doors, out onto the flagstone patio, and over to the deep part of the swimming pool. With a shout of "We commit thee to the deep" they threw the commander, chair and all, into the pool.

The shore patrol officer from the Fleet Bar arrived in time to witness the supply commander sail into the pool and come up spitting and sputtering, although somewhat cooled down.

"There," John laughed, bending over the pool solicitously. "Don't you feel better, sir? You old folks should watch your blood pressure. Tsk. Tsk."

John turned and walked into the arms of Lieutenant Commander Bill Barnes, the OINC of VC-3, and at the moment the Fleet Shore Patrol Officer.

"Alright guys. That's enough. Who threw him in the pool?" Bill could hardly keep from laughing. The supply commander, a portly gentleman, looked so comical with his uniform plastered to his fat body, his bug eyes flashing, and his mouth opening and shutting like a fish.

"I'll court martial you - all of you!" he finally screamed, turning to the Shore Patrol Officer. "Arrest them and throw them in the brig!"

"I'll take care of it, Commander. I'm taking them into custody and returning them to the ship." Once he was sure that injured commander was okay, and had departed the area, he turned to the four culprits, standing there with innocent looks on their faces.

"Alright, who did it," Bill Barnes asked, trying hard to look grim, and not to laugh.

"We all did, sir, and it was fun. He deserved it." Mike Turns volunteered.

"Hear! Hear!" the bad ass' added, and broke out laughing again.

"Just how many beers did you guys need to do this?"

"We don't drink, sir," Dave Herbert replied solemnly.

"Oh shit, at least two cases, Bill," John added. "We've been here all day."

"Well, get your stories together." Bill shook his head, and tried not to smile. "CAG will want to see you bad apples. I'm taking you back to the ship in my jeep."

"Good. I was wondering how we'd get back. Now we don't have to walk."

"You guys better clean up your act before CAG gets hold of you." With that remark he headed them out to the jeep, shaking his head and smiling.

The next day John and the others were put in hack, and confined to quarters by CAG for the remainder of the in-port period. The CO then called CAG to his cabin." Did those aviators do what I'm told they did, CAG?" the CO asked, laughing heartily.

"Yeah, they did, sir. They can be some real bad asses, but they're damned good fighter pilots. The commander probably deserved it - the damned chair-bound paper pusher! Incidentally, I remember one night in Jacksonville when a certain aviator whose name I won't mention took his girl friend for a ride in a Corsair. Where in the hell did you put her in a single-seat fighter?" CAG asked, laughing so hard tears came to his eyes.

"Where else? On my lap, right behind the joystick," the CO responded smiling at the memories.

"Behind the joystick, Skipper? Which joystick? Behind or on top?" Mike was laughing so hard he couldn't talk. "You really didn't do it in the cockpit, did you?"

The Skipper began to bang the table repeatedly with his fist, laughing until tears ran down his face. "I tried, Mike. I really did, but there was no way you could do it in a Corsair! I'm glad these young tigers don't know what hellions we were, or we'd never be able to instill any discipline in them! Let's go to the club, and get a drink."

CHAPTER 5

2739 Maple Drive
San Diego, California

Sylvia was in the kitchen when the telephone rang. She picked it up on the way to the stove to check on the rolls she was baking for an Officer's Wives Luncheon.

"Just a moment please," she said into the mouthpiece as she opened the oven door to check on them. "Thank God for long extension cords," she murmured and then addressed the phone. "Hello. I'm sorry to keep you waiting."

"Hi Sylvie, honey. This is Brad Masters from out of nowhere," the caller announced.

"Brad. Well, how nice to hear from you. How are you? It's been ages!"

"How are ya, Sylvie? Yeah, long time no see! John home?"

"No, Brad. He isn't. He deployed to Korea two months ago on the Phil Sea."

"Oh hell! I wanted to see both of you! I'm in town TAD for a week. I'm really sorry to miss John, but I'd still like to see you! Maybe we could go to dinner? Give you a chance to get out with an old friend."

After the Academy, Brad had gone through Corsairs with John and then was selected for the Jet Training Unit at Olathe, much to John's great consternation.

"Well, gee! I don't know! Can I trust some East Coast sailor? I hear they're very bad with women! And a jet jockey too!" She laughed. "Well Brad, I trust you! I'd love to see an old friend! Do you have wheels or do I need to pick you up somewhere? We'll have a drink and then go to dinner. It'll be fun to get out for a change!"

" Great! Can you pick me up, Sylvie? Say the North Island O'Club at seven? And you pick the restaurant. I don't know San Diego."

"Can do, Brad. I'll meet you in the bar. How about Anthony's for seafood - or would you rather stay in Coronado? We can go to the Hotel Del."

"Anthony's sounds terrific! See you at seven, Sylvie."

"Bye Brad." Sylvia hung up.

What fun, she thought, *a night out with someone other than wives, and Brad's so fascinating - done so many things. What's his squadron? VF-11 - the Red Rippers, I think John said. They fly Banshees at Oceana. Oh, I'm really sorry John's not here! We could have had a blast! What shall I wear? Exotic? Sexy? Simple? Mmmm. Simple it is, going out with another man! It's such fun to go out! I didn't realize how much I've missed it. I haven't dressed up to please a man since John and I last went to Anthony's!* She sobered momentarily. *But be careful, babe. Don't overdo it. Don't want anyone getting any funny ideas! Yeah - but Brad's so harmless! After all, he and John were roommates at the Academy, and he's happily married to Ann. So - what the hell! You only live once.* She stripped off her clothes, looked at her slender body approvingly, and stepped into the shower.

The water was warm and the spray felt good. She lathered the scented soap over her arms and upper torso, smoothing the fragrant bubbles over her breasts.

Damn these things are tender! Maybe I'm going to get my period tomorrow or next day. She mumbled to herself. *I'm late again. Sure wish I were regular!* Her hands slid the remaining suds down and across her stomach. *Hmmm. I've missed two periods since John left. I wonder if I could be pregnant? Nah, I feel great! No throwing up or anything, and I miss my periods all the time.* She rinsed herself in the pounding spray. The last of the bubbles floated down the drain, and she got out of the shower.

O'Club
NAS North Island

Brad was seated at the bar when Sylvia entered. He rose when he saw her, went forward to greet her, and gave her a big hug and kiss to which she responded. It did not go unnoticed by certain other patrons.

"Syl, you look wonderful! Smell good too! This Navy life must agree with you." Brad smiled at her and thought, *God, she's more beautiful than ever. Seems more grown up. John's a lucky dog.*

"How's Pam," Sylvia responded, as she smiled at him. "You didn't bring her with you?"

"No, I came space A, an NATS flight out of Andrews. She's back home in Norfolk, doing her pottery."

"I'd really love to see some of her work, Brad."

"Come back east on vacation when John boy gets back and stay with us. If you can tear yourself away from this beautiful place! Norfolk's not like this. You and John are lucky to be in San Diego." Brad gave her his best winning smile.

"Except for a little thing called a war," Sylvia retorted.

An ordinary short dumpy-looking woman approached with a smile on her plump face and arms outstretched.

"Sylvia! So good to see you out!" Mary Boone trilled, at the same giving Brad a thorough head to toe inspection. "And this is my husband, Ozzie." She turned to Ozzie and added, "Sylvia and I play bridge together at the OWC."

"Hello Mary," Sylvia answered. "This is Brad Masters, a very old and dear friend of ours who's in town TAD from the East Coast. He was John's best man at our wedding."

"Well, how nice. Will you join us for a drink to celebrate Ozzie's promotion to Lieutenant Commander?" she beamed at Ozzie who shrugged his shoulders and then shook hands.

"Oh, we'd love to Mary, but we are on our way to Anthony's for dinner and we don't want to be late for our reservation! You know how crowded they are, but thanks just the same. Anyway congratulations on the promotion." Sylvia replied politely.

"We won't keep you then," Mary responded. "But, if you have time, do bring Brad by for a drink! He's staying at your house, isn't he? Being good friends, that is?" Mary smiled maliciously.

"Absolutely not! Not when John's not here!" Sylvia snapped back, turned and left, Brad following behind.

"That little bitch. She's having an affair. Poor John," Mary said to Ozzie as they left the Club. Ozzie shrugged his shoulders.

"So what."

Coronado Ferry
En route San Diego

Sylvia expertly maneuvered the green convertible onto the ferry that would take them over to San Diego.

"What a beautiful city this is, Sylvie. Look how the lights sparkle on the water and reflect off the low clouds." Brad moved closer to Sylvia and put his arm around her. Sylvia took it for a brotherly move and did not pull away.

The breeze was fresh, coming across the water of the bay.

"There's a slight chill in the air," Brad continued. "Are you okay?" He tried to pull her closer, but Sylvia deftly moved to one side.

"I'm fine, Brad."

The ferry jockeyed into the slip and they went ashore. Anthony's was just a few hundred feet away, sitting on the water with a spectacular view of the harbor.

The restaurant was crowded and, although they had reservations, there would be a thirty minute wait.

"That's okay," Brad quipped. "We can sit in the bar and enjoy the view."

The headwaiter seated them at a cozy table for two next to a large window with harbor view. The room was filled with soft jazz from the Muzak, tinkling glasses, and the low hum of conversation and laughter.

" Bring us two large martinis on the rocks," Brad told the headwaiter as he left.

" Oh Brad, look! There's the Coronado Ferry approaching the slip! Isn't it a lovely night. I do wish John were here." Sylvia bubbled with the excitement of a night out.

The waiter quickly arrived with their martinis and Sylvia looked doubtfully at them.

" Hey! I always thought you liked martinis, Syl! You used to drink them all the time." he teased.

" Well, I used to, but I haven't had any since John deployed to Korea. I normally just have a glass of white wine - if that," Sylvia responded, still uncertain about the drinks.

" Oh, what the hell," Brad laughed. "You probably won't have another chance until John returns! Anyway, you've got someone you can trust to see you safely home if that's necessary." He laughed.

Sylvia laughed, "Oh well. What the hell is right. Why not?" She raised her glass and clinked Brads. " To John's safe return,"

"To us," Brad responded.

In a few moments, the maitre d' arrived at the table with the menus. "We are ready for you now, sir. Would you like for the waiter to bring your drinks?"

"No thanks. That's not necessary. Bottoms up, Sylvie. We'll have some wine with dinner." Sylvia upended her martini, and finished the last two swallows.

The lights were dim, the chairs soft and comfortable, and the large glass window gave a fantastic view of the harbor and the boats gently bobbing at anchor.

"The specialty here is seafood, Brad," Sylvia said as she opened the oversized menu, took a quick look, and closed it. "I'm going to have abalone and a salad. What about you?"

Brad ordered for Sylvia and then he ordered the grilled shrimp for himself. "And let me have the wine list, please," he added, presenting the waiter with the closed menus.

"Oh Brad, all I'll have is one little glass of chardonnay. No more."

"That's okay, Syl. I'll have a couple and it's cheaper by the bottle."

"Hey! What's that stuff you're getting, Syl?"

"It's a west coast delicacy. You have to pry it off the rocks with a tire iron and beat the hell out of the meat to relax the muscles." she giggled. "Mmmm- Dee-licious!" she sighed and licked her lips.

Dinner proceeded on from the appetizers to the main course and ended up with delicate Italian pastries for dessert. The conversation was animated and quick with long trips down memory lane, the Academy, June Week, the wedding, flight training, and finally Brad's wedding to Pam in Pensacola. As the conversation flowed, so did the wine, with Brad topping off Sylvia's glass frequently whenever it dropped slightly, so that she did not notice how much she was drinking.

Then came coffee and a brandy for Brad. Sylvia declined the brandy.

She shook her head, "I think I've had more than enough, Brad."

When the waiter arrived with two snifters, Brad said, apologetic, "I'm sorry. He made a mistake. Why don't you just enjoy the aroma and maybe a little sip or two."

The pleasant evening was beginning to wind down. "I really have enjoyed this, Brad, but I think I ought to be taking you back to the BOQ," Sylvia said. She felt flushed and heady from the wine.

"You aren't going to show me your home, Sylvie? Pam will be so disappointed if I can't describe it to her! How about one small nightcap and a quick tour of the house; then you can take me back to the Q?"

"I don't know, Brad. I've really had more to drink than I should, and I don't want to drive home and then back to Coronado. Yet I don't want to disappoint Pam." She replied, her speech a little slurred.

"Don't worry about the driving. I'll just grab a taxi from your place. Would you like for me to drive home for you?"

" Please. I think so, Brad."

"Just give me your hand, Sylvie. It's foggy and the street is wet," Brad offered as they exited the resturant. Sylvia didn't have much opportunity to avoid it. Brad had her hand firmly in his before she could respond.

2739 Maple Drive
San Diego

The Green Hornet pulled to the curb and stopped. Brad got out and looked at the view. A thin layer of fog covered Coronado and the harbor, but Mission Bay was clear. Sylvia opened the car door and climbed out with unsteady movements.

"What a gorgeous view, Sylvie!" He exclaimed. "Come over here and enjoy it with me." Brad smiled and pulled her to him. "Lucky you, Sylvie honey! You really have the good life. Good husband. Good friends to take care of you while John's gone." as he gave her another hug, running his hand down her back. Sylvia began to be aware of him, the faint masculine scent of his aftershave, mingled with the smell of pure maleness, something which she had not experienced since John left. She began to feel it in her entire being.

"Well, since you're now safely home and I'm taking a taxi, why don't I fix us a little nightcap? Brandy?"

Sipping the brandy, they toured the house, Brad wanting to stop and look at everything - to tell Pam all about it. The snifters were almost gone, empty as they completed the tour. Brad went out the French doors onto the terraced backyard and began to pick some oranges to take back with him. Sylvia leaned in the doorway and watched his smooth lithe movements.

Uh, he's a handsome dog, she murmured to herself. *Good build with square shoulders and a slender waist, muscular legs, and a classic face like those of the ancient Greek statues. Oh yeah, and that curly black hair, too.* Without being conscious of it, slow stirrings were beginning deep within her loins, building toward a conscious desire.

I wish John were here. I need him so. Oh, I need him so! She whispered as her desires came fully to the surface.

Brad came back into the house his arms laden with oranges.

"Whoa. Here, help me Sylvie," he laughed, as he pushed the oranges toward her. Some dropped to the floor rolling away. As they both bent down to get them, Brad leaned over further than needed and forced a collision. As Sylvia lost her balance, he grabbed her to prevent her falling to the floor. She fell into his arms instead.

"Hey! I got you, honey! It's okay! I'll help you during these tough times."

He ran his hands down her back and held her below her waist. Sylvia took his response as another brotherly expression of affection.

95

She had never been in this situation before, and had no idea what was happening to her. Alcohol was fogging her brain and generating a strong sexual desire. Everything was becoming dreamlike and so confusing! She laid her head on his chest and sighed, "Nice to have good friends."

She smelled the male scent strongly now and felt the heat of his body and his firmness. Her sexual stirrings began to take hold, as her latent desire for John began to dominate her being.

Where's John when I need him, she whispered, now close to tears

Brad rubbed her neck, held her closer, and purred, "I'm more than a friend, Sylvie baby. I'm what you want me to be."

Sylvia looked up at him, her eyes damp with tears. "Oh Brad, right now I wish you were John." A fantasy was rapidly growing uncontrolled within her.

"I can be," he whispered, smoothing her hair back off her damp cheek. He kissed her tenderly, and led her to the couch where he gently pushed her back against the cushions and bent over her, his mouth searching for hers. Sylvia's emotions exploded into overpowering need within the fantasy that Brad was John. *Let him do it! Let him do it!* her body cried, as she wrapped her arms around his neck.

"Oh John, John," she murmured softly, closing her eyes. Brad recognized the significance of her call. He was now John.

He smiled triumphantly to himself, and tipped her head back, pushing his probing tongue deeply into her mouth. He then unbuttoned her blouse, and slid the bra straps down off her shoulders, rubbing her erect nipples back and forth with the palm of his hand.

"Ohhh - John, John," she moaned, rolling her head from side to side as Brad took a breast in his mouth, tongued the nipple, and moved his hand under her full skirt to lower her panties.

"Oh John! Please!" Sylvia's body shook with emotion.

"Sylvie baby, it's so good for you. You need it, baby. You really need it."

It was the wrong thing for Brad to say. He had already scored. All he had to do was keep his mouth shut and work on her - let her have her fantasy.

"I need it?" Sylvia's eyes suddenly snapped open, the curtain of deep sexual desire ripped aside by the reality of the statement. Suddenly sober, her head cleared. "I need it alright! I need my husband to do it to me - not you, you son of a bitch!" Furious now and in control of her emotions, the sexual feelings were transformed into flaming anger. She shoved him back hard and jerked his hand from inside her panties. "You bastard. A friend? Friend indeed! Get out!"

Recognizing his mistake, Brad took the direct approach, as she struggled to get up. "Oh, Sylvie baby, I love you so much! I've always loved you! It's okay. John and Pam will never know."

"You bastard! You snake! All you wanted was a piece of ass! Get up off me!" Shaking with white hot anger, she shoved him away far enough to give him a knee in the groin. Brad collapsed on the floor, holding his balls and writhing with pain.

"Damn you, Sylvie. You bitch! You shouldn't have done that," He staggered to his feet, his eyes blazing.

Sylvia ran to the kitchen. Turning in the entrance, she yelled, "Get your ass out of here, Brad! Now!"

Infuriated, he stared at her. "You little prick teaser. You can't do this to me. You know you want it!" He yelled and started towards her.

Sylvia snatched up the phone and dialed the Operator, who came on the line promptly.

" I need Police to 2739 Maples. Emergency. I need help now!" She hung up.

" Get your ass out of here, you son of a bitch, and fast! Unless you want more trouble! They'll be here in a few minutes."

"You goddamned cunt!" Brad grabbed his coat, cursed her again, backing out the door.

The black and white arrived in four minutes. "What's the problem, young lady?" the policeman, a ten year veteran asked.

"I'm sorry I had to bother you, Officer, but the problem is solved." Sylvia answered him, still shaking from the ordeal

The old cop smiled. "Just for the record, ma'am. What happened?" He took out a notebook and pencil from his chest pocket.

"Well, I went to dinner with a male friend of mine and my husband, and then came back here for a nightcap. He made advances and tried to take my clothes off."

"You Navy, Ma'am?"

"Yes"

"Husband deployed?"

"Yes officer, on the Phil Sea. But this person was my husband's best friend. He was best man at my wedding!" Her eyes filled with tears.

"Just let me tell you something, young lady. And learn it good before you get into some real trouble. Don't ever have a man to your house when you are alone. I don't care how good a friend he may be. They immediately get the hots for you, believing you invited them there for that purpose. Always invite another couple, or a girl friend."

He continued in a fatherly way. "They particularly like the wives of the deployed Navy men. They think you can't live without it. I was a Chief Boatswain's mate before I became a cop. Take my word for it."

"Thank you, Officer." Sylvia said, looking ashamed.

"This will go in my log, but no where else. Nobody else will know about it. Okay?"

"I really appreciate that," Sylvia murmured, as she closed the door, tears of embarrassment coursing down her flaming cheeks.

"Nice kid," the officer said to his partner.

"Jesus! Good-looking woman. I could go for her myself!" the Partner laughed.

O'Club
North Island

"You just trumped my ace, Sylvia, and gave them the game and rubber," Peg said, looking closely at her partner. Sylvia did not reply, just looked at her hands as they fidgeted with a swizzle stick.

"Oh Sylvie's just having a bad day," Mary Boone smiled maliciously. "She seems so distracted. She needs to get out a little more and have some fun, Sylvie. When's the last time you were out for fun?"

Peg looked at Sylvie and then at Mary, and said, "Tally up the damages, Mary, while I go to the ladies room. Wait for me, Sylvie, please."

Sylvie and Peg left the club and walked down the steps under the long awning, but nothing was said until they were outside in the parking lot.

"Mike's gone TAD to Alameda tonight. Why don't you come home with me. We'll have some wieners and beans or do something easy on the grill. I'll feed the kids, pack them off to TV, and then we can sit on the patio, and enjoy the evening. It's going to be a beautiful one."

Sylvia looked at Peg and burst into tears, "Oh Peg, I'm so miserable!"

"Alright, honey. Get your car, and follow me to my place. I'll give the kids something to eat. Then we'll have a drink, maybe two, a little food and talk about it."

Peg cooked some quick hamburgers and fed the kids while they made small talk.

"Okay, the house apes are out of the way. Wine or beer for you? I don't think you need anything hard."

"White wine if you have it please."

"Okay, it's in the frig, and get me a beer while I do some cooking," Peg replied.

Peg put some more hamburgers on the grill, tossed a quick salad, and opened a pack of potato chips and a can of peanuts.

"What's wrong, honey? And don't tell me there's nothing. You weren't with us all afternoon. Four gross mistakes at bridge, mistakes that you never make, and then there's that catty remark Mary made. Better tell me what it's about, Syl. Get it off your chest, honey. I'm a good listener."

Sylvia burst into tears again, looked for her handkerchief, and blew her nose. After a long pause to get control during which Peg waited patiently, Sylvia wiped her eyes and then told Peg everything.

When she was finished, Peg smiled sympathetically, "Well, not to worry, honey. You're still very naive and too trusting to operate in this society. It's not Worthington, Ohio. If it's any comfort, you're not the first and you won't be the last. You were lucky, my dear. You came to your senses and realized that John wasn't there. If you had done it, you'd carry the guilt for a long time. The bastards play on that. Get you sexually aroused with supposedly innocent moves while you're wishing for your husband, and then slip it to you when the heat of passion has overwhelmed you - before you realize it's not your husband - or - you're so hot you just can't stop. Bastards! Real bastards!"

"Do I tell John?"

"Absolutely not! He'll begin to wonder what you did to start it. They always blame the woman. And if it makes you feel any better, I was there once. I was down to my panties." she snorted and then laughed. "Some gd Captain. He made admiral too! The snake."

"Oh, Peg, I was so foolish." Sylvia murmured, looking down into her glass.

"We all are at one time or another, honey. Just forget it." Peg's face brightened. "Weren't you going for a job interview at Kibbe's boutique? What happened?"

"Didn't I tell you? I start Monday in the sportswear department. It's only retailing, but it'll keep me busy. They like my designs for swimwear and they are going to show them to someone who manufactures them when he visits. Isn't that great?"

O'Club
North Island

"Six no trump. Bid and made. Game and rubber, ladies. I'll tally up the damages, if you'll give me a minute," Peg said, pencil and score card in hand. While Peg did the calculations, the other three ladies participated in the OWC's favorite pastime - gossip.

"You know that pretty Sylvia Sullivan?" Mary Boone smiled sweetly like a Chessy Cat, and smoothed her mousy hair "Well, you should have seen the hunk she met at the O'Club bar the other night. Greeted him like a lover - all hugs and kisses. When I invited them to our table for a drink, she declined. Said they were late for a dinner reservation. Ha! Reservation my foot! She just wanted to get him out of there and by herself!"

Peg glared at her. "Funny you should mention it, Mary - but I know who he is, what he does, and his relationship to the Sullivan family. There's no hanky panky going on like you just inferred," she snapped, her eyes flashing with anger. "So I don't want to hear any gossip because I'll know where it came from - dear." Peg said the dear with sarcastic emphasis. "Is that clear?"

And the wife of the CAG is a powerful person in the carrier Navy.

Paul Corrigan

CHAPTER 6

Ready Room #2
USS Philippine Sea

It was midnight. Lieutenant Commander Bill Barnes entered the Ready Room through the double blackout doors that prevent light from shining outside. He stopped in the rear of the room, drew a cup of coffee, and then proceeded to his seat to await debriefing by the Air Intelligence officer.

He propped his feet on the chair in front of him, pulled out a pack of Luckies, and fired up. The AI would be there soon, and Bill relaxed while he waited. The caffeine in the coffee and the nicotine in the cigarette gave him a jolt and perked him up - something he needed after three tiring hours of night flying around mountains and through canyons. That was tiring enough, but it was followed by a night landing aboard a fully blacked out carrier showing nothing but a single range light on the mast and the centerline lights in the landing area.

Will we ever get a really good radar in our planes so that we can see the mountains more accurately, and maybe even see the outline of the carrier's deck? He thought, as he sipped his coffee and dragged on his smoke. *But I can't complain. I had a good night. The quarter moon with only partial overcast really helped. I could see things. Got six trucks out in the open plus that poor son of a bitch that*

I saw sneaking under a tree to hide when he heard me. Bill took another drag and chuckled. *The poor SOB thought he was safe. He blew sky high when I hit him with the fifties. Didn't even use the two point five rockets.*

"Hey Danny, didn't hear you come in," Bill said, turning around to see the AI coming up the aisle from the rear of the ready room.

Danny Lynch, the ship's AI, slipped into a seat, raised the attached table, and plopped it across his lap. He took out his pen, put his ever-present notebook on the table, and paused for Bill to begin.

"Got seven trucks altogether, but the interesting news is Yang-doc."

"You mean at the horse shoe?" Danny interrupted.

"Yeah, that's it. On my first pass I saw lights and movement that went out when they heard me. With the partial moon I could get fairly close to the cliffs, but I couldn't see anything moving. So I hy-yockied out of there and looked for more trucks. Then I returned."

"You aren't supposed to revisit, Commander."

"Yeah, I know, but night ops is not like daytime. Anyway the second time around - the same thing. So I departed the area again. This time when I returned I did a gliding approach with power reduced, so they wouldn't hear me. There were lights all over the place and men working to install beams. They're doing something big there, Danny."

"Thanks, Commander. The duty steward has some chow being held for you in the Wardroom."

"Good. I'm ready to quit. It's been a long day ah - night that is." He raised his body wearily, stretched his arms, and shuffled off to the Wardroom

Ready Room #2
USS Philippine Sea

John sat in the back reading a book. There were no flights going out and the room was almost empty. The Squadron Duty Officer was half asleep, his head nodding, when the phone rang.

"Ready Two. Duty Officer here."

"Yes sir, he's here. I'll send him right down."

The duty Officer hung up and called to John. "John, CAG wants you in the Photo Interp spaces, pronto."

Photo Interpretation Room
USS Philippine Sea

CAG was there with the senior photo interpreter when John entered.

"Come over here, John and take a look," CAG waved him over and then pointed to the stereo lens set up over some black and white stereo prints. John came over to the table, moved the stereo stand aside, picked up the two prints, and held them up to the light to look at them.

"Hey, what are you doing, John? I said look at them in stereo."

"He is," the AI laughed. "He's just showing off."

"You mean you can see stereo without the stereo lens," CAG asked skeptically.

"All you have to do," replied the AI, "is to decouple your eyes so that one eye looks at one print and the other eye at the second print. Then you move the two pictures back and forth until you get the right distance for your eyes. Voila! Stereo vision!"

"But cross eyed people can't do it." John added seriously, looking at CAG to see if he took the bait.

"Are you saying your CAG is cross eyed, Lieutenant?" CAG growled at him.

"Absolutely not sir," he answered, trying to keep a straight face and then said, "Also, people with very narrow squinty eyes have trouble, too. The spacing of the photos is too far apart for them to do it." John held up the two photos, slid them back and forth in exaggerated movements, squinted, and made faces pretending to look for the stereo.

CAG laughed. "Alright, funny guy. Let's get serious."

John put the stereo pair under the lens. "It's Yang-doc but nothing out of the ordinary. Trestles cut, bridges down, rock slides."

"Bill Barnes said he saw a lot of activity there last night."

"Those UDT types smoking something again, CAG?"

"Be serious, John. These are yesterday's photography. Larry took them. Nothing resembling what Barnes reported."

"CAG, as I said earlier," the AI interjected. "The deep shadows around the cliffs and in the areas of the escarpments make it very difficult for us to see details using vertical photography. We need some stereo obliques."

"Yeah, I know. There's been no indications of activity and I wanted to avoid low altitude obliques because of the risk." CAG admitted. "Now it seems we must have them."

"I'd like to suggest, sir, that we do it early in the morning. We may catch some late night activity just finishing up, and we should gain tactical surprise since we normally don't schedule recce flights until 0900 - 1000 hours."

"Good idea," CAG responded, and turned to John. "I'm scheduling you tomorrow morning for Yang-doc. Get the bridges, the cuts in the cliffs, and the river bottom as much as you can. And, John - don't take chances. You hear? No revisits if you miss something. That flak is heavy and at 1000 - 1500 feet altitude they'll be all over you. Don't dally. Move in and move out quickly."

"Yeah, I sure wish we had cameras with lenses fast enough to allow us to fully use the jet's speed. Two hundred and twenty five knots! Hell, we should be doing 350, but the cameras won't stop motion at that speed."

"What's the latest flak count," CAG asked, turning to the AI.

"Sir, twelve 37 mm quad mounts with forty eight tubes and twenty 20 mm twin mounts with forty tubes plus a multitude of fifty caliber swivel mounted machine guns. All located and focused on the 3000 foot envelope around the horse shoe turn. Most of it sits on the high plateau within the turn of the horseshoe. At your altitude they'll all be pointed at you. That's eighty-eight tubes plus the .50 calibers on the plane the entire time over target. A real hornet's nest - especially for a single recce plane."

The weather was crystal clear when John launched at 0700 for the Yang-doc mission. He began his approach from fifty miles out at 350 knots, flying low up the river valley so that he was screened from observation by the hills. As he approached the target, he popped up to 1200 feet and rolled into a tight port turn following the horseshoe of the river and taking stereo obliques of the bridges, the cuts in the cliffs, and the general pattern of the river bottom. There was no flak. John smiled and thought to himself, *Good tactic. I caught them napping, but look what they're doing! The cuts have been deepened, there's piling stockpiled inside the trestle, and something down in the river bottom.* John pulled a hard 5g turn to bend around and get the last three bridges, but he couldn't make it.

They all seem asleep down there, John chuckled. *I'll just peel off to the south, hop over three ridges and return to get the remaining bridges.*

As he slid over the fourth ridge going away from Yang-doc, he noticed a heavy discoloration of the soil near the main road.

Oh Oh. Some heavy stuff has left the road there and probably went up that valley. Looks like they've covered the tracks and brushed the area over - but they can't change the discoloration, he laughed, taking obliques of the area. *I think I'll just mosey up that little valley and see what I can see.*

The valley contained three small badly weathered buildings that were in various states of disrepair, but what caught John' eye were three fresh boards not weathered like the rest of the roof.

My, My. There's activity here. I don't see anything else in the valley, but I've seen enough warning signs. I'll just roll out at the end of the valley, reverse course like I'm going back to Yang-doc, and then take the whole valley in stereo.

Yang-doc, North Korea

John planned his approach to Yang-doc to fly directly over the major gun emplacements on the plateau so that the guns would reach maximum elevation tracking him, and then have to slew 180 degrees to get him outbound. By then he would be gone. As he came over the last ridge at 1200 feet, he was jinking hard to port and then to starboard to present a difficult target. All 80 tubes opened up on him as soon as he cleared the ridge. Despite the jinking John could see the tracers passing over the wing within his line of sight from cockpit to tip tank.

"Jesus! Get your ass out of there!" yelled his escort, Joe Smith, his voice elevated a few octaves with excitement. Joe was flying Eagle 109 in a position about 1500 feet above and behind John.

John was already pulling back sharply on the stick when a loud explosion buffeted the airframe. Shrapnel filled the cockpit, pinging off the steel bucket seat, which held the parachute on which he sat.

107

Gauges shattered, the canopy cracked, and blood flowed into John's eyes, blinding him.

"I'm hit in the cockpit! I can't see!" John screamed as he pulled back even more sharply on the stick, which was now getting heavy due to loss of hydraulic boost.

"Okay, John boy - ease off the back stick. You're clear of flak and climbing steeply through 4000 feet."

"John, you're in a sixty degree climb," Joe shouted anxiously. "You're going to run out of airspeed. Roll off on a wing, and let it fall through - or you're going to stall! John! John! Do it now!!!"

In the cockpit a confused and frightened pilot began to comprehend his condition. The stick shaker began to violently shake its warning of incipient stall. As John rolled off on one wing, the plane shook and fell off into a near hammerhead stall. The nose fell through sharply and the plane was now screaming towards earth in a steep dive.

"Pull back on the stick! Hard! You stalled out, John. You're now in a steep dive, wings level, and accelerating through 300 knots. Pull back more, John. Give me 4g's! Now!"

The nose began to rise as the plane pulled out of its dive dangerously close to the ground and right in the middle of the AAA zone at Yang-doc. The guns opened up again, and a 50 caliber machine gun stitched the right wing. The thunk of the bullets as they passed through the skin and hit interior parts was frightening to an already panicked pilot. The plane began to climb as John pulled more g's trying to get away from the guns.

"My God! I'm hit again! What am I doing? I can't see, Joe! I'm blinded!" John cried as the panic of being blind gripped him. "My eyes are covered with blood!"

"Easy, John, easy. I'm here and can guide you. Let's get you straight and level first." Joe replied, keeping his voice calm and well modulated. "We got you under control, buddy. Left aileron now John; now neutral. Your nose is falling through. Now right aileron quickly! Now back pressure on the stick. Good. You're leveling off. Wings are level. That's it. Good. A little more back pressure. You're in a slight dive. More back! More back! Okay! You're in level flight. Hold the pressure on the stick, and trim it out. That's good. Let go of the stick. Okay, John. You're straight and level, and trimmed out. But you're heading west, and we need to go south to get over the MLR and into friendly territory. Then if you lose control you can punch out.

"Okay, John. Let's do a damage assessment. Any sign of system damage?" Joe continued.

"I can't see the gauges but from feel I know the hydraulics are gone. Engine sounds normal. I've got a radio, thank God! But the other electrical, who knows? Let's turn it around, Joe and head southwest to King-18." John's confidence was rapidly returning now that the plane was under control.

"John, I recommend you punch out after we cross the MLR. You'll never be able to put it down at K-18."

" No dice. I've got good stuff in these cameras. I'm going to bring them back somehow."

"Okay John. If you say so." Joe replied in a soothing voice. "I'm going to check in with Yo-do."

"Yo-do Angel. Eagle 109. I'm escorting Peter Peter 60 who has been hit in the cockpit. He's bleeding badly and blinded by blood. With my help he can control the airplane. We are in a slow turn to port twenty miles west of Yang-doc at 4000 feet. We intend to rollout heading southeast towards K-18, but he may have to punch out after we cross the MLR. Squawking emergency on my IFF."

"Roger Eagle 109," Yo-Do came right back. "We read your emergency squawk and are tracking you. Angel 15 will be airborne in five to intercept your track. Keep us advised."

"Roll out now, John. Gently. A little right stick. That's good. Nice and easy. Stop your roll. Okay. You lost some altitude. Use your trim tab to bring your nose up an RCH. Hold it steady. I'm sliding into position to inspect for damage."

"Joe, I'm now able to see the instrument panel for a few seconds - barely able to see it. Most of the instruments are shattered. No fire warning light, but the warning system may be destroyed."

"You got a big hole in the belly of the plane with torn metal just below the cockpit. That's where he got you. And the starboard wing is punctured with bullet holes, but no indication of bad structural damage."

"Eagle 109. You just crossed the MLR, and are ten miles inside friendly territory. Your heading for K-18 is 109 degrees."

"John, you're well inside the MLR. Everything's going okay. If you decide you want to punch out, I suggest you wait until over K-18."

"No ejection. Yang-doc is hot as hell. The ship needs the photos. And I may have some other hot stuff, too."

"Okay John, here's what we're going to do. Do you remember the pilot on the Happy Valley who was blinded? His wingman brought him all the way to the ramp and a cut. I'm going to do that for you, buddy."

"Eagle 109. Yo-do. Come right to 112. You are ten minutes out from K-18. They are expecting you. Shift to 127.3 and contact K-18 tower. Good luck."

"Roger, thanks for the help, Yo-Do."

"How you doing, John?"

"Joe, I can see a little better now. The blood seems to have eased off a bit. I can now see the instrument panel and I can see my wing tip intermittently, but it's hazy. The vision fades in and out."

"Eagle 109, K-18 tower. Do you read me?"

"Roger K-18. We're almost overhead. We plan to check slow flight here at 4000 feet. If Peter Peter can handle it, we'll fly a section approach with Eagle 109 on the wing, guiding Peter Peter until he's over the runway or can see the runway." There was a long pause before K-18 answered.

"109. This is the Command Duty Officer at K-18. I think the recce bird should punch out. Your plan is too risky, and we don't want to lose the pilot."

"K-18, my photos are too valuable to lose them by bailing out," John snapped back.

"Yes, but we don't want to clobber our runway either. Our skipper says to punch out."

"Bullshit," fumed John into the mike. "I'm declaring an emergency. Under ICAO flight rules, the pilot in command of the aircraft handles the emergency and I elect to land this bird at K-18 with or without your help!"

There was another long pause. "Okay, Peter Peter. You're the boss. We're standing by to help. I wish we could foam the runway, but we don't have the equipment."

"Tower This is 109. Can you give us a clear channel for the approach?"

"Roger, shift to 127.3. Eagle 109 and Peter Peter acknowledge."

"109 Rog."

"Peter Peter. Roger."

"Here we go, Joe. Give me stick and rudder orders," John said grimly. "I am blowing my landing gear down now with emergency air." There was a pause. Joe waited to see if the gear came down.

"Damn! The explosion must have cut the line from the air bottle. No air bottle - no gear. I guess we land in this configuration - gear up, flaps up. Okay, now I'll do slow flight." John slowly pulled the throttle back and at the same time trimmed out the back pressure on the stick as he kept the nose from falling through. Very very slowly - so that he could maintain control.

Eagle 109 tucked in tightly on one wing, and Joe gave quick concise orders to help him maintain level flight.

"What's my airspeed, Joe?"

"125, buddy."

"Okay, we'll do it at 125. It handles all right. Let's start down." Joe put Peter Peter on a straight in to the runway and dropped him down to 1000 feet to begin his final approach.

"Okay John, you're lined up with the runway. Looks like no crosswind. Crash gear in place. Ease your throttle back an RCH and let's set up a good glide slope."

"Oh Jesus." John suddenly said, cold sweat breaking out on his forehead.

"What's wrong, John?"

"I'm getting dizzy. Must be loss of blood."

"Get your ammonia vial out of your first aid pack, and sniff it whenever you get dizzy. We got this far - damnit we are going to do it!"

John came in low and flat with Joe tucked in tightly on his port wing

"A little left."

"Okay."

"Up nose slightly."

"Use the tab, man! The tab!"

"Okay, good lineup. Speed about 120. Looking good, John."

"Come left an RCH. You're drifting off centerline."
"Okay. You're lined up. A hair right stick."
"Good. Hold that."
"You're close, John. See the runway?"
"Not yet."
"Straight ahead, John. On centerline."
"You're almost over the runway."
"I got it! I got it!" John yelled as he whacked back the power to idle, dropped the nose and then flared.

Peter Peter touched down to the screech of tearing metal, shedding debris as it slid down the runway in a blaze of sparks. Crash trucks and the meat wagon, both with red lights flashing and sirens wailing, raced behind. John put the throttle into idle cutoff, closed the master fuel control, and shut down the electrical system. He could barely see the sides of the runway, and his vision was beginning to fade again. Using his rudders, he tried to head the plane off the runway so Joe could land, but he couldn't see the runway any more. The curtain was closing on his vision. The plane slid off the runway, hit a culvert, bounced over it, spun around losing part of a wing, and came to a halt a few feet short of the GCA building which the occupants were rapidly vacating on the other side.

The fire truck was alongside in seconds, and a monstrous firefighter in a silver asbestos suit and helmet climbed up on the plane, straddled the cockpit, and easily lifted the inert body of John Sullivan out into the waiting hands of six firefighters. The remaining firefighters stood by the foam nozzles and hoses in case the plane should erupt into flame.

John regained consciousness lying on a surgical table in the K-18 dispensary. Doctor Jake Arnold was inserting a needle into his wrist for plasma, and the corpsman was rigging a stand for the plasma bag.

Joe stuck his head in the door. "Can I come in, doctor?"

Doctor Arnold turned and looked at the face of the worried wingman.

"Come on in, sailor. We don't stand on formality here. Besides I have questions I need to ask you."

John moaned softly and slowly opened his eyes, trying to focus them. "How you doing, Lieutenant?" Arnold asked.

"Everything's hazy, Doc, and I hurt like hell!" John smiled weakly.

"Just relax, son. Your eyes and optic nerve are okay. You lost vision from shock and loss of blood. We're fixing that. Pumping some plasma into you, and then some whole blood as soon as they fly it in from Kimpo. Then we'll take some of the easy pieces of shrapnel out of you, patch you up, and leave the rest of the job for Tokyo. You were very lucky, son. A large section of shrapnel penetrated your neck and just missed the main artery to the brain. About a quarter inch further to the right and you would have died within a minute - your blood pumped out of you. You're a lucky man. We have a Medevac due in here in two hours. They'll take you to Tachikawa Air Base in Japan, and then by ambulance from there to the Army General Hospital in Tokyo."

"You luck dog," Joe interjected. "Those pretty Army nurses in Tokyo just love to take care of war heroes!"

"Thank God for the steel pan we sit on, or I wouldn't have anything for the nurses to play with." John managed to whisper.

"You didn't want your pencil sharpened by the Gooks, huh John?" Joe laughed.

"The only pencil sharpener I like is between a woman's legs," John smiled, but the Demerol was taking effect. He rolled his eyes and was gone.

"By the way, Lieutenant, what's your blood type?" Arnold asked, looking at Joe.

"Type A, sir. It's on my dog tag. Why?"

"Good. That's John's also. I can start a transfusion now and not wait for the delivery from Kimpo. You're now grounded for two weeks, my friend. Sorry."

"Wait until CAG hears this. He'll have to send another pilot to get my plane." He began to roll up his sleeve.

Army General Hospital
Tokyo, Japan

The Army General Hospital in Tokyo was the largest military medical facility in the Far East. The MASH field units in Korea, and the Navy's hospital ship, USS Consolation, in Pusan harbor, supported it. However, all the serious casualties eventually ended up at Tokyo General. The hospital was housed in a three story concrete building that had survived the fire bombings of World War II. The facility encompassed several outlying structures and included a small manicured Japanese garden.

First Lieutenant Sandra Hall was having an early breakfast of coffee and toast in the cafeteria that served the staff before her busy day began as head nurse of Surgical Team A. As usual it began for Sandra at 0430 when the alarm went off, followed by a shower and all the other routine activities required prior to putting on a stiffly starched white uniform, either a skirt or slacks, depending on what the day would bring. It was now 0545 and she had time for a leisurely few moments before reporting for duty at 0630.

Tall and slender, Sandra had inherited her mother's cool patrician beauty. She had a trim athletic body, and moved as gracefully as a ballerina. Her heavy honey blonde hair swung softly along her cheeks, and nestled just above her collar, where it turned under. Yet, what most men who met her remarked upon were her gray-green eyes.

Sandra was a product of Chevy Chase, Maryland, a fashionable, and established suburb outside the nation's capitol. Chevy Chase was old money, old families, many of whom regarded politicians as frightful people. Sandra had set her family on its ears - well, her mother actually - by refusing to go to the college - cum finishing school - that her mother and grandmother had attended. Upon graduation from high school during World War II, Sandra decided to attend Johns Hopkins University where she majored in biology. She so impressed her professors that at the end of her sophomore year, she was appointed to the prestigious nursing school at Johns Hopkins Hospital.

During her training she met an Army major, conducting research at Johns Hopkins' extensive laboratories. The major was quite taken with her professional ability, including her knowledge of biology, and convinced her to join the Army Nurse Corps with initial assignment as his assistant at the Army's Walter Reed Hospital. When the Korean War broke out, she was immediately transferred to Tokyo General as part of a war augmentation of the facility.

Sandra was finishing her toast, and preparing to get another cup of coffee when a vivacious redhead with an infectious smile and bright sparkling eyes bounced up to her table carrying a tray loaded with food.

" 'morning, Sandra. What's on the agenda today? Is your butcher shop down in Surgery all ready to go? I've got a bunch of victims up on the ward just dying to come down and let you play with them," Second Lieutenant Mitzi Gray said, all in one breath, as she set the tray down and dropped into a chair. Mitzi was the ward nurse of the surgical ward on the second floor.

Mitzi was a native of southern California - sun-baked and fit from cavorting up and down the beaches at La Jolla and Pacific Grove for most of her twenty-three years. She was also a complete extrovert with seemingly bottomless vitality.

"Good morning, yourself Mitzi. You're just bubbling as usual. Don't you ever run down?" Sandra asked before she took the last bite of her toast. Then she saw Mitzi's tray. "My God, Mitzi! Are you going to eat all that? You'll become fat as a pig!"

"Sure!" Mitzi responded, effervescently. "I'll burn it all off this morning! But, I'm going light at lunch because some guy's taking me out to dinner this evening." She grinned at Sandra.

"Another one?" Sandra laughed. "Don't you ever get serious with just one?"

"Why should I? It's a free dinner, and the guy seems nice enough. I just hope he's capable of some conversation. He's a captain from Washington on TDY."

"Is he married?" Sandra queried.

"Probably, but what the hell, Sandra, I'm not going to bed with him! You know me - No veil, no tail!," she laughed again, and then giggled at her joke.

"Yeah well, he'll probably try to get you over to the never-ending party at the Riding Academy, and then upstairs to his room. He's staying there isn't he?" Sandra said, referring to the Tokyo Bachelor Officer's Quarters by its nickname.

"Sure - where else? But I don't go to the Riding Academy anymore. When I first arrived here, a major got me above the first floor before I realized what it was all about. When I saw all those naked Japanese dollies running up and down the halls, I made a real quick exit. I'll date 'em, have fun with 'em, and let 'em pay for dinner - but no sack time! No way!" She paused to catch her breath.

"Hey - what about you, pretty lady? How's your love life these days?"

"Still looking for Mister Right, Toots, but I'm beginning to despair," Sandra laughed, as she finished her coffee.

Mitzi sighed, "I had this real heart-throb in high school. Cool guy. I really liked him. He was lots of fun, a great surfer, but a bit of an airhead. Definitely not marrying material." She bubbled on and then turned serious. "Haven't you ever had any real love interest, Sandra? A stunner like you?"

Sandra thought a moment and then replied with a faint smile, "Yeah well, I guess I did, but it didn't last. Actually I had the ring on my finger when I canceled the wedding. A nice guy, but I just didn't love him! He lived in Chevy Chase and was going to law school. I'd dated him ever since high school, and we had some great times together. Used to take the streetcar every Saturday night to Glen Echo and dance 'til two. Our streetcars had three tracks in town, but they ran on an overhead electrical connection in the outlying areas like Glen Echo. On the way back to the city, the cars stopped and got connected to an underground third rail - always with a great stream of sparks. I was watching that one night coming back from Glen Echo, when it dawned on me - there were no sparks in our relationship! So I broke the engagement! He was a nice guy, and he took it better than I thought he would. Said it was better I knew then, than after we were married. Like I said, he was a nice guy."

"What about all those middies at Annapolis? Surely you could find a good one there?" Mitzi queried, excited about all those men available in one spot!

"I never went there," Sandra replied. "Never could get interested in a man whose job was killing. I believe in saving life - not taking it." Then she laughed at the incongruity of her situation. "Yet here I am patching up military men who get ripped apart in Korea. I'm dedicated to saving their lives - yes - but I'm not sure I want to marry one! That's probably why I don't date too much here."

"But don't you want to get married and have kids?" Mitzi persisted, chewing her bacon.

"Sure - of course I do. All of us do, Mitzi. But the right guy just hasn't come along. I've got several years to go before I hit the big 3-Oh, and lose my girlish looks."

"Well, we can't wait too long." Mitzi replied, studying her piece of bacon. "We all get old and wrinkled - just like this bacon! And then all those guys will want something younger - plus," she added. "all the good men will be gone! Time is of the essence - Confucius say."

"Speaking of good men, Mitzi," Second Lieutenant Lou Semper broke into the conversation, as she joined the other two and placed her tray on the table. "Have y'all seen that hunk of a man that came in last night - the Navy lieutenant that's peppered with shrapnel?" Her long Texas drawl stretched out the phrases.

"Oh yeah." Mitzi popped in. "I meant to tell you, Sandra! This guy has beautiful blue eyes that I could just fall into. And his smile. Wow! Now that's a man! I could do some equestrian riding with him! I'd like to get him in the saddle at the Riding Academy!" Mitzi jumped up from her chair and mimicked a rider on a horse.

"This guy's not for you, Mitzi! I think he's for Sandra," Lou drawled on dryly and laughed. "Really! His personality and hers would fit together like a hand in a glove."

"Yeah, I guess you're right," Mitzi sniffled and then grinned. "I bequeath Mr. Hunk to you, Sandra! He's all yours! I guess I'll just have to find me another riding partner!" she laughed.

"Okay girls. That's enough about men and our rather forlorn love life. Let's go carve on a few of them. Maybe we can save the women they love from some heavy tears." Sandra rose, brushed the crumbs from her slacks, and headed for the surgery suites.

Surgical Suite #2
Tokyo General Hospital

"Okay, Mitzi. We're ready for the shrapnel case. Send him down. Maybe I'll fall in love with him." Sandra called up to the ward.

"Lieutenant Sullivan is on his way down now," Mitzi responded. "And when he gets there, why don't you propose to him after you get him on the operating table? And if he says no, or you decide not to keep him, let me know, I'll take him!"

Sandra laughed at Mitzi's antics, and then she turned serious. "I think we're all beginning to suffer from battle fatigue. Too many broken men to put back together. Too much blood. Too much human waste. We need some time off, Mitzi, to recharge our batteries."

The gurney with Lieutenant John Sullivan on it pushed its way through the swinging doors of Surgical Suite 2, and stopped at the nurse's station.

"He's all yours, Captain," a young intern said, handing her his chart board. John looked up, his eyes glazed, and tried to get up, but he was strapped down.

"Hey, take it easy, big boy," Sandra said quietly, checking his pulse and peering into his eyes whose lids she held open with her thumb and forefinger.

John looked at her, his eyes crossing and uncrossing from the sedation. "Shit, lady. You are the most beautiful thing I've seen in a long time."

"Hush now. You probably say that to all the girls," she smiled down at him as she logged his vitals onto his chart. She looked at him again. *A good looking man, Mitzi's right. Something about him. Maybe I could go for him.*

"He's gone," she said to the aid. "Wheel him into the operating room and let's get started."

John opened his eyes again. "I'm madly in love with you, sweetheart. Will you sleep with me tonight?" John mumbled.

Sandra smiled wryly and touched his forehead with the palm of her hand. "You're gone, my handsome knight. You'll never know."

She turned to the nurse's aid standing nearby. "Okay, take him in."

2739 Maple Drive
San Diego

Sylvia was washing her hair in the sink. Her hands were full of suds when the phone rang.

"Damn, why now, God?" She was tempted to just let it ring. Instead she wrapped her head in a towel and went across the kitchen to the extension.

"Hello, Sullivan residence."

"This is the AT&T International Operator. One moment for the Tokyo operator."

"Oh my God!" Sylvia cried out. "Something has happened to John!"

"This is Tokyo. I have a collect call for anyone from Lieutenant junior grade John Sullivan. Will you accept the charges?"

"God, yes," Sylvia replied with great relief, but still concerned. "John? Is it you? What are you doing in Japan? R&R? I don't remember one at this time. Are you okay?"

" Whoa!" John laughed. "Yes, I'm okay. but I got my skin decorated. You know those decorative patterns that some African warriors wear - the little lumps? That's me!" He chuckled again. "Your name is spelled in lumps on my chest!"

"What in God's name are you talking about? You don't make sense."

"My darling Sylvia. I got hit in the cockpit and took a lot of shrapnel on my legs, arms, and face."

"Did it hit any vital spot, John?" Sylvia interrupted, now concerned.

"The family jewels are okay. Not a scratch - if that's what you mean." he laughed.

"Don't be a smartass, I already told you! I mean all of you - but then the family jewels are important," she giggled like a school girl

"I'm really okay. Just kind of done in from the ordeal of it. For the next week you can reach me here in Ward J, U.S. Army General Hospital, Tokyo. After that I'll be back in the squadron."

"Well, Mister Fighter Pilot, have I got news for you! You were a pretty good shot that last night you were home. I'm pregnant! How about that!" she laughed. "Pretty good aim for a fighter pilot!" She beamed.

"Oh baby, what wonderful news!" His voice softened. Huskily he said, "Really wonderful! Maybe I'll get a little girl just like you. But girl or boy, who cares! You okay? What does the doctor say?"

"I'm healthy as a horse! Unless you get extended in WESPAC, you should be home for the launching! The doctor says mid - November. The sixteenth to be exact!" She cradled the receiver in her shoulder and stretched her arm that was going to sleep.

"I can't wait," he replied. "But there's some bad news, I'm afraid, honey. Ray Hale bought the farm a few weeks ago. Strange accident." John said, frowning with deeply furrowed brows. "A strange accident."

"Well, the squadron news isn't too good here either. I went to the VF-112 luncheon where that stupid Janet showed the pictures of

119

Ralph Winters dancing with that nude Japanese girl. Sally Winters is talking to a lawyer. I hope there's no divorce, but she was terribly embarrassed. Mrs. Towsan - how do you guys say it? - chewed Janet a new asshole. That's vulgar I know, but that's the only expression that does it." She rolled her eyes.

"Changing the subject to a more personal note, John dear. Were you at the Komatsu too?" Sylvia asked sweetly. "Were you dancing with those nude Japanese sweeties?"

John laughed, "No, that's the night I got put in hack for throwing that supply weenie into the pool." He laughed again and then turned sober. "But I have visited the Komatsu with the other guys. I drink sake, watch the floor show, and never, never touch the merchandise!"

"I trust you, darling. I know you won't cheat on me. But be forewarned. If you do, I'll know it and I'll cut your balls off! Better yet I'll rip them out by the roots and stuff them in your mouth." She idly stretched the curly phone cord. "What do you call those people with no balls?"

"Well, you can call them either Air Force pilots or eunuchs." He laughed at his bad joke.

"Well Stud, you'll be one, if you play with those gee-shies." She paused. "Honey, just keep safe and come home. That's all I ask. And with that we'd better hang up, my darling. I miss you so much, and love you so."

"I love you too," John replied as the phone went dead, and each was left with their own memories.

Photo Interpretation Room
USS Philippine Sea

Lieutenant junior grade Wolfe was assigned the job of examining John's film which was returned by COD aircraft, a converted Grumman World War II TBF, used for Carrier On Board delivery of mail and vital parts.

"Wow! Look at this! There must be twenty Russian T-34 tanks in this valley. This has to be the tank repair facility we've been searching for. Take a look."

The other photo interpreter put the prints under his stereo vision device. "Yes indeed. Mr. Sullivan sure hit the jackpot. I wonder what triggered him to take the photography?"

"I'm going to do the P.R. Report and then I'll ask Commander Jenkins, the flag air ops, to take a look."

One quick look and Jenkins asked for an immediate conference with Rear Admiral Stein, Commander Task Force 77, who was flying his flag on the Phil Sea.

"Captain Oliver," the admiral said to his Operations Officer after looking at the stereo prints. "Plan a two carrier maximum strike effort for tomorrow. Notify the Commander, Eighth Army, General Ridgway, what we have and what we plan to do. And info General MacArthur."

"Do you want confirming recce this afternoon, Admiral?" Captain Oliver asked.

"Hell no! Stay away from that area! Don't spook them. They thought the recce bird was just playing games with the defenses at Yang-doc. They knew he got hit there. No, it's perfect! Plan the strike, and send that youngster Sullivan up to see me. I'd like to know what prompted him to take the photos."

"He's still in the hospital in Tokyo, sir. Will be for another two weeks. Do you want me to send him up when he returns?"

"Yes, please do."

CAG entered the admiral's cabin. "May I speak with you, sir?"

"Come in, CAG. Have you seen the film of Sullivan's? The tank repair facility?"

"Yes sir. And have you seen the photos of Yang-doc?"

"No, I haven't. Should I?" the Admiral replied.

"Yes sir, you should. They're as important as the tank facility. They show a remarkable ingenuity by the Gooks to repair the road and rail line to a point where they can really move some cargo - all the repairs designed to be non-observable with the vertical photography, but the low obliques caught it. We need a major effort to put them out of business. First, we've got to destroy the triple A, so the Spads can get in there with the heavy stuff."

"I'll look at it CAG, but it will have to be tomorrow. We need to get the tanks now, before they move."

"I agree, sir. But let's get both," CAG laughed. "That damned John! He really did a job. God bless him!"

CHAPTER 7

USS Philippine Sea
Yokosuka, Japan

It was late March and the Philippine Sea was headed for Yokosuka and its third R&R period. The combat-weary recce aviators decided it was time to take a real R&R on one of the package tours offered by Special Services. Each pilot had almost one hundred missions, and it was beginning to wear on them. No one wanted to go to Kyoto to see the temples, or to Mount Fuji to climb the mountain. However, they had all heard about Akakura, a resort in the Japanese Alps run by the Army.

"That sounds like fun," John said, reading the bulletin with its words of enticement for snow and sports. "Has anyone skied before?" All heads shook negative in unison.

"What the hell," responded Dave Herbert, going to look over John's shoulder at the bulletin. "Worst that can happen is that someone will break an arm or a leg! Then he won't have to fly the next time on the line. Great idea!" He laughed, his dark eyes glinting at the thought of taking some risk, for Dave was a risk-taker. He loved the thrill of it. John leaned back in his chair and waited for Larry's comments.

"Hey! I vote for Akakura and a broken leg," chirped Larry, his rubber face forming itself into the image of Bacchus, the happy god of wine and frivolity. "I'm tired of getting shot at. Besides, I'm not up to any more temple tours or sitting around the Riding Academy in

123

Tokyo looking for action either - which I never get anyway," He laughed uproariously, and the others joined in with suitable comments on Larry's apparent inability to snag a woman.

"Larry, you'll remain a virgin all your life!" Dave poked fun at him.

"Maybe you can snag a live one at Akakura, Larry, but I doubt it!" John laughed at Larry's expense.

"Okay guys! Let's vote. All in favor?" John asked. Three hands were raised. Unanimous for broken legs!

"Where do we get the skis?" Larry queried.

"The bulletin says that they have everything from skis to splints," John answered.

"Well, what if I break my leg or" he looked at Larry, "more likely Larry! Are there nurses to hold my hand?" Dave wanted to know.

"Dave, you're too suave to get mixed up with nurses," Larry laughed.

"Try me," Dave grinned. "I'm not a virgin like you, Larry."

The three pilots hopped the train from Yokosuka to Tokyo, an easy trip that they done many times before. In Tokyo they were met and escorted to the train for Akakura, and the overnight trip. No one had to interpret the Japanese signs, or worry about getting, God forbid, on one of the milk run trains that took forever to go anywhere.

There were no Pullmans, but they had a compartment to themselves with comfortable seats. John grabbed a seat next to the window facing forward, and stretched his long legs. "Man, let's get this show on the road. I'm ready." The others, now seated, heartily agreed, and eagerly anticipated a well-earned rest from combat.

The train's cars were short and stubby with only two axles and four wheels. Inside, the passageway was on the left side of the car like a Pullman, and the compartment was spacious. The engine itself resembled a child's toy from some miniature railroad. Small, and squat with metallic silver coloring, it was steam-driven with two oversized main drive wheels on either side, and an old-fashioned cow-catcher in front.

The train left the Shinjuku station at dusk, and passed through residential areas consisting of small doll-like homes and buildings where a few lights could be seen, casting a soft yellow glow as the day faded. The little engine chugged on through the residential area and eventually small plots of farmland began to appear in muted tones of brown, green, and gray. From his window John could see small rice paddies, small haystacks, and it seemed - small cattle. It all appeared as a study in miniature. He found himself watching the changing countryside with delight and a sense of peace came over him. The men, for once, were quiet. There was no conversation as they traveled into the evening, each alone with his own thoughts.

Darkness fell and everything turned gray and black; eventually the whiteness of snow dappled the landscape, a soft restful scene that emphasized the quietness. The whiteness of the snow and the blacks and grays of the thatched roofs, roads, and rice paddies became a study in chiaroscuro as a full moon rose slowly over the tranquil scene.

It's like watching an old-time movie in black and white, John mused. *You can almost feel the frames of scenery change in unison with the sound of the wheels and the flicker of the telephone poles as they flip past . . . .* His eyes closed and he drifted into welcome slumber.

The sturdy engine labored up increasingly steep grades throughout the night as the temperature dropped sharply and the peaks of the mountains and walls of the canyons shut out the rest of the world. The intrepid aviators wrapped blankets about themselves and huddled together for warmth as the womb of the earth closed in around them.

Army Lodge
Akakura, Japanese Alps

The sun was up when the train arrived at the Akakura station. The reflections off the snow blinded the eye with infinite light, and the glare to the east was impossible to look into. The weary engine puffed noisily to a stop, emitting large gasps of steam, all the while panting as though trying to recover from the long pull up the mountains.

A snowmobile that looked like a tiny Army half track waited for the three aviators. An ancient-looking man in a stovepipe hat with a dirty gray scarf wrapped around his neck waited at the half track for the arriving passengers.

"We go Akakura! We go Akakura!" The old man kept saying over and over in a monotone voice through large yellowed teeth. He looked like a centurion with long stringy white hair and beard, a weathered face with deep creases in leathery skin, and gnarled hands. "We go Akakura." His eyes twinkled as he surveyed his new customers, grinning broadly.

"Wow! What a place," marveled Dave. "Just look at all that snow piled high! Must be at least ten or eleven feet! And the miniature station, with a peaked roof to make the snow fall off! The building's not tall enough for a regular sized man to enter! I'd never make it!" He stretched; glad to be off the train.

"Just remember," John commented, laughing. "The Japanese are not big people. Be thankful that you didn't have to sleep in a Japanese Pullman!"

The steep mountains rose on all sides, enclosing the station in a basin. They were completely covered with snow although some formidable black outcroppings pushed themselves up through the white blanket. The air was bracing and clean.

Dave took a deep breath, exhaled it and said, "Breathe that clean, sweet mountain air. God! It's so good!" Changing the subject, he added, "Okay troops, let's go find the skis, the lieder hosen, and the alpine hat with a feather. Onward!"

"Ah . . . Don't forget the hot buttered rum," John said, adding his two cents and following Dave through the snow to the half-track.

It was a short trip to the lodge. The half-track scooted through the doll-sized village with its tiny doors and windows peeking out of the drifts, and then climbed again over the hard packed snow, until moments later it pulled up in front of the lodge itself. The charming old building was made of gray stone and dark wood, with heavy support beams between the stone sections. Two large chimneys dominated a steep black tile roof. The windows were lovely - patterned in leaded glass, while the wood around them, and the gables were intricately carved with small designs of birds and animals.

The half-track stopped at the main floor of the two-story lodge, which actually was a three-story building. There was a ski shop on a lower level, but it was completely covered with snow. The new arrivals went down steps carved in the snow to reach the main entrance. Spirits were soaring.

"Welcome to Akakura," greeted the tech sergeant manager who was standing in the entrance. "Welcome to U.S.Army hospitality." He grinned broadly, holding out his hand.

John shook it and introduced the others.

"The maid, Kimiko, here," The manager continued, pointing to her, "will show you to your accommodations."

Kimiko, in the traditional kimono and obi, looked shyly at the new arrivals, and covered her mouth with her hand as she smiled and bowed.

"Gentlemen, my name is Sergeant Joseph. I will be your host to see to your comfort during you stay with us. We have two dormitories on the second floor - one for men and one for women. You'll sleep on Army cots and mattresses, and there are plenty of blankets. It gets very cold here at night. There are shelves to put your things on, and the latrine is down the hall."

Larry couldn't wait any longer and he interrupted the Sergeant. "A ladies' dorm? You have some real women here?" Larry was excited at the prospect.

Sergeant Josephs smiled tolerantly. "Yes, as a matter of fact we have three arriving later this morning. Three nurses from the hospital in Tokyo. But, please remember that you are officers and gentlemen," he added somewhat facetiously.

"Real women!" John grinned expectantly. "I knew we picked the right tour." The trio laughed. Things were looking up!

"Gentlemen, let me have a few more minutes of your time for orientation, if you don't mind," the Sergeant continued. "On the lower levels are the showers and hot tubs. The former are American, and the latter Japanese. The hot tubs are really great! The hours for them are posted, and I regret to say that unlike the Japanese, I cannot offer you mixed company hot tubs. Army regs, you know." He smiled apologetically, and chuckled.

"Behind me is the great room. It has a bar, a high beamed ceiling, some really comfortable deep leather chairs, and a twenty-foot fireplace that will be blazing this evening. You'll enjoy it after a day on the slopes, I guarantee it."

"And hot buttered rum?" John added expectantly.

"Yes sir, all you want."

"Downstairs is the ski shop for whatever you need, and outside to the left are the beginner's slopes with Japanese instructors to teach you basics - like how to stop, and how to cover the sitz marks you make when you fall. We don't have a lift. Instead we have a half track that keeps running up and down the mountain, taking skiers up, and bringing down broken legs and ankles," the Sergeant said with a deadpan face that suggested many broken legs and ankles.

"Very funny," replied Larry. "But being expert skiers, we need only the up service. Right guys?"

" So they all say. Gentlemen, I am at your service. Enjoy your holiday." Sergeant Joseph shook hands all around, turned, and left.

"Let's pick a bunk, stow our gear, and head for the slopes." Larry laughed.

An hour later the trio were trying it out on the beginner's slope with the Japanese instructors trying desperately to get them to do it right. At last, most of them could snow plow and stop, and by noon they were tired of it.

"I've had enough of this shit," said John. "Let's get a sandwich from the chow line, and we'll try the big stuff."

After some food, they were ready to have another go at the mountain. The half-track dropped them at the mid-level of the run. Above that the slope was steep, twisting and wicked as it plunged down the side of the mountain. The three men stopped at the edge of the down slope and readied themselves, checking their skis in the bright sun.

"Okay, guys, here we go!" John shouted and pushed off. About twenty feet down the slope one ski got away from him, and he landed spread eagle with his face in the snow, and his aviator sunglasses awry.

"Hey, guys, what do we give him for that landing?" hooted Larry, making signals like an LSO. "It's surely not an OK-3! How about an OK-1 with a comment that he dove for the deck!" Dave and Larry were now doubled over in laughter.

"Hey John baby, if you want to know how to do it, look at this," Dave pointed up the slope where a small Japanese boy was coming down the run about sixty miles per hour. He was literally skimming from one high point to another, his little legs bending and extending like pistons.

"The smart little show-off bastard," John muttered to himself. "He can do that as easily as I can ride a bike! I don't think I like him."

The young boy turned slightly and waved as he flew past, powdered snow flying behind. It was definitely a condescending gesture to the dumb American.

"The little shit," John called to his buddies. "Did you see that?" But they were already rolling in the snow in gales of laughter. "You bastards," he said, but he smiled.

By the end of the day all the intrepid warriors were going down the mid-level slope at varying degrees of speed with only two or three sitz marks to be covered on each run. By late afternoon they were exhausted and headed for the lodge, spirits high from the glorious day and exercise.

True to the Sergeant's promise, the hot tub was as wonderful as it looked, and it did a great job of taking out the aches and pains.

"Ahhh - I sure wish this was coed," sighed Larry, as he slowly moved his tired arms and legs through the steaming water. "All that exercise made me horny. I'd just like to have something here that I could play with and tickle about now."

"Yeah - You've got a one track mind, buddy," said Dave, sinking back into the hot water.

"Hey! Just look at that!" Larry bragged to the others, elevating his hips to the water's surface, revealing his erection. "Gentlemen, meet King! Up King! Up gallant fighter!" He flexed his muscles causing the organ to bounce up and down to the hoots and hollers of his comrades in arms.

"Poor Larry," John laughed. "If he had a girl here, he wouldn't know what to do with her." He received a mouthful of water as Larry stood up and splashed violently.

"Yes sir," John continued. "He couldn't even tickle her fancy much less anything else."

"Aha ha ha!" They howled.

"I'll have you guys know I'm going to get laid before this cruise is over - some good looking, super girl," he sputtered.

"Sure, Larry," John snickered. "The only place you'll get laid is at the Komatsu for a price. Some yen for your yen!" he hooted.

John and Dave roared and splashed more water at Larry.

"Okay. You guys just watch," Larry announced. "I'm going to get a piece of ass with one of these girls arriving today."

"Yeah - right. I'll believe it when I see it," Dave laughed.

"I wonder where they are," John asked. "Let's get dressed and head for the hot buttered rum. That's where we'll find them."

But they weren't in front of the big stone fireplace. There were a few Army types from Tokyo who were three-quarters' blotto, but no women.

"Sergeant Josephs, where are the women?" John asked as the sergeant stopped by.

"They were tired from the trip and are resting. They'll be at dinner which begins at eight o'clock. We have steak tonight."

"Well, they must not be swingers," Larry said sourly, "or they'd be down here with the hot buttered rum." The Sergeant shrugged and left, shaking his head at their antics.

John took a swig and exclaimed, "Hey, this rum is great! And what a setting! I'm almost in heaven, sitting here in a massive leather couch in front of a roaring log fire with real fur rugs on the floor. Tall ceilings, heavy beams, deep cushioned chairs, dim lights. You know, someone could score in that dark corner back there, and no one would be the wiser. Oh well, hell!" Frustrated, he got up and walked to the window to look out at the falling snow.

"Hello everyone! How's the hot buttered rum?" called a sweet feminine voice. All three heads immediately turned in the direction of the query, their eyes locking on the potential targets.

The aviators stood up as three young women approached the fireplace area where they were sitting. Larry introduced the Navy trio.

A tall tawny blonde responded. "I'm Sandra Hall, and this is Mitzi Gray and Lou Semper. We're all nurses from the Army hospital in Tokyo." She paused and, turning to John, she added, "Say, John, weren't you in our hospital about a month ago? Shrapnel in the legs?"

"Yeah, I was, but how could I not remember you?" he replied, searching his mind for her name and where he saw her.

Sandra laughed, "When I saw you, you were going into surgery, and were feeling no pain! In fact, just before you faded completely, you looked at me and said something like - Hello sweetheart, I love you! Will you sleep with me?" She smiled at him, and laughed a low husky laugh.

"And I thought he was just getting senile! You know, too many g's - too much combat! But I can't believe he propositioned you right on the operating table! What a guy!" Larry hooted

The group roared with laughter as Sandra smiled at them, and replied, " You guys could only be naval aviators with a remark like that. Right? Not pilots - that's Air Force."

"Yeah, Lou and I remember John well." Mitzi said, looking at John. "You remember me, don't you? The surgical ward nurse?"

"Of course," John replied. "And Lou too."

"Well, I want you to know we drew straws for you, flyboy, and Sandra won. You're hers now." Without drawing a breadth, Mitzi continued, "Well, are we going to stand here all evening or are you going to buy us a hot buttered rum?" she laughed. She practically sat in Larry's lap. Sandra then sat down next to John, and Dave got third choice, Lou Semper. But, not a bad third choice, a pretty blonde with a glowing complexion, and an infectious smile. A real Texas darlin'.

You are one good-looking woman, Sandra, John thought to himself. *Beautiful long legs, slender and shapely, nice tits, and tall. Umm nice! She must be five foot seven or so. That great swinging hair - and those eyes, gray-green. The kind that just pull you into them. This could be a great evening.* His attention returned to the group and the happy chatter.

"Hey guys! We're in luck," Mitzi announced. "There's a combo here from the Army band in Tokyo for the next five nights. They come up for a week and in return for their music, the week is free. We can live it up and dance all night! Or at least 'til they stop!" She did a little dance step.

"Great," Larry responded. "For a change, no off-tone Japanese guitars."

"They are not guitars, dumb-dumb," Dave laughed.

"You can say that again!" Larry snorted.

The hot buttered rum arrived and after a toast to everything and everyone, the warmth of the roaring fire took over. Each one retreated for a moment into their personal reverie as they looked into the crackling blaze, just enjoying the peaceful atmosphere, the war forgotten for the moment.

"What do you do in Tokyo besides carve people up?" John asked Sandra as they sank back in the deep leather cushions of the massive couch.

"Not much," she replied, shifting to tuck her long legs underneath her. "After you run out of sight-seeing and shopping, what else is there? That's why Akakura is so great for me. It's active, not passive like sight-seeing is. I'm not a big skier, but at least it's a diversion! And you, John Sullivan. What do you do besides fly?" She raised her mug for another sip and looked at John. *Mitzi was right. What a hunk this one is! I wonder if he has anything to talk about besides airplanes._*

John put his empty mug on the table and answered her. "Oh, I watch movies in the Ready Room. Listen to the raunchy comments of the aviators about the scenes and dialogue. They can turn a lousy movie into hilarious entertainment. And read. I read a lot."

" Hey gang, let's liven this up," Mitzi yelled at the group. "Where are the dice? You guys know liar's dice, don't you?" Larry immediately rose and got the dice from the bar.

"I'm the best liar's dice player in the world," he boasted, broadly.

"How do y'all play it?" Lou drawled, leaning forward.

"It's easy, if you're a good liar like Larry," Dave laughed. "You roll the dice and tell the person on your left what you rolled - rather what you want him to think you rolled."

"For example, you roll garbage, but you tell the person on your left that you rolled three fours. He in turn either believes you or calls you. If he believes you and accepts the garbage as three fours, he can pass it along, or he can roll again, and start the liar's chain over. If he calls you, and you have three fours or more, he loses and buys a round."

"Now that sounds like fun. No wonder naval aviators play it. They can lie their way into a girl's pants, and the poor girls believe them. Give me the dice. I'll start." Mitzi said gaily as she grabbed for the cup. She then rattled the dice in the cup and upended it on the table so that no one, but her, could see the results of the roll.

"I've got four sixes," Mitzi bragged. John didn't believe her and lifted the cup. To the squeals of delight from Mitzi, everyone saw four sixes. John shook his head in disbelief and signaled the bartender for another round - on him, of course.

The next roll started with John. It was garbage, but he called it three three's. It traveled full circle increasing in value until it reached Mitzi who was on John's right. Obviously she had to call or roll again because John knew what was under the cup. Without thinking she passed it to John as five fives. John smiled. Larry, who had passed it to her figuring she would just pass it on, rolled off his seat laughing. Sandra laughed and said, "You'll learn, Mitzi. These naval aviators play to win."

Mitzi lifted the cup, saw the garbage she had passed to John who had rolled it originally, and threw the cup at Larry who was rolling on the floor in laughter. She then jumped on top of him and gave him a very large and very sexy bite on the ear in the process of wrestling him.

Dinner was announced, and the six went in to find candlelight, fine table linens, excellent food, and superb service. The dining room itself was charming and intimate, with a small dance floor in the center. The Army did it right. Conversation never lagged during the sumptuous meal. Stories were told, jokes abounded, and the wine flowed as the little group relaxed and enjoyed the camaraderie among themselves.

The band arrived and was greeted by the girls who knew most of them.

"Hi Mitzi," yelled the bandleader. "What are you doing with a bunch of old naval aviators? All they want to do is get in your pants!" The rest of the band joined the laughter as they set up their equipment.

"There are worse things you know!" retorted Mitzi. "You know me! No veil - no tail!" And with that she gave Larry a hug and a quick kiss to the hoots and hollers of the band and the aviators.

The band started off the set with the slow strains of Stardust. "This is one of my all time favorites," John said to Sandra. "Shall we?"

John took Sandra into his arms as they slipped onto the little dance floor. It was nice to have a woman in his arms again, he thought as they moved together to the sweet music. "It's so perfect. I must be dreaming," he reflected.

"You are very light, John," Sandra said softly, after a few turns.

"And you are a wisp. I hardly know you're in my arms," John replied without thinking about what he said.

Sandra ignored his faux pas and replied, "Then hold me tighter, you silly goose, and put your head closer where you can smell my perfume."

"Promise her anything, but give her Arpege," he laughed softly, already enjoying the subtle woodsy scent that wafted from her as she moved her body to the haunting music. "You sure do smell good, Sandra."

He then pulled her close. Their bodies were of similar height, and they moved together like a hand in a glove just as Fred Astaire and Ginger Rogers did in all the movies. It was a great dancing posture, but it also could be very arousing.

"Sorry about that," John said quietly and laughed, as she felt his erection pressing against her thigh.

She looked at him and smiled and laughed softly shaking her head.

"Well, you're responsible for it!" he laughed again, and pressed against her harder as they took another turn.

"Sorry about that," she murmured, and moved her hand from his shoulder and rested it softly at the base of his neck so that he could hold her even tighter.

Then the feel of the music took over. They whirled, twisted, parted, and spun, moving in unison together as if they were one in the midst of the other dancers. Each seemed to know exactly what the other was going to do. Nothing else existed for either one of them, except the music and the moment. The band ran through a melody of: *Tiger Rag - How High the Moon - Deep Purple – Moonglow -* and *Frenesi* before taking a break. John and Sandra headed for their table to the applause of the others.

"You were superb, John," Sandra laughed, breathing hard.

"Well, I could be if only you'd let me do it," John teased, semi-seriously and slightly winded from the dancing. "You can only do that kind of dancing with someone who really knows how to dance."

Sandra smiled and acknowledged the compliment as they rejoined their table.

"I didn't know that you could even dance, John," Dave teased, as they sat down. "I thought all you could do was fly airplanes."

"From now on he's Twinkle Toes. They'll love that in the Ready Room," laughed Larry.

"Hey. C'mon now. You guys leave him alone, or you'll give him an inferiority complex, and he won't be able to dance at all," joked Sandra. "Then I'll have to dance with you clods." More laughter.

A few moments later the band returned, and the happy group enjoyed the changing rhythms of the music and just being away from reality. Everyone was relaxed. The music was great and they were having fun.

As the evening was drawing to a close, the band struck up a favorite of the air group - *Give me a kiss to build a dream on and my imagination will thrive upon that kiss . . .*

The song held a personal touch. It was poignant, sad, and yearning - just the way aviators felt when alone with their thoughts about their loved ones. It came from a movie with Dorothy Malone, who was the hottest stuff on film in the Ready Room. All the guys thought - "If Mickey Rooney can score with someone like that, then there's a chance for me."

Again John held Sandra closely as she snuggled up to him while they danced, her head resting against his shoulder, her breasts pulsating against his chest. Two pair of hot hips swung together in erotic rhythm. Back at the table Dave poked Larry, and lifted his eyebrows. "Well now, would you look at our boy go! Man! Now there's a little item!"

The band quit at 0100 and everyone drifted away reluctantly. John walked Sandra to the ladies' dorm.

"It was a wonderful evening, John. I really enjoyed it," She said, holding out her hand and smiling. But John pulled her to him and kissed her instead, something he'd wanted to do all evening. He drifted again into the woodsy musky scent as he nuzzled her neck, and murmured, "You taste just like I thought you would - like summer wine."

Sandra gave him her easy smile and pulled back, shaking her heavy hair and saying softly, "Um, that was nice, John. But don't get carried away. You guys just returned from combat, and you're really wired. Let's just keep it slow and easy - and not do anything crazy. I like you, Lieutenant Sullivan, but slow and easy for now. Okay?"

In the dimness of the hall John looked at her and gently ran his thumb across her full lower lip. "Sandra, I've never met anyone like you." He whispered, and drew her to him again.

She sighed softly. "Oh John, that's just the combat followed by the wonderful ambiance here. Let's enjoy what time we have, and not let it get away from us." She put her hand on his cheek. "Good night,

John," she whispered, opening the door to her dorm, and slipping inside.

Sandra leaned back against the closed door, her entire body warm with the heat of desire. She closed her eyes and whispered, *Well, what are you going to do about this, Sandra?*

The morning shone bright and early. Clear blue sky and a hot sun. The guys were up early, but the girls were already at breakfast.

"Beat you to it, you old slow pokes," said Mitzi. "Come on! Let's hit the slopes!"

It was embarrassing to the men who thought they were aces after their efforts the previous day. The girls were pretty good skiers, no doubt about it. Obviously they'd been at Akakura many times, and they now helped the guys learn a few tricks, and then dared them to go to the top. The dare, of course, was taken, although they had some second thoughts when they saw the slope. Dave went first, picked up some good speed, and then went ass-over-tea-kettle as he tried to turn to avoid a tree. Fortunately he missed the tree.

John went next, and didn't miss the tree. He sideswiped it and ended up with cuts and scratches. Everyone made one trip down with near-disastrous consequences, but no broken bones, and they unanimously agreed laughingly that they needed a little more time on the lower slope.

Again the hot tubs felt great after the day of strenuous activity. As usual the horseplay turned to talk about sex.

"That Mitzi is something else," Dave said. "But I don't see what she sees in old lover boy Larry! What a waste of talent! Take my advice, Larry. When they pull their pants down, and spread their legs, all you have to do is poke the hole with the fur around it." He guffawed.

"Don't get it in the wrong hole, Larry. It's the one in the front," laughed John, as Larry pulled Dave under water.

"You guys can laugh all you want, but we'll see who has the last laugh," Larry retorted, laughing and splashing more water, and then moving to the jets on the other side of the tub.

"And John baby," Dave said quietly so Larry couldn't hear. "What about Sandra? I never saw a woman with such hots as Sandra has for you, John boy. Big time!" He paused. "You really kinda go for her too, don't you?" He squinted at John. "We all could see it when you two were dancing last night."

"Yeah, I guess I do," John replied slowly. "I've never had it for anyone like this before - except for Sylvia."

"Well, she really goes for you too," Dave laughed. "You're like two kids - hot to trot - but be careful, buddy. You're getting in pretty deep." He looked intensely at his friend.

"Dave, it's so damned bad that if she gives me the slightest come on, we'll be in the sack before the day is out." John sighed, leaning back against the wall of the hot tub, and letting the steam and the pulsing water of the jets work on his muscles.

"Does she know you're married, John?"

"No, she doesn't."

"You haven't told her?"

"No," John shook his dark head and looked down at his hands. "I can't, Dave. I'm afraid it will all blow up and I'll be left with nothing."

"That's not fair, John. You've got to tell her. Then if she still wants to screw you, that's her problem."

"I know you're right, Dave. I've got to tell her and I know it's wrong not to, but I just can't seem to get control of myself. It's crazy!"

"Well, you've got to, John." Dave shook his head. "I know you. You'll never forgive yourself later if you don't tell her now. "

John sat brooding. Finally he straightened up, and looked at Dave.

"Well shit. I guess that's it. I'll tell her tonight. Thanks, friend." As he started to raise himself out of the hot bath, Dave put a hand on John's arm.

"Wait a minute, John. We're not finished here. What about Sylvia, who's pregnant with your child?" The water stilled and the mist rose as the tub heated the room.

"Damn you, Dave," John clenched his jaw, his muscles working. "You didn't have to bring that up too, did you? I feel guilty as all hell right now! Just don't make it any worse! I love Sylvia with all my heart, but this thing has really got hold of me and I can't shake it. Korea seems a million miles away - and San Diego even further!

I'm sorry, but I love Sandra too, and she's here. That's the way it is."
John turned his head and looked away.

"You damned shit head!" Dave growled. "Only one night here
and you and Larry are going to make complete asses of yourself, right
here in Akakura! I'm glad I'm with Lou and we're acting like adults,
instead of a couple of hormone-driven kids!" He smacked the water
angrily with his open palm.

"How come, buddy. No balls?" John snapped back viciously.

Dave's face was hard as he answered.

"For your information, asshole, Lou was badly hurt by a doctor
she fell for. Same thing. He was married and didn't tell her, the
asshole! Last night when you were tripping the light fantastic, we
agreed - no romance - no hanky panky - just friends and
companionship. I suggest you and Sandra do the same thing - if
you're smart. It ain't worth it, friend. It just ain't worth it!"

With that remark, Dave climbed out of the hot water and
headed for the showers, leaving John to stew over his problem.

"Whee! Tonight's the night," whooped Larry as he jumped out
and stood under a cold shower. "Wow! TTN!"

The three aviators had showered and were starting to put on
their clothes when Larry suddenly stopped dressing and exclaimed.
"Hey guys! You know the ladies' hot tub session begins in five
minutes?"

"Yeah, we'd better hurry and vacate," John cut in, as he dried
himself with a large fluffy towel.

"That's not what I had in mind," Larry laughed. "Our nurses
are the only women here. Everyone else left today. Why don't we
hide in the pool and jump up when they come out of the locker room!
We can have a little skinny-dipping with them. Wahoo!"

"Or you can blow the whole thing, idiot," John replied, his
anger gone by now.

"Aw, come on, John! It's just a harmless little fun! These
nurses have seen it all before. What about you, Dave?" Larry asked.

Dave shot a glance at John. "Aw, Larry, I don't think it's such a
hot idea." He paused, the idea of the prank beginning to grow on him.
"Well, okay - I guess I'm game. But, they'll get mad as hell at us!
Hopefully, it will all blow over if we don't do anything ugly."

"I still don't think so," John interrupted. "These women are too nice to pull something raunchy like that. Forget it."

"You a candy ass, John? It's all in fun! What's wrong with a little fun and games?" Larry wasn't going to give up so easily.

"I just don't think it's a good idea, Larry," John said quietly.

"Tell you what, guys," Larry persisted. "We'll just pretend that we lost track of time. Then if they get mad, we can claim it was an accident!" Larry smiled, visualizing the coming drama.

Dave was weakening. "Good thinking, Larry," he said. "This could be fun! I haven't done this since I did it at the age of six when little girls had no whiskers!"

"Yeah, let's see the whiskers," Larry laughed.

"It's a bad idea, Larry," John said shaking his head.

"Aw, John. Come on! You've always been game. What's wrong, old Candy Ass!" Larry needled him, and threw an arm across Johns shoulder.

"Well, to hell with it! Let's go," John capitulated, and tossed his shorts on the floor "We'll hide the clothes under a locker."

"These naval aviators are really fun people," Lou drawled as she slipped out of her bra and panties in the locker room and then admired herself in the mirror. The three nurses had undressed and were putting their clothes away before heading into the hot tub room.

"Ohhh- they're a wild bunch," Mitzi added and giggled. "But I love them. I could play with them forever." She did a bump and grind, rotating her pelvis vulgarly with her hands clasped behind her head, her round breasts bouncing up and down. "That Larry's the one for me. And how!"

"Well. They're wired alright," Sandra admitted dryly. "But it's the effects of combat, and they're hyped because of it. John said each of them have over a hundred missions and four more months to go! I hope none of them get shot down."

The three walked across the locker room and opened the door to the hot tubs. The lighting was dim, and the moisture coming off the hot water made the visibility poor with the heavy steam and mist.

Larry, John, and Dave were sunk down in a corner of the pool their heads barely above the water's surface. Larry could hardly keep from laughing.

"Okay, now guys," Dave whispered, as the women started to get into the water.

"Oh hell!" Dave said standing up, his penis dragging the top of the water. "Is it that time already ready? Damn! We didn't realize....."

"What the hell are you guys doing here now?" Sandra shouted angrily, and then began to laugh because she realized it was a fraud.

"Whee! Let's go skinny-dipping," shouted Mitzi, taking a cannonball jump into the pool, and splashing everyone.

"Well, that settles it, Lou," Sandra said, smiling ruefully. "I guess we have no choice but to skinny-dip for a while. We can't leave Mitzi alone with these three wild men." Sandra slipped down into the pool and sat in a corner. Dave came over through the water and lifted Lou down, and they sat together. In the meantime Mitzi was bear wrestling with Larry. She finally got him by the hair and pulled him under. When she let go, Larry slid up her legs, put his nose just below her navel, and hung on tightly, hollering, "How's this for gaining tactical position, guys?"

Mitzi smacked him on the side of the head, and the sideshow ceased for a few minutes, as everyone laughed.

John eased over and sat near Sandra. "You guys are insane - absolutely crazy! What are you going to do next?" She turned her head, and kissed him playfully on the nose. John could see her pink nipples floating just below the surface of the water. The movement of the water itself was constantly changing and distorting the shape of her body, producing an erotic kaleidoscope. He began to get a magnificent erection. Noticing what John was suddenly sporting, Sandra said, "Hey guys, that's enough of this nonsense! Let's get out of here before we all get in trouble. Anyway, it's time to get dressed for dinner! And I could use a drink about now."

She rose from the seat and headed for the locker room, John following behind her. Reaching for her clothes, she stumbled over a low bench and fell. John was there in an instant to pick her up. As their wet bodies touched, the voltage sparked between them, and she was suddenly in his arms, her eager mouth searching for his. Her soft lips parted breathlessly, and suddenly his tongue was probing and exploring. John took his lips from hers and lowered his head to kiss her erect nipples. As he caressed her, she moaned and pulled his head closer to her breast. John quickly raised up and grasped her, pulling her body to him, his erection hot and throbbing with desire. She responded instantly, wrapping her legs around his hips, preparing to pull him into her.

"My God! What am I doing?" She choked, immediately dropping her legs, and pushing John bodily away from her, her entire body shaking with emotion.

"No, John! No! No! I can't do it with you," she gasped.

"Why not, Sandra? Why? We both want it. You know we do," he said hotly, reaching for her.

She spun away from him.

"Let's get dressed and go upstairs. Then we'll talk." She quickly threw her clothes on and ran from the locker room.

Angry and frustrated, John put his clothes on and followed her. By the time they reached the great hall and sat down on the couch in front of the fire, carefully keeping a distance from each other, sanity had somewhat returned to them.

"Oh God, Sandra. I'm sorry. I'm really sorry. I don't know what got into me. I just suddenly had to have you. Right there! Right now! I'm sorry," John looked contritely into her eyes, the sexual fire that scorched him earlier having now been extinguished. "I'm really sorry, please believe me."

"Damn! Damn! Damn!" said Sandra softly, turning her head away. "Why are the best always married?"

"Who said I was married?" John said quietly, looking at her.

"I know you are, John, and you know I know." She sighed. "Too much electricity is flying between us." She looked back at him. "You want me, and you know I really want you. Right?"

"Yeah. You're right, Sandra," John responded, leaning forward and resting his elbows on his knees. "If I weren't married, you and I would have been making sweet music together that first night. I'm sorry, really sorry. I have a pregnant wife at home and I know I'd regret it. It wouldn't be fair. Frankly, I wanted you, and I was ready to do it, even without telling you I was married. That's how bad it was. Dave gave me the father lecture. Made me promise to tell you, which I should have done at the very beginning. I apologize for not doing it."

" Well. That's two of us, John. Too damned good for our own good!" She laughed softly but her eyes glistened. "I won't make love to a married man. I love you, John. I have since the first time I ever saw you. I love what you are. You're special somehow, but this isn't our time. If your marriage ever falls apart - and I do hope it doesn't - call me - I'll come running." She smiled and put her hand on his arm.

"But in the meantime, there's no reason why we can't enjoy each others company as friends, is there? We have a few days left, if you can stand the ache." She smiled. "I want this to be our time - our memory of Korea or should I say Japan? But you're restricted to a brotherly kiss on the cheek, and don't you dare lay that thing on my leg when we're dancing," she smiled.

"I'll take lots of cold showers," John promised, laughing. Then more seriously, he continued. "But you know it still might get away from us."

"I'll take that chance," responded Sandra, leaning back into the warmth of the old leather couch. A log fell, and the blazing fire subsided into glowing coals. The two of them sat quietly in front of the fireplace, each one immersed in their own private thoughts. Gradually the room began to fill with other guests, and happy hour began to the sounds of laughter and the chink of ice. Someone added another log to the fire and the evening festivities began.

Suddenly, Sandra sat up and said, "Whatever happened to Larry and Mitzi? I thought they'd be here by now."

"Mitzi said they might go for a walk, or something," John said lazily.

Sandra smiled to herself, "I wonder if she found a little hideaway out there? Crazy Mitzi is hyperactive and very ingenious. I wouldn't put it past her."

What John and Sandra didn't know was that MItzi and Larry were burrowed deep in one of the couches in the far corner of the great room where it was very dark with no through traffic patterns.

When Larry came down with his coat to go for a walk, Mitzi had grabbed him by the seat of the pants as he headed for the main door.

"Nope. Not that way, dum-dum," she purred. "Follow me. I have plans for you." And she quietly tiptoed to the dark corner of the great room with an eager Larry in tow. Once there she pushed him down into a deep couch, and fell on top of him, pulling a woolly blanket over them in the process. Horseplay and jokes were completely forgotten as their teasing kisses gave way to those of real desire. Moaning in pleasure, Larry slid his hand up Mitzi's smooth thigh to explore, expecting to find her panties. Instead his fingers found a moist silky treasure of another sort awaiting him.

"Oh God!" he groaned, as Mitzi's pelvis rubbed rhythmically against his powerful erection. "Oh God!" He slid his trembling hands away from her lower body as their kisses deepened, and his tongue sought hers. Raising her sweater he undid her lacy brassiere, freeing the round white breasts he sought to touch. His hands brushed her taut nipples as he cupped them. Mitzi slowly drew her lips away from his, and raised her body, offering her breasts to his eager mouth and tongue. Her nimble fingers then quickly unzipped his pants. Grasping him in her hand, she slowly slid her fingers down the long smooth shaft. Larry groaned with pleasure and desire. Mitzi moved again, raising her hips and slipped herself over him. As he slid into the dark warmth of her, Larry gasped and shuddered as the long months of celibacy pumped out of him.

"There," purred Mitzi, and she leaned down to kiss him playfully, while Larry lay exhausted under her, his energies spent. "That gets rid of all that old stale stuff you've been carrying around. Now we can get down to some real loving." And she cuddled next to him.

Time stood still as the two lovers slipped back into their world of oblivion, and they sought each other again and yet again in the darkness of the night.

The roaring fire was gone, and only a few glowing embers remained as the pair reluctantly crept out of the deserted great room and upstairs to their respective dormitory beds, each smiling in mutual contentment.

The days went by quickly as the couples alternately tried serious skiing interspersed with horseplay. In the evenings Mitzi and Larry took their evening walks , much to the amusement of the other four.

Unable to explore each other's bodies, John and Sandra also took long walks, some with snowshoes, and explored each others' psyches. The walk to the little village of Akakura was particularly stimulating and rewarding. They found a small restaurant serving local dishes, and Sandra knew what most of them were. Over sushi and sake they got to know each other.

"What makes you want to fly airplanes, John? And why do you want to do a job that involves killing people?" Sandra asked, sitting across from him late one afternoon after many glasses of sake.

"Flying does two things to you. First, you escape from earth. Free - restrained only by the force of gravity. You move easily in three dimensions. The space belongs to you - the sights, the motion, the power of nature. Second, you control something powerful that is an extension of your body and mind. You and the plane become one. You think - and the plane does. You don't think in terms of the stick and throttle movements. You think a turn and the plane does it for you. There is a great sense of power - a great sense of immortality, if you wish. You become closer to infinity," he answered.

"Yes, but the risk - the fear of crashing," Sandra probed.

"You control that fear. You don't think about it. Even in combat the fear is suppressed by the job you have to do. It's the idle time that is the worst. Every time I sit in the cockpit on the flight deck in bad weather or pitching seas waiting to start engines. I always ask myself why I do these crazy things and the fear creeps in. Predawn launches are the worst. Once you start the engines and get active, you forget to be afraid. There isn't time." He turned the tiny sake cup in his fingers.

"The fear that gets you the most is when you've lost control. It can grab you and make you do foolish things. Remember when I came to Tokyo with shrapnel?" He put the cup aside and looked directly at her.

"Yes, I do," Sandra replied quietly.

"Well, I got hit in the cockpit and I was completely blinded by the blood in my eyes. I totally panicked - couldn't see - couldn't control the plane. My first reaction was to punch out, the worst possible thing to do. I couldn't think rationally. Thank God for my wingman whose calm voice settled me down. And only a month before, I criticized my OINC for panicking and bailing out when he was too low to survive. And there I was over Yang-doc, doing almost the same thing because my fear took control of me."

"But why a job killing people? What makes you want to do it?"

"Unfortunately, the country needs a military, and I am a warrior. I took an oath to defend the Constitution from all threats, foreign and domestic, to obey the Commander in Chief and other lawfully appointed officials, even if it means killing people. Fortunately, I believe in this war. It's a just war against an obvious aggression."

"But what happens if it's a war you don't believe in?"

"Depends. If I can't support the war, then I must resign my commission in protest, but when that time actually arrives - it's difficult to know when. There's a famous quote -' My country - may she always be right; but right or wrong, my country.' Also there are times when apparently lawful orders must be disobeyed. I can conceive of cases where the results of obeying an order could be very wrong - where the order might do serious damage to the country - and it is not recognized by superiors."

Sandra sighed, moved by what he had just said. "Oh John, I wish we could be together, but I know it can't be done right now. It would be so wrong for us to do it." She looked at him sadly.

"I know," he replied, taking her hand across the table.

All too soon it was over. The little train left the station at nine-thirty in the morning. The ancient man in the stovepipe hat and dirty gray scarf was there to smile with his twinkling eyes, and repeatedly intone, "Bye-bye. Bye-bye."

This time the train's car did not have compartments. Instead, there were old-fashioned, straight-back seats. However, the car itself was nearly empty, and the six could spread out. Mitzi curled up against Larry, and both were soon asleep. Sandra rested her head against John's shoulder, their arms linked together.

"I think Larry finally made out," Dave whispered to John from across the aisle.

"Do you really think so? Naw! They were just two puppies playing."

"I think ole Larry scored in the big league," Dave insisted, smiling broadly.

"I'll bet you ten dollars he didn't," John laughed. "Larry's a babe in the woods."

"You're on for ten bucks, old buddy, but I don't know how we prove it."

Sandra opened one eye and smiled. Then she ran her hand tenderly along John's face, and said, "Well, you just lost ten dollars, big guy." Whereupon she closed her eyes and went back to sleep.

After seven hours of chugging down hills and around hairpin turns, the train finally arrived at Tokyo Station. Mitzi and Larry embraced deeply and clung together. John held Sandra close and whispered, "You're a wonderful person, and I love you very much. I just wish I could do something about it."

"It's sayonara for us, John. That's the way it is." She looked at him. "There's no future for us, but I will always cherish these past eight days. I love you, too." She kissed him lightly, turned, and walked rapidly away, tears blurring her vision.

"Oh, you fool! You fool! Your utterly stupid fool! You should have let it happen! Morals be damned! You'll never find another one like him. Another like him doesn't exist! Better to have loved and lost than be left with nothing at all," she cried, tears running down her cheeks, as she dashed to the closest exit - unmindful of the clamor of scurrying Japanese rushing to their trains.

John sighed in resignation as the tall figure disappeared from sight into the onrush of humanity.

"Let's get a good stiff drink before we catch the Yokosuka train," He said glumly to his two companions, and they turned to look for the closest bar.

Every R&R period after that, Larry was the first off the ship and the first one on the Tokyo Express. He had a standing reservation at the Tokyo BOQ.

Months later, towards the end of the cruise, John got a formal invitation:

Doctor and Mrs. David Philip Gray
request
the honor of your presence
at the marriage of their daughter
MARTHA ANN
Second Lieutenant
Army of the United States

to
Lawrence Andrew Duncan
Ensign United States Navy
on Saturday, the twenty-fifth of November
one thousand nine hundred and fifty one
at four o'clock
Grace Episcopal Church
San Diego

A small card inside bore the invitation to the reception: dinner followed by dancing at the Hotel del Coronado. John fingered the creamy heavy envelope and smiled to himself.

Paul Corrigan

CHAPTER 8

USS Philippine Sea
En route San Diego

John lay in his bunk reading a novel. There were three more long, long days before the ship arrived in San Diego. The crew was wired; no one could sleep. Twenty-four hour poker and smoke games were going on in the wardroom.

Although the ship was quiet, a few members of the crew were working. CAG knocked on the door to John's stateroom and entered without waiting for his response.

"I've got some news for you, John. I was just selected for Captain."

"Great CAG! Congratulations!"

"Not only that," CAG continued. "But I'm going to AirPac as the Aviator Detailer where I will wield a lot of power over who goes where."

"Don't forget your good friend here, and get me out of recce, like you promised," John smiled back at him.

"Not to worry, tiger. I've already done it - at least started it. The current aviator detailer whom I'm scheduled to relieve is a close friend, and we're working on placement of Air Group Eleven pilots. I had to pull in a few chits to do this, but you're going MiG bashing! After your post-deployment leave, you will report to VF-112 at Miramar for duty for three months, and then be assigned to the

3049th Air Force Fighter Squadron at George Air Force Base to check out in F86's. After a four-month training period, you'll be sent to Kimpo Air Force Base at Seoul to the 334th Squadron of the 4th Fighter Interceptor Wing. Use the time at VF-112 to refresh on fighter tactics - lots of simulated air engagements, and you'll be ready for the F86's. Your tour at Kimpo will only be six months. The Air Force doesn't like to give Navy pilots on exchange duty much chance to get five MiG's and become an ace.

"It took some real arm-twisting to get you the exchange slot, John, but having friends always helps. An old World War II Air Force buddy of mine is the USAF fighter detailer in the Pentagon. He flew P-38's in the South Pacific when I was flying Hellcats. I saved his ass once and he owed me. Anyway it's all greased."

Without waiting for John to respond, he continued, "Larry will get his request for Naval Intelligence School at Suitland approved. He's not the best fighter pilot in the world, but he'll make a super intelligence officer. He's quick, fast and has an inquiring mind. Besides, he may bust his ass in fighters, and we have to keep him safe for. . . what's her name - Mitzi! I guess she really did a job on him at Akakura. Incidentally I got an invitation to the wedding. Tell him that Peg and I will be there. Dave Herbert goes to VF-112, but I think I can get him a test pilot job with a friend at Point Magu. He's happy. The only one unhappy is VC-61. They are screaming but it won't do any good. It's locked in," CAG smiled, pleased with himself.

"I don't know what to say, CAG, but thanks for the opportunity."

"Just get me five MiGs, Ace," CAG answered, getting up to shake John's hand and then heading for the door.

North Island
San Diego, California

At 1015 on November 4, 1951, the Philippine Sea nosed her bow into the channel entrance. All personnel were at dress ship, each man spaced evenly along the side of the flight deck. Six large tugboats met the big carrier as she slowly traversed the channel into the inner harbor. With whistles blowing and streams of water from high-pressure nozzles shooting into the air, the tugs announced the return of the Philippine Sea from the wars.

The pier was alive with activity and excitement, as the big carrier made its turn to come alongside. Children in their Sunday best were running and jumping everywhere as the brass band blared forth lively music. A large collection of balloons and a multitude of signs welcomed the crew individually and collectively - some with lascivious promises of future activity. *Welcome home VF-112,* a large sign located the position of the VF-112 loved ones. *The school bus arrives home at 1500,* said the sign announcing the loving time available to couples before the house apes got home. Many wives sent the kids to school for just that reason - knowing that there would be no time for mom and dad until midnight if the kids came down to see the ship arrive!

Wait 'til I get you in bed, Jimmy, a sign held by a lovely blonde announced to the world - and hopefully to Jimmy!

The mooring lines went over - sent on their way to the pier by a shot-line. The lines went on the bollards, and the band struck up a noisy version of "Anchors Aweigh", followed by the Marine Hymn, the Washington Post March, and other Sousa favorites. Sailors on the flight deck spotted their loved ones, and waved their white hats. Wives and children jumped up and down from the sheer joy of the reunion. The pier was pandemonium! A line of shore patrol kept happy people from being pushed into the water by the jostling crowd.

A loud cheer went up as the crane placed the forward brow on the edge of the hanger deck, and COMNAVAIRPAC himself boarded the mighty ship to welcome them home. The aft brow went in place, and a surge of sailors began to leave the ship.

Sylvia was standing with the VF-112 wives in a smock that only served to emphasize her advanced condition. Patricia Ward, the wife of Joe Ward, the LSO, stood beside Sylvia looking for her husband, "Do you see him yet, Sylvia? Oh my God, there's Joe on the flight deck." And she started waving frantically.

"I don't see him, Patricia," Sylvia replied. "Where is he?"

"On the flight deck just forward of the island! Oh, there's John with him! Don't they look handsome?" Patricia squealed with happiness.

"I see him! I see him!" Sylvia yelled, jumping up and down before the baby objected and violently kicked her in the ribs.

151

"Stop it, kiddo! Your Daddy will be angry with you for kicking me," Sylvia said in mock anger. "Your time's coming."

A vivacious-looking woman with short curly auburn hair and a turned-up nose walked up to the wife holding the VF-112 sign and announced, "I'm Mitzi Gray, and I'm looking for Sylvia Sullivan from VC-61."

"That's me," shouted Sylvia and Mitzi turned to look for the owner of the voice.

"You just have to be Sylvia," Mitzi laughed. "My God, the new Sullivan must be due any minute!"

She came over and gave Sylvia a hug, as best she could. "I'm Mitzi from Akakura! I know John told you about me. I'm looking for that boy friend I acquired on the ski slopes - Larry Duncan from the recce detachment!"

"Gee Mitzi, I'd recognize you anywhere! John wrote me about you and Larry. Congrats on your engagement! And if you'll look up at the flight deck just forward of the island, you'll see Larry standing next to John!"

"What's an island?" bubbled Mitzi. "I'm Army! I don't know all these nautical terms," she said, peering up at the huge carrier.

"Stand behind me and look up my extended arm. You'll see him."

"I do! I do! Larry! Larry!" Mitzi waved frantically. Larry still didn't see her. So Mitzi found an open area, and did a few cheerleader movements followed by some very sexy bumps and grinds. The sailors loved it. Larry saw her and began to wave wildly and then did an Irish jig.

By prior arrangement with their husbands, the VF-112 and VC-61 wives waited for the brow to clear and then went aboard to meet their loved ones on the hanger deck.

Some wild hugs and kisses were followed by tender and possessive moments. Then the laughter and chatter began, and kids were given attention.

John tried to hug Sylvia and buried his face in her neck. He stepped back and surveyed the expanded girth of his wife.

"Do it soon, babe," he laughed softly and hugged her again.

"It won't be long, John. The baby's dropped and we're all set to go. I'm just glad you made it home." Sylvia leaned her head against his chest and purred contentedly. Slowly the group broke up and headed for the brow and home.

2739 Maple Drive
San Diego

"Someone's been here," Sylvia said as John opened the door of their house. On the dining room table was a large casserole, a bottle of champagne on ice, and a basket of French bread. A sign said "Welcome home, Champ. Dinner's all prepared. P.S. Salad's in the frig."

"God bless the neighbors," murmured Sylvia. "I'm so tired. I don't think I could have fixed it."

Balboa Naval Hospital
San Diego

The night was short. At 0330 Kathleen Ann Sullivan weighed in at seven pounds two ounces. At 4:30 AM John Sullivan saw his new daughter through the glass of the hospital nursery.

"God, she is just so beautiful, Sylvie! What a beautiful child! Looks just like you," John said proudly, as he reentered Sylvia's room after seeing their baby for the first time.

"Oh John," Sylvia teased. "That wrinkly little thing looks like me?"

"Don't you dare call my little girl wrinkly, Syl! She's beautiful! So lovely. And her skin is so soft. Maybe a few wrinkles - but just a few because she's a fat little thing! A chubby rascal!" he laughed.

"You really must love that baby, John." Sylvia smiled at him, and ran her hand along his cheek. "Goodness, what a proud Papa you are, sweetheart."

"She's beautiful," he repeated for the fourth time. "And her smile," he continued and then stopped short and frowned. "Syl, we haven't picked a name. We've got to give her a name!" He panicked.

"She didn't give us a chance to name her, darling! You've only been home fifteen hours! Okay, what name, my husband? Ummm - what about Pamela? I like that." Sylvia sank back against the pillows, and waited for an answer as John puckered his forehead in thought.

"Well, that's a nice name, Sylvia, but what's so special about it? There's lots of Pamelas around. This is a special baby, Sylvie." John replied seriously. " My little girl has to have a name with a special meaning." He smiled at her.

Sylvia laughed at his intensity. "Alright, John, your turn. What would you like? Better make it good!"

"How about Kathleen?" John queried expectantly.

"That's as Irish as Paddy's pig!" Sylvia laughed. "'Aye an' begorra!' Whatever would Bernice say? An Irish immigrant name for her granddaughter!" She wrinkled her nose in imitation of Bernice, and then she laughed, as she teased her husband, who seemed so serious about his new daughter.

"Aw, c'mon, Sylvie. What's wrong with Kathleen?" John's feathers were ruffled.

"How about Elizabeth or Ann? Elizabeth is an old Houghton family name, and Ann is my grandmother - Bernie's mother," she continued.

"How about Kathleen?" John persisted stubbornly.

"What's so special about Kathleen?" Sylvia countered.

"It's special to the Irish, Syl. I've never seen an Irishman who didn't get tears in his eyes whenever they played the song - *I'll Take You Home Again, Kathleen.* My grandfather always retreated within himself and his eyes got moist whenever he heard it. I think the old boy must have had an early love named Kathleen."

"Well, it's a beautiful name I have to admit, after all, and the nicknames are cute, too - Kathy, Kate, Katie, Kit, and more." Sylvia thought about it a moment. "You're serious about this, aren't you John?"

"Yeah, but you have to be happy about it, too," John said quietly, taking her hand in his. "What else do you like besides Pamela?"

Sylvia looked at him for a moment, and then said, "My grandmother's name is Ann, as I told you." She paused again. "Tell you what - my big Irishman. Why don't we name her Kathleen Ann. Then Bernie can't complain about it. Then, it's one for you, and one for me!"

"A done deal, sweetheart!" John smiled and kissed her forehead. "Now you go to sleep and rest, little mother. I'll see you in the morning."

John stopped at the nursery for one more loving look at his new daughter, Kathleen Ann. "You and I are going to have great times together, Kat," he said to her.

As he left Balboa Hospital he stopped and looked back at the building. "Well, I made it home for the launching. No skill, just luck!"

George Air Force Base
Victorville

John checked in to the 3049th Fighter Squadron, and was assigned one of the small bungalows reserved for married students. The action began the next day, and the pace was fast. John was scheduled to fly two flights a day each of which took three hours to fully complete - brief, fly the mission, and debrief afterward. Ground school took two additional hours. Because of the heat, the day started at 0600 with the first flight at 0700. Fridays were frequently free to allow maintenance to catch up with the gradual accumulation of gripes.

The Air Force did not have enough F-86's to meet its global commitments. The need to rearm Europe was the first priority in the minds of the Air Staff, and support to the war in Korea with its combat attrition was second. The Air Force had difficulty supplying the training squadrons which had third priority. Yet they had to keep them manned because pilots in Korea were exceeding 140 missions in less then six months, and it was becoming a morale problem. Only 180 F-86's were produced in 1951, and technical problems and lack of spares had grounded forty-five percent of the Sabres that year. The Air Force had only 44 F-86's in Korea to counter more than 450 MiG's

"What do you think of the bird, Lieutenant?" Colonel O'Grady, the Wing Commander asked John, as they stood at the bar in the O'Club. John had just bought the bar in celebration of his solo flight in the F-86 Saber. It was expected of all new members of the team when they completed their first flight.

"It's a great fighter, Colonel. Quick response, high roll rate, great turning radius at high g's, and good climb. However, the fuel cells are small. Doesn't take long to run out of gas," John smiled.

"And there are no filling stations along the Yalu," the Colonel chuckled. "You're okay as long as you have your externals, but as soon as you drop them to engage, you are on a short tether. When you get to Kimpo, you will find that you frequently have to shut down your engine and use your altitude to glide back, and then light off for landing. Later in your curricula we'll have you practice a few dead sticks, including a few where you dead stick it all the way to landing. It's essential that you know how the bird handles with the engine shut down."

"That ought to be sporting! Did anyone ever land short, and plow into those barracks near the end of the runway?" John asked.

"No, John," the Colonel replied laughing. "We do them on the dry lake at Edwards. The runway is laid out as far as you can see, and there's acres of flat surface around if you land short. It's amazing how good you can get at it even though you're coming down at 8000 feet a minute. As long as you keep the proper airspeed you have good control, and the gyro-horizon keeps you oriented. The trick is not to kill your airspeed before you have the runway made."

The harbinger of imminent departure made its appearance all too soon. The trusty B-4 bag again sat at the front door along side the sea bag. John was fully packed and ready to go. He would fly to San Francisco where he would catch a commercial flight to Tokyo, and then Government air from there to Kimpo - either a Gooney Bird or a C-54.

Sylvia sat dejectedly on the sofa with her legs curled up under her, watching John do the last-minute things. They had had their farewell night the evening before, and they both were drained of emotion.

Well, here we go again, Sylvia thought sadly. *I wonder how many times we'll go through this. Ain't fun! Hopefully, the next time it'll be for a routine peacetime deployment, not war!* She was fighting the urge to cry.

"I had some additional wool sox in here somewhere, Syl," John called from the bedroom where she could hear him rummaging through the drawers.

"They're hanging in the shower, John. I washed them yesterday."

Lindbergh Field
San Diego, California

The trip to Lindbergh Field was subdued. John checked in with PanAm and they went to the coffee lounge. "Take care of yourself, my darling. And our little Fat Kat, too," John said, as the hand on the big airport clock jerked away the remaining minutes. "Pan American announces the departure of flight 431, non-stop to San Francisco, now boarding at gate twelve." A tender kiss and a protracted hug at the gate and John was gone. A dejected Sylvia, her face damp with tears, turned to leave when she was enveloped in a strong pair of arms.

"Let's get Kat from the baby sitter, and then you'll spend the night with us," Peg said softly while Mike stood tall behind her. "This is not the night for you to be alone."

CHAPTER 9

Kimpo Air Force Base
Seoul, Korea

Air Force 91734, a venerable gooney bird, dropped its gear and flaps, and turned on short final to runway 03, completing the final leg of its trip from Tachikawa, Japan. The plane touched down about 300 yards from the end of the runway with a comforting splat as the tires hit the blacktop and began to roll.

"Air Force 734. Kimpo. You are cleared to the parking ramp in front of base operations. How many souls and how much cargo?"

"Rog, Kimpo. I have fifteen souls, three thousand pounds of cargo, plus mail."

"Great on the mail, 734. We haven't had any in a while. Do you have a Navy lieutenant aboard?"

"I got a naval officer, but damned if I know his rank. I never could figure out their rank structure."

"Not to worry," Kimpo replied. "Neither can I."

"Is there a problem Tower?"

"No, it's just that the 334th is expecting him, and wants to be informed when he arrives."

"Rog that."

The DC-3 turned into the throat access to the ramp, and was picked up by a taxi signalman who walked the plane forward, and then spun it around next to another DC-3, the prop wash blasting dust and debris onto the adjacent buildings. When the dust had settled, the Operations Duty Officer stepped out of the tower building, and headed for the DC-3 whose cargo door had now been opened, and the passengers were beginning to deplane.

John jumped down from the door, brushed off his travel-weary uniform, and looked around.

"So this is the famous Kimpo Air Base where all the hot shots live." he grinned. "Not impressive. Definitely not - even in this bright sunlight which is a treat from all the nasty weather in Japan."

"Sir, are you Lieutenant Sullivan?" the ODO asked, approaching John through the milling airmen who were looking for their baggage on a pallet that had just been unstrapped.

John looked up, saw the railroad tracks of an Air Force captain on the ODO's collar, and saluted.

"Yes, sir, I am."

"Welcome to Kimpo. The 334th asked me to watch out for you. Colonel Jake wants all his new pilots welcomed as soon as they arrive."

"Colonel Jake?"

"Yeah, Colonel Jason Wolfe, the Commander of the 4th Fighter Interceptor Wing which owns the 334th where you are going. We all call him Colonel Jake."

"I thought the Air Force was a little more formal than that," John laughed.

The ODO's eyes twinkled. "Not here in the toolies. Just look at the buildings. Does this look like a standard immaculate well-groomed Air Force Base? Come on, Lieutenant! Anyway it's Colonel Jake to everyone. He doesn't stand on formality - and he's a great fighter pilot!"

An airman brought a note out to the ODO, who glanced at it, and looked at John grinning. "The 334th is putting on a special show for you, Lieutenant. We've got an F-86 from the 334th coming in dead stick. Great indoctrination for you." He turned to the rest of the passengers, and called out. "We got an F-86 coming in dead stick -

that's no power - in a few minutes. If you want to come with me over there," he pointed to the taxiway throat, "we can watch the show."

John scanned the sky looking for the bird. A glint of sunlight caught his eye, and there was the F-86, falling it seemed, like a rock. John estimated the plane at 8,000 feet. It would be all over in a minute.

"Jesus, he'll never make it," an airman standing next to John said in awe.

"He's gonna crash for sure," said another.

"Just wait and see. These guys are good at this." the ODO smiled.

"I don't care. He'll never make it," the airman insisted.

"He'll make it," John quipped. "Besides it looks like fun!"

A young, shavetail lieutenant stared at him, and snapped angrily, "You Navy guys don't know shit about flying!" Then he saw the wings and shut up.

John laughed at the ninety-day wonder. "I still think they're fun. I've done a few myself at Edwards."

"That's right," the ODO interjected. "They train you to do them while you're at George, don't they."

"Yeah, they sure as hell do."

"Look at him now, Lieutenant," the ODO said as the F-86 passed through 1,000 feet, seconds away from crashing. He appeared headed straight into the ground. "He'd better break his glide," the ODO mumbled, a worried look on his face.

"Another few seconds. . ." John started to say, and then smiled. "You can see the heat waves coming off his tail pipe. His engine's spinning up. Must have some fuel left."

The plane broke out of its steep downward drop, and headed for the runway, touching down on the threshold.

"Good show!" John laughed. "What a welcome from the 334th. Did you guys plan this just for me?"

"Sure we did, Lieutenant! Always ready to show off just for the Navy. But, look at that," the ODO pointed to the Follow-Me truck and the mule with a tow bar headed down the runway behind the F-86. When the plane stopped, the tow bar was attached and the plane towed to its line. It had run out of gas!

"What a reception. That's real flying, plus a little luck!" John murmured. "

"Okay, Lieutenant. Here's your transportation now," the ODO pointed to a jeep that had stopped at base ops. "Good luck, Lieutenant. I'll see you around."

"Hang loose, Air Force." John lifted his bags, and headed for the jeep. Then, he stopped again, and turned to the ODO.

"You know, Captain. It scared the shit out of me watching it from the ground. Up in the plane I have control, and it's okay. Not scared at all. But, here on terra firma. Oh shit!"

The ODO smiled, "I understand. Good luck and good hunting, Lieutenant."

The jeep deposited him at the 334th FIS administration building, a long quonset hut filled with desks, typewriters and maps. A small day room occupied the rear. It was rather decrepit, but far better than the other buildings which were mostly tents over a wooden floor and half-walls up the side. They were well ventilated - summer and winter. The wood stove in the center took the chill off in winter, but the wind still whistled through.

John was assigned to Red One Flight, a four plane combat element. The pilots lived together in a four-man tent where the jeep now deposited him. He dragged his duffel bag to the door, opened it, and went in. The tent was gloomy with late afternoon lighting, and it took a moment for his eyes to adjust.

"Hey, Sailor," someone called. "Get a drink and drag up a chair. We've been waiting for you."

With his eyes adjusted to the low light, John saw three men in aviator flight suits seated around the stove. A tall heavy-set man got up and handed him a bottle of Johnny Walker and a grungy glass.

"I'm Captain Rex Taggart, leader of this ragtag group. That's First Lieutenant Leo Strong, the section leader, Red 1-2, and that lazy bastard over there is Sam Lewis, Leo's wingman, Red 1-4. I'm putting you on my wing initially as Red 1-3. We may want to change it around after I see what you can do."

"I'm glad to join your ragtag outfit," John replied smiling. "But I'm not sure I care much for this Kimpo place, and your accommodations are definitely substandard. Much better on the carriers, I must say." He laughed.

Leo chuckled and held out his hand. "He'll do, Rex. He'll do. Anyone who doesn't like Mud City is okay in my book."

"You really shouldn't belittle our little home away from home, Navy," Sam Lewis added, grinning. "I know it's not as grandiose as those lovely staterooms on board ship, but it's home! And wait until our life sized Marilyn comes back. She'll add real beauty!"

"Marilyn?" John quizzed.

"Marilyn Monroe! We have a blowup of the famous nude picture. It's in the photo shop for enhancement." Rex said, interrupting Sam.

Sam continued, ignoring Rex, "we call this beautiful place the Emerald Palace, just like the Wizard's in the movie, The Wizard of Oz."

"Well, Oz it isn't, guys," John smiled.

"You know what I mean, Navy," Sam explained. "And the beautiful village that we live in is called Mud City."

"The Emerald Palace of Mud City?" John laughed incredulously. "What do you guys smoke here? Or should I just say - how romantic?"

Rex took up the badgering. "Let us show you the features of our little home here. You, of course, saw the entrance with the exquisite natural pine walkway leading from the carefully rutted road to our welcoming door. We tried planting flowers in the mud under the windows, but the rodents ate them."

"At least, they didn't eat you guys," John laughed. "I've seen some pretty big rats - four legged and two legged."

Rex ignored him and continued, "Inside we have planks of natural wood, extending five feet up from the floor, and matching the decor,"

"We have a fully cross-ventilated air conditioning system, using screened openings above the planks. It can get quite breezy and it doesn't keep the snow out, but they have an automatic temperature control. Observe." He got up and kicked Sam Lewis in the shins. Sam in turn got up and closed the heavy wooden panels that dropped down over the screened opening.

"Voila! As we French say! Very efficient! And we have the latest automatically fired stove. We call it the Old Pot Bellied Stove. It almost gets the temperature above freezing on a mild winter day." Leo kicked Sam again who threw two small logs in the stove's gaping door. "Automatic! Like everything else here." All the guys were laughing at him. John smiled and waited for the other shoe to drop.

"The only problem is that the junior man becomes the automated system." Leo laughed and the rest chuckled.

"That's you boy," Rex added, and hit John on the shoulder.

"You mean I don't have a batman to perform that little chore for me? Goodness, who serves my morning tea, and cleans my boots?" John said, smiling innocently.

That brought a hoot from Rex. "This guy plays dirty. Be careful, gang."

"As I was saying before I was rudely interrupted," John added. "At first glance, all the excellent features are not obvious. And we really need to call Rex, the Wizard of Kimpo," loud hoots from Leo and Sam. "I guess I owe the Air Force an apology," John continued. "Maybe I should write the Secretary of the Air Force, and thank him for the air conditioned accommodations. But, help me with the spelling, guys. When I write the Secretary, do I spell Air Force with an 'a' or an 'o'?"

Rex roared, "Your choice, John. Sometimes I think it's a farce, too. But, believe me, buddy, Mud City's for real, and so are the MiGs that want to shoot you down!"

"This Navy guy can really dish it out, Rex," Leo interjected.

"He'll do alright here in our little community" Rex took his glass and refilled it.

"Rex, I can't help noticing the emblem of the 334 FIS on your patch - what's that? A boxing pigeon?"

"Yeah, John, it is," Rex replied, repositioning himself, and cautiously waiting.

"I don't mean to sound disrespectful, Rex," John laughed. "But why the pigeon? Is it symbolic - like maybe you guys just want to give everyone the bird!"

"John, John, you really are a dirty player!" Rex laughed. "But you should remember our little pigeon coos, just like all the women do when they're around us." Rex finished his glass and poured another.

"Well, guys, enough fun and games. We're off duty tomorrow," Rex changed the subject. "We'll get you suited up, John - show you around - how to crawl back from the club; you know, important things like that. We do have a club, sort of. We'll visit the flight line, and give you some tips on how to survive here. Also the day after tomorrow's a great day for our little home. We get our life-sized Marilyn Monroe back. Some guy in the photo lab is really good at color enhancement. He does really great fur pieces. It'll give you a hard-on just lying in bed looking at her."

"So John. No fly tomorrow. Drink up. There's more where that came from. And this evening we'll start your formal indoctrination at the Club. Great night for a crawl back!" Sam added as he took John's glass and refilled it.

"And, John," Rex added laughing at him. "Don't worry about feeding the wood to the stove all night long. The gooks actually do it for us, and I understand we're going to get a kerosene stove with a large outside tank before the bad weather sets in."

Officer's Club
Kimpo Air Force Base, Korea.

"Hey, John, grab a beer, and come on over to the corner table. I want to talk to you."

John broke off his conversation with Leo, snatched two beers out of the hand of the bartender to his great chagrin, and headed for the table.

"Watch it, sailor," the bartender yelled and then laughed. "Rex will eat you alive," he predicted.

"Sit down, John. Let's talk about you and flying," Rex said, slipping a large rock under the broken leg of the wobbly three-legged table which had only partially survived the insults of the many raucous victory parties.

John sat down slowly onto a chair to see if it would hold him.

"Okay, shoot," he said, guzzling half of one bottle and handing the other bottle to Rex.

"John, I have close to sixty missions with two MiGs to my credit. I got there by being smart and aggressive. I want three more MiGs before I leave. To get there, I need a really good wingman. I need to know who you are and what you are before I put you on my wing. A lot of flight leaders think of themselves as being all alone in the sky, and some get shot down that way. Not me - when you need help, you want to know you'll get it - especially from your wingman. Understand?"

165

"Yes sir, I do. Navy fighter pilots are taught the integrity of the two-plane section, Rex. Sometimes in a dogfight you can't help but lose your section leader - especially when someone jumps you. That's expected, but other than that we're taught to hang in there."

John leaned back in the chair, whose leg promptly splintered and dumped him on the floor. "Damn! I spilled my beer!" John grumbled, rising up and grabbing another equally antiquated seat.

"That's the way, John boy! You have the right attitude," Rex laughed. "To hell with the chair and your ass! Save the beer!" The smile dropped quickly, however, and Rex looked John in the eyes. "Why are you a fighter pilot, John?"

"This'll sound corny, but I grew up wanting to fly. Why, I don't know. I just know that I always have. I like to fly. No, check that! I love to fly, and being a fighter pilot is the greatest flying there is." He took a swig of beer. "And I think I'll be good at it. Damnit! I know I'll be good at it!"

Rex grinned. "Well, that's honest enough, John. You need to think that way."

"What way?" John asked defensively.

"That you're the best." Rex shrugged. "Shit, we all do, don't we? It's the other guy who is going to get it."

"Done much killing, John?" Rex said softly with a slight, almost teasing smile.

John felt himself flush. "No, I've almost been killed a couple times myself, but I've been a reconnaissance pilot all my time in jets." He smiled self-consciously. "Which means my whole time as a carrier pilot. When I returned from Korea, I began to prepare for this assignment. Then it was fighters, and fighter tactics, but no live targets. And you don't really know what you are, Rex, until you have one in your sights."

Rex nodded. "Yeah, I knew that. What do you think of killing a MiG pilot?"

"You know, I haven't thought much about it. I know that the MiG is flown by a man, but, I guess, well, he knows the chances he's taking. Just like us. But, Rex, the bottom line is I want that MiG. I don't give a shit about the pilot."

Rex digested John's response silently. "What's your greatest thrill flying, John?"

"Making a successful carrier landing."

"Do you get a charge out of that?"

"Yeah, I do. I really do. When you take the cut and head down for the deck, you hold your breath until you catch a wire and are dragged to a stop. Then the elation hits you. You get a great feeling of satisfaction in yourself." He allowed himself a jab at Rex. "That's something you Air Force guys never will know about as long as you build runways ten miles long."

Rex gave a bark of a laugh. "That's true, John. But let me tell you a lot of Navy pilots have blessed every goddamn inch of that runway when they've come in on a dead stick landing or with their hydraulics gone."

"Touche."

Rex continued. "Well, kid, you might change your mind about thrills when - and if - you bag a MiG." He leaned forward and loudly whispered. "You know, some guys have said it was better than their first lay."

John couldn't resist the opening, "tell them to try it a second time - the lay that is."

Rex saluted with his bottle.

"Why are you here, John?" Rex said, handing him another beer. "Exchange guys don't come here unless they worked hard to get the position."

"Well, Rex, a friend of mine, a Navy Captain, called in a lot of markers to get me here. Said I was a natural fighter pilot, and he wanted me to have the chance to do some real dog fighting before the missiles came in and took the challenge away."

Rex shook his head. "No, John, not how did you get here. But, why did you want to be here? With all respect, fuck your captain friend. If he wanted people to get in some old-fashioned dog fighting, I'd tell him to get his ass over here to Kimpo and strap on a Sabre!"

John fought back his anger, and took a swig of beer before answering. "Rex, the reason why I'm here is not for my captain friend, but for me - me alone! I want to know if I can do it - be a fighter pilot like the guys I grew up reading about. I don't want to leave the Navy never having gotten the chance."

Rex said nothing. Instead, he reached into the zippered pocket on his left arm and pulled out a pack of Luckies and a Zippo lighter. "Cigarette?"

"Thanks, Rex," John took one, and tamped it on the back of his hand while Rex fired up the Zippo. Both of them took a drag and then cupped the cigarettes in their hands to block the wind and hide the glow.

"Well, you passed the first half of the exam," Rex said brightly. "Now get us two more beers and let's see what they taught you at George about the F-86 and the MiG-15." He inhaled deeply and blew the smoke out his nose as John headed for the bar and refills. The bartender saw him coming, and threw two unopened bottles end over end and a church key after them. John neatly picked all of them out of the air.

"Rex hasn't eaten you alive yet, Sailor Boy?" the bartender snickered. "Well, don't get too cocky. He can still chew you up and spit you out."

"He doesn't like tough meat," John replied and returned to the rickety table. He popped the beers with the church key and began to talk.

"I know we're flying F-86E's because I saw them on the flight line."

"Very good, John. You get a B+ for alertness. Now continue."

"The A-model is what I flew at George. But, I'm told they're inferior to the MiGs in every aspect of their flight envelope."

"They are indeed, but we - meaning the Air Force - were still able to get a four-to-one kill ratio over the MiG for one simple reason, my friend. Our pilots are better. Just remember that. You may have an inferior machine, but it's what you do with it that counts. Just like your pecker!"

"Yeah, but it's still nice to have a newer machine like the E that can out turn the MiG below angels 30, and out-dive it anywhere. Also it's supposed to be far more maneuverable, and we have the advantage of the A4 radar ranging gun sight."

Rex grinned, "Well, you have been doing your reading. But you forgot those beautiful .50- caliber machine guns," Rex added.

John was genuinely surprised. "That's an advantage? Those 23mm and 30mm cannon in the MiG do a lot of damage."

"Boy, I can see those idiots at George still haven't wakened up." Rex shook his head. "Those cannon are great against B-29s. Using a 23mm against a fighter is like using a rifle against a quail.

You need to put out lots of lead - real fast if you want to bag a MiG. Remember you're moving fast and the target is, too. You get a shot, and then - BAM - you lose it. So, you've got to be quick on the trigger and put out a lot of bullets in what we call a 'snap shot'. Rex was now leaning over the table, looking directly at John. "Get me?"

John nodded and Rex leaned back. "Sorry, John, but those jackasses at George can really piss me off." He took a deep drag. "Now, what else can the MIG do?"

John cleared his throat, and continued, "the MiG still has a 5,000 foot ceiling advantage, and can out-accelerate, out-climb, and out-zoom the 86E. Yet the engines in the MiG and the 86 are both derivatives of the British Nene. The Brits licensed them to the Russians in '47. If so, why does the MIG have a slight thrust advantage, and a better thrust-to-weight ratio."

"Don't know why our engineers can't get the same thrust. Beats me," Rex replied. "But, remember that the MiG is lighter - doesn't have the armor plate behind the seat, a bullet-proof windscreen, and other goodies that makes the 86 more like a Mercedes." Rex stopped for a moment to light another Lucky, and then continued, "A warning, John. You can out dive a MIG, but don't forget that it has the faster acceleration initially because of the thrust-to-weight ratio. A MIG can close on you and get you before gravity begins to kick in, and you pull away. If you want to dive, shake him loose a little first."

"What really bothers me is that with the altitude advantage, the MiGs choose the time and the place of engagement. All we can do is wait for them to come down and fight."

"True enough, John, but, if they want to go after the fighter bombers, the F84's or the B-29's, they have to come down, don't they? And after all, that's what we're really here for - to keep them off the bomber's backs. "

Rex smiled savagely, and took a belt from his beer. Again, he leaned forward. "John, now what I'm about to tell you, you have to keep under your sombrero. You understand?" Rex's voice was just above a whisper. Intrigued, John nodded.

"We're up against Russian pilots," he said quietly.

"Bullshit!" John snorted.

Rex's eyes grew hard. "Listen, Sailor Boy, that ain't no bullshit." He began to tick off points on his fingers. "One, all of a sudden, there are some good, I mean really good, bad guys up there.

Now usually they fly a class of pilots up there in MiG Alley to train them, and they take a while to get aggressive - two maybe three weeks. Not these guys. They come right at us. Second, a friend of mine in intelligence told me he heard Russian on the tactical circuits. When I asked him again a little while later, he clammed up and told me I didn't know what I was talking about." Rex raised an eyebrow. "Third, it makes sense. Shit! The Ruskies want to know how they stack up against the first string. How do their planes handle? How good is their training? How good is our training? So, let those assholes at George keep their heads in the sand. You just remember what I said - when some Russian's crawling up your ass and you can't shake him."

John said nothing for a moment. "Well, Rex, thanks for the tips."

Rex lighted another cigarette and exhaled loudly. "I'm sorry, John. It's just that those assholes stateside keep telling us things we know just aren't true. Christ!" He shook his head again. Then he grinned sheepishly. "Typical loud-mouthed fighter pilot, huh?" He winked.

John felt relieved. "Hey, Rex, I know a lot of them."

Rex tossed back the rest of his beer. "Okay. You pass the first two exams, Sailor. Now let's belly up to the bar and do some serious drinking. We don't fly tomorrow!" Rex waved at the bar. Leo and Sam detached themselves and came over to the table. "Well, boys," Rex announced. "John, here has received the wisdom of Rex, and admitted that the Navy can learn something from the Air Force." He smiled at them all. "Now we drink."

At 4 AM Red One staggered out of the club and the four men weaved their way towards their hutch, alternatively singing, *Nothing Can Beat the U.S. Air Force* and *Anchors Aweigh.* Their interlocked arms were as much for stability as camaraderie.

John had passed the final exam.

"How we doing today, Lieutenant?" Jimmy asked, helping John to strap into his F-86E. "Your first flight today, sir!" the plane captain continued, making light banter. "Be careful and don't try too hard the first time out. Okay? You and me - we'll get us some MiG's so I can paint them on the nose. But, for today, take it easy. Also, sir, you need an emblem and a name. What do you call your girlfriend?"

"My wife's name is Sylvia. Why?"

"Well, sir, we got to put Sylvia on the nose - her name and maybe even a painting, too. I know some guys who do it. This bird is now Sylvia!" he announced and patted the plane's side lovingly. John chuckled.

Time passed slowly as John waited to start engines. *Strapped in and waiting! Always wait!* he growled. *Wonder what the problem is? Just like sitting on the flight deck waiting for a predawn launch. At least it's not pitch black! This is the worst time - sitting, waiting, wondering - the fear beginning to push its way through the bravado!* John looked up at the overcast sky, and shuddered.

Despite what Rex says - you still live and die alone. All by yourself in this aluminum can! What is it, an aluminum coffin or a protective womb - or both? It certainly has the characteristics of a womb. I'm connected to it by umbilical cords. It gives me life. Feeds me oxygen, and activates my G-suit to save me in high g-combat turns. It protects me. Gives me armor plate behind my seat and bullet proof glass in front of me. It's a womb, alright.

And it gives me a gun sight, a pickle button, and controls to make me a killer. So what are we? Gun fighters from the untamed west? With notches on our gun handles? Red stars on the sides of our plane to show our kills. Or are we aerial knights - like I told Rex - with honor and integrity as our code? The code has always been there in air combat. Von Richthofen - all the vons from Prussian families. A gentleman's war - a warrior's way to die - not even a parachute! There were no common men as pilots in the German Air Force in World War I. The code even held in World War II. Is it the romance of the knights protecting helpless maidens? Killing the dragon? Or are we just paid killers? I don't think I answered Rex well on that.

The radio gave a squawk of static, and then announced, "Red One this is Kimpo Tower. Start engines. You are released."

"Kimpo Tower. Roger. Starting engines," Rex replied.

"Roger, Red One. Runway 03, Altimeter 29.94, Wind northeast 15, Ceiling two thousand broken. Visibility five miles in light rain. Call taxiing."

The four pilots gave the windup signal, the starting units belched, and the turbines began to whine.

" Red One, you are cleared number one for a flight takeoff.-break- Aircraft waiting takeoff clearance on the parallel taxiway move immediately to the parking area on the opposite side of the runway. You are cleared to cross the active. All other aircraft hold position. Combat departure by Red One."

Red One lined up on the runway. Rex in the lead, John on the right wing, the second section of two aircraft on the left wing. Rex advanced the throttles to full power, got a thumbs up from each pilot, and released the brakes. The flight rolled down the runway in formation and lifted off. They were on their way to MiG Alley with no wasted gas on an airborne rendezvous.

Red One reached thirty thousand feet just north of P'yongyang with the low cloud cover breaking up just south of the North Korean capital. Glancing ahead, John could see the outline of the Yalu River as it snaked its way west out of the mountains and across the coastal plain to the Yellow Sea. As his eyes became adjusted to the haze, John could discern the city of Antung on the Manchurian side. By squinting and then relaxing, John's eyes picked up MiG-15's lifting off the many airfields in the Antung area.

"Close it up a little, 1-3," Rex said, jerking John out of his mental Travelogue.

The MiGs were clearly visible now as they climbed out of the ground haze.

Jesus, there must be forty of them, John murmured. Ahead he could also see the F-86's waiting, twelve of them plus Red flight joining in a less than a minute.

They'll stay on the Chinese side of the Yalu until they are joined up and reach their desired altitude. Then they'll cross over to North Korea, and it will be forty MiG's to sixteen F-86's. Lousy odds. John mumbled. *And with the higher ceiling of the MiG's, they also start with the altitude advantage. Shit!*

The MiG's, now at 35,000 feet, turned south to leave the sanctuary. They closed the F-86's now at 30,000 feet, but made no move to descend and engage. The F-86's tracked them while the MiG's headed south and maneuvered their formation. Then suddenly they left their altitude to zoom down on the 86's.

"Here they come, guys!" Rex banked sharply to port to meet them head-on. When the MiG's reached 2000 feet above the F-86's, they suddenly pulled out of their dive, and climbed back to 35,000 feet, turning north towards Antung.

"What in the hell are they doing?" John screamed in frustration as Rex turned the flight to patrol along the border until Bingo fuel was reached.

For the entire week the MiG's refused to engage. Even the MiGs launched to go after the F-84's would climb out from Antung, see the F-86's on CAP patrol and return to base.

John was fit to be tied. "What's wrong with those candy asses? Why won't they engage?" he yelled in the Day Room after returning from another fruitless mission in which the element spent the afternoon boring holes in the sky.

"Easy, John. You'll get your chance. They're just doing their training - which I might also add is good for you, too - getting the feel of the E - and learning the terrain!" Rex laughed at him. John gave him a dirty look and left the Day Room.

The next day Red One was lazing around over Sinanju near the coast when Rex pointed towards Antung. John looked, squinting his eyes to see through the haze. His heart skipped a beat. Thirty MiG's were climbing through 20,000 feet headed for the Yalu. Rex turned north to meet them.

Red One took the MiG's initial attack head on with some ineffective nose shots. Then he turned hard starboard, pulling his nose up sharply to gain altitude and kill airspeed in a half yo-yo maneuver. He rolled on his back with John in good covering position, and there below were two fat MiG's. Rex reversed his roll and homed in on the tail of the first MiG.

"Try for number two, John, but don't lose me doing it."

John maneuvered to get behind MiG number two who was trying to position himself on Rex. John closed rapidly. He was just about within range when the MiG pilot became aware of the F-86 on his tail. He pulled up sharply, rolling into a port turn, and climbing steeply. His g's were not that high, and John could have stayed inside him easily, but that would have exposed Rex's six o'clock position. Reluctantly, John broke off and headed for Rex who was closing on the leading MiG. John rolled inside Rex's turn radius to cut the corner and gain position. At the same time he kept one eye on the MiG that he had been chasing. It had pulled up steeply, killing airspeed so that it could turn tighter. The maneuver, if properly executed, would also put the MiG in position to drop down onto John's tail, using its altitude to regain the airspeed it had lost. But the pilot failed to recognize his favorable position and the opportunity was lost.

That's how us wingmen get killed, John thought to himself, as he now concentrated his attention on Rex who was slowly closing his target. The MiG, as yet unaware of the danger, was trying to close a section of F-86's in front of him. Suddenly, Rex's plane popped into view in the MiG pilot's rear-view mirror. The MiG whipped into a steep bank to port and pulled his nose up slightly, killing some airspeed - a fatal error because Rex had a slight altitude advantage. Rex easily stayed inside the MiG'S turning radius, and took advantage of the MiG's mistake to close rapidly. The six .50 caliber machine guns barked.

The MiG's rudder exploded and the canopy shattered.

Shit! Too high! Rex cursed. But it wasn't too high. The pilot was dead. Rex easily closed the MiG, which was falling off on a wing. Another burst ripped the engine compartment, and gray smoke began to pour from the tail. The bird slowly rolled over and headed for the ground. A few seconds later it exploded.

"I got him! I got him! And no question about the kill. John saw it. That gives me three!" Rex let loose a wild whoopee into his oxygen mask.

John was just as ecstatic as he watched his Red leader make the kill. *Good ole Rex! I'm proud to be part of this team! Proud to be with these guys.* But the thought didn't last as Rex whipped into a 6g turn and then pulled back into an almost vertical climb.

"Damn!" John grunted through clinched teeth as the g forces caused his whole body to shudder under the magnified weight. The g-suit was squeezing him to death.

"I hope I can stay with this guy," John grumbled, as Rex kicked off on a wing and came roaring back down in another yo-yo maneuver onto an unsuspecting MiG below him. But Rex was too close and too fast to get the shot off as he sped by below the target.

But, John, following behind, wasn't too fast, and he got off a quick burst as the MiG suddenly whipped off to starboard, spoiling his aim. *That SOB knew what to do,* John admired the MiG's maneuver.

As suddenly as it started it was over - in only ten minutes, but it seemed a lifetime.

John checked his fuel, and was shocked at what he saw. "My God! I've only got 200 pounds!"

"Where are you Red 1-3? And what state?" Rex called as he turned south and headed for Kimpo.

"At your seven o'clock, Red One. Fuel below bingo - 200 pounds."

"Roger, buddy. You better shut down if you want to make it home. You've got good altitude to glide back at least part way. I'll be astern of you."

With a shiver of concern, John shut down his engine. "Kimpo Red One Three, returning dead stick. Squawking emergency."

"Roger, Red One Three, we have you fifty miles out. Say fuel state."

"Two hundred pounds."

"Roger that. Steer 213. If you have the altitude, we'll put you downwind at eight thousand feet."

"No good, Kimpo. Don't have the altitude. Bring me in at the ninety. I'll probably break out of the clouds there."

John began engine start at four thousand feet. By the time he broke clear of the clouds at twenty five hundred feet, the engine had spun up, and he had ample fuel, 100 pounds, to make the runway.

Rex and the second section landed in trail behind him, after Rex did a few sharp victory rolls. The four F -86's pulled into their parallel parking slots on the tarmac, and shut down. John's plane captain jumped up on the step to help unbuckle the pilot.

"You fired your guns, Lieutenant! I see the black smoke around the gun ports. Get one?" the kid asked excitedly.

"Naw. I got a shot, but missed," John grumbled. "But Captain Taggart got one."

"Jeez! Great! I hope some day my plane will get one."

"I'll do my very best, Jimmy."

John jumped down from the plane and strode over to Rex's bird.

"Congratulations, Boss. Great shot!" John called, taking Rex's clipboard from him as he deplaned.

"Hell, John! Am I riding high! It's my third kill, you know. Too bad I bombed that yo-yo. I should have had kill number four. Well, can't be greedy." Rex beamed at John and slapped him on the back. "Damned fine flying, Navy. You hung in there all the way. Makes me comfortable to know you are back there, and I can concentrate on the kill."

Leo and Sam ran over from their planes. "Did you get him, Rex?" Leo yelled as he approached. "I lost sight of you."

"Got him, Leo. I got him good!" Rex replied, his face beaming. Leo pumped his hand and hugged him. "I think a little celebration is in order. Colonel Jake doesn't like us to go to the O'Club in our dirty gear, but he forgives us when we get a kill." Rex laughed, and jumped into the front seat of the jeep which had just stopped to retrieve them. The other three squeezed in back.

"Let's go to the O'Club, driver," Rex yelled as the three in back began to sing raucously.

The word soon got out and the Club began to fill with laughing fighter pilots, fighting the latest battles. Hands were twisting and flying in all directions as the pilots maneuvered their planes against imaginary kills.

"How about the confirmation, Rex?" one of the revelers asked. "Anyone see it?"

"Yes sir, my wingman did," Rex boomed out, as someone poured a beer over his head.

"Wingmen don't count, Rex. They'll lie, cheat, and steal for their leader," someone yelled back.

Rex suddenly got serious. "I'll have you know my wingman is a Loot-nant, junior grade, in the United States Navy - regular Navy! And he's an Annapolis man. They don't lie!" His seriousness disappeared as fast as it came.

"This ole wingman of mine, Loot-nant John Sullivan is okay," Rex wrapped his arms around John's neck, and pulled him towards him. "This ole Navy guy hung in there behind me all the way, and it was his first mission."

"Lost your cherry today, Navy?" someone yelled.

"Hey! These Navy guys lose their cherries early in life." Rex laughed. "Don't they, Navy? Sure wish we had a good liberty town nearby where we could go and fuck some women. That's the thing I hate about this war - no women to play with after the kill. Take England in World War II. Now that was a civilized war. All those limey girls we were saving from the Nazis. They were most appreciative. Here's to the limey ladies! They did it with class!" Rex held up his beer can high to the roar of approval from the crowd.

"What's all the cheering about?" called a tall hawk-faced individual in a pressed flight suit with a pair of eagles on his shoulders. Colonel Jason Wolfe, Commander, Fourth Fighter Interceptor Wing, entered the room.

"Hey, Colonel Jake. Rex got one!"

"And Green Flight got a second one!" someone yelled.

"So I hear," Jake laughed, and grabbed a beer from the bartender. "Congratulations, guys!" He tipped up the beer and drained it. He then turned to Rex. "Good show, Rex. Did you have your new apprentice with you?"

"Yeah, I did, Colonel Jake, and he was damned good. Hung onto my wing like he was glued there."

Colonel Jake turned to John, his hand outstretched. "Welcome aboard, Navy. Glad to have you with us. If you can hang onto Rex, you'll do okay."

"Is Captain Rex Taggart in here?" a tech sergeant called from the doorway.

Rex looked around and grinned. "Hey Bilko. You got my Marilyn ready?"

"Sure do, Captain. I'd deliver her right now, but it's raining and I don't have wheels. Can't get the honey wet. She might wrinkle!"

"Aw shit, Bilko. Can't you scrounge some?" Rex replied disappointed.

Colonel Jake looked at Rex, "What's the trouble, Rex?"

"Aw, our Marilyn is ready, but we don't have transport. Damn! That would be a great present tonight."

"You talking about your famous picture? What's wrong with her?" Jake asked.

"Well, Colonel, Sergeant Bilko just gave her a new fur piece," Rex laughed.

Jake turned to Bilko. "You go tell the Sarge at transportation that I said to give you a deuce if necessary to move her. Then we'll all go down and christen her."

"Yes sir, Colonel! Right away, sir!" Bilko grinned a toothy grin and departed.

"What are we going to christen her with, Rex?" Leo asked.

"The Navy uses champagne," John laughed.

"We can't break a champagne bottle across her bow. We'll ruin the picture!"

"To say nothing of her titties and the new fur piece!" someone hooted.

"Tell you what, Rex," Jake laughed. "We'll christen the whole tent. The Marilyn House! I think they have one in Annapolis, but they spell it differently. I'll personally break a bottle of beer on the stoop. Would that make it official?"

"Great, Colonel Jake!" Rex replied, and then called out to the crowd. "You are all invited to the commissioning of the Marilyn House." He turned to John, and chuckled. "Father Sullivan here will do the invocation!"

"Dear Father in heaven," John intoned, looking up sanctimoniously at the dark sky. "We are gathered here to commission this ignoble structure which houses one of the most beautiful pus . . .ahem - I mean - women in the world. God keep her and her cute little brown patch safe from Bed Check Charlie and other hazards of war. Amen."

"Amen! Amen!" the crowd chanted, as Colonel Jake broke a beer bottle on a stone at the entrance. Then they all went inside to see the lovely apparition.

"What a beauty!" everyone exclaimed, admiring the beautiful Marilyn and her new brown patch.

"Congratulations, Bilko," Rex said, shaking his hand, and giving him an envelope of cash for his efforts.

"Say - Marilyn's a blonde and the fur patch you guys put on is brown," someone piped up. "Do blondes have brown whiskers?"

"Sure, they all do," someone replied. "They're all fake blondes anyway."

"How about black?"

"Yeah, I knew a blonde who had a black one. Damned good looking, too. She tried to bleach it once. Didn't work too well, and she couldn't sit down for two days!" he howled.

"Did it work okay afterwards?"

"Don't know. She kicked me out for suggesting it."

"Hey, Jim. You're wife's blonde. Is hers brown?" Spike asked, laughing.

"You'll never know!" Jim replied.

"I already do," Spike replied, and the wrestling match was on, ending up outside in the Korean mud. Having expended all of their combat tensions, the group slowly dispersed to lie in their bunks, and think about home.

The Red One team sat in their hutch, idling the morning away, doing their housekeeping chores, and as usual talking about flying or women.

"I think we need to take a weekend in Seoul, guys, the next time we have three days off," Rex offered, as an opening conversation piece.

"What's there in Seoul to make it worth the trip? A dinner of kimchi?" John asked.

Sam stopped sweeping the hutch, and looked at John. "Aw Navy. Have you no faith in the U-S-A-F to take care of your needs? They got great food, and superb whorehouses! Let's see - there's kimchi. For example - Kimchi soup! Kimchi salads! And the latest - frozen kimchi - in winter only, you understand."

"Ugh! And forget about the whorehouses too. I wouldn't touch them with a ten-foot pole!" John replied, his face showing his disgust.

"Come on, Navy, quit bragging. Even you Navy guys don't have one ten feet long!" Rex laughed. "And obviously you don't know anything about Seoul. We'll stay in the BOQ on the compound where all the big wheels are located. It's comfortable, and they have a nice Club - at least by our standards. The food's superior to the shit we get here, and there are women! Civil Servants and occasionally Army nurses from one of the MASH units. They're wilder than March hares! You may not be able to lay one of them, but at least you can look."

"Okay! I'm in," John volunteered. "Maybe I can lay a nurse. I tried once. She said no."

"What? The Navy's white stallion got rejected?" Leo laughed hard, and almost fell off his upper bunk.

"Now don't you guys ride him. He'll get a complex," Rex chuckled. "What time are we on this afternoon, Sam?"

"Launch at 1400, Boss Man," Sam replied. "Maybe we'll get lucky today."

"Yeah, I hope so," John interjected. "I've got fifteen missions already, and nothing to show for it. Every time I get in position, something happens to blow the opportunity. The target maneuvers away and I can't close because I can't leave Rex, or when I do close, he breaks sharply just as I am ready to fire - and I can't follow him. Shit! Not a damned thing to show except combat flight time in my pilot's log!"

"Not true, John." Rex snapped at him. "Not true at all. You keep those MiG's off the backs of the tactical air guys - the F-84's doing the dirty job of interdiction, and the B-29's with their crazy ideas of strategic bombing in a tactical war. If you weren't out there every day keeping the MiG's busy at altitude, they'd be all over those poor suckers. Even so, the B-29's lost four planes in one raid last week. The MiG's broke through and had a field day." He laughed, and then headed outside for the latrine across the wooden planks and through the mud. At the door of the tent he stopped and turned around.

"While I'm thinking of it, let's talk fuel, John," Rex said, looking at his wingman. "At the end of the mission you were down to 200 pounds and had to dead stick part of the way, while the rest of us had 600 pounds. You're jockeying the throttle too much. Can't afford to throw away gas trying to look pretty and impress everyone with your flying skills. A hundred pounds of fuel could be the difference between getting home and ending up in a POW camp. I'm not going to chew your ass if you get a little sucked, but I will when you waste gas. Okay?" He continued outside.

"Kimpo Tower. This is Red One. Flight of four. Starting engines. Combat mission."

"Roger Red One. Cleared to runway 03. Altimeter 30.02. Wind north at five. Scattered cumulus. Visibility ten miles in haze. Call taxiing."

Rex looked at John in Red One Three, parked next to him. John turned to look at Leo parked on the other side. He got a thumbs up from Leo, then turned and gave a thumbs up to Rex. Rex acknowledged and pressed the start button. The compressors began to turn as the rest of the flight initiated their start procedures. The igniters sparked the fuel, and the sound of the jet engines rose in a crescendo of noise along the flight line. The plane captains pulled the chocks as the tower cleared them to the active and immediate takeoff.

The flight lined up on the runway and on signal from Rex began to roll. Once airborne they turned north and headed for MiG Alley.

Looks like thirty bandits today, John said as he watched the MiG's rendezvous north of the Yalu. *We've got twelve again. And here they come!* John smiled, as the MiG's swept south of the river. This time the MiG's broke their large formation while still above the F-86's, and then dove in flights and sections trying to single out stray F-86's for attack.

Most of the MiG's had lost their altitude advantage and were pulling out below him as Rex pulled into a steep climb, trading airspeed for altitude. He rolled on his back with John in good covering position, and there below were two fat MiG's. Rex rolled off into a dive, homing in on the first MiG.

"Try for number two, John, but don't lose me."

John swung out wide and reversed to get behind the number two MiG, who was trying to position himself behind Rex. John closed rapidly. The MiG seemed oblivious to John's presence. The shot was perfect as John's six .50-caliber machine guns spit out a lethal batch of projectiles. The bullets stitched up the fuselage across the wing root and into the cockpit. Parts flew off the airplane, the canopy released into the slipstream, and the pilot ejected.

"I got him! Jesus, I got him! I got the son of a bitch! My first kill!" John screamed, his adrenalin pumping hard and the excitement spilling out of him! Rex was right. There's nothing like it - not even women! The elation passed as he added full power to close Rex who was now in a tail chase after a much smarter MiG pilot. Rex soon broke off the fruitless effort when the MiG headed for the Yalu.

"Break right!" John yelled, as two MiG's dived down on Rex's tail. John also became the hunted, as two MiG's jumped him and, forced him to break off his attack. Two other F-86's rolled in to help Rex. John whipped into a 6g turn and the MiG's slid to the outside of the turn.

"Good! They can't get me from there." John grunted through his teeth, as the g forces pulled his body down. The lead MiG opened fire with its 37 mm, but could not get the correct lead for his weapons from the outside of the turn. The projectiles went wide of the mark. The MiG pilot suddenly broke off, and John was left to find Rex.

"Where are you, John," Rex called. "Let's head home."

"Roger, I'm disengaged. Fuel state. 450 pounds. Waggle your wings."

Rex did as requested to help John identify him.

"Gotsya."

The section of F-86's with Rex in the lead hit the break over runway 03 at 350 knots. Rex kissed off to John with the comment on the radio, "Do your stuff, Sailor!" Red One Three pulled his nose up and did three victory rolls before he turned downwind to land.

On the ground Jimmy saw the victory rolls and started yelling, "He got one! My pilot got one! My F-86 killed a MiG!"

Everyone was running now to see the excitement. It attracted the attention of the Wing Commander who had just deplaned nearby.

"What's up, Jimmy?"

"He got one! Did a victory roll!"

Colonel Wolfe was waiting as John climbed down.

"You got one, John?" Wolfe smiled at him.

"I did! I did! Lost my cherry! SOB never saw me! He was after Rex!"

"Good show, Sailor," Rex ran up and wrapped his arms around John in a bear hug. "How was it?" he asked.

"Just like you said, Rex! There's absolutely nothing like it!" John's face beamed with pleasure and his eyes darted happily from person to person as he lifted Rex up and swung him around.

"Here comes our naval hero!" Sam called, as John and Rex got out of the jeep in front of the debriefing tent.

"Naval hero, my ass!" Leo chimed in. "One lucky son of a bitch! Did you see that MiG just pull in front of him and wait to be shot? Like a woman waiting to be laid."

"Doesn't make any difference, guys, does it?" Rex said, walking through the door with his arm around John's shoulder. "He got one! You bastards probably would have missed the shot that he had!" Rex laughed.

"Aw, Rex. We're only teasing!" Leo replied, his face beaming at John's good luck, "You did a great job, Sailor. We're proud of you."

"Yeah, congratulations, John! I can confirm the kill," Rex added, looking at the debriefer. "I saw the pilot eject. Four more and you're an ace!" Then he shrugged. "However, the Air Staff will pull you before then. Air Force Aces only, here."

Rex turned to the debriefer who had been waiting patiently. "Let's get this thing over so we can go to the club and get shit-faced! We deserve it!"

"God! There must be fifty of the bastards coming out to greet us." John mumbled, as he watched the MiG's maneuver at 40,000 feet, heading south. "And again there are only twelve of us!"

The battle was soon joined, not unlike a swarm of angry hornets, a wheeling and twisting mass of men and machines trying to position themselves, and gain advantage. Rex was close to the tail of a MiG-15 who was maneuvering violently trying to shake him without success. John was loosely hanging in on Rex, cutting inside the turn whenever possible. Amid the noisy calls for breaks and help came the clear voice of Leo. "Red 1-2. Need help. I'm in trouble. Lost my wingman and this guy is all over me."

"Red 1-3. Red One. I think I have this guy that I'm locked onto. Don't want to lose him. Can you break off and help Leo?"

"Rog, I have Leo in sight. Breaking off." John flipped over on his back and pulled through to gain airspeed and reach Leo quickly. But he was too late. The MiG managed to close and get a shot off. Leo's plane was hit in the wing and tail section. The canopy blew off, and Leo ejected. The plane flew another second and then began to come apart. The port wing folded up and ripped off. The empennage separated, and the fuselage with the starboard wing still attached went into a flat spin.

A white fury enveloped John as he swung into position behind the MiG whose pilot saw him and whipped into a 6g turn, but John was there before him, pulling over 9g's to get well inside the MIG's turn. His fury was such that his taut muscles helped the g-suit keep him from blacking out. The F-86 grunted and groaned at the abuse, but John kept pushing until he was well within range. The long burst of his .50's was more than necessary, but John kept pouring it into the MiG until it blew up.

It was a quiet group seated in the Red One Flight's tent. There wasn't much to say. Rex was going through Leo's things, sorting and packing, and preparing a small package of personal effects to be sent to his wife.

"Sam, why don't you go down to the Class 6 and get some more whiskey. We're going to need it tonight."

When Sam had left, Rex turned to John and said, "I need a replacement for Leo, and I don't want an outsider in the slot. Sam is good, but not good enough to fill Leo's shoes. I'm not supposed to do it, but I'm going to anyway. You are now the section leader for the second section. Sam will fly my wing, and we'll get you a new wingman." He stopped and looked at John for a moment. "You're good, John, damned good. You have two kills now, almost as many as I do. As section leader you've a good chance of making Ace - but," he chuckled, "do it quick before the Air Staff realizes what's happening and transfers you."

"Thanks, Rex. I appreciate the vote of confidence," John replied.

The door of the hutch opened and the Wing's leading metal smith walked in.

"Who was flying 320, gentlemen?" he asked, his lips set grimly and his eyes angry.

"I was," John volunteered. "Why?"

"Sir, you popped a dozen or more rivets along the main spar of the wing! If the spar's bent, we'll have to replace the entire wing! Damnit!" he blazed.

"I'm sorry," John started to say but Rex interrupted him.

"No, he's not sorry! He did what was necessary to get the kill. So get off his back! Besides it was a vengeance maneuver. The MiG he got had just shot down our buddy, Leo. So get your ass out of here, you damned tin bender!"

On the first flight as section leader John reaped a bonanza. A pair of MiG's were on Rex's tail, and another pair were headed down to go after Sam. John saw them and converted his altitude advantage to air speed, closing the distance quickly. The two MiG's were separated by about a hundred feet and seemed oblivious to John's presence. The MiG's flipped into a tight turn following Rex's maneuver, but John was already on the inside of the turn. He eased up on the stick and let his pipper walk back onto the second MiG. Although it was an angle shot, John was on target with the first burst which tore pieces off the port wing. John quickly shifted to the lead MiG and fired a long burst which tore the fuselage in half just forward of the tail. He then shifted back to the second MiG who had rolled out of his turn and was headed home, but because of the damage to his wing, couldn't use his speed advantage to break clear. John laid a long burst up his tail pipe and the plane exploded.

In the meantime Rex had dispensed with his target. Red Flight had downed three MiG's in a single mission!

John came in low over the runway, nearly supersonic fifty feet off the deck. At the far end of the runway he pulled up vertical and disappeared into the clouds doing rolls. He reappeared shortly entering the downwind for landing.

"You got another one?" Jimmy yelled, bouncing up and down like a kid. John shut down and jumped down exuberantly to be greeted by Colonel Wolfe and a band of yelling pilots.

"I got two! I got two!" John's voice exploded through the noise.

"And I got another one!" Rex yelled, and the two of them yelled and danced with glee. Some one found a can of beer and poured it over them. Both Rex and John were one short of ace.

The O'Club was bedlam. John was drenched with beer, poured by happy comrades. Colonel Jake arrived with a bottle of champagne in each hand. He popped the corks, handed one to John and one to Rex and said, "Okay guys! Let's see a chug-a-lug!"

Three months of his tour were gone, and John already had seventy-five missions. But like the Ides of March, nothing was going right. On one flight his fuel transfer wouldn't work and he had to abort. On another flight he threw a hot turbine blade, and had to return to base. To make matters worse, John's new wingman, Tom Collins, was a nice guy, but he didn't have the skill and experience necessary to hang in on the violent maneuvers of combat. He'd learn eventually, but until he did, John's six o'clock position was frequently exposed, which affected his ability to concentrate on the target.

Red One lounged in the Day Room on alert to cover a flight of F-84's on a bombing mission near the Yalu.

"HQ will call us when the 84's are airborne." Rex briefed his ragtag crew in their scroungy flight suits, dirty yellow life jackets, and scuffed ankle-high boots. They didn't smell too good either. It was cold and the al fresco showers of ice water were not inviting.

"We'll climb to 20,000 initially and cruise back and forth along the Yalu. The first one to spot the 84's, signal with your hands. Of course, if you see MiG's do the same - but don't be reluctant to use the radio to warn me. Okay?"

Rex continued to drink his coke and munch on a large ham sandwich.

"Eat up, John," Rex said, observing that John was not partaking. "It could be your last meal for a while, if you have to punch out."

"My stomach is tied up in knots about this flight. If I eat, I'll probably just barf all over the plane captain," John replied.

"And, of course - ace that you are - you won't get shot down either," Sam chuckled before he stuffed an entire sandwich into his mouth.

"You could eat shit and enjoy it." John smiled and patted Sam's fat cheek.

"Red One, man your planes," the squawk box announced.

"Here we go, guys," Rex said, grabbing the knee board that clamped to his thigh in flight, and his packet of maps, nicely sized to fit by his seat.

"Get us another one, Lieutenant," Jimmy said, strapping John in.

"I'll do my best, Jimmy," John smiled and tousled the kid's red hair.

"All aircraft, this is Kimpo Tower. Red One, four F-86's on combat departure. Clear the runway and taxiways, 937 cross the runway to the warmup area on the opposite side."

Red One lined up on the runway, executed a formation takeoff, and headed for the Yalu and 20,000 feet where they entered a lazy max endurance racetrack pattern to wait for the action to start.

Tom Collins, John's new wingman, pulled up close to John and pointed down at three o'clock. John looked and saw the eight F-84's, and gave Tom a thumbs up. Rex, who had been watching, also looked down at three o'clock, and gave John and Tom a thumbs up.

It was a beautiful sunny day, clear with some towering cumulus, but the pilot's minds were not on the beauty of it. Generally relaxed, but with an underlying tension that would produce quick reaction, they continually scanned the skies for signs of MiG's. Fighter aircraft were always difficult to see at altitude, the eye having a tendency to focus close in when it had no visual reference. But today there were the towering Q - the cumulus that went up to fifteen thousand feet. They helped to provide a distant reference for the eye to focus on.

A sudden glint of sunlight on a shiny object caught John's attention at eight o'clock. Looking down he saw nothing at first, but as he squinted he began to make out a flight of four MiG-15's crossing the Yalu and heading for the F-84's

There was no time for hand signals. "Tally-ho! Eight o'clock down. Four bandits at ten thousand feet," John said into the mike.

Rex looked and saw nothing. He continued to scan the area, but could not pick out the MiG's against the gray and brown of the hills.

"No joy, John. You have the lead. Let's go get them - break- F-84's north of Sonchon. This is the 86CAP. You have bandits closing. We are engaging."

The MiG leader saw the 86's, and rolled into a head-on with John. Both fired, but missed. As John passed below the MiG he rolled hard to port in a 6g turn. The MiG pilot broke starboard, matching John's turn to form a classic scissors maneuver. It now became a question of who could turn tighter to end up on the tail of the other. The MiG's wingman pulled up into a high yo-yo to get on Rex's tail as Rex and his wing man tried to box the MiG leader between himself and John. The other section of MiG's turned in the opposite direction forcing Rex to break off, and John was now alone, his new wingman having disappeared during the violent maneuvering.

After completing three scissors maneuvers, John was slowly gaining the advantage, using all the 86's superb maneuverability at that altitude to turn inside the MiG. Suddenly the MiG pilot broke out of the scissors to do a high-g yo-yo, trying to drop on John's tail. But John had anticipated the move and countered, ending up astern of the MiG, but out of gun range.

"This Americanski is good," the Russian grunted through the clenched teeth of a high-g turn.

Back and forth the fight seesawed, each pilot trying something new only to be quickly countered by the other. They were slowly losing altitude, and John was gaining position to fire when the Russian rolled on his back and pulled through.

"Jesus! He'll never pull out in time," John said, doing a partial Split-S himself to follow the MiG. The F-86 began to gain on the MiG in the dive.

At the last minute the MiG rolled out of the dive, and dropped down into the nap of the earth, flying down gullies, skimming ridges, and weaving through clumps of trees.

John pulled into position behind him trying to get his guns to bear on the target, but the MiG was so low that he was blowing up dirt from the dry riverbed! At this altitude John had a slight speed advantage and the MiG couldn't run away. John's eyes glinted as he began to savor a kill, but he still couldn't get in position below the MiG to bring his guns to bear. Unfortunately, all F-86 guns are mounted to shoot slightly upward, and the MiG was simply too close to the ground - almost dragging his belly in the dirt!

Suddenly the MiG slowed, hoping John would overrun him. John came alongside the MiG for an instant before he could react, and then countered by doing a high-g roll over the top of the MiG, slowing down to regain the position astern. However, in that fraction of a second alongside the MiG, John saw the leather helmet worn by Russian pilots, the red star of the Soviet Union on the fuselage, and the cyrillic lettering near the tail. The MiG was now flying a little higher, and John tried a burst. It went over the top of the MiG.

"Damn! Damn! Damn! I've got to get him somehow," John cursed, his adrenalin pumping as the excitement of the chase overwhelmed all prudence. He smelled a kill and would do anything to get one. Another futile burst from the .50- calibers. John was practically bellying into the ground to get low enough to shoot upward.

Then an idea hit him. He pulled up sharply, rolled onto on his back to bring his guns to bear. In the inverted position, they were now pointing slightly down. " I got him! " John yelled, as he pickled off a burst which was dead on target, but the Russian, recognizing John's intent, pulled up just as John fired, spoiling his aim. John was now beginning to red out from the negative g's. He quickly rolled upright, his port wing tip dusting the ground in the process. The MiG, which had increased his altitude to negate John's upside-down shot, now dropped back onto the floor as the two planes crossed the Yalu, and the Chinese anti-aircraft weapons, protecting the Antung complex, opened up on them.

"Oh shit!" John screamed in defiance and frustration. He pulled up steeply to get out of the gun's range, and reversed course to depart the sanctuary which he was violating.

The MiG dropped its gear and flaps, landed at Antung, and taxied to the line. The canopy opened, and Colonel Yevgeni Antonofski, Commander of the 196 Istrebitel'nyj Aviatsionnyj Polk, stood up in the cockpit and narrowed his eyes as he looked back at the retreating F-86.

"You are good, my friend. Damned good! Makes it even more worthwhile to get you. And get you I will! I saw the 'Sylvia' painted on your nose. I know you now and we'll meet again." He saluted the now vanishing F-86, and stepped down from the cockpit.

A new arrival in Manchuria, the Russian colonel was charged with improving the training and performance of the Chinese pilots, in addition to directing his own regiment of Russian pilots. The Russians wanted to equalize the embarrassing disparity in kill rates between the Americans and the Communists, and test the capability of the Americans. The Colonel was himself a multiple fighter ace with twenty Germans to his credit in World War II. He was already an ace in Korea with five kills; four F-84's, and one F-86.

Kimpo Air Force Base
Seoul, Korea

The Day Room echoed with John's shouts of frustration. "I had him! Goddamnit! I had him! It's not fair to let him go! These fucking rules! What stupid asshole made them! Damn him anyway!" John's emotions spewed out of him in a torrent of invective, and vile language. He pounded the walls with his fists, and paced back and forth like a caged tiger, all the while salivating as his anger exploded out of him

Rex came up and put his arm around him. "Easy, John boy. Easy. You should have gone after him into Manchuria. Next time, just turn your IFF off so that the American radar at Chodo Island can't see you, and go after him. A year ago Major Robbie Risten flew right over the airfield at ground level to get one he was chasing. The SOB blew up right over the flight line and destroyed three additional MiGs. Lots of guys do it, but if you get him over Manchuria, you can't claim it."

"Yeah! Sure! And if someone reports me, I'm out of here. I'm Navy! I can't get away with that! There are those who would report me. I've got kills and they don't. Shit! Let's go to the club and get drunk!" He turned and headed out the door, Rex in trail to keep him out of trouble. After four neat shots of scotch, John began to settle down, and his hands stopped trembling.

"You know, Rex, I told you in our long discussions when I first got here that I wanted to kill the machine, not necessarily the pilot. I was wrong. Today I wanted to kill the pilot because he wouldn't let me shoot him down. I was so angry that he got away from me. I just wanted to kill him - and I would have, too! Strange - isn't it. The cavalier in me disappeared. Just like that!" He snapped his fingers.

"It happens, John. Don't worry. You're still yourself. It's the emotion overwhelming you. I told you there's nothing like a kill." Rex raised his glass. "Here's to you, Sailor. You're okay!"

Over North Korea

Colonel Yevgeni sat comfortably in his MiG-15 at 33,000 feet, slowly scanning the F-86 formation 3000 feet below him. It was his intention to let the other MiGs drop down to engage the F-86s while he remained aloft at 33,000 feet, waiting for the appropriate moment to jump a straggler for a quick kill.

In the meantime he used his twenty-power Leica binoculars, that he took off a dead German, for a close-up inspection of the individual F-86's, looking for the one with Sylvia on the side.

"There she is!" he shouted. "The lovely lady whose owner is now trying to close two MiG's. Good!" Yevgeni muttered. "The pilot of Sylvia is trying to engage and his wingman is sucked back out of position."

Yevgeni rolled into a steep dive to rapidly close John's aircraft.

"Red 1-2. Break right!" John's wingman had enough sense to warn his section leader even though he was effectively out of position to help. A quick look confirmed the threat. John broke off his engagement to his great frustration and whipped into a high-g turn. The Russian struggled to get inside the turn, but the 86's maneuverability and John's 8g effort prevented that from happening.

John tried a yo-yo to get behind the Russian without success. Rolls and other twisting and turning maneuvers couldn't seem to break the Russian loose. He was slowly but surely closing John who now called for help.

"Red 1-2. Get this guy off me!"

"Roger. I'm coming," responded Rex.

In desperation, John tried a 9g vertical pull-up with the intent of rolling over the top, and escaping in a dive in the opposite direction.

The maneuver caught Yevgeni by surprise. He responded a fraction of a second late, and it was enough to put him well outside John's vertical turn. About to give up and try another day, he looked down and saw two F-86's flying together like they were on a summer outing. Yevgeni smiled and rolled down onto the trailing F-86 who seemed totally oblivious to his presence. But John had also seen the two F-86's as he went over the top. His situational awareness mechanism sensed the 86's position and their vulnerability to the Russian. John reversed course, dropped down to regain airspeed, and close Yevgeni who now became the hunted. There was the Russian in front of John. Yevgeni had dismissed John, both as a target and a threat. He saw easy pickings with the F-86's in front of him. He was just about to fire when he saw John's plane swing down on him well within range. Before he could react, John's machine guns poured a long burst into the MiG tearing the engine apart. The fire warning light came on, the tailpipe temperature soared, and the engine made horrible noises, forecasting its disintegration. Yevgeni ejected.

"I got him! He's mine! It's number five! I'm an ace!" John yelled and tried to jump up and down in his seat against the constraints of the seat belt. His nerve ends tingled and his muscles twitched, stimulated by the massive dose of adrenilin pumping into his system. The excitement stimulated his sex organs, and he felt like he would have a orgasm. He kicked his feet and pounded on the canopy, his feelings exploding in the joy of it.

"Nice shot, John, and congratulations!" Rex who had answered John's call for help, swung in alongside him. "I confirm it, ace!"

Yevgeni opened his chute at 10,000 feet after a 15,000-foot free fall. The chute blossomed, and swung Yevgeni back and forth as he began his slow descent. Embarrassment flooded his face, but the skin was too cold to show it.

That was Sylvia. It sure as hell was! And I thought she was gone - out of the action. A great maneuver on the American's part! I'm shamed! Me! A hero of the Soviet people! Holder of ribbons! Killer of German aces! He shrugged in his chute harness and shook at the thought. *All the more reason to bag him! And at least even the score! Now let's concentrate on not breaking an ankle on landing. I need to get back into the air!*

"Kimpo Tower. Red 1-1. Tell the Colonel I'm bringing home an ace!" Rex called in.

A mob was gathered around Rex's plane to congratulate him. Rex shut down, and stood up in the cockpit as Colonel Wolfe climbed up on the step, thinking Rex was the ace.

"Not me, Colonel! Not me! That damned Sailor beat me to it!"

Wolfe stopped and looked at him until the comprehension hit him. Then he smiled, "Great for him, but the Air Staff will be furious with us for letting a Navy pilot into the Air Force's exclusive club."

Rex laughed, "That's the way it is. I just knew he'd do it. Can we delay reporting it a few days to give us time to enjoy it?"

"Yeah, I guess we can. It'll be two or three weeks before they finally get a set of orders out here to relieve him. And I refuse to do it without written orders. He's too valuable to lose, Rex."

"In the meantime, let's join the party. Everyone's over at John's plane sloshing around in beer. John should have the grand daddy of hangovers tomorrow!"

Rex and John were alone in the hootch drinking beer when John brought up the problem of his wingman.

"Collins just doesn't have it, Rex," John opened the discussion. "Frankly, he doesn't handle his plane well. His reactions are slow and he does not have the drive to force an engagement. He'll lay back and watch. I don't think he's a coward. He just doesn't have the will."

"Yeah, I know, John," Rex replied. "I've seen him, but there's nothing I can do until we get some new replacements. Anyone you get now from another flight will just be another guy that someone doesn't want. Maybe in a few weeks. I told Colonel Wolfe about it. He'll give me first choice."

"He scares me, Rex. He's unpredictable, and he's never where he should be."

"Okay, John. Got the message. But you probably won't be here long anyway. Your next mission is 93. The Air Staff will kick you out soon."

"I want a hundred missions, Rex. I really do."

Mission ninety-five was a disaster from the start. The belly tanks transferred their fuel erratically, and then stopped completely before they were empty. The A-4 gun sight swung its reticule all over the windscreen, and then quit.

"What's next?" John grunted, as the MiG's came roaring down at them. At least the drop tanks released properly into the slipstream, and he was free to engage as a big fat MiG-15 lumbered slowly across in front of him at Mach .8 airspeed instead of the normal Mach .9. John set his teeth for the inevitable high-g maneuvering, and dropped down on top of the pigeon who continued blithely on course!

"How sweet! A real knock off!" John hit the armament switches which he had forgotten to engage, and pickled off a burst with the firing button on top of the joystick. Nothing happened. The MiG, now aware of the danger, began to maneuver violently while John desperately tried to clear his guns.

"What the hell's wrong with them?" he screamed, not knowing that a critical electrical connection dangled loosely in the nose.

The flight continued to deteriorate. Two sections of MiG's swung in on his tail, and his wingman suddenly was nowhere in sight! "Damn! They've got me boxed. I can't maneuver in either direction without exposing my six to one or the other. Well, here we go for a little dive!"

John rolled over and pulled through in a screaming Split-S, hoping he would accelerate fast enough to quickly open the range from the pursuing MiG's. The lead MiG fired a burst of his 23 mm cannon as John opened, and was rewarded with a lucky shot. One of the projectiles penetrated the forward engine compartment of the F-86, but now John had the luck. It did not explode! Instead, it plowed through various engine parts, and impacted the armor plate behind John with a mighty splat! John was now out of range, but the MIG's kept up the pursuit until they reached 8000 feet altitude. Then they gave up the chase.

John applied more power to begin a climb, but the fire warning light began to flicker and the tailpipe temperature rose dangerously to the red line on the gauge.

"I'd better head home. It's just not my day today!" John turned south towards the front line, the MLR. Five miles north of it the TPT went completely into the red and the fire warning light came on steady. John shut down the engine, turned the fuel master valve off, switched the IFF to Emergency, and called Kimpo.

"Kimpo. This is Red 1-2. I have a fire warning light and have shut down my engine. I will try to glide to friendly lines, but I'm not sure I can make it"

"Roger. Red 1-2. We're tracking your Emergency squawk, and have requested a flight of F-51 ResCAP plus an angel chopper for pick up. Keep us advised."

"Roger Kimpo. Got any Navy ADs available. They're a lot more capable than the F-51."

"I'll try, Red 1-2."

But, John was lucky again. Strong upward thermals over the North Korean lines gave him the little extra boost that was needed to reach the MLR. The first UN emplacements passed under John's wing. A few seconds later at 1500 feet, he punched out. The chute opened, blossomed, and swung just once before depositing John in the remains of a tree five hundred yards behind the MLR.

John was hanging by the risers, helpless to get down by himself when a jeep with a driver and one passenger came barreling down a nearby rutted road, and screeched to a stop below the tree. The passenger stood up, stared at John and his predicament, and then he laughed at him. He wore the silver eagle of a bird colonel.

"Flyboy, you are one lucky son of a bitch!"

John smiled back at him, "That's all I ever need, Colonel. Just a little luck."

The colonel chuckled, "Smart-ass Flyboy! Now don't you go away!" he said, with a sarcastic grin on his face. "Just stay where you are. I'll get someone to get you down."

John laughed and then mumbled, "Smart assed, dogface!"

The colonel heard the mumble, and fixed John with a beady stare and knitted brows.

"Oh shit, I've done it now!" John waited.

Then the smile returned to the colonel's face, "You're gutsy, Flyboy, real gutsy. I like gutsy people. I'll send someone back for you."

2739 Maple Drive
San Diego

Sylvia was baking bread when a neighbor, Mary Lyons, rushed in. "Sylvia, have you seen the morning paper? John's on the front page. He's an ace, got his fifth kill the day before yesterday. Now they'll send him home. Can't risk losing an ace!"

Before Sylvia could answer, the phone rang. "Yes, this is Mrs. Sullivan. . . No, I haven't seen the paper, but a neighbor just told me about it. . . Yes, I'll be home tomorrow if you want an interview." She hung up. "That was the Tribune. They want to interview me. Let's see that paper and find out what this is all about."

"It's all over for John. They'll send him home," Mary Lyons repeated, and beamed at Sylvia, happy to be the bearer of the good news.

But it wasn't quite over for John. Three flights later on mission 96 in a massive dogfight, he got kill number six - a tough MiG pilot who almost outmaneuvered him. But almost isn't worth much in aerial combat.

CHAPTER 10

Kimpo Air Base
Seoul, Korea

John kicked the door open and dragged in boxes of critical supplies, four bottles of scotch, two gin, a case of Bud, and ten boxes of Cheezits.

"Stocking up, Sailor?" Rex Taggart asked as he rolled out of his bunk to help the Navy. "I hate to tell you this, John boy, but even you can't drink all that in two days."

"I got time, Rex."

"That's what I'm telling you, Loot - nant. You are on your way home. I've been told to see about cutting your orders."

"Damn!" John replied. "When?"

"I'm supposed to take you off flying status now, but I don't have a relief assigned yet."

"Rex, damnit. You know this afternoon's my hundredth mission. Please don't take me off until tomorrow," John countered.

"I'm supposed to do it now, John." He stopped and then smiled. "But I don't have a replacement and it's my considered operational judgment that a three plane flight is hazardous to my health which you have protected very well these last few months. Okay Navy, until a replacement arrives, which probably will happen tomorrow, you remain in flying status."

197

"Thanks, buddy. Who ever said all Air Force pilots are a bunch of shits?"

"Probably the same one that said all carrier pilots are candy asses," Rex chuckled. "Suit up, John. You go today."

"Kimpo Tower, Red One. Flight of four, starting engines. Combat mission."

"All aircraft at Kimpo. This is the tower. Combat mission departing. Hold your position, or clear the parallel taxiway. Air Force 10735, clear the active immediately to the warm-up pads to your right."

"Red One. Flight of four rolling. Power now."

"Roger, Red One. Good hunting."

Red One passed north of P'yongyang at 35,000 feet in a loose tactical formation.

"They're already engaged," Red One announced to the division. "We'll be there in five minutes. Check your armament."

MiG Alley
North Korea

Colonel Yevgenie was back in the saddle, the ankle which he had injured on landing following his bailout now fully recovered. He was leading a flight of 33 Chinese trainees, but he real mission was personal - to even the score with the F-86 named Sylvia. As usual he had his Leica binoculars in hand and was scanning the F-86 formations for Sylvia.

"There she is!" he exclaimed, "and as usual the wingman is getting sucked behind." Yevgeni signaled his own wingman to take the lead and engage the F-86s. The wingman acknowledged, broke off to port, and headed down to engage, the flight of trainees following behind him.

"Okay, guys. Here they come." Rex announced. He broke right with his section while John picked up a straggler crossing in front of him, and maneuvered hard to attain firing position. John's wingman was sucked even further behind, and John's six o'clock was exposed.

Yevgeni chuckled to himself. "That wingman of Sylvia's is a real asset - to me!" He put his binoculars away, rolled off on a wing, and swept down to engage Sylvia.

Assuming his wingman was still in position, John's total concentration was on the victim MiG, when someone yelled, "Red 1-2. Break right now!"

Automatically, John whipped into a 6g turn, and checked his rear view mirror. There was a MiG-15 on his tail, inside his turn and closing rapidly! The 6g turn didn't bother him at all.

Oh shit! Where did he come from? John exclaimed as he tightened the turn and dropped his nose to keep up his airspeed. An 8g turn didn't bother the MIG either. He held position inside the turn and was slowly closing.

"Red 1-2! I'm in trouble! Someone get this guy off me!"

"Rog, Red 1-2. I'm coming," Taggart replied.

"Damn! Damn!" was all John could say. He tried to further tighten his turn, but he blacked out momentarily from loss of blood to the brain. His back pressure on the stick slacked off, the g forces dropped slightly, and the MiG gained firing position. A projectile from the Russian's second burst hit the skin of John's fuselage at an angle, just forward of the wing root. It exploded on contact showering the air inlet duct of the engine with shrapnel whose pieces were then ingested by the turbine. The shrapnel also damaged the aileron boost system. With the decrease of g load, John quickly regained consciousness, but it was too late.

"Red 1-2! I'm hit. I'm hit!" John yelled into his mike as the F-86 slowly rolled into a port nose-down turn, descending with gray smoke streaming from the exhaust.

"Easy, Red 1-2. I'm on him," Taggart answered. "Get your ass out of here."

"I got him! I got Sylvia!" Yevgeni yelled, elated at his good fortune. He moved in for the coup de grace, but Rex was rolling into position on Yevgeni's tail! The Russian's concentration on killing Sylvia blinded him to the threat until, too late, he saw Rex swing into position. Rex's six .50 calibers barked and stitched the fuselage and wing of the MiG-15. A few seconds later the MiG exploded - another victim of target fixation. Yevgeni had wanted Sylvia too much! And Rex was now an ace!

The F-86's wing was heavy, but John managed to level off. The engine was vibrating severely as he swung the plane around to the south towards Kimpo. But he had no fire warning light and the smoke from the tailpipe had stopped. Things were looking up!

"Must have been hydraulic fluid," John thought as he checked in with Kimpo.

"Kimpo, Red 1-2. Disengaged and headed for home plate. I'm hit in the engine compartment, and the engine's vibrating badly. I'm shutting down now."

"Roger, Red 1-2. We're tracking you. Be advised that we have an indefinite ceiling at 500 feet and a mile visibility. Clouds are up to 10,000. Weather is deteriorating rapidly."

John got out his whiz wheel and checked. He had enough fuel, if the weather would just hold. But he did not have the altitude to glide all the way. He'd have to light off the engine just south of P'yongyang to make it. The big question was whether the engine would hold together when he started it. John continued to descend dead stick at 8000 feet per minute through dense gray-white clouds that swirled around his canopy. Fortunately, the turbulence was light, and his attitude instruments continued to perform.

At 5000 feet, south of P'yongyang, John did an air start. The engine vibrated, but seemed okay at 80 percent power.

"I don't have far to go. I'm about fifty miles north of the MLR. Just another five minutes, please Lord."

Seconds later, the engine vibrations began to increase and the fire warning light came on as the entire plane began to shake. Sweating heavily, John stared at the red fire warning light and hoped. Now the tailpipe temperature began to rise rapidly. When it passed the red line, the plane shook violently. The engine was coming apart! John switched his IFF to emergency and shouted into his mike, "Mayday! Mayday! Red 1-2 ejecting!"

John then pulled the ejection levers on the sides of the seat. The canopy blew off and the seat fired, sending him thirty feet into the slipstream - well clear of the tail surfaces. He reached down, unbuckled his seat belt, and kicked clear of the seat. Then he located and pulled the ripcord. The chute streamed out behind him and blossomed, jerking him upright, the risers taut above him. Looking around he saw nothing but a white mass of drifting cotton. He couldn't see the ground below him

Jesus, there'll be no RESCAP today, but at least I got a Mayday out, and Kimpo radar was tracking me.

But John was wrong. His radio had died. The engine fire had shorted out the antenna, and his Mayday call did not get out. The aircraft flew another twenty miles before it exploded in the air, the flash hidden from the ground by the heavy overcast.

Kimpo Tower
Seoul, Korea

"Sir, we just lost Red 1-2. No radio transmission," the radar operator reported to the supervisor.

"Okay Max. Mark it and give me the coordinates. We can't do anything about it in this soup. Even the helos aren't flying. We'll probably have to wait until tomorrow to put up a RESCAP. By then it will be too late."

Twenty miles to the west of where the F-86 exploded, Lieutenant John Sullivan hung in his parachute amidst the dense clouds waiting for the ground to reach up and grab him. Too late he saw a large wooded area below towards which he was headed. John desperately pulled the risers, trying to direct his chute towards a small clearing, but without success. He plunged through the dense foliage - the long branches cruelly breaking his fall. A searing pain swept up and engulfed him as his right leg was ripped open from knee to hip by the jagged tip of a broken branch

He impacted hard on his other leg and collapsed, the parachute falling on top of him and covering him. He lay there a few minutes recovering from the shock and then moved slightly to examine the extent of his injury. There was a deep gash in his right thigh running the length of it, but no evidence that an artery had been torn. He painfully rose and discovered that he could stand on it and walk, although with difficulty. He then located his first aid pack in the parachute seat, dusted the wound with sulfa powder, and wrapped the pressure bandage around it. Next he cut additional strips from the parachute and further bandaged the wound. He then gathered up the chute and hid it in a nearby rotten tree trunk.

Suddenly aware that he was in enemy territory, he dragged himself to the edge of the trees and scanned the scene below him. The woods lay along the down side of a low ridge. Below it a meadow swept down a gentle grade for about three hundred yards to a rutted dirt road where there was a small village of mud huts with thatched roofs. A few scrawny black and white cattle grazed listlessly in the meadow. On the far side of the village the land was flat with low dikes holding the water for a rice paddy. A benjo ditch ran between the muddy road and the paddies.

God! It looks just like the Japanese countryside that we went through going to Akakura, except it's more primitive, less orderly, and much dirtier, John reflected. It all seemed very peaceful, but John knew the enemy was out there. The dominative sensory experience was the odor that pervaded everything - the smell of the human excrement used by the Koreans to fertilize the fields. Overlaying this smell was the stench of fermenting kimchi.

"My God, it stinks," John gagged and gasped for air, overcome by the all-pervasive smell. "I sure hope I don't have to walk through all that shit," he mumbled, smiling weakly.

He unloaded his survival equipment from the seat pack of the parachute and hid the remains under some brush. He then lay down again at the edge of the woods to observe the area for movement, particularly the movement of militia. There was no sound and no activity. He knew his plane was still flying when he bailed out. What he didn't know was that it had exploded in flight twenty miles away and, therefore, there was no wreckage resembling a crashed plane to alert the local militia.

John took stock of his situation and tried to recall the things said in survival training at the Marine Base, Camp Pendleton. He had a canteen, three K-rations, four sticks of jerky, four candy bars, a compass, a flashlight, poncho, .38-caliber pistol, a hunting knife, and three weeks' supply of iodine tablets for water purification, probably the most limiting factor of all his possessions. After the iodine ran out, he would be forced to drink from local streams, and only God knew what was in them. He reviewed the survival rules. Avoid the ridgelines, roads, paths, and habitation. Keep to the forest edges. Watch for children or old ladies gathering firewood. Travel at night. Keep a low profile. John prepared to wait.

Three hours later there was still no sign of militia searching for him. "No sense in moving if no one is looking for me. If they knew I had landed in the area, there would be search parties out by now," he reasoned. "I'll just stay until morning to see whether a RESCAP or search planes show up." He then checked his signal mirror, cleaning its polished surface. It was his only means of communicating with the search aircraft.

Night came quickly, and the moon came up. *Holy Shit! I forgot about the moon!* John thought as he lay watching the weather begin to clear. Although a light drizzle continued to fall, he could now see patches of stars where the clouds had been swept away. _*Moonlight is a double-edged sword. It cuts both ways. It'll help me find my way, but it'll also make me more visible. If I'm careful, however, I can use it to my advantage.*_

Suddenly there were sounds of movement in the valley. By moonlight John could see about twenty soldiers moving slowly down the road. Afraid that they might be looking for him, he pulled back more deeply into his cover, but they continued to straggle along the road, chattering in Korean or Chinese with their rifles slung upside down as protection against the drizzle. John watched them until they were out of sight.

Damn! I forgot they move mostly at night because of the road interdiction effort. But, they're moving slowly and making no effort to keep quiet. Hopefully I'll hear them in time to hide.

Morning arrived with no sign of RESCAP or search planes over John's position. The USAF had initiated an intensive search effort, but the search was concentrated twenty miles to the southeast where Kimpo radar last tracked his aircraft. As the day wore on with no sign of them, John became more and more convinced that he would not be rescued by air. It was also apparent that the North Koreans were not searching for him either.

I'll just have to walk out, and he began to organize his meager possessions for travel, including additional strips of the parachute to provide dressing changes for the wound which at this point was red and angry, but as yet showed no sign of infection. His body was stiff from the long night on the cold ground.

He fingered the amulet attached to the flight suit - the one that Sylvie had given him. *Okay, lucky piece. Let's see you do your stuff.* John got up, shouldered his possessions and slowly started walking.

The trip was slow and painful, but the terrain was not mountainous or even terribly hilly which made walking much easier.

After four hours he sat down on the edge of a glade to rest. He had made good time, and his leg was doing okay, but his ribs hurt like hell.

Must have bruised them, when I went through the trees.

Suddenly he heard a rustling nearby. He became alert, his senses keen, fear rising sharply within him, causing the adrenaline to pump rapidly. Looking around slowly for any threat, he touched his pistol in its holster to make sure it was in position. Seeing nothing he began to relax a bit.

Must have been a small animal.

Then, without warning, a small girl stood in front him. His adrenaline peaked again and fear gripped him, but he managed to control it. They stared at each other, the wounded man and the child. She made no move to run. Instead she reached into the pocket of her dirty smock and pulled out a piece of dried apple. She broke it in half, put half in her mouth, and shyly offered the other half to him, saying something in Korean. Despite the fear, John smiled back, and put the dried apple in his mouth. Touched by her generosity, he reached inside his flight suit and pulled out a piece of candy bar that he had partially nibbled. He broke it in half, offered half to her and put the other half in his mouth. She studied him, said something in Korean, bowed to him, and took the candy. A faint smile broke the serious lines of her face as she turned and continued along the edge of the glade, picking up small twigs as she went and making no effort to run towards the village. When she was out of sight, John's first reaction was to run like hell, and then he realized with a strong sense of fatalism that she was no threat.

If she tells the village, they'll find me regardless of what I do. So I won't waste my energy running. I'll need it later. There are many South Korean sympathizers in the north. Many ROK officers have relatives, even family in North Korea. Maybe I just lucked out again! He rubbed the jade talisman on his flight suit, picked up his pack, and started out again walking towards the MLR as dusk was falling.

The most difficult part of the journey, besides the fear of the unknown, was crossing roads, and circumnavigating villages. Getting around the villages was a matter of luck and timing. John found the best time was around 2200 when the village had settled down to sleep, and the dogs were not yet alert. He had discovered that later in the night the slightest movement or noise would attract the animals' attention. At the first three villages that he went around, dogs barked and someone came out of one of the thatched huts to look. Seeing nothing they had gone back inside. After that the barking ceased.

Maybe I've acquired that right odor after lying in benjo ditches and wading through rice paddies, he grimaced. *Or should I say ripe odor! Ugh! I stink!*

On the sixth night his aviation buddies almost did him in. John was lying in a benjo ditch, watching traffic on a main artery with the intention of crossing when it was clear. Two trucks had just passed him, and there was no sign of marching troops or A-frame coolies. He was about to make his move to cross the road when he heard the sound of a prop plane with its engine throttled back close to idle.

That SOB is after those trucks. John pulled himself deeper into the ditch and covered his head with grass. Now the truck drivers also heard the plane, and were frantically pulling off the road, trying to reach a nearby grove of trees, as a dozen troops scrambled from the rear of the last truck and ran for cover.

The plane's engine roared to life as the pilot dropped his nose and dived for the trucks. A ripple of 2.5-inch rockets swished off the wing racks in a blaze of light. A second later the front truck exploded as the plane wheeled up and around to conduct a strafing run with its .50-caliber machine guns.

An F4U-5N night fighter, John murmured. *It's that damned Marine outfit at Kimpo. I love what you do guys, but please do it elsewhere! I've got to get across this road before first light, or they'll find me for sure. If I go back into the rice paddies, the locals will spot me when they come out to work in the fields. Now I've also got a batch of soldiers milling around up there near the grove of trees. There's good cover across the road if I can only get to it.* He chewed his lip nervously, debating his next move.

It was now 0300 and the flames from the burning truck had almost died down. In the faint light John could see some men working under the raised hood of the surviving truck, with the soldiers clustered around the workers watching them.

Well, it's now or never, John growled, rising up from the benjo ditch and cautiously approaching the road. One more anxious look at

205

the soldiers barely visible in the dark, and then he scurried across the road. As he did so, he thought he saw one of the soldiers turn around and look back towards him.

John hunkered down in the weeds alongside the road, and then crawled into some nearby rushes, all the time watching the soldier who was still looking in his direction. Very slowly the soldier started walking back down the road in the direction of his hiding place.

Shit! What the hell do I do now? If I turn and run for the woods, he'll see me. If I stay here, he may stumble on me. John took his .38-caliber revolver out of his shoulder holster, checked the cartridges, and cocked it. *I'm going to sit tight here and wait. If he finds me, I'll shoot him and hope the others don't hear it. The .38 is not too loud, but if they do hear it, there's nothing I can do. I might as well sit here and shoot until they shoot me or I run out of ammunition.* John positioned himself for the encounter.

The soldier approached slowly and cautiously, his rifle at the ready. John sat and waited, the fear gone, but the adrenaline pumping heavily. About six feet from John the soldier stopped and scanned the rushes, standing still like a bird dog for thirty seconds. In the background could be heard the banging and clanking of the men trying to fix the engine of the truck, overlaid with the shouts and gibberish of the observers.

I won't wait for him to see me! If he keeps coming towards me, and I know he'll find me, then I'll shoot him before he can do anything.

The sharp crack of John's .38 split the air - at the same time that the truck's engine started running, and backfiring convulsively. The soldier fell to the ground with a small hole in the forehead. The other soldiers continued to concentrate on the truck. John rubbed the talisman and smiled. Without further hesitation, he headed out as fast as he could, and continued a forced march without rest for twenty-four hours. There was no sign of pursuit.

At the end of ten days John ran out of parachute strips to change his dressing. After that he just tried to clean the wound each time after being in the ditches or rice paddies, and then put the soiled bandages back on. The wound was showing signs of festering, and it was very painful.

2739 Maple Drive
San Diego

"Sullivan residence," Sylvia said, answering the phone while she blew her fresh nail polish dry. Kat was finally content in her playpen with some toys, and Sylvia had a few seconds to herself.

"Sylvia, this is Peg. Can I come over for a few minutes?"

"Peg, I'm just getting ready to go to the store. Why don't you come by in an hour so you can stay awhile, and we can visit?"

"I'm leaving now Sylvia. Please don't leave before I get there," Peg hung up.

"What the hell?" Sylvia responded, irritated at Peg, and her preemptive manner. "That's not like her."

Sylvia checked the grocery list again and added a few new items - then crossed the hall and looked out to watch for Peg's car. After a few moments she saw an official Navy sedan slow and turn into her street. With great trepidation she watched as the car slowly continued up the street towards her house. Sylvia's worst nightmare was actually happening in slow motion. The icy fingers of fear began to clutch and grab at her chest and she had difficulty breathing.

"Oh God! Please don't let it stop here!" She whispered to her pounding heart. The black sedan inched its way up to the curb and stopped. The doors opened and Peg and Mike got out of the car and started up the walk, followed by two other officers.

"No! No! No! Please, God, no!" In her horror Sylvia couldn't believe that this was happening to her. Not to her! Not John! It just couldn't be! There had to be a mistake!

She opened the door and stared in disbelief at Peg coming up the walk.

"Is he .. ?" Her eyes said the rest.

"Oh Sylvie, dear! I'm so sorry. John is missing in action," Peg said, as she ran to her and wrapped her arms around her like a mother protecting an injured child. "Oh my poor child, come into the house and Mike will tell you what we know." Peg stroked Sylvia's hair as she led her back into the living room, whispering softly, "Oh Sylvie, darling. It'll be alright. You mustn't lose hope - missing isn't hopeless! We're here to help you through this."

Her eyes bright with unshed tears, Peg gently moved the stunned Sylvia toward the sofa. Sylvia allowed herself to be maneuvered to the familiar couch and stared out with unseeing eyes. Peg sat down next to her, wrapping a protective arm around her.

"Sylvia, this is Chaplain Bristol and Doctor Ames from Balboa. Mike, tell Sylvia what we know, please."

Mike sat down and took Sylvia's icy hands in his huge paws.

"It's not much, Sylvie. John was hit by a MiG twenty miles south of the Yalu River. He was headed back to Kimpo with a damaged engine which he had shut down. He told Kimpo Tower that he did not have the altitude to glide all the way and that he would have to use his engine again when he ran out of altitude. When he was south of P'yongyang, he called the tower and said he was starting his engine. Kimpo radar was tracking him. Shortly after engine start, he disappeared from the scope.

"The weather was shitty and an air search couldn't begin until the next day. The search aircraft found nothing in the area where the contact disappeared - no plane, no debris, no flashing mirror signals and interestingly - no apparent searching by the militia." He paused and sighed.

"So we just don't know, Sylvia. The plane could have blown up with him in it or he could have bailed out. If he did, he's either evading or he's a POW. The Air Force is sending a plane every day to look for a signal mirror flash from him. So far, no luck, but we mustn't give up hope." Mike took his handkerchief from his pocket and wiped the tears from his eyes, tears that he had been trying so hard to hold back.

Kat, sensing something was wrong, began to wail in her playpen.

Mike searched his mind trying to make sense of the data. *He's probably gone. The plane probably blew up with him in it, guessing from what information we got. Damn! Chances of his surviving are really slim. The best we can hope for is that he punched out and couldn't send a Mayday, in which case the gooks'll have him.*

Sylvia just sat there, staring straight ahead with no comment. When Kat started to cry, she rose to gather the unhappy infant in her arms. The Chaplin gently spoke. "Mrs. Sullivan, you'll find comfort in prayer and in your religion. God will not desert you in your time of need."

Angered at his sanctimonious words, Sylvia looked at him, her eyes focusing for the first time, her lips pressed in a hard line.

"Chaplain, I know you have to say all these fine words to feed me some pabulum so I'll calm down. But, the truth is, God just dealt me a crappy hand! He and I are going to have some serious discussions about his conduct! I won't believe all this baloney! I want my husband back, and that's what's going to happen! John is not dead! Nor is he a POW! He's alive and he'll get back. I know him too well to believe otherwise! Somehow he'll do it!" She took another breath and addressed the doctor, who was slowly shaking his head at her performance.

"Thank you for coming Doctor, but I will be fine! I'm not going to flip out! Please leave some sleeping pills with Peg for me; I might need them. And now I'd like to be alone with my friends. Please leave me."

"Thank you, Chaplain," Mike said quietly. "And take the car. We'll make it back by ourselves."

As the door closed behind the two officers, Peg bit her lip and mumbled, *My God! She may not be able to accept the fact that he's lost! He's either dead or captured - and that's worse. You just don't walk out of Korea! The odds are against it!*

Mike sat down in the armchair, fighting the urge for one of his cigars, and waited for Sylvia to respond.

Her face was grim and tearful, but she said nothing. She rested her cheek on tiny Kat's soft hair. Suddenly, her facial muscles relaxed, the tears stopped, and she spoke softly. "John will be back. I know he will! You just wait and see. I know he will!" Turning to Peg, she added, "would you please call my mother for me. Tell her what happened. I'll talk to her as soon as I can get myself together - but I can't now. The number is in the directory next to the phone. I need to be alone for a while with my baby. Thank you both." With that, she rose and went into the bedroom and closed the door to grieve in private.

Peg turned to Mike as she picked up the phone, "Mike darling. Why don't you go on? I'll stay here with Sylvie for a while, and make some calls. As soon as the word gets out, this place will be flooded with people. Check the booze before you go and get what's needed, will you? Also ice. I'll take care of the food. A few calls to the other wives and we'll be loaded with eats. Thank God for good Navy friends at times like this. Oh, why did this have to happen to such good people? Why does it have to happen at all!" She bit her lip and regained her composure as the call to Ohio was answered.

Bernice and Franklin arrived in L.A. on the American Airlines All-Nighter from Chicago. Franklin rented a car at the airport and they drove the three hours to San Diego silently - each of them alone with their own thoughts. Sylvia greeted them at the door and Bernice was surprised at her composure. When asked about it, Sylvia replied, her shoulders straight, her head up and her eyes bright.

"I'm a Navy wife. My husband is a fighter pilot. We know about death. We know about POW camps. We know about loneliness - and we can handle it. We are expected to handle it. It is part of our code - the Wives' Code." Her lips quivered and she collapsed into her mother's arms in tears.

Main Line of Resistance
North Korea

John lay under a rotten tree trunk which had fallen across a narrow gully. It was the only piece of foliage remaining in the area. The shallow valley in front of him was barren, pockmarked by shell craters with a few lonely splintered tree trunks. Two or three muddy rutted roads crossed the barren land, and numerous footpaths wove a latticework of random patterns across the area. The main trails headed south. The ground gently rose up towards a ridge where John could see earthworks near the top leading down to log and earth-covered bunkers on the down slope side.

John had lain there for twenty-four hours already, watching and waiting like a cat stalking its prey. His body was stiff and sore from travel. He tried to sleep whenever possible, but he mostly dozed, his senses always on the alert. His body was greatly weakened from lack of food, and his mouth parched for water. The last drink had been three days ago. John moved his cracked lips and tried to scratch three weeks' worth of beard and stubble that covered his face. He was filthy and miserable and his wound was infected.

This is a great hideout he said to himself, shifting slightly to ease his discomfort on the hard earth. *I've watched the movement of the troops and the A-frame peasants carrying supplies and ammunition from the rear. And I've learned a lot about the location of the gook's emplacements and lateral movement among the bunkers. Most important, I now know their command structure. There obviously is a break in the command layout between emplacements on the immediate left and those on the right. There's a gap between two bunkers which the troops do not cross. It must be the flanks of two battalions, maybe regiments. What did the Marines say at Camp LeJeune during our summer training? Try to find the locations of two units and hit them in between, because that's the weakest point. I know where that is now and that's where I'm going through!*

I also think I know where the front line is. I've seen and heard sights and sounds that could only be the front. It's got to be over that ridge where the flares and star shells light up the night whenever the machine guns chatter or the mortars whoomp. The no man's land has to be over that ridge. Please God, let it not be far! I've got just enough strength left for one more big push, and then I'm through. I know it. John sighed and closed his eyes to rest in preparation for his move through no man's land.

John lay in a shell hole just over the top of the ridge, and tried to smile. There it was - the no man's land between the opposing forces! From his position on the down side of the crest with North Korean emplacements on both sides of him, John could see the rise on the opposite side of the shallow valley, and on it were the UN emplacements.

They have to be ours because they're not exposed in this direction, and they sit close to the top of the ridge. If it were another level of gook stuff, the bunkers would be exposed here on the down slope with openings visible, his mind fully alert and active. *I also see a nice defilade off to the right. If I can get to it, I'll be screened from the gooks. Just have to worry about the Americans who will have the area well covered, I'm sure. It looks like a relatively smooth and shallow grade. Maybe there'll be some breaks in the barbed wire. Anyway here we go!* He fingered the small jade amulet, now encrusted with mud and filth.

John slid down the embankment, and began to crawl towards the UN lines, moving when the scud blocked out the moon's light, and lying dormant when it broke up.

First Cavalry Sector
Main Line of Resistance

"Jesus, man! Did you just fart, or what? It's been stinking up here for two hours! One fart after another! Smells like a goddamned shithouse. Maybe one of the new guys crapped in our communication trench - the fucking bastard," PFC Bruce Johnson griped, leaning against the sand bags that shaped one of the forward bunkers of the First Cavalry defenses. "Shit, Corporal, I sure could use a fucking smoke about now. Phewy!"

The bunker was situated in barren land, facing north across no man's land towards the gook emplacements. What little previous vegetation there was had also been removed to provide clear zones of fire - the killing zones. The bunker itself was dug into the ground four feet and sand bagged around the top with small ports between some of the bags. A wooden platform allowed the occupants to peer over the top or slide their rifles and BAR's through a port. It also provided a dry place to sit above the eternal mud that comes with war. A narrow communications trench connected the outpost to the rest of the trench complex and led to the bunker where the company commander, an Army Captain, had his command post.

"I sure wish I had a cigarette, buddy. This night is long and it's damned cold. How much longer before we're relieved?" PFC Johnson bitched again.

"It's 0400 now. Two hours to go," Corporal Adams replied, blowing his breath into his gloves to warm his hands.

"Sure would like a cigarette. Need one bad. Damned bad!"

"You light up out here, asshole, and if the gooks don't get you, the sergeant will. And if he doesn't get you, it'll be me. I don't want any fucking gook mortars coming down on me because you want a smoke. And keep your fucking voice down."

"Shush. I hear something," the hair on the PFC's head stood on end and the back of his neck prickled, as he carefully unslung his M-1 Garand rifle, laid it silently on the parapet, and placed the butt against his shoulder.

"What is it?" Corporal Adams asked softly, looking warily over the parapet. Then he heard it - an American voice in a stage whisper.

"Hey guys, I'm Lieutenant junior grade John Sullivan. I want to come in. You can check me out first if you want. I'm an exchange pilot from the Navy with the 334th Fighter Squadron at Kimpo. I was shot down in my F-86 four weeks ago in MiG Alley. My mother's name is Mary Ellen O'Connor. What else do you want to know?"

"Jesus, if he's for real, he's right in the middle of our minefield! Johnson, get the Sergeant of the Guard! On the double!" After Johnson had scuttled away, Corporal Adams quietly addressed the stranger out in no man's land.

"Okay, Lieutenant Sullivan. Answer some questions, but keep your voice low. Who's the coach of the Cleveland Browns' baseball team?"

"Hey guy, the Browns play football. Their coach is Paul Brown."

"Okay. What university is trying to steal him?"

"Ohio State. They want him back."

"Okay. Who's the slugger for the Yankees?"

"Joe DiMaggio."

"What town?"

"New York."

"His wife?"

"Marilyn Monroe, but I think they're separated."

The Sergeant of the Guard arrived. "Who is he?"

"A Navy exchange pilot with the 4th Fighter Interceptor Wing at Kimpo - the 334th squadron. I've asked him sports questions. He knows the answers. I think he's for real and not some goddamned gook."

"Corporal, get the lieutenant up here and have the bunker contact the 334th squadron to confirm what he says."

"Sergeant, he's in the middle of our minefield."

"Jesus! Okay. Lieutenant Sullivan, listen to me," the Sergeant whispered over the parapet. "Tell me exactly where you are."

"I'm on the edge of a large shell hole next to a large flat rock, sticking up a little above the ground."

"That's our turn point! Get the map!" exclaimed the Corporal.

Lieutenant Roger Blackston arrived. "He checks out at Kimpo. Let's bring him in."

"Lieutenant, you got a compass?" the Sergeant asked John.

"Yeah," John replied.

"Okay. Follow these instructions carefully. You're right in the middle of our mine field."

"Holy shit! That's all I need," John muttered.

"Okay, listen. Come out of the shell hole at the point of the rock. Take ten steps heading 190 magnetic. Then twenty steps 195. Then left to 170. From there come in very slowly, standing so we can see you."

"I'm not sure I can stand."

John raised himself up and tried to push himself out of the shell hole. In his weakened condition, he couldn't do it. "Give me a minute, guys. I'm having trouble getting myself out of this crater." John tried again but slid back down, exhausted by the effort.

"What's the trouble, Lieutenant?"

"I'm too weak to climb the side. It's slippery. Haven't had anything to eat in three weeks and no water in three days. Let me rest and try again."

"Where're you going, Sergeant? " Lieutenant Blackston asked, as the Sergeant put his rifle down, and started up over the parapet.

"I'm going out there and bring that poor son of a bitch in, sir! He's almost home, but he's almost gone! I'm not leaving him out there to die! I planted those mines myself, and I know where every fucking one of them is." He quickly crawled over the top of the parapet and headed out for John.

The Sergeant reappeared about five minutes later, half dragging John who was desperately trying to stand and walk.

"Jesus, look at him!" Lieutenant Blackston cried out in amazement. He jumped up on the parapet to help the Sergeant drag John into the bunker. His clothes were in tatters and his hair and beard covered with mud and green slime. And he stunk! God, did he stink! But his eyes were bright and his teeth shone through a wide grin.

"I made it! I made it! By God! I made it!" John said softly, his voice cracking with emotion. He began to shake all over as the tension in his body subsided.

PFC Johnston held his nose and replied, "Lord, Lieutenant. You smell like a walking shithouse."

"Yeah," the Corporal added. "That's all the farts I been smelling." He raised his hands, smelled them, and wrinkled his nose disgustedly. "Now I stink too."

"My friend," the Sergeant continued with awe in his voice. "You are one lucky son of a bitch. You walked all the way through our minefield. You should have been blown to bits." He shook his shaggy head in disbelief.

"You got any injuries, Lieutenant?" Brackston asked.

"Yeah, my right thigh. It got ripped up by trees when I came down in my chute."

"Okay. Corporal, take him to the aid station. Let them look at him. Then take him to battalion. Maybe they can clean some of the stink off him and give him some clothes. I'm sure the intelligence guys at battalion want to quiz him."

Company Aid Station
First Cavalry Division

"Let's take a look at it, Lieutenant," the corpsman said, peeling back the bandage. He took one look and closed it up.

"Hey, aren't you even going to change the bandage?" the Corporal growled, dragging on his cigarette.

"Just get him back to the battalion aid station immediately."

"I'm supposed to take him to intelligence."

"Corporal, I said take him to battalion aid. This man's sick. Let intelligence debrief him there. Get a Stokes stretcher and two troopers to carry him. He'll never make it by himself."

Battalion Aid Station
First Cavalry Division

"You smell a whale of a lot better now, Lieutenant," the doctor smiled at him. "Now that you've been doused and scrubbed in our makeshift shower."

"That's a great contraption, Doc, with the fifty-five gallon drum and the hose coming down from it."

"The best we can do, and the only one in the battalion," the doctor chuckled.

"I never knew clean skivvies could feel so good."

The doctor cleaned John's wound, bandaged it, and inserted a IV needle into John's wrist. He then hung the IV bag on a rod attached to the Stokes stretcher.

"Lieutenant, we have a chopper coming in at first light to take you to the MASH."

"What's a MASH? I don't understand this Army lingo," John asked weakly.

"It's the Mobile Army Surgical Hospital, a full-blown hospital right here at the gates of hell!"

"What's wrong with my leg?" John asked, concerned.

"My friend, you have one helluva case of gangrene. I've given you a massive dose of penicillin - more than I should probably, but the infection is really bad."

"Lieutenant," the intelligence officer said to John at the end of his interrogation. "I've drawn a map of your movements approaching our lines, based on what you told us. Does this look correct?" He handed John the paper.

"Looks good, sir."

"Now look at this one," he continued, handing John another sheet. John looked at it, and then looked at the first paper.

"They look the same."

"My friend," the intelligence officer replied. "The second sheet is ours. It shows the safe passage route through the minefield. You followed it like you had the map. Talk about luck," he laughed, and then suddenly stopped and said, "Tell me, Lieutenant, what made you take that route?"

"It was the natural way to go," John replied. "I reconnoitered your approach from the opposite ridge - where the gook emplacements are. The route I took looked like the easiest way to get up the hill, and I was so tired that I couldn't have gone any other way. In short, it was the easiest way."

The intelligence officer stared at him for a moment, trying to decide if he was telling the truth or making up a story. Then he said, "Thank you, Lieutenant. You just did us one big favor. It looks like we picked a route that telegraphs the directions. If you can do it, so can the gooks. I think we'd better review how we laid this access down."

3049 MASH Unit
South Korea

Colonel Jason Wolfe, Commander, 4th Fighter Interceptor Wing, and Captain Rex Taggart, Red Flight Leader, joined Colonel Langston Sharp, Commander 3047 MASH at the helo pad as the medevac chopper carrying John went into hover, blowing dirt and debris as it prepared to land on the pad fifty feet away. Two patients, one of them John, were lifted off the helo's struts in their Stokes stretchers, and placed in the waiting ambulance to be transported to the hospital a short distance from the pad.

"You want to say hello, Jake, before we take him in for examination?" Colonel Sharp asked.

"Hi Sailor," Rex said, slipping inside the meat wagon, and shaking John's hand. "That hundredth mission was a bitch, wasn't it, buddy?"

John tried to smile. "Thanks for coming, Rex. It's good to see a familiar face."

"And you know the boss, Colonel Jake," Rex said as the Commander of the 4th FIW slipped in alongside Rex, and found a seat.

"Hey John, that was quite a feat, walking out like you did. The E and E guys will want to talk to you about your tactics for escape and evasion."

"Not much to say, Colonel. Just kept walking south," John attempted to chuckle.

"Why don't you two ride in with him, Jake. I'll meet you in my office," Colonel Sharp said, closing the doors to the meat wagon. He stood back to let the ambulance clear, and then watched as it made the short trip, his hands on his hips and his jacket slung open. "They aren't going to like the news they're going to get. Battalion said he's got a horrendous case of gangrene. We'll probably lose the poor bastard. And after all he's gone through to get back. Rotten shame!"

Commander's Office
3047th MASH

"Gentlemen, your pilot is in bad shape. He's got a massive gangrene infection. Gangrene can be treated with penicillin, if you get it soon enough. But, that may not be the case here. These infections, when left unattended for any period of time, tend to overwhelm the type of penicillin we have at this unit. If it spreads any more, he's dead," Colonel Sharp said, summarizing John's condition. "This guy also has a couple of cracked ribs. Must have happened when he landed in the trees. The breaks are fused now. We'll have to break them and reset them. How did he ever walk out with the pain?"

"How did he do it?" Jake laughed. "It's called desire, Colonel. You can do it, if you want it bad enough. There are also people who just give up. When they do, they're dead. This guy's a survivor! He doesn't give up!"

"We should take the leg off right now. But he's so weak, he probably won't survive the operation. We're in a dilemma, Jake. We need to get him to Tokyo General as soon as possible, but a medevac trip to Tokyo in a gooney bird is a long process. If we don't send him, he'll probably die. If we do send him, the trip will probably kill him. If we take the leg off now, he probably won't survive the operation."

"You need to get him to Tokyo quickly?" Colonel Jake asked.

"Yeah Jake, that's his only chance. The sooner the better."

"How about an ETA in two hours?" Jake pulled his ear lobe.

"Great - but wishful thinking," the head of MASH replied sadly, shaking his head.

"Can I use your phone?" Jake asked, already picking up the receiver.

"This is the First Cav switch, sir," came the voice of the operator.

"This is Colonel Wolfe, Commander 4th Fighter Interceptor Wing. Please patch me to base operations at Kimpo."

"One moment, sir,"

"This is Major Rose, the Operations Duty Officer. Can I help you?"

"Jimmy, Colonel Jake from the 4th."

"Yes, sir, Colonel. What can I do for you today?"

"You still got that T-33 from Tachikawa parked out front - the one you showed me when I had coffee with you this morning?"

"Yes, sir. He's still here. Due to leave any minute."

"Hold him, Jimmy. Do not let him leave! Better yet, if you can find the pilot, put him on the horn," Jake said in a command tone that left no doubt in Major Rose's mind of the importance of the request. Jake could hear Major Rose as he yelled, "Hey, Buzz. Colonel Jake wants to talk to you. Pronto, buddy. Move it!"

"Colonel, this is Buzz Steward, pilot of the T-33. What can I do for you, sir?"

"Who you got in the back seat, Major?"

"A light bird from staff getting his flight time."

"Good. Tell him he's not going back with you. My orders. We'll get him out later."

"Okay by me, Colonel," the pilot of the T-33 replied delightedly. "He's been a royal pain in the ass the entire trip. He'll scream to high heaven."

Colonel Jake laughed, "Okay. If he's there, put him on."

Jake could hear Major Rose calling for the light colonel.

"Yes sir," the light colonel said to Jake.

"This is Colonel Wolfe, Commander 4th Fighter Interceptor Wing. I'm sorry to inconvenience you, but we have one of our pilots who walked out of North Korea after being shot down. He's in bad shape, and we've decided to medevac him in the backseat of the T-33. Sorry."

"Colonel, you can't do that! I'm on flight orders and I need to get back. I have a dinner engagement with the general." Jake looked at Rex, pointed to the phone, and gave the French salute by throwing both hands up at the shoulder. Rex smiled and played hearts and flowers on an imaginary violin.

"Well, Colonel," Jake replied sarcastically. "I think this boy's life is more important than your dinner engagement. And I'm sure the general will understand."

"But Colonel, why can't he go on the regular medevac flight? If you bump me, I will, of course, have to file a report of this with my general."

Jake lost his temper. "Listen to me, asshole! You are not going! My orders! And I hope you're not stupid enough to try to give me trouble later! If I get any static, I guarantee you that your next duty station will be the island of Shemya at the tip of the Aleutians. It's so isolated that the charter flights refueling there don't let their stewardesses get off the plane! Now shut up and put the pilot back on!"

"Yes sir, Colonel. Didn't hear what you said, but it must have been great!" Buzz laughed.

"Buzz, the ops duty officer will cut you written orders, based on my verbals, to keep you out of trouble. You are now an official medevac flight. Make sure those guys at Tachikawa have an ambulance waiting. Also contact Red One Flight at Kimpo, if you need flight gear. They can give you John's spare. Have a good flight."

Colonel Wolfe hung up and turned to the hospital commander. "Can Lieutenant Sullivan ride in my helo?"

"Sure, Jake, it's a short flight."

"Great! He'll be on his way out of Kimpo in less than an hour."

"How about a quick cup of coffee while they get him ready, Jake? It'll be about ten minutes."

"Not a bad idea. Black, please. And will you notify the chopper pilot of the departure time and the patient's condition?" Jake put his cap on the coffee table and dropped into the adjacent chair, waiting for the cup of java.

"You know, Jake, Lieutenant Sullivan has some kind of amulet that he cherishes. The nurses told me about it. It's a piece of circular jade. He had a fit when one of them tried to take it off of him. Says it got him out of North Korea. She finally put it on a thong around his neck and he was satisfied."

"Yeah, I've seen it," Rex laughed. "I think some Chinese honey gave it to him in Hong Kong. They must have had a really good time. But I'm not one to talk about superstitions!" He pulled out his wallet and showed a St. Christopher medal. "Flyers are very superstitious, doctor. I won't fly without my Saint Chris. I misplaced it once and grounded myself for three days until I found it."

Jake laughed, "I have a lock of my wife's hair in a small plastic container. That's my lucky piece. Won't fly without it." The two flyers smiled and looked at each other in acknowledgement of their feelings about luck. The doctor just shook his head.

One of the nurses came to the door. "Colonel, we're ready to launch."

"Okay, Rex. Let's kick the tire and light the fire. It's time to get the hell out of here."

"Right Jake," Rex replied, picking up his hat and heading for the door. "As the shepherd said when he saw the wolf - Let's get the flock out of here."

"Thanks, Colonel, for MASH's help. You're great as always," Jake said and gave the Colonel a solid handclasp.

"Always glad to help the troops, Jake. That's what we're here for."

USAF T-33 # 85115
75 miles west of Tachikawa

"Tachikawa Tower. Air Force 85115. Seventy-five miles west for landing. I'm a designated medevac flight."

"This is Tachikawa. Say again. You're a what?"

"115. I'm operating under medevac orders. I have a very ill and wounded passenger in the backseat. He needs immediate transfer by ambulance to Tokyo General."

"Air Force 85115. Roger. The duty officer will meet you at the T-33 parking area."

"Negative, Tachikawa. You're not putting me out in the toolies where it will take forever to get any action. My passenger is very sick. I want to park where you put the medevac flights."

"Roger 115. I'll inform the duty officer."

Air Force 85115 pulled into the parking area reserved for medevac flights and shut down. The base operations duty officer, a pudgy and visibly annoyed major, climbed up on the plane's steps while Buzz was completing the shutdown checklist.

"What in the hell are you doing, Major? And who's the guy in the backseat?"

"I'll explain later," Major Rose replied, standing up in the cockpit and forcing the duty officer off the steps. Jumping to the ground from the last step and removing his helmet and oxygen mask, he continued. "Where's the ambulance?"

"Let's get your passenger out of the plane. He can walk into base ops while we settle this little matter," the Duty Officer fumed.

Major Rose gave a gesture of despair and stuck his face belligerently into the face of the duty officer. "You don't seem to understand English, Major. I said I want the ambulance that was supposed to be waiting for my arrival, and I want it now! My passenger is incapable of walking by himself to the waiting room. Until we get him into an ambulance and on his way to Tokyo General, there is nothing to discuss. Now where's the goddamned ambulance?"

"I'll order it as soon as we settle this," the duty officer snapped, his face red with anger.

Major Rose reached out and jerked the walkie-talkie out of the duty officer's hand.

"What's the CO's call sign?" Rose demanded.

"Tiger One, but you can't call him. That's for emergencies only," the duty officer shouted furiously, reaching out to retrieve his walkie-talkie.

Rose shoved him back. "Can't I?" he retorted, putting the unit to his lips.

"Tiger One. This is ops duty."

"Roger, ops duty, Tiger One here. Why are you using non-standard voice procedures?"

"Sorry sir, but I don't know the correct ones. I'm Major Rose. I just brought a T-33 in from Kimpo with a medevac patient and I can't get an ambulance for him."

"A T-33 operating as a medevac? Isn't that a little unusual, Major?"

"Yes sir, but I've got an F-86 pilot who was shot down over North Korea and walked out. The MASH CO said he would die if we didn't get him to Tokyo Hospital fast. Sir, this is a real emergency!"

"And just who authorized this unusual procedure?"

"Colonel Wolfe, sir."

"Jake Wolfe, the Commander of the 4th Fighter Interceptor Wing?"

"I think his first name is Jason, but yes sir, the 4th FIW."

"Major, you'll have your ambulance in five minutes. If Jake Wolfe authorized this, that's good enough for me."

The radio crackled with static as a new voice came on the circuit. "Sir, this is Sergeant Lyons at the medical transportation garage. Sorry to eavesdrop on your conversation, sir, but the ambulance just left. Be there in two minutes." The colonel could hear the siren in the background.

"Thanks, Sarge. You do good work."

"Any time, sir."

CHAPTER 11

Army General Hospital
Tokyo, Japan

Captain Sandra Hall, her face lined with fatigue, dropped wearily into a chair near the emergency desk at Tokyo General. She had just completed five surgeries as part of Surgical Team A and was exhausted. She had two more hours to go.

And then a hot bath, a drink, and something to eat - if there's anything in the frig, she sighed. *I'm really beat.*

An aid came through the emergency entrance. Through the open door Sandra could see an ambulance backing up to the unloading platform. "Captain, we got another one just arrived from Tachikawa. Driver says he's in bad shape."

"Okay Joe, I'll look at him," Sandra replied, getting out of her chair, resigned to another two hours of work before the bath.

The aid pulled the gurney to a stop in front of her. As she leaned over it to examine the patient, he rolled his head toward her, and murmured something unintelligible.

"My God! John Sullivan!" she exclaimed.

"You know him?" the aid asked.

"Yes, I do. Where's his record?" Sandra asked as she took his pulse.

"He's in from the 3047th MASH in Korea. Driver said something about being medevac'd by T-33. How about that, Captain?" The aid said, making conversation.

"Never mind, Sammy. Let's get a look at that wound," she said, pulling the tape off one end of the bandage while Sammy peeled back the other. John didn't move despite the obvious pulling of hairs as the tape came off his skin.

"Oh my God! Look at that!" she exclaimed, frightened. "Sammy, page Doctor Meadows! Use the patient emergency code!"

John, John. What have you done to yourself? Sandra softly lamented as she bent over and laid her hand against his cheek. He was on fire!

Doctor Meadows pulled the green mask from his face, exposing a grim-lipped mouth. He and Sandra walked over to the nurse's station.

"It's a bad case of gangrene, Sandra," he announced, his face puckered with concern. "It may have gone too far already to save his leg. We may have to take it off."

"Oh, Doctor Meadows. Don't say that! He's a fighter pilot," Sandra cried out in anguish.

"Well, we'll see what the experts say in the morning. But, I'm afraid we have no choice. Amputation is the only solution!" He looked at her for a moment, and then turned and left.

Surgical Lounge
Tokyo General Hospital

The surgical staff met at 0800. Sandra sat in a soft lounge chair, her body exhausted with fatigue from the all-night session caring for John. She had stopped in the cafeteria for coffee and a doughnut and then had gone to her locker to change her uniform and brush her hair, but she still looked out of tired, bleary eyes.

"Okay guys," the Chief Surgeon said. "Let's go. Doctor Walsh, what's on the agenda?"

The surgical resident replied. "First on the list is Lieutenant jg John Sullivan. A massive case of gangrene. Prognosis poor. Assigned team A."

"Sir," the Chief of Surgical Team A began. " We've slowed the spread of the infection significantly, but have not stopped it. It is our opinion that the infection will continue to spread despite the massive penicillin dosage that we are giving him. We're playing a delicate game, trying to build him up enough to survive surgery, and yet not wait too long. I estimate we have no more than three days max. We are feeding him intravenously and his body is beginning to respond. His temperature is moderate down from what it was when he arrived. If it begins to increase, the leg comes off." He leaned back in his chair and looked across the conference table at his colleagues for concurrence.

"Doctor," Sandra interrupted before any of the doctors could respond. "I've been reading about the new and more powerful strains of penicillin being tested by NIH. What about using them?"

"They're experimental and we'd have a hard time getting them. Besides, it would take too long," He replied, shaking his head negatively.

"But can't we try, Doctor?" Sandra persisted.

The doctor smiled thinly at Sandra, trying not to show his irritation at being questioned by a nurse. "Sandra, from your actions in the ward, it's apparent that you are emotionally involved with this patient. He's not just another patient to you, is he? You're constantly at his side. In fact, you're beginning to lose medical perspective. There are other patients that also need attention," he gently chided.

"But Doctor, the man's a pilot - a Korean ace. It'll kill him if he loses his leg and can't fly!" Sandra blurted out.

"It'll kill him if he doesn't," the doctor smiled tolerantly.

COMNAVAIRPAC
North Island

It was late afternoon and Captain Mike Moran looked distastefully at the pile of papers on his desk. "Jesus, doesn't it ever stop?" He leaned back in his chair, propped his feet up, and took a coffee break.

"I'd rather be flying," he mused, sipping the black coffee, while he idly looked at the ceiling. The intercom buzzed him to attention. Mike dropped his feet, sat up straight in the chair, and flipped the switch.

"Yes?"

"Sir, it's ComFairJap's secretary on the phone. The admiral would like to talk to you."

"Good morning, Mrs. Lane. You're up early this morning. How's the admiral today?"

"Good morning, Captain Moran - or should I say good afternoon because I'm talking to you," Mrs. Lane answered. "He's grousing as usual. He retires next month and he doesn't like it."

"Why don't you all take up a collection, and buy him that F7F that he flies out there?"

Mrs. Lane laughed. "That would do it. That certainly would do it. Anyway he wants to talk to you. Good news, I think. I'll get him on the line."

"Hello, Mike," Admiral Dan Murcham said. "It's good news today. That young tiger of yours, John Sullivan? The one that was shot down over North Korea?"

"Is he a POW?" Mike interrupted, tensing and hoping desperately that John was alive.

"Hell no, Mike! That kid actually walked out of North Korea! Would you believe it? The First Cav picked him up at the MLR, and he's in Tokyo General now. The Navy liaison officer there called me just a few minutes ago. He's sending a message to Washington, info to you, as we speak now. Just thought I'd preempt it and call you personally."

"He walked out? How did he ever manage that?"

"I don't know. The details are sketchy, but I talked to Colonel Jake Wolfe at the 4th at Kimpo. He told me that he walked through the First Cav's minefield without blowing himself up. Jake also said he's in bad shape - so bad that Jake commandeered a T-33 at Kimpo to take him to Tokyo."

"Thanks for the call, Dan. Can I use this to notify the wife?"

"It's not official and you're supposed to wait - but hell, I wouldn't, Mike. Do it! I wish I could be there myself! Oh, for your info, Mike, I've made the decision this week to retire in San Diego. So Mary and I will see you soon! Give my love to Peg." The Admiral hung up the telephone, leaned back in his chair and said softly. "Thank you, God, for good things! This Sullivan is one lucky man. He must be one gutsy son of a bitch to do what he did."

He leaned forward to hit the intercom button, "Maggie. I feel so good. Do you know what I think I'll do?"

"Yes, Admiral, I certainly do." She laughed heartily. "And I'm way ahead of you. I called ops while you were on the phone to Captain Moran, and told them you'd be down to fly the Tiger Cat shortly."

Moran Residence
Coronado

" Moran residence."

"Peg! Wonderful news! John Sullivan is alive in Tokyo! Don't ask details! Get over here as fast as you can and we'll go to Sylvie! Brief you in the car!"

"She just called me, Mike. She's at home. I'm out of here now! Pick you up in front in ten." Peg hurriedly replaced the receiver, grabbed her coat and purse, and ran for the door.

2739 Maple Drive
San Diego

Peg knocked and opened the door. "Sylvie? Sylvia! Where are you? Are you home, darling?" she called and entered with Mike close behind her.

"Hi Peg. I was sewing," Sylvia said, coming out of the bedroom area. Then she saw Mike. Her face fell and tears started as she looked behind Mike for the chaplain and doctor. She leaned against the wall not sure that her legs would support her.

"No Sylvie! No! He's alive!" Peg yelled. She grabbed Sylvie and hugged her tightly. "Alive!"

Sylvie wiped tears from her eyes and managed a weak smile, shaking her head in disbelief. "Thank God, he's alive! Which POW camp? Is he hurt? When did you hear - who told you?"

"No Sylvie. No! He's free in Tokyo!" Sylvie stared for a moment in wonder before the room spun on her.

"Mike! Grab her! She's falling!"

Sylvie recovered consciousness lying on the couch, reality finally registering. "Oh Peg! Is it really true?" Sylvia said softly. "Is he really in Tokyo? I can't believe it."

229

Paul Corrigan

"He's at the Army's General Hospital in Tokyo and I understand he's quite ill," Mike interjected. "But he's alive and in capable hands. My good friend, Dan Murcham, who's ComFairJap will get more information for us ASAP."

"Thank God! He's alive! He's alive! I must call my parents right away," she said, heading for the bedroom phone.

Mike fixed himself and Peg two stiff drinks from the bottle of good scotch which Sylvia kept in the cupboard for special occasions. He carried them into the living room, where he and Peg sat and beamed at each other.

Tripler Army General Hospital
Honolulu, Hawaii

"Doctor Stone's office," his secretary answered the telephone.

"This is the Tokyo operator. I have a person-to-person call from Captain Sandra Hall for Doctor Stone."

"One moment, please. I'll find him for you." The secretary hit the interphone switch. "Doctor Stone, you have a person-to-person call from a Captain Sandra Hall in Tokyo."

"I'll be right there."

Stone entered his office through the side door and picked up the receiver.

"Sandra, so good to hear from you. Is this social or business?" he laughed.

"Doctor Frank, it's serious business, but ..." she paused. "It's personal, too."

"Oh-oh. When you talk like that, you must need something. Okay babe, shoot. What's the problem?" He leaned back in his chair.

"Frank, we have this Navy Lieutenant here with a really bad case of gangrene in the thigh. He got shot down flying F-86's in MiG Alley, bailed out and landed in a tree which ripped open his thigh. Then he walked out of North Korea. Spent over four weeks doing it, lying in benjo ditches and rice paddies to avoid capture. His fever is 101 down from 103. He's emaciated from lack of food and drink, but he's coming around. The surgeons are planning amputation." Sandra had trouble holding the tears back.

"That's probably the prudent course of action," Stone slowly replied. "But I suspect there's more to this, Sandra, or you wouldn't have called me."

"Yes, Frank. Yes, there is. This man is an ace, six kills to his credit. One hell of a fighter pilot. Flying is his life, Frank. It'll kill him to lose his leg and not fly again. Can't we save it, Frank? It means so much to him."

"And what's your personal involvement, Sandra?" Frank was now curious about the relationship.

"Deep - deep - very deep, Frank," she sighed. "I first met him at Akakura on R&R a few months ago."

"Is he your lover, Sandra?"

"No, I only wish it were so, but he's married, and well, you know me."

"Yes Sandra. I do." The doctor nodded.

"I love him so much, even if I can't have him. I'll do anything to save him - save him intact so that he can fly again. It's his life. Will you - can you help me, Frank?" Sandra pleaded, now sobbing softly.

"I owe you a lot, Sandra, for what you've done for me in the past. For you I will do it!" Doctor Stone smiled, remembering the many times that Sandra's keen eye had saved him from a bad mistake.

"Thank you - Oh thank you, Frank," she murmured gratefully.

"I have a new experimental strain of penicillin, just in from NIH. It just may be strong enough to reverse the spread of infection, but I need him here now to do it."

"Oh God, Frank! They'll never turn him loose from Tokyo General. They've already made up their minds to take the leg off. The head of the surgical team in charge of him told me to stop spending so much time with him."

Frank smiled and then replied with a dry chuckle. "Sandra, I've been around this organization too long to let a little thing like that stop me! Despite the fact that Sullivan is in Tokyo General, his parent organization, the Navy, has the final say about his treatment. It so happens that the Navy's Chief of the Bureau of Medicine and Surgery is an old friend of mine. He owes me a few favors. Get the lieutenant's medical record, call back, and read it to my secretary so I can have it. She takes great shorthand. Do you want to come with him, Sandra?" Frank smiled because he already knew the answer.

231

"Oh Frank, could you?" Sandra's eyes lighted up at the thought.

"Okay. We'll try then, Sandra. With a case this critical, I'll need someone I can trust to watch him continuously. Now be a good girl and get that record to me immediately. And don't worry, my dear," Doctor Frank said gently. "If I can't save him, no one can."

Army General Hospital
Tokyo Japan

NAVAL MESSAGE

PRIORITY   DTG 071645Z

FROM: CHIEF BUMED

TO: ARMY GENERAL HOSPITAL, TOKYO

INFO: COMFAIRJAP, FEAF, 4FIW, USAF BASE TACHIKAWA, TRIPLER GENERAL HOSPITAL

SUBJECT: LTJG JOHN FRANCIS SULLIVAN, USN, 498101 , TRANSFER OF

UNCLASSIFIED

1. CHIEF BUMED REQUESTS TRANSFER OF SUBJECT OFFICER IMMEDIATELY TO CARE OF DR. FRANK STONE, TRIPLER GENERAL HOSPITAL, HONOLULU.

2. FEAF HAS AGREED TO PROVIDE IMMEDIATE MEDEVAC SERVICE FROM TACHIKAWA. TRIPLER CONCURS WITH TRANSFER.

3. REQUEST TOKYO GENERAL PROVIDE QUALIFIED NURSE FAMILIAR WITH THE CASE TO ACCOMPANY PATIENT AND ASSIST DR. STONE IN SPECIALIZED TREATMENT FOR A PERIOD NOT TO EXCEED THREE WEEKS. TDY CHARGEABLE TO BUMED.

4. DIRLAUTH ALCON. KEEP BUMED ADVISED OF PROGRESS

The Chief of Surgery entered the office of the Commanding Officer and threw the message on his desk,

"What the hell is this!" he exploded.

"It looks like BUMED is exercising its authority over the patient to alter his treatment," the Commanding Officer replied, throwing the paper back at the Chief of Surgery.

"They can't do that! That leg needs to come off!" The Chief of Surgery shouted, his face livid with pent-up anger.

"Oh yes, they can, and there's nothing you or I can do about it, but protest - and frankly that won't do any good either. When I first saw the message an hour ago, I looked up this Doctor Frank Stone. It seems he's one of the foremost authorities on infectious diseases. He works closely with NIH on testing new drugs, and in that role has immediate access to the latest medicine even before it hits the market. Someone figured it out and had the weight to make it happen. If this kid has enough reputation to be medevaced by a T-33, then there are people who will watch out further for him. Remember, Doctor, he's a fighter ace. There aren't many, and those that are, are held in high esteem. So just relax and do it." The CO paused and then added, "And send Sandra Hall as the nurse. It's obvious they want her, and she obviously has a thing for the patient. We wouldn't want to screw this up, my friend, or the feces will hit the props."

The Chief of Surgery just stood there glaring at his boss.

Finally, the Commanding Officer rose and leaned over his desk supporting himself on his rigid arms, his fists set firmly on the desktop. "Doctor, just do it. Let the Navy decide what's best for their man."

4th Fighter Interceptor Wing
Kimpo Air Base, Korea

Colonel Jake looked at Rex and laughed. "I wonder if they're upset at Tokyo General - people going over their heads! That Doctor Stone really pulled a coup. Or - the nurse Sandra did it. It was obvious that Stone wanted her there. I wonder if your little old wingman had something hot going there. Gotta watch those Navy guys, Rex."

"Yeah, judging from what you've learned, Stone is a real hot shot. I hope he can save John's leg. We can't afford to lose pilots like him, even if he is Navy!" Rex replied, reaching in his pocket for a smoke.

"Agreed! Now get out of here and let me get some paper work done. I'll meet you at the Club, if I can call it that, and we'll toast the sister service while we get shit faced. Neither one of us is on the flight schedule tomorrow. Now get!" And Jake turned his attention to the pile of papers on his desk.

2739 Maple Drive
San Diego, California

Sylvia was in the shower when the phone rang. "Damn. I'm either in the shower, changing Kat, or baking a cake whenever that damned thing rings. Okay! I'm coming! I'm coming." She grabbed for the nearest bath towel, wrapped it around her body, and tossed another one over her hair as she headed for the bedroom.

"Sullivan residence."

"This is the Tokyo operator. I have a person-to-person call for Mrs. John Sullivan." The distance crackled on the line.

"This is she," Sylvia replied, nervously chewing on a fingernail, and suddenly frightened that something had happened to John.

"Go ahead, Ma'am. Your party is on the line."

"Mrs. John Sullivan?" A female voice queried.

"Yes?"

"I'm Captain Sandra Hall, an Army nurse at the Army's Tokyo General Hospital. We have your husband here - he just arrived from Korea. Although he's heavily sedated, he asked me to call you and tell you he's okay."

"Oh thank God. How is he, Captain? It's been so hard not knowing." Sylvia's voice was soft with unshed tears that were close to spilling over as she spoke.

Sandra hesitated a moment before she answered, not sure exactly what to say.

"I will be frank, Mrs. Sullivan. Your husband is a very sick man. He ripped open his right thigh when he landed after he bailed out of his F-86. He then walked through rice paddies and benjo ditches for miles behind enemy lines to escape. To do it, he had to lie in and walk through all the human excrement that exists in the ditches and paddies."

She paused and Sylvia shuddered at the mere thought of what John had done.

"Your husband has a terrible infection called rehustox condron, more commonly known as gangrene. He has a particularly vicious strain which is out of control. We've got to stop the infection or - to put it bluntly - he will die." Sandra bit her lip.

"Oh God, what can be done?" Sylvia whispered, terrified.

"We've arranged for an immediate medevac flight to Tripler General Hospital in Honolulu. There is a Doctor Stone at Tripler who is one of the best in the world on infectious diseases. If anyone can save him, Doctor Stone can." Sandra took a deep breath and then continued. "Because of your husband's condition I will travel with him on the medevac."

Oh-oh. What does that mean? Sylvia wondered silently, as fear clutched at the stomach. *Something's not right! I can feel it! Why is she so concerned about John? She's just one of the nurses isn't she? Or is she? She seems to know a lot about John. I don't like this!* The icy fingers refused to go away, as Sylvia replied, "I'll get a plane reservation right away, so I can be there in Honolulu when he arrives."

"I'd wait, Mrs. Sullivan, if I were you," the cool voice replied.

"Please. It's Sylvia."

"As I was saying, Sylvia. I would wait. He will arrive heavily sedated, and we'll probably keep him that way while we try to get the fever down and the infection under control. He'll need complete, undisturbed rest for at least a week to ten days. I will call you daily, and when he begins to show improvement, then come. It would be best that way."

"Alright Sandra. If you say so," Sylvia responded slowly, her heart and spirits rapidly failing. "I trust your judgment. When he does come out of the sedation for a moment, please tell him I love him! And if he begins to get worse or anything, call me right away. Please promise me you'll do that. I must be there if he begins to fail. I love him so much. I really do."

"I understand, Sylvia. Please have faith in me. John - your husband - is a very special person," she paused. "- to all of us here. I met him some time ago - before he went to Kimpo."

This time the warning bells sounded loud and clear. Sylvia shook her head to clear her mind. *Who is she? Why is she going with*

235

him to Honolulu? When did she meet him - and exactly where? What is this all about? Whatever it is, I don't like it - not one bit! Something's not right here.

After a moment she spoke, "Thank you, Sandra, for calling me! I've been so worried and upset - and it's a big relief to know my husband is in such good hands. I know you will all do your best. Please keep me informed. I'm so worried."

"I'll be happy to do that," Sandra answered.

"Goodbye, Sandra - and thanks again for calling."

Oh John, John. Come back to me! Don't leave me alone. Sylvia hung up the phone, leaned against the wall her head bowed, and began to sob. *Oh John, John,* she repeated, her body thoroughly chilled by what had been said and not said.

Hickman Field
Honolulu, Hawaii

The C-54 from Tachikawa was met by a long string of ambulances and staff cars. Colonel Frank Stone, U.S. Army Medical Corps, was the first one to embark when the plane's door opened. Sandra greeted him as he entered. "Doctor Stone, it's so good to see you again."

"Thank you for coming, Sandra. I know the trip was tiring. Now where's our patient?" Sandra directed him to John's litter.

"How is he, Sandra?" Frank asked, gently checking John's pupils.

"The fever still hovers around 102. It spiked once or twice during the flight, but I got it down with alcohol sponge baths. He's resting quietly now and breathing okay. No signs of congestion or incipient pneumonia. But it's been a long flight for him. Thank God for sedation, or he never would have made it."

"Good girl. You did what was needed. We'll get that fever down with the new drugs, starting now." He opened his medicine bag and handed Sandra a new plastic IV package to replace the one currently being used. "This bag contains the latest penicillin strain developed by NIH. If this doesn't do it, nothing will. Watch him closely, Sandra, for any adverse reaction to the drug." Stone snapped his medicine bag shut, as the head nurse called to him from the cargo door, "We're ready to deplane your patient, Doctor. I'm sending you two aides to carry the litter."

Sandra and Doctor Stone followed the litter down the steps and watched as the aides put John in the ambulance parked on the tarmac below.

"Has anyone notified his wife that he's here at Tripler?" Doctor Stone asked.

Sandra quietly replied. "Tokyo General called her and notified her of his arrival in Tokyo. They sent a telegram announcing his transfer here. At John's request I also spoke to his wife after the transfer was arranged. She'll come to Honolulu when you say it's okay." Sandra looked away.

"Am I going to have to deal with a love triangle - menage a' trois so to speak - while I try to cure him?" Stone looked at Sandra quizzically.

"My sole concern right now is John and his health," Sandra replied fiercely. "Everything else - including my love for him, is secondary and of no immediate concern for now. I hope Mrs. Sullivan feels the same when she arrives. I think she sensed that there was something between John and me when I talked to her. Just a feeling I have - but there'll be no squabbling between us, believe me. John's life is too important - to all of us!"

"Okay Sandra. I believe you. But keep in mind that the problem is not yours alone. John's going to be touched by it, and unless he has already solved the problem in his own mind, it's going to prey on him. We need to minimize that - at least initially."

"I understand, Frank."

"I have a staff car, but let's both ride in the ambulance. I'd just like to observe him quietly, and the trip to the hospital is a good time to do it."

Tripler General Hospital
Honolulu, Hawaii

Sandra finished taking John's temperature, which was down considerably, when he opened his eyes, looked at her without full focus, and said, "Sylvia honey, when did you arrive?"

Sandra smiled and patted his hand. "It's Sandra, John. Sylvia isn't here yet."

John continued to stare at her with a puzzled look. Then he grinned. "Yeah. I'm still in Tokyo. When do I leave for San Diego, Sandra? I just had a dream about it."

"John, you're in Tripler General. Remember? You and I flew here by Medevac from Tokyo. You probably don't remember the trip."

The puzzled look continued. "Really? Where's Tripler? I don't remember it in the San Diego area."

"It's in Hawaii - Honolulu. Can you sit up a little, John?" Sandra reached down and cranked the headrest lever, elevating John's head about eight more inches.

"That's good, Sandra." He smiled at her, and then frowned in concentration. "What were we talking about? Oh yes, the hospital. In Honolulu? I don't remember coming here, but I do remember Sylvia would meet me somewhere."

"You're not ready for company yet, John. You need to be more alert before she comes. It will take some time to adjust down from the heavy sedation you had."

"Oh yes, I do fade in and out, don't I?"

"Yes, you do," she smiled. "And that's enough talk for now." She reached over and picked up his pitcher. "I'll get you some fresh water, and you rest for a while."

She needn't have said it. He was gone already.

"How's he doing, Sandra?" Doctor Stone asked, as Sandra sat down in the easy chair in his office.

"The temperature is slowly and steadily coming down, Frank. No more sudden spiking either. But he's terribly confused. Can't seem to remember where he is. And he confuses me with Sylvia."

It's normal, Sandra. So many things have happened to him since they picked him up at the MLR, when his energy level was near zero. Another day or two without help, and he just would have gone to sleep and never awakened. And the confusion level may get worse as he begins to cope with the problem of you and Sylvia. He's in no condition to address it, and won't be for some time. Watch the frustration level, Sandra. He could explode any time for the smallest reason. Don't let him hurt himself."

"Alright, Frank. We'll do our best." She sighed, rising from her chair, and heading for the door.

2739 Maple Drive
San Diego

"This is Honolulu calling. Doctor Stone for Mrs. John Sullivan."

"This is Mrs. Sullivan."

"Go ahead, sir. Your party is on the line."

"Mrs. Sullivan?"

"This is Sylvia Sullivan, Doctor Stone. I know who you are from Sandra Hall's call."

"Thank you, Sylvia." The doctor spoke warmly. "The three of us have a very difficult task ahead of us. I need for you to be strong and brave, and not give up hope. I think I can pull John through, but I must tell you that even in the best of times, I sometimes lose. But not often, and not this time. This young man has gone through too much to lose him. It's important that you have hope and always display a positive attitude around John. The will to live is a very important part of the treatment." Doctor Stone looked up at Hippocratic oath, hanging on the wall by his desk - with the shield and serpent of the caduceus which signifies the doctor's creed.

"Doctor, I will not lose hope!" Sylvia replied in a firm determined voice.

"Good. I am a specialist in infectious diseases. I work closely with the National Institute of Health in Bethesda, Maryland, and I have access to some new experimental forms of penicillin. That's what will pull him through. The standard penicillin just can't cope with the strength and vitality of this disease. Your husband is a lucky man. One or two days more in North Korea and it would have been too late for anyone to save him. Twenty-four more hours without penicillin and it would have been hopeless. But we'll save him, Sylvia," he said gently.

"Oh Doctor, please cure him. I'll die without him." She sobbed quietly.

"Sylvia, please listen. I just received an even more powerful strain of the penicillin from NIH. We are giving it to him now. We'll know its impact in two or three days. Sandra has been able to stabilize him, and you should thank God for her, because she recognized the problem when he arrived at Tokyo General. Then she got hold of me. Tokyo would have taken his leg off, and failed in the process. You are lucky she was there."

"My God!" Sylvia sniffled, biting her knuckles until the blood ran. "He'd die anyway if he couldn't fly again! It's his life!" She gripped the phone.

"So I understand from Sandra. She apparently met him some time ago at a Japanese ski resort on R&R. She and two other Army nurses were there at the same time as your husband. For that reason she recognized his name and checked on him when he arrived at Tokyo General."

Sylvia took a deep breath and closed her eyes. "I didn't know that, Doctor. He didn't tell me. But I am deeply indebted to Sandra for what she has done. It means so much to me and to our baby."

Doctor Stone smiled at the human pathos, and continued.

"There's no sense in your coming out now, Sylvia. He's heavily sedated and in isolation. If he begins to deteriorate, Sandra or I will call you. In a week or ten days we should be able to get you out here for a visit. Okay?"

"Yes, Doctor. I'll do as you say." She wiped the tears away with the back of her hand, and sighed softly.

"Take it easy, Sylvia. I'll be in touch." With that Stone hung up and Sylvia released from the tension, began to cry in earnest.

Tripler General
Honolulu, Hawaii

"Miss Hall!" The Candy Striper at the nurse's station called. "You're needed in Lieutenant Sullivan's room right away!"

An aide was scurrying out of John's room when Sandra arrived.

"He threw the jello at me, Miss Hall! Said he didn't like raspberry!"

"Okay Annie, I'll handle it." Sandra patted her arm, and opened the door.

"You come back in here again and I'll throw something else at you, you little bitch!" John's voice roared through the partially open door which Sandra now swung wide open.

"John Sullivan! You just stop that! You're not a child, entitled to have temper tantrums!"

"Well, she made me do it! Said I never should have gone to Korea. Should have deserted. The bitch!"

"Nevertheless, John you had no right to throw something! Now just calm down! I'll get another aide to work with you. Right now we need someone to clean up this mess." She glared at him, turned, and left.

2739 Maple Drive
San Diego

Peg knocked on the door of the Sullivans' house.

"Yoo hoo, anybody home?" She stuck her head in and called.

"I'll be there in a minute," Sylvia shouted from the bedroom. "Make yourself comfortable and fix yourself a drink. You're going to need it. And make me one too, while you're at it - will you?"

"Uh-oh," Peg murmured, and headed for the kitchen and a heavy scotch and water.

Sylvia quickly splashed her face with cold water in the bathroom before she came out to greet Peg, a happy Kat in tow.

"Oh Peg, I'm so scared," Sylvia began. "John is in Honolulu at the Army's Tripler General Hospital."

"Why there for God's sake? Why not Balboa? What's wrong?" Peg reached for the baby. "Come see Auntie Peg, darling."

"Because an Army doctor there is a world-renowned specialist in infectious diseases, and John apparently has a bad case of gangrene in his right leg. Could kill him, Peg." She leaned back on the sofa.

"Sweet Jesus have mercy! I know about gangrene," Peg said softly, crossing herself. Peg took both of Sylvia's hands in hers as Sylvia continued.

"Anyway, they were looking at amputation in Tokyo when an Army nurse intervened - I think that's the right word," she said hesitantly, "- and got him transferred to Tripler. The nurse apparently knew that this Doctor Stone was Mister Big on infectious diseases. The nurse - Sandra's her name - recognized John when he medevac'd into Tokyo from Korea. It seems she had met John before at Akakura - on R&R when John and the other Peter Peters were there. What bothers me is that John didn't tell me about her." Her eyes filled with fresh tears which she dabbed with her handkerchief.

"Oh Oh. Sounds more like I&I to me," Peg retorted angrily, dropping Sylvia's hands and getting up from the sofa.

"I&I? " Sylvia asked. "What's that?"

"Sylvia dear," Peg said with a wry smile, "You are still a very young Navy wife. I&I is a more accurate description of R&R. Stands for Intoxication and Intercourse. "

"John wouldn't do that. . . . . would he?" Sylvia murmured. "We're married, Peg." She paused as doubts began to grow inside her. "Now she's there with him, and here I am in San Diego. Alone! God have mercy on me! I don't know what has happened - nor do I know what to do." She sat down again on the sofa and put her face in her hands.

"You just listen to Peg, honey," Peg said, raising her up and wrapping her arms around her. "I don't know if there's been any hanky-panky or not, but remember this, Sylvia. It appears this woman saved his life. Give her credit for that. But it doesn't mean she can have him! Nevertheless, there has to be a close relationship there of some sort. If she hadn't known him before he arrived in Tokyo, she might not have paid any attention to him other than the usual routine. So thank God she did know him, or he'd be dead by now!"

"I know you're right, Peg," Sylvia admitted. "But I don't like it."

"It's also true that you don't know how they feel about each other although the fact that he didn't tell you about her makes me suspicious too! You know women can sense these things. But you'll know soon enough. Go to Honolulu as soon as the doctor gives the okay; make your presence as his wife known to all. Be at your very best, and, above all, be strong! Meet this Sandra and make your own judgments. Mike and I will help in any way we can, you know that, dear. Now try to relax. We'll take it one step at a time. Drink your drink, and I'll fix something for you to eat."

The Sullivan phone started to ring off the hook when word got out that John had walked out of Korea and was at Tripler General Hospital in Honolulu - friends, classmates, shipmates, and even people who didn't know him, were telephoning with congratulations and warm wishes. The articles in the San Diego Tribune, Washington Post, and New York Times had excited the nation. It was even on San Diego's new TV station.

The phone rang again as Sylvia was changing Kat, stabbing herself on the diaper pin in the process "Damn! Damn! Damn! Why are you ringing now?" She snorted and grabbed the phone off the hook. "Sullivan residence and hold the line for a minute!"

She put the last pin in Kat's diaper, plopped her in the playpen, and gave her the squeaky yellow duck to play with.

"Okay, I'm here," Sylvia laughed, pushing her hair back from her face.

"You sure sounded pissed when you answered the phone, babe," Larry Duncan laughed and then turned serious. "We just heard about John and his ordeal. I didn't know that he had bailed out and was missing! Mitzi just talked to Sandra at Tripler, and we wanted to call you to see how you're doing and what we can do. Here's Mitzi. Hang in there, Sylvia!"

Larry gave the phone to Mitzi. "Hi Sylvie, how are you holding up? What great news that John walked out! I know how thrilled you must be." Mitzi bubbled over, jubilant at the turn of events. "But, I guess the leg is still a big problem. However, Doctor Stone certainly is the best, and Sandra is no slouch either. She's worked with Stone before and knows what's needed. If you need help, just say the word, and I'll be on the next plane to San Diego." Mitzi stopped, out of breath.

Sylvia laughed. "Thanks Mitzi. I've been so frazzled I haven't thought to call anyone, but the papers took care of it. I've heard from literally everyone! Your friend, Sandra, called me from Tokyo, and told me about John's condition. It was she who got him transferred to Doctor Stone's care! I didn't know anything about her, or Akakura for that matter, except that you all were there at the same time and that's where you and Larry found each other. John never said anything about Sandra, and you never mentioned her at the wedding either!" Sylvia said, twisting the phone cord around her fingers as she waited for an answer.

Mitzi hesitated for a moment and then trilled on. "I'm sorry, Sylvie. I just assumed John had told you all about Akakura. It was R&R for all of us. I never thought that he wouldn't have mentioned Sandra," she said, trying to make light of the issue. "I guess I didn't think anything about it, and therefore made no point of it at the wedding. Gee, I'm sorry," Mitzi replied, as she chewed her lip.

God forgive me for the lie, she said to silently herself.

"He really did tell me all about Akakura - I thought - but he never mentioned Sandra. So I'm kinda confused, I guess," Sylvia replied quietly.

"Well, you'll meet Sandra when you go to Hawaii," Mitzi continued, avoiding a direct reply. "She's really a great person and lots of fun! I know you'll like each other. You can talk to her then."

Damn you, John Sullivan. You really screwed this up, didn't you? Mitzi groused. At the other end of the wire, Sylvia wondered just what was going on. *She's avoiding the issue. Something is definitely wrong here,* Icy fingers gripped her stomach once again.

"How's Kat, Sylvie? Walking yet?" Mitzi countered, changing the subject. "Bet you look like a million dollars in spite of it all. You always do! When do you leave for Tripler, and how long will you stay? Will your folks take Kat? Probably would be best if you didn't have the baby with you this time," Mitzi said, out of breath again.

"I'm fine, Mitzi. I'll go to Hawaii as soon as Doctor Stone says it okay. And yes, I'll talk to Sandra then." She smiled at Mitzi's motor mouth.

Why didn't John at least mention Sandra? Mitzi sighed. *Now it looks funny, which it sure as hell is! But I don't want to be the one to tell her about it. Not me! God! That's all they need, the poor people!*

"Sylvie, I'll be on the next plane if you need me, ya hear?" Mitzi repeated her offer.

"I'll let you go, Mitzi. Thanks for the call." Sylvia hung up the phone and went in to the living room to check on Kat.

"Mama! Mama!" the little Fat Kat squealed, and banged the playpen with her favorite yellow duck. She then reached up with chubby little arms to be picked up and hugged.

Peg's right. Something smells here, and a diaper it is not! She kissed Kat and then checked the diaper's back. *Well, we'll find out when I go to Honolulu. Boy! Will we!*

Tripler Army General Hospital
Honolulu, Hawaii

"How's he doing, Sandra?" Doctor Stone stopped at the nurse's station on the second floor.

"Temp is down to 100, Frank. Isn't that great!" Sandra smiled, her face etched with fatigue.

"Sandra, you've been here for six days, almost day and night. It's time for you to get some rest. I'm putting Susan in charge full time for the next twenty-four hours while you sleep. Take a sleeping pill. But, before you do, look at this." He held up a vial of medicine. "This is the latest version of the medicine John is getting! Basically the same chemistry, but stronger with a wider spectrum of effectiveness. Walter Reed got it and sent it by special courier. We'll start him in the morning! I'll call Mrs. Sullivan and tell her to come out for a few days." He paused and looked at Sandra, "How much complication will we have, Sandra?" His eyes questioned her.

Sandra looked directly at the doctor. "It all depends on Sylvia, Frank. If she's not worthy of him, I'll take him away from her, just like that," she replied, snapping her fingers. "If she's deserving of John, it's up to him to decide when he recovers. I won't interfere. I told him no, once when he wanted to sleep with me, but I won't do it again. I won't push him into it either. It's funny, but the strong sexual feelings for him have subsided somewhat. After nursing him the way I have, and all we've been through in this crisis - I can't feel the way I did before. Yes, I still love him, but in a different way. I can't explain it, Frank. Whatever it is, I don't have to have him, but I won't see him used or abused by any woman either. I'm sure he can take care of himself with men, but women? I'm not so sure." She looked away.

"You've been wonderful, Sandra, but the stress of this menage-a-trois. . . It may begin to get to you as you watch him trying to cope with the problem. He's going to be even more confused, frustrated, and probably irrational. He'll love you one day and Sylvia the next. He'll be incapable of addressing the problem, although he will try with conflicting and frustrating results. We need to give him time to get well first. Something needs to drive him in the right direction, but I don't know what."

Sandra laughed and said, "I do." Stone gave her a quizzical look.

"Flying, Doctor Stone." She smiled. "That's his real love. Not one of us mortals!"

Doctor Stone took her hands in his. "My dear, you are something else. But don't worry, it will solve itself, somehow." He looked at her for a long moment, and then he added, "You saved his life, Sandra. He owes you a great deal - and so does his wife. Even if they had taken the leg off in Tokyo, he would have died anyway. The infection was too pervasive. Without this new NIH strain of penicillin he just wouldn't have made it. I'll make sure you aren't hurt in the Army because you kicked over the apple cart to do this. As I said before - you are one helluva person! Now go to bed and get some rest. You look terrible!" He laughed at her shocked reaction.

Moran Residence
Coronado, California

Peg was pruning her prize roses in front of the house when the phone rang. She put the pruning shears in her apron, wiped her hands on the front of it, and entered the front door.

"Hello, Moran residence."

"Peg! It's Sylvia! I just got a call from Tripler, from Doctor Stone. The fever is breaking! I can see him! I can go see him!" Sylvia cried happily. "I'm so excited! Bernice is coming out to stay with Kat so I can go to Honolulu! I can't wait! But I have a real problem, Peg. The airlines are all over-booked! I can't get a seat, and I can't get a hotel room either! What shall I do?" Her voice trembled.

"Don't you worry, honey! That's what we have that big Captain for. I'll just turn this over to Captain Mike Moran to solve."

"Oh thank you, Peg! I hope Mike can help."

"Syl, just don't worry about it. Mike and I will solve your transportation problem, if we have to row you out there ourselves!" She smiled to herself.

Sylvia laughed, "You'll probably have me sleeping in a tent on the lawn at the BOQ. Well, if that's what I have to do, I'll do it." She paused and then continued. "Peg, Bernice is arriving on the night flight tonight! Isn't that wonderful!"

"That's great, Syl. You'll have time with John - just the two of you. That's much better!"

And you'll need the time, Peg added to herself. _It won't be easy._

Tripler General Hospital
Honolulu, Hawaii

Sandra quietly entered Doctor Stone's office, sat down, and waited for him to recognize her presence. He stopped writing in a chart, put his pen on the desk, and looked up.

"Oh! Sandra. I didn't hear you come in."

"I talked with John in the sun room just now. He's much more alert."

"Yes, he is, Sandra," Stone replied, leaning back in his chair. "I must say he's coming along well enough that he won't need your watchful eyes soon."

Stone got up, walked around his desk, lifted Sandra to her feet.

"Do you want to go back to Tokyo next week, Sandra?" Stone asked, looking intensely into Sandra's eyes for some indications of her real feelings. "It may be better for everyone - especially you, the one caught in the middle."

"Thank you, Frank, but I think not. I want to see this through, and I want to be near him for at least a while longer. I also want to meet his wife and judge their relationship. That will tell me where I stand. I need to know."

Stone smiled understandingly. "You have a real bear by the tail, my friend. If it gets to be too much, let me know."

2739 Maple Drive
San Diego

Peg arrived at the Sullivan residence and entered with a knock and a call, "It's Peg, Sylvie."

Sylvie with the Fat Kat in her arms came out of the kitchen.

"Mike's got it all arranged, Sylvie! You leave on Friday on a Navy C-54 non-stop to Barbers Point, departing in the evening about 2200. That'll give you and Bernice some time together before you leave. You have reservations at the Makalapa BOQ, and you'll have a point of contact out there to help you!"

"Thank you so much! - so very much! And thank Mike for me as well! I'm so excited." Sylvie exclaimed as she put Kat down with a cookie. "Can I get you a drink, Peg?"

" Just a coke please, Sylvie," Peg responded as she sat down on the couch. "I want to talk to you, darling. Girl talk about what you must do before you go."

"Well, here I am with a coke for you, and ears to listen."

"Sylvie, it's crucial that you make the best possible impression in Honolulu, and there are a few things you should know to prepare yourself," Peg began, taking a sip of her soda. "So just listen to old Peg awhile."

"Men change when they go on deployment. They change even more after combat; and the change is greatest after they have been wounded. When they come back from deployment, they frequently disrupt a smoothly running household, take charge and preempt the wife and her authority, spoil the daughter, damage discipline, and displace the son as the man of the house. And, Sylvie, in many cases the man has matured and the woman's been left behind. Divorces are made from events like that. It can be really stressful."

"You experienced some of it when John came back the first time, but you had no kids, and you were the same fun-loving young thing that he left. He liked that. Although combat changed him, I don't think you noticed - you were so busy having a baby, and that little tyke has helped bring you two together even more strongly." Peg paused again to look at Sylvia, and was satisfied that she was receptive.

"But this time, Sylvie, it will be different. Playing house will not be enough. Neither will fun in bed be enough. You can't just be pretty - which you are, my dear. You need to present this man with a mature, confident, beautiful woman who has the sophistication and ability to grow with him. And grow he will! He's already an ace, and Mike tells me he's a shoo-in for deep selection to full lieutenant. The board is meeting now to select. John is not just a fine pilot, according to Mike. He's got a wonderful analytical mind as well. He and I both think he could achieve flag rank.

"So, Sylvie darling, put away the little girl from Worthington, Ohio. It's time to mature and develop alongside him. If you don't, he'll run away from you as a person, and you'll lose him - even if he stays at home, which, knowing John, I don't think he will. You must match his development!

"I've seen this happen many times, Sylvie. So take a long look at yourself. You'll know what to do. I have great faith in you." Peg drank the rest of the coke, patted Sylvie on the hand, and went to pick up the Fat Kat who had her arms out for her Aunt Peg.

"You are a darling," Peg said, nuzzling her. Kat responded and then held out her hands for her mama. "You tell Mama to get with it. Just remember we love you, Syl. Got to run." And she blew a kiss and went out the door.

Salon Jean-Philipe
Coronado, California

Jean Philipe lifted the heavy silky hair off Sylvia's shoulders and held it in his hands, just below her chin.

"Mmm. Ah oui, mademoiselle - We do zee little trim? Eh?"

Sylvia looked at her reflection in the huge circular salon mirror. "Oh. I'm not sure, Jean Philipe! I'm used to it like this. It's so easy to pull it up in a ponytail," she said hesitantly. "But I want to look special right now! I'm going to Hawaii to see my husband. He's in the hospital there. He's the Navy pilot who was shot down over Korea and walked out."

"Iz 'e zee one we read about in all zee newspaper?" Jean Philipe asked.

"The very one," Sylvia answered softly. "So you see, it's really important that I look special. It's important to me," She repeated, remembering Peg's advice.

"Ah, Mademoiselle - you have beautiful hair - oui - but zis ponytail affair iz for school girls - which you are not! You are a pretty girl ziz way - but I zink iz time to turn you into zee beautiful young woman!" He picked up his shining scissors.

Two hours later, Sylvia opened the heavy glass doors of the salon, and walked out into the brilliant September sunshine. Heads turned to look at her as she passed. She sneaked a glance at her reflection in the shop windows along Orange Avenue, and was pleased at her transformation. Jean Philipe was true to his word. She was no longer just a pretty girl. The bouncy ponytail had been replaced by a sleek swinging bob that grazed her chin. There was a hint of blush on her cheekbones, and her eyes were just a little smoky. Everything was perfect - except her dress.

249

Several doors down the street she paused to look at the chic sportswear in Kippy's windows. Without a moment's hesitation she opened the door and went inside.

Naval Air Station
North Island

The Navy C-54 bound for Barbers Point, Hawaii, was ready to board its passengers. Sylvia, in trim stylish slacks and blazer, was saying goodbye to Peg, and trying not to cry.

"Let's get her on board and get her settled, Peg. It'll be a long night for her," Captain Mike Moran said, walking up to the Chief Petty Officer in charge of loading.

"I just can't thank you enough, Peg!" Sylvia said, hugging her friend tightly. "You've both been so good to me."

"Now don't get emotional, Sylvie! You'll make me cry, and a CAG's wife is not allowed to cry in public." Peg made light of it and hoped she could keep her cool.

"You're all set, Sylvie! A car will be waiting to take you to the Makalapa BOQ where you have reservations for a week, and a Hertz car - and then a week on Waikiki Beach, at the Halekulani Hotel courtesy of CAG and Mrs. CAG! I know the manager." He grinned broadly as Sylvia hugged him too. "I love you both," she said.

"You certainly have a way with women, Michael Moran - all the good-looking women hugging and squeezing you," Peg laughed, tears forgotten.

"And remember, Sylvie. If you have any problem, just call Rear Admiral Jim Davies at CINCPACFLT. He's ACOS for Operations and an old fighter pilot. He'll make sure the wife of a Navy Korean ace is taken care of." Mike patted her shoulder, winked, and gave her a thumbs up.

"Mrs. Sullivan, we're ready to board you," the Chief in charge of the flight said. "May I help you, Ma'am?" he added, offering Sylvie his arm. Sylvia blew Peg and Mike another kiss and headed for the stairs to the big C-54.

Naval Air Station
Barbers Point, Hawaii

"Navy 15436, Barbers Point Ground Control. You are cleared down the parallel taxiway to the access throat for base operations. Park in the VIP slot in front of ops. Do you have a Mrs. Sullivan aboard?"

"That's a Roger, Barbers Point."

"She is to disembark first. She's got quite a reception committee here." The radio crackled with static.

Aboard the aircraft Sylvia brushed her hair, put on fresh lipstick, and looked at herself in her tiny compact mirror. The new hair style had traveled well, and she had enough glow left from her summer's tan to look reasonably healthy

Not good, but not too bad, all considered, she commented, observing the faint circles of fatigue under her eyes. *My mouth tastes awful,* she grimaced, searching in the bottom of her bag for a breath mint.

"Give me your attention," the cargo master announced through a hand-held megaphone from the rear of the cabin. "When the plane stops, keep your seats until Mrs. Sullivan has disembarked."

The C-54 taxied through the throat and onto the parking ramp. A line of staff cars and the usual operations buses were waiting for the passengers to disembark. The engines shut down and the cargo master opened the large cargo door at the rear of the plane.

"Mrs. Sullivan, we're ready for you. Please come down here and stand with me while they put the steps in place," he said to Sylvia, offering her his hand to help her.

Sylvia stood at the door and looked out. *There's a Navy Captain and car waiting for some big wheel,* she thought, *And there's an Army sedan with a woman officer standing in front of it. Could be Sandra.*

The ground crew put the steps in place and Sylvia started down.

That must be she, Sandra critically examined the woman standing in the plane's door. *Pretty, very pretty indeed, and she carries herself well. She looks tired, too. She did the best she could with her face, but the fatigue is there in spite of it all. Huh! I should talk. Look at me.* Sandra laughed to herself. *She looks like someone John would go for. Well, only time will tell.*

"Welcome to Hawaii, Mrs. Sullivan," the tall, handsome Navy Captain said as he put three leis around her neck and kissed her on each cheek. Sylvia smiled at him and was quick to note that he was a naval aviator and sported a impressive collection of fruit salad on his chest, including the Navy Cross and a DFC with a gold star.

"Mrs. Sullivan, I'm the Special Assistant to Rear Admiral Davies and have been tasked by him personally to see to your welfare while in Hawaii. He sends his warm regards, and asks you to relay them to your husband. The Admiral's a great admirer of your husband's combat performance in Korea. We have a car to take you to Makalapa BOQ, but perhaps you'd rather go directly to the hospital. If so, Captain Hall will take you." He waved to the tall slender woman in the Army uniform standing unobtrusively to one side.

"Mrs. Sullivan, may I present Captain Sandra Hall from Tripler. She looks after your husband." Turning to Sandra, he added, "Sandra, come and meet Mrs. Sullivan."

"Hello, Sylvia, I'm glad you're here. Did you have a good flight?" Sandra said, stepping forward and offering her cool hand.

"Yes, thank you. I did. How's John?"

"He continues to improve. However, he still has some fever and is still slightly sedated. He asks for you. Do you want to go directly to the hospital, or to the BOQ first to freshen up?"

"I want to see John. I'll freshen later."

"Good," the Captain interrupted, smiling as he gave Sylvia his card. "My driver will take your luggage to the BOQ and I'll leave you in the Captain's good hands. Have a pleasant stay." He waved a friendly salute, turned and entered his staff car.

Sylvia and Sandra stood stiffly for a moment, warily examining each other. "Shall we go, Sylvia?" Sandra finally said.

"Yes, please, let's do. I can hardly wait to see John."

The drive to Tripler was quiet and reserved. Sandra pointed out interesting sights, and Sylvia asked several questions about them. Beyond that each was left with her own thoughts. As they approached Tripler, Sandra turned to Sylvia and said, "I should prepare you for what you will see. John has been through hell and close to death. He has lost fifty pounds, and is still so weak that he cannot stand by

252

himself. He will fade in and out when you're talking to him. When he does, let him go. It's the sedation, and he needs rest."

"Thank you for warning me," Sylvia replied quietly. "Be assured my sole interest is John's welfare, and I'll keep my visits to whatever schedule is best for him. Right now I'd like for him to know I'm here. As soon as he starts to fade, I'll leave. Perhaps you can join me for breakfast somewhere." Sylvia smiled for the first time.

"If John is resting okay, I'd love to join you because we need to talk," Sandra answered quietly. "Why don't we go to the Halekulani on Waikiki Beach? They have a wonderful buffet breakfast, and we'll be away from the Navy."

"That sounds wonderful, Sandra. I'd like that."

Sandra parked the car in an official parking slot. The two women walked across the pavement and entered the Hospital. The elevator took them to John's floor, and they continued down the wide corridor to the end room.

Sylvia entered John's room with Sandra behind her and came to an immediate stop two steps inside when she saw John, who lay in a bed on the opposite side of the room. Although Sandra had warned her, she was not prepared for what she saw. John's eyes were closed, but she could see how deeply sunken they were in a face whose color and texture looked like slippery gray mud. His cheeks were hollow and sunken like his eyes, his chin line prominent with the waxy skin stretched tautly over the bone. His hands and arms had no flesh on them and his body was cadaverous.

"My God, the poor man," Sylvia put her hand to her mouth momentarily. Then as Sandra watched her, she straightened her body, put her shoulders back, and with a smile walked over to the bedside. She took his hand and kissed him gently on the lips.

"Hello, Stud. Want to go dancing with me tonight?" she said, forcing a radiant smile.

John opened his eyes slightly and looked at her. As recognition finally dawned on him, his eyes opened wide and a feeble smile broke the harsh lines of his face.

"Sylvie, honey. Oh Sylvie, you're here at last," he said in a near whisper and then began to choke on his own saliva, spittle oozing from his lips. In a flash Sandra was there to wipe his mouth and use a syringe to excise the remainder.

"Okay, big guy. Take it easy. Sylvia is here." Sandra put her hand on his.

"I'm so glad," John smiled at Sylvia, closed his eyes, and went back to sleep.

"He's gone, Sylvia. I'll get the ward assistant in here to baby sit and we'll go to breakfast."

Halekulani
Waikiki Beach

The Royal Hawaiian, Halekalani, Outrigger Club, Queen Surf, and the Moana, with its magnificent banyan tree, ruled the white strip of sand that was Waikiki Beach. Of the five, the Halekulani was assuredly the most charming resort on the beach. Its design was unique and open to the sea. The spacious grounds were lush and beautifully landscaped with palm trees and an array of colorful blossoms. A small building with no doors, made famous by a Charlie Chan movie, offered informal dining at the water's edge. The hotel rooms themselves were individual bungalows scattered along beautiful winding garden paths.

Sylvia and Sandra took a table by the railing next to the beach. A fresh breeze blew in across the surf, carrying the sweet fragrance of tropical flowers into the dining room. The opulent buffet offered a magnificent selection of colorful exotic fruits, as well as an abundance of hearty breakfast fare.

"This is heavenly, Sandra," Sylvia said between bites of fresh pineapple and sweet rolls. "I'm really hungry. I haven't eaten in fourteen hours."

"Then enjoy it!" Sandra smiled. "I don't come here too often. The food is so delicious and the ambiance so inviting, that I'd put on ten pounds in no time. However, I'm really going to treat myself today. I'm tired and hungry."

Sandra took a sip from her cup, and carefully placed it back in its saucer.

"Sylvia, we must talk now. About John," she began.

Sylvia put her fork down and looked calmly at the attractive blonde woman across the table. "Okay Sandra. Let's talk about it."

"First, let's discuss Post Combat Syndrome for a moment. It's something you need to know about." Sandra began. "I'm not sure you'll find it in a textbook on psychiatry, but all of us nurses who deal with the carnage of combat know it exists. I spent some time in a MASH unit, the first real hospital behind the combat lines. Believe me, it's for real!" Sandra paused, thinking how to say what had to be said. Sylvia, poised, remained quiet, wondering what was coming.

"Post Combat Syndrome is sort of like PMS, on a very large scale. It takes over your being, and you do crazy irrational things, and say things you don't mean. When these guys come back from combat, they live for the moment. They're just so damned happy to be alive. They're wired, and full of electricity. They have been living with death, their mortality always at risk, always in the forefront of their minds.

"When the pressure comes off, they experience - not all, but many - a compelling drive to reestablish their immortality. A compelling need to leave their seed so they can live in their progeny, a compelling urge to plant that seed! Their sexual drive is greatly heightened. It's an unbridled drive put there by nature for the survival of the species, a part of the natural evolution of man. The strong survive and procreate; the weak die! It's been that way since man first went to war!"

"But what's that got to do with us?" Sylvia asked warily. *What is she trying to tell me?* she wondered. There was a long pause, as the two women assessed each other.

"Sylvia - John had the Post Combat Syndrome at Akakura - and - he had it with me."

Sandra stopped and looked at Sylvia, who in turn thought, *so here it is. Peg was right. Thank God for Peg. I was forewarned.*

"Alright Sandra! So continue. When did you sleep with him? And how many times?" Sylvia snapped, her eyes blazing with anger.

"Funny thing, Sylvia. I didn't. But we almost did. I fell in love with John Sullivan the first time I laid eyes on him. Who wouldn't have? There were three of us nurses and the three Peter Peters from the Phil Sea. The guys were wired from their recent combat missions, and we nurses were wired from all the carnage we had dealt with. After two days of great fun, it got serious, but I realized that John was married."

"Didn't he tell you?" Sylvia asked incredulously.

"No, he didn't, and I didn't ask. I repeat - we were wired. It wasn't important to ask. There was only the moment - away from combat - away from the carnage. Korea was a million miles away - and I'll be honest - so was San Diego! We were all living for the moment! The sexual attraction was getting high by then - not just us - Larry and Mitzi too. We all went skinny-dipping in the Japanese hot tub - against facility rules. John cornered me by the lockers. It got hot and heavy, and I made no attempt to stop him - at first. He wanted to sleep with me. I told him that I wouldn't sleep with a married man."

Sandra stopped for a moment. The pause was pregnant with emotion. Sylvia felt sick and cold, her appetite forgotten. She stared at Sandra as if she had two heads.

"I have to be honest with you, Sylvia. This has to be gotten out in front now - for John's sake - for all our sakes. I love him. I may not have slept with him, but I love him all the same. And he loves me - not necessarily the same way he loves you - but he does. That's the agony of the thing."

Sylvia sat there staring out at the ocean, crushed at what Sandra was saying. She gazed down at her folded hands. Then her head snapped up, her eyes flashed with anger. "You bitch! You goddamned bitch! You play footsie with my man - probably screwed him like a bitch in heat!   Then you give me this bullshit about post combat syndrome. That's just a cover up! So much bullshit!" Sylvia threw her fork on the table, grabbed her purse, and ran for the exit with Sandra trying to catch up. At the entrance Sandra reached out and grabbed Sylvia's arm. "Let me drive you to Makalapa. We meet with Doctor Stone at 1400."

Sylvia glared at her. "I'll be there. And here's a taxi. I don't need a ride from you."

Tripler General Hospital
Honolulu, Hawaii

"Well, how did it go with Sylvia?" Dr. Stone asked as Sandra entered his office and dropped into a chair.

"I told her about John and me. She was not too happy," Sandra chuckled. "You might say she went ballistic. Called me a bitch and walked out. Can't say as I blame her."

"She'll cool down when she realizes how much you've done for John."

" Maybe she will, and maybe she won't. I just don't know."

Sylvia sat in a straight-backed chair at John's bedside, holding his hand and praying for his recovery. The conversation with Sandra had shaken her, but her determination to see John through this had taken hold, and she was in control of the panic that had raced through her veins that morning. Her appointment with Doctor Stone was for 1400, but she had deliberately arrived at the hospital earlier so she could spend some time alone with her husband. She knew that Sandra would be present the entire time, if she came as scheduled.

You must get well, sweetheart! Kat and I need you, and have so much love yet to give you Sylvia looked at her wasted husband.

Get well John! Think it! Feel it! Believe it! she murmured quietly to him, trying to impart her own strength and will to the weakened man.

"Hi darling, I've been dreaming about you." John's eyes opened and he smiled. "Shall we go skinny-dipping on the beach?" His eyes were bright and focused and his mind seemed less fogged by the effects of the drugs. Sylvia squeezed his hand and smiled.

His dosage must have been reduced. A good sign.

"How's my baby? How's my Fat Kat?" John asked about Kat for the first time.

"She's wonderful, John! Active and inquisitive! Crawling and trying to stand. Bernie is with her so I could come and be with you without the worry of a one year old. They can be so very demanding." She smiled.

"How are you, Syl? I've missed you! Sorry I'm in such bad shape - but I walked out! Believe it or not - I walked out! I did it on my own. I survived!" His eyes glistened.

"Yes, yes you did, and I am so proud of you." She spoke softly. "I love you, John. Get well so we can take you home again," Sylvia bit her lip, and smiled as she rose to kiss his lips. She whispered, "I miss my stud. Hurry up and get well. We've wasted too much time."

"Sweet Sylvia. I'm trying so hard. Please be patient with me. The Stud of old will rise again from the wreck I am right now," John replied. His eyes began to cross again and his mind wandered.

"Red 1-3! Break right now!" he muttered. The engagement resurrected itself and John went back to a dream world to fight his battles.

He's going, but at least we are having some lucid moments where I can touch him and imprint my love on his mind.

"Oh there you are," Sandra said, all business, as she entered the room with a thermometer in her hand. "I've been looking for you. Doctor Stone is waiting. Let me get John's temperature and we'll go. The temp was normal this morning - 98.6. Isn't that great! Maybe we can get some real food into him now - get his weight back."

"Sylvia, your husband will recover. He's out of danger," Doctor Stone said. His entire face beamed as his eyes and mouth smiled at her. Doctor Stone was very satisfied with himself. He had saved another patient. "He still needs a lot more hospital rest and care, but he can go outside in a wheelchair now. I would say we can send him home to you in about three weeks. Doctor Payton at Balboa will care for him. John will be attached to Balboa for duty, and will report in weekly, or as Doctor Payton directs. Please understand that this is not convalescent leave. That will begin when he's released from Balboa and will last thirty days.

" What he needs, Sylvia, is a lot of tender loving care - and patience - lots of patience. Men like him tend to become irascible during the healing process. With what he's been through he will have mood swings and be unpredictable. Just be patient, Sylvia. Time heals all wounds.

" Now let's talk about you and Sandra. I want you to know just how much she has done for John." Sylvia started to interrupt, but Stone raised his hand. " Hear me out, Sylvia. It's important that you know this for John's sake. Yes, I know Sandra's in love with him, and I know all the circumstances. It was Sandra who saw John in the emergency room in Tokyo when he was medevac'd from Korea. If she hadn't intervened and called me, they would have taken his leg off, and he would have died in the process. It was only the more powerful experimental penicillin that I was able to get from NIH that saved his life."

Sylvia's face turned ashen at the thought of what might have happened. "I suspected, Doctor, but I didn't know."

"Sandra has set all her emotions to one side while she nursed him to health, and I think she'll leave it that way as long as John's here at Tripler. What happens in six months when he's recovered depends on you and John. He needs to go back to San Diego and recover - regain his strength and stability with you. Sandra says you are good with him, and right now that's what he needs." Stone paused to let this sink in. Then he continued. "So for now - for John's sake do not let any antagonism that you may feel about Sandra as a competitor show through." He concluded by looking into Sylvia's eyes.

"I won't, Doctor. And I do understand about Sandra. By mutual agreement we could have a truce."

Stone smiled at her. " I'll speak to Sandra."

Stone looked up when Sandra entered his office. " How's it going?" he asked.

"John is doing remarkably well. Sylvia takes him on long walks outside in the garden every day. She's a tower of strength, Frank."

"I judged as much," Stone remarked.

"When I first met her, I thought to myself, a sweet young thing. June Week wedding, lots of fun and games. You know - typical officer's wife. Put that last in quotes," she quipped.

"Yeah, I know. The ugly parody? How does it go? Oh yes - The officer's wives, the officer's wives. That's what they'll be for the rest of their lives."

Sandra laughed. "I've heard it, but it's really not true of most of them. Did you know that Sylvia is a well-known fashion designer. She got the position on her own while John was in Korea." Sandra paused. "And she's no pansy either. She really chewed me out when she learned about Akakura. She didn't think much of post-combat syndrome either." Sandra chuckled. "She's a fighter, Ralph. That'll be good for John the next six months."

"And what about you, Sandra?" Stone asked.

"It's time for me to go, Frank. John is rapidly recovering and Sylvia has taken over as head nurse."

"And the future?" Stone asked in a low voice.

"I don't know, Frank. I really don't know, but I sense my options with John are closing on me - and not just because of Sylvia either."

"How so?"

"Frank, when I first met John, I would have married him in a heartbeat, if he hadn't already been married. No questions asked. And I would have bedded him even quicker. But now, I don't know. If he wants me in six months when his mind is clear, he can have me. I won't deny him twice, but marriage? I'm not sure."

"Why Sandra?" Stone asked. He already knew the answer.

"Frank, I've spent months with John as we pulled him back from the brink of death. Our relationship has changed, but more important...." She paused and her breath caught in her throat. "It's the sitting at home in the evening waiting for him to come home - no, clarify that - wondering if he'll come home alive or in a body bag. Every night - every goddamned night on the days that he flies. I don't think I can handle that. The emotion of it, day after day would rip us apart. He's a warrior, Frank. Always will be. He'll never quit flying, and I'd never ask him to." There was a long pause filled with emotion. Sandra looked up from her hands. "Yet, if he divorces Sylvia and asks me, I'll marry him, Frank. I love him that much."

Stone smiled gently, rose from his chair, and went around to Sandra. He lifted her from her seat and wrapped his arms around her. "Go back to Tokyo and bury yourself in your work. Help heal those broken bodies coming out of Korea. That will also heal your own soul. You're a healer, Sandra. You saved John's life. You can save many more. And remember," he tipped her head up to look into her eyes. "I'm here if you need me."

"John, good to see you're getting around so well. You'll be out of that wheelchair soon," Stone said, peering into John's eyes with the pinpoint beam of light from his equipment.

"Sylvia has been a big help, Doctor, pushing me everywhere in this contraption. She's a great woman driver," John chuckled.

"We're going to send you back to the Navy very soon, John. To Balboa hospital in San Diego for your recuperation. That'll take some time," Stone warned. "Try to be patient. I know you want to get on with your life, but you need time to let things heal."

"Yeah, Sandra keeps telling me so," John laughed. "But, you know I reached the highest pinnacle of my life in Korea, Doctor. I became an ace, every fighter pilot's ultimate dream. Equally important I survived. I fought in the war, achieved ace, and I walked out of there." John said in a quiet tone, his mind focused on his good fortune.

Stone laughed. "If that was the pinnacle for you, what will you do for an encore, or is it all downhill from here?"

John grinned. "You mean, go back to Korea and rack up more kills. No, I don't think so. The dice had to roll just right a number of times for me to get out of there alive. I have great respect for this war. It almost got me once. I won't give it a second chance. Besides," He continued with a twinkle in his eye. "There are many more mountains to climb in aviation. Breaking the sound barrier. Flying at 75,000 feet. Aviation is only going to grow as newer and better planes are built. I want to be there."

"So you'll continue flying?"

"It's my life, Doctor. I want to grow with aviation as it grows." He paused. "But I need to be smarter. I want to go to the Post Grad School at Monterey. If aviation is going to get more complex, I need to know more to stay ahead of it"

Stone had been watching John closely as he talked. *His mind is sharp. No damage there from the protracted fever. And he's beginning to get his sense of life back. That's good!* He smiled at John. "Just keep thinking that way, Lieutenant. There's a whole world ahead for you."

"I know. I can hardly wait to try it on for size."

Halekulani Hotel
Waikiki Beach

The faint strains of Hawaiian music drifted on the soft breezes. Sylvia sat on the beach enjoying the warmth of the sun on her body. She leaned back against a striped canvas beach chair, her long legs stretched out in front of her on the sand. She had just returned from Tripler where she had taken John for a protracted walk in his wheelchair. For the past two weeks Sylvia had been in constant attendance at the hospital, sitting quietly while John slept, stopping in the chapel to pray, pushing John in his wheelchair outside in the lush tropical gardens, and most recently walking him up and down the corridors of the hospital.

His progress has been remarkable, she reflected as she soaked up the hot Hawaiian sun. *Now that he is regaining his strength, he's becoming restless and irritable. He wants to do everything right now, and he just doesn't like the restraints imposed by the hospital. Soon they will release him and I will have the problem of trying to be loving and supportive as we begin to reestablish our personal relationship while trying to hold him back when he wants to do too much! How do I cope with that? That problem and Sandra at the same time! What will I do? What will John do?*

I was shattered when Sandra told me about Akakura. I felt betrayed. He actually had her in his arms when they were both naked - skinny-dipping together! How could he? Imagine - a married man and his wife pregnant! Far worse than what happened at the Komatsu with VF-112. His big hard thing pressed against her naked belly! Ugh! I want to throw up every time I think of it! How could he do this to me - to us? Sylvia shuddered and tried to concentrate on her book, but her mind kept coming back to John, Sandra, and herself.

Sandra says it's the Post Combat Syndrome, she sniffed. *Men just want to fuck - fuck anyone to reestablish their damned macho ego - immortality! Hah! You let them out of your sight and they try to get into the first female they meet. How nice! Sounds like she didn't do much to stop him either! Bastards! I get livid when I think of it.*

Sylvia took a sip of her coke, and let her thoughts seek their own way.

Well - to hell with it! I love him, damnit! I love him and I want him back. Okay. Hey! Just a minute, Sylvia sweetheart - you really can't say too much, can you? What did you do? You almost let Brad Masters boff you while you supposedly were thinking it was John! You let him undress you, play with your tits, and then run his hand down into your crotch. God! And if you had let him go all the way - what would you have said? Oh, I thought it was John! Sure you did! Bullshit, Sylvia! You just wanted to be laid, too. No - that's not true, damnit. I had too much to drink. All I could think of was John inside me. Honestly!

She paused and stared out to sea where one of the native outrigger canoes was cutting the waves as it headed for shore.

Okay Sylvia. If you can excuse yourself, why can't you accept Sandra's Post Combat Syndrome? She's been there and should know.

She did it herself, didn't she? She has no reason to cover up John's unfaithfulness - well almost unfaithful - or wanting to be unfaithful - whatever the hell it was! The real bottom line is that he didn't do it. A fine line maybe - but if they had done it - well - after having seen Sandra, I may never have gotten him back.

The bottom line, old girl, is you still have a husband, at least for now. He could still bolt, but you still want him. So forget about Akakura. Let it die. And forget your almost-affair with Brad Masters, too! You didn't do it with him! John didn't do it with Sandra! You're even!

Now only one more part to this whole mess. Sandra saved John's life. He could interpret feelings of gratitude as a continuation or even an expansion of his love at Akakura. If he goes after her, she'll let him this time and your whole life could blow up! You can't let that happen. She shifted on the beach chair and sighed.

Conclusion - You want him. You want to live together like you did before this goddamned war. You want the joy of marriage. So grow up and get on with your life! Do your best to show your love. Show off your assets while you replace Sandra as his nurse. John's body is recovering nicely, but his psyche still has a long way to go. Help him with that. As Peg and others have repeatedly told you - patience - patience - patience! Now would be the time to bring the baby out for a visit. He adores Kat, and all's fair in love and war! Isn't it?

Sylvia got up, and brushed off the sand, pulled up the straps of her bathing suit, and walked across the sand to the water to the admiring glances of the men on the beach.

CHAPTER 12

Navy Ace Returns Home Today
Exclusive by Nancy Reed
San Diego Union

Lieutenant junior grade John Sullivan, United States Navy, returns to San Diego today after a long recovery period at the Army's Tripler General Hospital in Honolulu. The Navy Ace, who flew F-86's on exchange with the Air Force in Korea, has six MiG-15's to his credit. He was himself shot down on his last mission - his hundredth. He successfully bailed out of his crippled aircraft thirty five miles north of the front lines, managed to evade the North Korean militia, and walked out arriving at an outpost of the First Cavalry Division a month later in a state of collapse with a near fatal gangrene infection in his thigh.

The Army medevac'd the lieutenant to the General Hospital in Hawaii where he was put under the care of Doctor Frank Stone, a renowned specialist in infectious diseases. Using experimental drugs from NIH, Doctor Stone managed to reverse the dangerous spread of the infection, and saved Lieutenant Sullivan's life without the need to amputate his leg. Lieutenant Sullivan holds the Distinguished Flying Cross for combat missions. He is married to the former Sylvia Houghton of Worthington, Ohio. They have one daughter, Kathleen.

Naval Air Station
North Island

The welcoming party gathered in the NavAirPac conference room next to the Admiral's office at 1500. The conference table was covered with a white cloth which was loaded with canapes. The bar in the corner, attended by the admiral's stewards, served wine and soft drinks, and featured fino sherry flown in from Madrid by a P2V returning from deployment.

" Sylvia, we have an update on the C-54." Captain Mike Moran said, after he got rid of a mouthful of canape. "They are one hundred miles out. The pilot just reported by HF radio to the tower. He'll be in the pattern in a half hour."

Admiral and Mrs. Bender saw Sylvia and came over to talk, accompanied by a distinguished looking officer with three stars on his shoulder boards. Tall and slender, he had a beaked nose, an aquiline face, and piercing onyx eyes.

"Sylvia, may I present Vice Admiral Wayne Brooks from Washington, the Navy's Gray Eagle." Admiral Bender said by way of introduction.

"Mrs. Sullivan, I'm delighted to be here for this reunion. All of us in Washington are tremendously impressed with the fortitude and audacity displayed by your husband in becoming the Navy's only ace in Korea, and then by shear guts and tenacity walking out of North Korea after he had to eject from his aircraft. I look forward to meeting him, but I won't spoil your reunion by talking to him too much right now about these things. I'll bring him back to Washington later for some conferences." With that the admiral excused himself and sought out the Mayor of San Diego.

"What's the Gray Eagle, Mike?" Sylvia asked.

"He's the number one aviator in the Navy, and a very powerful man. It speaks well for John that he came out to welcome him back." Mike replied.

"Mike, did you tell Sylvia the ETA?" the admiral asked. He was preempted by his wife.

"What a beautiful child, Sylvia. She has your eyes. What's her name?"

"Mrs. Bender, this is Kat and she's a handful," which Kat immediately demonstrated by trying to slip out of Sylvia's arms.

"Has John seen her yet?"

"No, I couldn't get her out to Honolulu in time. The hospital, of course, wouldn't let her in his room, and he improved so rapidly, that there wasn't time to make another trip."

"Daddy? Daddy?" Kat asked, looking at her mother.

"Yes, darling. Daddy's coming for sure," Sylvia beamed.

Peg Moran came up to join the group. "Here, honey, you come to your Aunt Peg and give your mama a rest." Kat eagerly held out her arms to Peg to be taken.

The C-54 made a circling approach to runway 27, smoothly touched down on the runway and taxied to the VIP parking slot in front of base operations. The pilot cut the engines, steps were wheeled into place, and a red carpet unrolled. Only then did the admiral move forward with Sylvia on his arm. Peg with Kat in her arms walked where she could easily hand the baby to Sylvia. The rest of the entourage followed behind.

The door opened and John stepped out on the top step.

"Go to him, Sylvia," the admiral said in a stage whisper.

Sylvia needed no more encouragement. She handed her flowers to the admiral's wife and ran to her husband, her hair flying in the breeze, her arms outstretched to embrace him. The photographer for the San Diego Union snapped the picture of a beautiful young woman running with sheer joy on her face to embrace a waiting husband. The picture appeared on the front page of a dozen papers across the country the next day.

Sylvia walked back with her arms around her husband, but John still managed a salute to the admiral who shook his hand, and then broke protocol to embrace him.

"Daddy! Daddy!" an excited voice shrilled and Peg gave Kat to Sylvia, the child wiggling and squirming to reach her daddy. She stayed in Sylvia's arms just long enough to slide across into John's arms.

"You little rascal. You little Fat Kat!" John beamed, and all sign of protocol disappeared.

"My God, Mike," Peg said in an aside, "He's just skin and bones. I can imagine how he first looked to Sylvia three weeks ago."

"Never mind, honey," Mike replied. "Sylvia will fatten him up."

"Yeah, but it's still a hard road for them. You remember when you came back from the South Pacific."

"I do indeed! Couldn't do it for weeks," he chuckled. "It's funny now - wasn't then. You begin to think you're a damned eunuch!"

Introductions were made, photos shot, and press queries answered. Then the Admiral intervened, "John, we aren't going to keep you here any longer. Interviews can be done later." The Admiral turned and flagged his aide who waved the official car forward. "Take Sylvia and Kat and go home. Enjoy your family."

The Admiral stepped back and saluted the returned hero as the car pulled away.

Naval air Station
North Island

Lean and trim at one hundred ninety pounds, Lieutenant John Sullivan scanned the instruments of his swept-wing Cougar, and called the tower as he rolled down the taxiway towards the warm-up area.

"Tower, Navy 126021. Ready for take off."

"Roger, Navy 126021. North Island tower. Cleared onto the active. Number one for takeoff. Altimeter 30.01. Wind 290 at ten. Have a good flight, sir."

"021. Rolling."

The swept wing Cougar accelerated down runway 27, lifted off, and headed out to sea.

"He looks good," commented the Navy captain standing next to the Operations Duty Officer, his binoculars focused on the jet.

"Nice lift off," said the Operations Duty Officer, looking through a similar pair of binocs. "Nice climb. He's not wobbling like most of them do the first time in a swept wing. How did you ever manage to get him the only swept wing F9F at North Island for his first flight, CAG." he said without taking his eyes from his binoculars

"His F-86 time helped. Why wouldn't it? He's got more swept wing experience than any other naval aviator. In fact, they'd had a hard time refusing a Navy ace. But, I made certain he'd get it," Mike Moran laughed. "You saw the photographers? I gave the PIO's the whole story. Then the operators couldn't refuse," CAG chuckled. "The big wheels are slobbering over the publicity. It'll be on the front page tomorrow and it'll be in every news magazine next week. The Navy ace that walked out of North Korea returns to flying again! How's that for a lead?"

In the cockpit the pilot looked at the beautiful blue sky, the fluffy white clouds, the blue Pacific below him, the green-brown land of Southern California, and grinned from ear to ear. He raised his hands over his head in the winner's clasp of a boxer, releasing an exuberant shout of pure joy. He then grabbed the stick and did five aileron rolls just for the love of it. Lieutenant John Francis Sullivan, USN, Navy fighter pilot, had come home to his first love - the eternal mistress of flight who captures the souls of men. And he caressed her like he would caress a woman.

2739 Maple Drive
San Diego, California

Sylvia paced nervously back and forth in the kitchen, stopping frequently to peer out the window, looking up the street for John's car.

"Will he ever get here," she groused, but her watch only showed the passage of a few minutes since the last look.

"Here he comes," she said, running to the front door.

"Hi sailor. How was it?"

"Fantastic! Absolutely fantastic!" John shouted, doing a pirouette, and handing Sylvia a dozen red roses that he had hidden behind his back.

"Oh John, whatever made you think of these," Sylvia said softly, surprised that he would think of her after his very first flight since Korea.

"Well, I thought that if I brought something nice, I might get a good piece of ass," he replied leering at her. "Just a little piece of tail from a good looking woman. Maybe even some torrid nook from a little hot tamale."

Sylvia drew in a deep breath and hoped. *He's more like the old days.* Then she smiled a big lascivious smile and said, "I don't know about a piece of ass, but I'm a bundle of love."

"Do you want to do it here on the floor or can you wait until we get in the bedroom?"

"Your choice."

He looked around, went into the kitchen, and returned. "How about on top of the frig? We've never done that."

"Any time, any place, sweetheart," and she did a bump and grind for him.

"Come here, you little witch," John swept her off her feet. "I love you."

Sylvia lay quietly next to John who had fallen asleep.

"That was almost as good as the good old days," she purred. "It will work out. Given time and some maturing, we'll be okay. Luck is with us - and so is God."

But there still was the question of Sandra, nagging at John who could not get her out of his mind.

Naval Air Station

North Island

"Sir, you have a visitor," Yeoman Miller said as Lieutenant junior grade Larry Duncan stuck his head around the door jam, and entered John's office without further invitation.

"Hey, Larry! Come on in! What are you doing here?" John yelled, jumping to his feet and walking around the desk to greet Larry with a firm grip and a friendly pat on the back.

"I'm on my way to Pearl to interview at PacFlt for an intelligence slot with them."

"That's great, Larry. You'll come out to dinner, of course," John said, waving Larry to a chair.

"Sorry, I can't, John," Larry shook his head. "I'm leaving on a C-54 in two hours. I just got time to see you and then get to the terminal for the one hour check in."

"Sylvia will be disappointed, but I'll tell her I saw you. How's Mitzi?"

"She's great! Always the live wire! Never runs down! She's disappointed that she couldn't go with me so she could see Sandra."

John raised his eyebrows. "Are you going to Tokyo as well, Larry?"

"No," Larry laughed. "Sandra's at Tripler. A permanent change of duty. I think Doctor Stone arranged it. Anyway it'll be great to see her again."

"Give her my love, Larry," John replied somberly. "I'd like to see her myself."

"You still haven't gotten her out of your system, have you, John?" Larry said quietly. "It's such a shame the two of you couldn't have put it together. Mitzi and I talk about it frequently."

"She's been constantly in my mind, Larry. I can't seem to shake her. Jesus, Larry, I had a monstrous ache for three days after we parted. I still want her, and I want her bad." John suddenly stopped talking, and time stood still. The silence was filled with unspoken emotion. He looked at Larry, his eyes closed slightly, their iris tightening into slits, and their shade turning steel gray. For a moment Larry was frightened, for he was well acquainted with John's moods, as reflected in those eyes - and he was not sure what - or - why - or - who it was meant for.

Then John relaxed, and smiled at him. "I just made my decision, Larry. Sandra said to contact her after six months when I knew my own mind - when I had recovered my health and it's been six months. I've been agonizing over it for weeks. Well, I'm headed for Honolulu on business in a few weeks, but I will not see her when I get there."

"But, John, why not? You know you'll never get over her!"

"Oh yes I will, Larry." John slowly replied. "I just did. Seeing you now, and having Akakura flash before me made me realize it had to be a one time thing."

"But, John," Larry began to cut in. John stopped him with a dismissive wave of his arm.

"I still love Sandra, yes. It has only deepened in the passing months. Recently I had an almost uncontrollable urge to bail out and go to her - but I knew in my heart it could never be. Regardless of my feelings for Sandra, I still love Sylvie and my child. I just can't dump her and chase a will-o'-the-wisp. Life isn't that way, Larry. We have responsibilities that we can't set aside."

John paused for a moment, and Larry sat quietly unwilling to break the spell that gripped his friend.

"Sandra and I had our time even if we didn't consummate our love. - - and if we had?" His face furrowed with deepening lines of concentration.

"I know now I couldn't have kept her long as a mistress, and I know now I couldn't have dumped Sylvie. If we had consummated our love, and had an affair, it would have eaten at us until it ripped us apart and destroyed our love. That's just the kind of persons we are. No, Larry, I will not see Sandra. She already knows it won't work. But, she'd try for my sake if I came to see her." John sighed, and smiled at his old buddy from the days at Akakura. "So, Larry, we'll both keep it in our hearts as a poignant moment in time when two loves touched, and parted, retaining only the memory. Only the memory? But, that's everything there is to life isn't it? The memories.. . ." John stopped, straightened his back, shrugged off the world, and bounced out of his chair.

"Let's get you to your plane, Larry. When you see Sandra, give please her my love."

After Larry had left, John leaned back in his chair, his face pensive and thoughtful.

"It's Sayonara, Sandra. I'll always love you, but the time has come to put it away. Sayonara, sweetheart."

THE END

Glossary

AIO	Air Intelligence Officer.
ASAP	As Soon As Possible.
Able Sugar	Ape Shit.
Air Boss	Department head on a carrier, responsible for the flight deck, hangar deck, and proximity air space.
ASAP	As soon as possible.
BAR	Browning Automatic Rifle.
Benjo Ditch	Run off ditches in Korea, carrying human waste.
Chandelle	A steep climbing wingover reversal.
Carquals	Qualifying landings on a carrier.
CO	Commanding Officer.
Comms	Communications.
CAG	Carrier Air Group Commander.
COMNAVAIRPAC	Commander Naval Air Pacific Fleet.
COMFAIRJAP	Commander Fleet Air Japan.
CRUDESFLOT	Cruiser Destroyer Flotilla (Staff or Commander).
DFC	Distinguished Flying Cross.
EF or FF	Standard query by young lovers. EF is eat first.
Fantail	The stern of the ship.
FASRON	Fleet Air Service Squadron.
FCLP	Field Carrier Landing Practice.
Gooney Bird	Venerable DC-3 transport aircraft.
Geishas	Used in the vulgar sense common among service men at the time.
High Dip	An LSO signal where the pilot responds by dropping the nose slightly and then returning to the original attitude. The plane loses a little altitude without gaining airspeed
I&I	Intoxication & Intercourse. Alternate definition for R&R.
LSO	Landing Signal Officer.
MASH	Mobile Army Surgical Hospital.

Medevac	Medical evacuation.
NSLI	National Service Life Insurance.
NATS	Naval Air Transport Service.
MLR	Main Line Of Resistance. The front line.
1MC	Ship's internal announcing system
NAVCAD	Naval Aviation Cadet
O'Club	Officer's Club.
Overtemp	Exceeding the upper limit for tailpipe temp
OK-1;OK-2	LSO evaluation of an approach, including the arresting wire that was caught.
PACFLT	Pacific Fleet
PIM	Position and Intended Movement of a ship or force
Port	Nautical for - On the left side
PriFly	Primary Flight. Domain of the Air Boss.
Pump bilges	urinate.
Ramp	The round down of the flight deck at the stern, a very hard metal.
RCH	A naval aviation vulgarity, meaning a very fine measurement, or just a little.
Roger	I acknowledge the transmission. Also the OK signal given by the LSO with arms and flags extended from the shoulder
Roger Pass	A carrier approach in which the LSO holds a Roger signal all the way.
Right Echelon	A formation where all aircraft are stepped down to the right.
R&R	Rest and Recreation.
ROK	Republic of Korea.
Spud Locker	Where potatoes are stowed on the fantail.
Space A	Space available
Starboard	On the right

Signal Dog	Enter the holding pattern and conserve fuel.
Signal Charlie	Cleared to descend and enter the landing pattern.
TAD	Temporary Additional Duty involving travel. TDY in the Army and USAF.
TLC	Tender loving care.
Triple A/AAA	Anti-aircraft artillery.
Towering Q	Tall cumulus clouds.
The Ninety	A carrier approach begins abeam the ship's fantail and completes a 180 degree turn around to the ramp. The 90 is the half way point where the LSO picks up the pilot with signals.
VF-112	Fighter Squadron 112.
YE	A navigation system putting out a morse code letter for each octant around the ship. Signal changes daily.
yo-yo	A movement like a yoyo. Converting airspeed to altitude and vice versa.
yellow gear	Support equipment.

ABOUT THE AUTHOR

Captain Corrigan flew jet combat in Korea in the Panther (F9F-2) and the Banshee (F2H-2) from the aircraft carrier, USS Philippine Sea (CV-47). He also flew special operations missions from the USS Essex (CV-9) during the same period. He holds the Distinguished Flying Cross and Air Medals for combat action.

The author spent thirty years in carrier aviation. He is qualified in the Corsair (of Pappy Boyington fame), Panther, Cougar, and Crusader. As a Navy Captain, he held such prestigious positions as Operations Officer, Carrier Task Force Sixty; Air Operations Officer, US Naval Forces Europe; Commander US Naval Activities, Spain; Deputy for Navy Command Control and Communications, Pentagon; Navy C3 Architect; and Commanding Officer, US Naval Station, Rota, Spain. He holds a masters degree from the University of Illinois.

Captain Corrigan's career has been wide and varied. It began in the Army Air Corps as an Aviation Cadet in 1943. While in Pre-flight he received an appointment to the US Naval Academy. He received his wings of gold in 1949, just in time for the Korean War. He served on the joint staff at Headquarters, Strategic Air Command (SAC) in Omaha, Nebraska.

Following retirement in 1975, he worked for Lockheed-Martin and then retired again to the West Indies.

He resides in the Sarasota area and is currently the Commanding Officer, Golden Pelican Squadron, Association of Naval Aviation, Sarasota.